LUCIA'S POLTERGEIST

LUCIA'S POLTERGEIST

FELICIA KATE SOLOMON

Matador
9 Priory Business Park,
Wistow Road, Kibworth Beauchamp,
Leicestershire. LE8 0RX
Tel: 0116 279 2299
Email: books@troubador.co.uk
Web: www.troubador.co.uk/matador
Twitter: @matadorbooks

ISBN 978 1789015 799

British Library Cataloguing in Publication Data.
A catalogue record for this book is available from the British Library.

Printed and bound in Great Britain by 4edge Limited
Typeset in 11pt Adobe Garamond Pro by Troubador Publishing Ltd, Leicester, UK

Matador is an imprint of Troubador Publishing Ltd

To Gloria and Peter;
For the creativity you taught me to believe in.

...you have the Jekyll hand, you have the Hyde hand...

Gwendolyn MacEwen, 'The Left Hand and
Hiroshima', *Breakfast for Barbarians*, 1966

So split and halved and twain is every part,
So like two persons severed by a glass
Which darkens the discerning whose is whose
And gives two arms for love and two for hate,
That they cannot discover what they're at
And sometimes think of killing and embrace...

Daryl Hine, 'The Doppelganger', 1960.

PROLOGUE

LONDON, 1989

LUCIA IS SIXTEEN YEARS OLD

She does not want to go home.

The bus approaches the bend. She pulls the string overhead to request her stop.

'Did you hear Ben Phillips pissed on Caisie's head at Lidiya's party?' Josie laughs.

Lucia giggles. She wants to stay with her friend, and go all the way to Kilburn to eat American ice cream and watch videos at Josie's house. It has been a long afternoon learning about microclimates in double geography, which she hates.

'All alight here, folks,' the bus conductor jokes. He always makes her smile, reminding her of Doctor Doolittle, with those red pimples on his fat face.

She stands. 'See ya,' she says.

'See you tomorrow.' Josie waves.

Lucia steps off the bus. It pulls away.

She swallows. Her heartbeat pounds through her neck.

Gripping her cold keys in her pocket, she walks, head held high. The air is fresh, the sky a clear baby blue and the white tail line of an aeroplane disperses. She wonders where that plane is headed, maybe Malaga, or even the golden paradise of Trinidad or St Lucia?

Her rucksack weighs her down; Lucia sweats under its heavy load. Her woollen jumper itches. She feels like a tramp in her brother's ripped suede jacket and her second-hand 501s with no top button on.

She thinks of her friend Mary as she passes the school for the deaf and dumb. The two girls often run up and down that slanting wall in the school's car park for something to do. The big, green electricity box on the corner unnerves her. It is where people often get bottled.

Lucia walks through the Holiday Inn complex. She stops to watch, through the glass, the tanned Italian boys, who dive bomb into the Mediterranean-blue swimming pool, and the rich women sitting in stripy deckchairs amidst mock palm trees. She wishes she could go in, but you have to be a member.

She does not want to go home.

She can't go into the foyer and sit in their armchairs again, so she takes a detour by walking through the car park. The loud fans above blow out warm air and make her waxed curls dance on top of her head. The howling car alarm makes the surrounding silence bite more.

Her tummy tightens then twists as she nears her house. Her pulse moves up to her throat.

A Porsche speeds by blasting out Tracy Chapman's 'Revolution'. A burst of spring breeze blows a shower of cherry-blossom petals onto her shoulder. That gust of wind chills her clammy skin. She smiles.

That moment was hers, and no one else's.

Only ten doors away, she kicks a stone and watches it jump, then bounce. Ah! Lucia inhales the tang of diesel coming from the old Bentley on the roadside. She savours the smell. The thought of where else she could go sprints through her mind. She wishes she had stayed longer at Maria's dad's pizza house. No rules, sitting by the drinks' fridge, eating a free slice of four-cheese pizza, watching the speed of traffic passing by on the Camden Road.

'Smile, it might never happen!' shouts a tattooed builder from the scaffolding above.

Lucia's pace quickens. She keeps her gaze fixed on her pixie boots, and swallows.

The kids from the white houses opposite are playing out. She wishes she lived in one of those modern houses instead of her shabby Victorian one. They all have brightly coloured doors with driveways. Serena and Patsy are standing outside in their maroon school uniforms, laughing and flicking their glossy hair.

She looks.

Their mums gossip in loud Irish accents and look like models from a Clairol advert. Why is that not her life? Frilly socks, private school and a flashy Mercedes. It's a Barbie-and-Ken world from where she stands.

She passes Mr. Stanley's house. The sandy-coloured bricks make her house's charcoal-grey ones look Dickensian.

She peers through their front bay window, but cannot see anyone. He must be out in the garden tending to his azaleas.

There are no more detours Lucia can make.

She stares up at the front door, which is a big, black door with a brass door handle. At the bottom of the stairs, two roaring, concrete lions sit on top of each stone pillar. She picks the paint off one of the pillars, and walks up the stairs.

She looks back at the young boys racing on their BMX bikes across their private garden, which is an endless run of grass separated from the street by wire fencing.

She pulls away her gaze. It is like wrenching a magnet off a fridge.

Lucia gulps. She opens the front door.

The smell of damp hits her, but seconds later the scent of strawberry candles and fruitcake wafts over from Petunia and Steve's flat.

She stands outside their door and listens. Lucia hears quiet talking and the sound of Vivaldi on low. She covets that family cosiness, basking in the comfort of leather sofas and flush carpets.

She looks up the winding stairway.

The hallway is church cold.

She walks up the stairs. The carpet is grey and shredded.

Her head is lowered; her jaw clamped tight.

The approaching sound of television talking to no one becomes close. Today's deodorant has faded, and she can smell her acrid body odour. She stops and massages her key inside her pocket, moving her thumb in and out of its wedges.

The blue-and-red stained-glass window rattles. It has a crack down the middle, but never breaks. Loose cobwebs hang from the lampshade above. No one ever cleans the communal hallway.

She walks up the last five steps.

The sound of the *Countdown* Conundrum is loud. It is her mum's afternoon addiction.

She presses her ear to the door and listens for clues as to what mood her mum is in.

She is in a mood. Lucia knows immediately by the sound of her mother's cough and from the tension she feels in her pelvis. Her mother's cough has no commitment and does not discharge any phlegm. It just dances around in her lungs and then resettles. This is the sign that it is dangerous inside.

She holds her breath.

In front of the flat, on the landing, is a pile of cardboard boxes covered by a pink wool blanket. Inside those boxes are her mother's divorce papers and out-of-date cheque stubs that she won't dispose of. Upstairs, she can hear Clara walking about listening to UB40.

There's a rat in mi kitchen, what am I gonna do?

Lucia puts the key into the lock. *I don't want to go in.*

She cannot turn back now.

I'm gonna fix that rat…

She looks down at the paisley patterns on her boot. *I wonder what Maria is doing?*

She turns the key.

Lucia opens the door.

CHAPTER ONE

LONDON, 1989

LUCIA IS SIXTEEN YEARS OLD

'Lucia!'

She stops. Her chest constricts.

'Yes, hello…' her mum mutters.

She bites the inside of her cheek hard, pushes open the door and drops her head.

Ten, then twenty faint coffee stains merge into one.

'Yes, Lucia…'

Cold blood trickles into the well of her mouth. It tastes of sour iron tablets.

Her mother emerges, swaying in the doorway and holding on to the doorframe for balance.

God, I hate you.

Lucia's lips are tightly pursed and her tongue thick. She looks up at her mum, who wears luminous, green socks (a freebee from a British Airways' flight); baggy tracksuit bottoms, and a matching top with crumbs scattered all over it. Her glasses are wonky, her hair stands on ends, and she has dried, white spit at the corners of her lips.

'Yes, Lucia, what is it?'

Lucia clenches her teeth and glimpses at the bubbles on the woodchip wallpaper. The sitting room behind where her mum stands is dark. The curtains are closed. The TV is at a deafening level of decibels.

She feels a thump in the hollow of her abdomen, followed by a contracting sensation. It is her automatic response to her mum 'in a mood', which is the term she and her brother Ben use to describe their mum's personality change. She doesn't understand what causes her mum's behaviour to turn. She leaves for school with one mum and returns to a different one.

She looks into her mother's glazed eyes. She is stony faced, with drooping eyelids that look like they carry weights. Lucia sees no emotion in her mother's eyes; they are vacant, just a black dot with bloodshot white around.

Lucia walks to her bedroom. Her mother stops in front of her and extends her arms.

'Are you g-o-o-o-o-i-n-n-ng to clean your r-o-o-o-o-om?' she stutters.

'No, I'm not. I've got homework to do,' Lucia replies, thrusting her way past. She slams her bedroom door shut.

She draws a breath, drops her rucksack and wipes the sweat from above her lip. The walls of her bedroom are a dirty pink. She flops onto her bed and brushes the backs of her hands against her Laura Ashley bedspread. It feels cool.

'Lucia?'

'What?'

It is a routine call of loneliness.

Lucia scrunches her hair, feeling relief from the pull on her scalp, and then finds a moment of refuge in the colourful sparkle on her special display shelf. Diagonal lines of Carol Sheen lip glosses stand in militant order. Greens, yellows, reds and purples glisten next to the neat rows of Hello Kitty and Twinkle Star stationery that she collects.

Cars roar past outside and a taxi engine chokes. Its sound lingers on. She listens for her mum's cough and waits for her intrusion. It is only a matter of minutes before it will come.

She has a millimetre of space, so pulls out her *Just Seventeen* magazine from under her table and reads. Her limbs relax. There is a massive centre spread on Bros; why all the fuss?

'Lucia!' her mum calls.

For God's sake, woman!

The sound sequence of the next three seconds is Lucia's traffic light to hell. It is a bar of notes that she has learnt to cope with for years, but it still freezes her upper body into tense alert.

Red.

Her mother coughs.

Amber.

She pounces down the hall. The floorboards squeak, bounce, then spring.

Green.

Thud! Her mother's hand hits her brass doorknob. The door flies open, and she stands in the doorway, breathing in a noisy, raspy way. She has a lit cigarette in her hand, ash curling. The frown between her eyes is a deep V shape, like the fork of a swallow's tail has been ingrained there. She forces a gluey smile at Lucia. Her docile eyes lift into a feigned look of surprise, as she grips her lower teeth onto her top ones.

'Your ash is going to fall on my carpet!' Lucia shouts, clenching her fist.

Her mum holds onto the radiator for balance, wheezing.

'What do you want, Mother?'

'Yes? Yes?' her mum murmurs. A vile characteristic of her mum's mood is her repetitious use of 'yes'. She says it in the intonation of a question for no reason and waits for a response.

Lucia stands. She meets her mother's gaze. She notices light dancing on her mother's eyeballs, and feels her water level rise within her, like liquid rising in a tank. It stops at her throat. She swallows. Her tears have nowhere to go.

'What, Mum? You're just standing there,' Lucia shouts with a crack of desperation in her voice. Tension rushes in between her legs.

Her mother's cigarette's ash falls onto the carpet.

'For fuck's sake, your stinking ash is on my carpet!'

Her mum rubs it into the carpet with her foot. It leaves a grey stain. She wipes her middle finger across Lucia's bookcase and stumbles over, holding her finger up to Lucia's face. 'Look, look at this! Thick, grey dust that hasn't been cleaned for weeks.'

'I don't care, Mum. It doesn't bother me.'

'You don't have a clue about the upkeep of a ho-ho-ho-me, d-o-o-o-o you?'

'No, Mum, I don't. Shoot me down.' Lucia's words come out in a sprint of anger.

She holds her breath, aware of her mum observing her, and stares out of the window at Taplow Towers, which is a concrete monolith soaring above the houses. She focuses on the rows of light squares, and counts the levels from the ground floor up to eighteen to see if she can see her friend Leanne Miani's flat. She imagines their compact kitchen, as Leanne's mum, Bev prepares bolognese pasta bows. She thinks of Leanne's cheeky dad, Vince, poking his bald head between the hanging beads, with a wink. She can just see them all having dinner together, and sharing a box of Quality Street afterwards in front of *The Krypton Factor*.

Her gaze lowers to Serena's window opposite. Serena and her brother, Dylan stick two fingers up at her, and then duck.

She looks back at her mother.

'Ar-ar-are you ever go-go-going to wipe a duster over here?' her mother stutters. She is unable to get through a sentence without stuttering when in a mood. She gets stuck bang in the middle of a word, paralysed by spasm, and her front teeth repeat on her bottom lip. Her mouth opens, she gargles with air, scrambling to finish a word, looking like the subject of Munch's *The Scream*. Then it comes like a sneeze. Her handicap saddens Lucia.

'No, I'm not.'

'Bone idle you are, utterly useless.' Her mother scowls with venom in her eyes.

Lucia tightens her buttocks. Her hatred races to where most people feel love and tenderness.

'Thanks for the vote of confidence. Shut the door on your way out.' Lucia looks back out of the window.

Her mother parts her stuck lips. Her cigarette is now burnt down to its butt. She stares at Lucia with intent and does not blink.

'You really do hate me, don't you?' Lucia says, looking back quizzically at her mother. The voice that comes from her throat is thick with rage, but quavering a little.

'I-I-I,' her mother begins to speak then falters for a moment. 'I-I-I think you are an awful person, actually.'

A bruise creeps across Lucia's chest like a moving cloud. *Awful?* 'How can you say that to your own daughter? You gave birth to me, Mum,' Lucia says choking on a sudden surge of tears.

Her mother staggers out, bashing her arm on the door.

Her room is now silent. Her possessions come into focus reminding her that this is her domain. Lucia thumps her Judy Blume book, cursing, 'Bitch!' under her breath. She stretches her cheeks back, holds her breath and fights to find an inner strength.

No, she isn't right. I am not awful. Her head throbs right behind her left eye.

Or maybe I am. Tension mounts within her. She lies on her bed, brings her hand between her legs and presses hard. She knows she should not do this. It doesn't work, but it takes her away from this nightmare for a second.

She pushes hard. The denim ridge on her jeans is thick.

It tingles, and then aches.

The more she pushes the more her mum's hatred goes away.

She feels a burst of fizz. It's not enough.

She tenses. *Come on, hurry up.* Tears fall down her face.

She conjures violent scenes in her mind to get the release she needs.

Keita Jalloh, naked, runs out of her kitchen. Her mum, in high heels and pink lipstick, follows with a black leather belt in hand. 'Come back here!'

'Please no, Mummy! No.'

Harder. Faster, nearly there.

The bedroom door slams shut. It locks. Keita screams and runs around the room. Her mum chases her, backs her into a corner and pulls her to the bed. She sits on her.

She sweats. Her hand aches. She keeps pushing; there are waves of tingling.

Keita wriggles trying to escape. Her mum pins her down, and lashes the belt against her naked thigh. Keita screams, flinching and flailing.

Lucia's limbs shake. She presses fast against herself. It clicks there.

The metal buckle cuts the air with a *whoosh* and beats Keita's black skin again and again. 'No mummy!' Keita cries twisting and writhing, hot tears running down her face.

Lucia replays the scene over and over, until she gets goose bumps and then goes over the edge. She feels a forced release. Her body shakes, tickles, spasms and then stops.

Everything is blurred. Lucia takes her hand away. A big square is indented into her hand. Now tired and blank, her vision is hazy; yellow and blue dots sail in diagonal lines. She feels worse than she did – empty. Her board games of Monopoly and Blockbusters come into view, but she still feels weary. She is hot and sore between her legs, and is angry that she hurt herself like this. Nothing is better. It was not enjoyable.

Lucia sits up and is able to hear her mum in the next room.

Her white, paper mache mask on the wall glares at her, with square holes as eyes. It looks like a ghost and offers no comfort.

She waits for that next sound cue. Her mother will be back.

Lucia runs her foot across the carpet, making rainbow shapes. It changes the shade of her polyester carpet from a dull blue to a brighter shade. She zones out into the dancing-hedgehog pattern on her curtain, wishing for something more modern.

The bright-yellow, dancing matchstick man on her Yazz and the Plastic Population nine inch, lights a spark in her. *Jazzy.* It gives her hope and clears her haze, like sun coming through a spell of grey cloud. *Zing.*

She puts the record on and turns up the volume. Her chest expands to the pumping beats.

We've been broken down
To the lowest turn,
Bein' on the bottom line
Sure ain't no fun.

She mouths the words in sync to the rhythm, lifting herself out of the funk.

(Hold on) hold on

'Lucia!'

She turns the volume up even higher to drown out her mother's call. The bass thumps. She sings.

The only way is up, baby
For you and me now

She shuffles her feet to the beat, punching her arms in the air. She glimpses at her Matisse print on the wall, and smiles. A feeling of optimism sweeps over her. Brilliant-blue, red, magenta pink chunky squares spiral into the shape of a snail. It is childlike. The memory floods back of the day her father introduced her to that masterpiece, that sweaty afternoon amidst Japanese tourists at the Tate. Escaping from the monotony of Turner and Constable, she found this painting. It stood out, drew her to its statement. *The Snail* is her find, her connection to her father. She stands still as she recollects that day.

'That's not art – I could do that,' she said.

'Yes, it is, darling, because he thought of it and you didn't,' her dad replied.

It reminds her of the faith her father had in her original mind, and his encouragement to express it. He taught her that creativity is what you make up, not what you think it should be. She recalls the warmth of his hand, and the love they shared of Seurat's bathers. It was a place she wanted to go to, with the sun twinkling on water and people lounging around a lakeside.

Lucia has not heard from her father for six months. The last letter she received promised that she could visit Yvonne and him in Spain. He has not phoned or written since.

She bites her bottom lip.

Boy, I want to thank you
Yeah, for loving me this way
Things may be a little hard now,

But we'll find a brighter day.

She sings along to Yazz, forgetting her grief for her absent father. *The Snail* is enough for her to hold onto. He loved her. He believed in her. No one can take that away.

'Lucia!'

(Hold on) hold on, won't be long

She is not awful. Her mum is wrong. Pulling in the support of the vibrant squares, she holds onto their power and locks them away inside a treasure chest. They are hers to keep.

She chants to herself, affirming a better future, 'One day I will be free. I will be my own person. One day, I will no longer be my mother's daughter.'

She thumps the air.

The only way is up, baby

'I will have my own life. I will be independent.'

(Hold on) hold on

Hold on, won't be long

No, no, no...

CHAPTER TWO

Westminster, London, 1980

Lucia is seven years old

The table is big.

'Lunch is ready now, darling. Sit yourself down,' Daddy says.

Everything is like a restaurant with candles in the middle, and big, white plates with roses on the sides. The knives are shiny and thick, not like Mummy's thin ones. I have orange squash. Daddy has a glass of red wine. There is a green bottle on the table with a napkin tied in a knot. Sometimes, I am allowed just one sip.

'I'll cut you a breast, my love.'

'Thank you, Daddy,' I say.

I look like I'm busy, because I am tracing the shape of the hills on my plate mat with my knife, so he doesn't look at me. Smells are coming from the kitchen, of lemon, steam and mud. Daddy is cutting the spitting chicken with a red knife. He is sweating. He wipes his head with the kitchen apron.

He sits at one end of the table and I sit at the other.

There is no noise. He is very far away from me.

I hate this bit, because I can't hide, so I start making triangles in my gravy with my knife.

But he sees me. 'Don't play with your food, darling. Eat it up. It's your favourite.'

My swede and carrots are bright orange. I love how Daddy mashes them with butter. The roast potatoes are crunchy. My favourite is the chicken skin; I save that until the end.

Daddy is looking at me as he chews. He hums, but, when I look up at him, his eyes move to the window.

I don't know what to say.

My hands are sweating. 'This is delicious, Daddy,' I say.

He smiles and says, 'Good, my love.'

He stops. He calls it 'pausing'. He wipes his chin with his napkin, hums and then taps his fingernails on the table. He is looking at the window again, but his eyes flick over to me. They are squinting and wobbling.

I don't know what he's thinking about. I need to find something to say. 'Is Nanny Rosa coming to stay soon?' I ask.

'Soon, love, yes.'

'Daddy...' I say.

'Yes, my darling?'

'Daddy, do you like living here alone or do you get lonely?'

He slices his chicken and puts it on his fork, but then he drops it. It hits his plate.

I'm frightened. I've said the wrong thing.

His cheeks go red. His teeth are grinding. His face shakes. He leans forwards. 'Darling...*Do...not...ask... questions*!' Now his face is really red. His spit lands in the middle of the table by the gravy holder.

I can't breathe.

Five round blobs of spit.

'It's that mother of yours,' he says, 'all her demands and questions, putting you up to it.'

I won't say anything now. 'Sorry,' I say.

I finish all my chicken skin, peas and potatoes. I don't like the Brussels sprout. They taste of soil.

I put my knife and fork together, and wait with my hands on my lap. I want to cry, but I know I can't. My head is hot. I want Mummy.

We don't say anything.

'Now, my darling, for dessert you can have loganberries or pears.'

'Loganberries, please, Daddy.'

He's not cross anymore. His face has gone white again.

I can hear a man and a woman walking outside, laughing.

'I love loganberries, Daddy,' I say. I am trying to make him happy again.

'Here, you go, my darling.'

It's a white, shiny bowl, with berries in a dark-red juice that smells orangey. I love it when Daddy pours the cream on top, because the red juice has curly, white swirls in it. I stir it together. It turns into a thick, candy-pink sauce. I call it fruit salad.

The loganberry pips crunch in my mouth and stick in my teeth. I finish mine before Daddy finishes his pears. Tinned pears are his favourite.

'Daddy, can we go to St. James' Park and feed the ducks this afternoon?' I ask.

'Yes, my love. We'll digest this first and then take a stroll,' he says.

That's good. By the time we get back, it will be night-time. Then it will be tomorrow, and tomorrow is when I am going back to Mummy's.

Daddy hums again.

Tap, tap, tap – his fingers again. He stares at me. He is thinking something.

I look down and pick my nails, under the table so he can't see. He doesn't like it when I pick my nails. He says I'll never get a boyfriend.

Big Ben strikes three times. It is three o'clock. That's good. It's only three hours until it's six o'clock, and that is night-time.

Today is nearly over.

*

The street is quiet.

All I can hear is Daddy's heel clinking on the ground.

He is holding my hand. His hand feels warm. I like it when his fingers tickle my palm. He hums again and frowns under his bowler hat.

There is a big clock on the church in front of us. It is black and gold. The clock says III with the small hand and IV with the big one. We pass Gerald and Sebastian's house.

Their mum has goofy teeth, and their dad has a swinging chair made from bamboo. Over there is a big building with a Union Jack flag over it.

'What's that, Daddy?' I ask.

'It's the Conservative Party,' he says, 'which is just back in power now, thankfully.'

On Barton Street, we pass posh houses for rich people. This one at the end has a metal tile on the brick, and it says *'Lawrence of Arabia 1888–1935'*.

This is where he lived. He was famous; he rode a horse, I think.

Now we are walking through a big, grassy square with the ground covered in old cobbles. I walk along the wall, but it is very thin, so Daddy holds my hand in case I fall. I put my left foot first, then my right in front of it, in a straight line, so I don't lose my balance.

I jump off at the end, and we walk past Westminster School. It's closed today, but Daddy says sometimes the boys stay there on a Sunday for choir practice. The door is open, and inside it smells of cabbage and cheesy feet, like a hospital, and there are lots of metal shields on the wall, all in different colours. One is gold and blue. It has a cross in the middle and five ducks. Another has two red roses in gold squares, with two angels blowing horns with *'Dat Deus Incrementum'* written on it.

'What does that mean, Daddy?' I ask.

'It's Latin, darling.'

I am allowed to ask questions, just not about him.

It's busy on the main street. Tourists are everywhere, taking photos of Westminster Abbey. Marcelo's ice-cream van is on the green lawn just outside it. Daddy buys me a 99 Flake with sprinkles on top, but then he says, 'Let me take a photo of you, darling, here, by the railings.'

I don't like this bit, because I don't know how to smile for him.

I say, 'Cheese.'

Click!

The ice cream drips on my anorak.

Opposite is a serious, big building called Scotland Yard. And the yellow pelican-crossing lights are flashing by the zebra crossing.

*

Pomp! Pomp! Pomp!

The brass band is really loud.

Daddy and me are at the park now. We are watching the band in the bandstand. We are sitting on the bench in front of the green, smelly water, and there is pigeon pooh all over the concrete path.

There are lots of men wearing black-and-gold suits with white hats on, blowing gold trumpets all together. I like the noise the trumpets make. Daddy does too because he taps the rhythm they are making on my shoulder with his hand and taps his foot, laughing. The men are blowing really hard; their cheeks are puffed out like balloons.

There are lots of people sitting in green-and-white stripy deckchairs. I can only see their heads. They are happy. One boy has a scooter, and he is riding up and down saying, 'vroom, vroom, vroom'.

'Daddy, can I feed the ducks?' I ask.

'Here you go, my darling.'

He gives me the Sunblest bread. It smells of mould, but I screw it up, so it is like plasticine, and I throw it into the green water. All of the ducks fly over, with a whhoooshhhhhhhhhhhhhhhhhhh, and land in a V shape on the water. Daddy laughs because they are all quacking and flapping their wings. I like the ones with the purple bit under their wing best, and the ones with the shiny, green heads. It's a bright green – like an emerald.

'Why are some purple and some green, Daddy?

'The green ones are the males, darling. They are called mallards,' he says.

I throw one duck two balls of bread. He catches it with his long beak, but then all of the others fight for my crumbs.

Daddy says he wants to look at the flowers now. We walk.

A baby is crying, and the seagulls are crying too. The flowers Daddy shows me are bright red. He says they are his favourite. He teaches me how to spell their name.

'Darling, repeat after me: R-H-O.'

'R-H-O,' I say.

'D-O.'

'D... O,' I say.

'D... E... N,' he says smiling. He is excited, because his nostrils are fluttering again.

'D... E... N,' I say.

'D-R-O-N. R-H-O... D-O... D-E-N... D-R-O-N! Now can you spell it altogether?'

'Yes,' I say, and I do it. 'R-H-O... D-O... D-E-N... D-R-O-N!'

'Well done, my love,' he says, and picks me up. I put my head on his chest and suck my thumb. He bounces me up and down. I like the smell of Daddy's aftershave.

'Now, how about a strawberry ice, for my clever girl?'

'Yes, please.'

He is still happy with me, because he is laughing and his nostrils are fluttering like butterflies. He is looking at me like he really loves me, and he carries me all the way to the Icemaid triangle with the wooden roof, where we buy our ice cream. He bounces me with one hand under my bottom and taps my back with his other hand. I lean my face on his shoulder.

I don't want him to put me down.

We sit on the white-plastic seats, under the umbrella that has *'Lyons Maid'* written on it. Daddy has a choc ice. I have my vanilla-and-strawberry ice lolly. We don't talk. I bite the ice off first and then eat the ice cream under it. The roses in the flower bed smell sweet. When the wind blows, it makes the rose-smelling breeze stronger.

I finish my lolly first and tell Daddy the joke on my stick.

'Who invented fire, Daddy?'

'I don't know love.'

'Some bright spark...'

He laughs and then kisses my forehead three times. His kisses are warm.

Then he says, 'Before we go, I want you to go and stand by that tree, and let me take another photo of you.'

Oh no. Not again.

'Where?' I ask.

He carries me over to the stone wall under the weeping willow tree. He says the light is 'fantastic', that it is a 'photographer's paradise'. I don't understand. I just cross my legs, and try to smile. But I can never do it when I try.

'Think of something happy, darling, like that ice cream!'

That does make me really laugh.

Click.

Click.

Click.

'That's it! Wonderful,' he says. 'Your eyes were genuinely smiling.'

Then he screws the cap onto his camera lens and puts it round his neck.

We start walking back home again through the park.

*

It is getting dark and cold. Daddy has his arm around my shoulder, but he is walking too quickly, so I have to hop and skip to keep up. You can see his long legs and my little ones in the black shadows on the pavement. They are following us.

We walk past a busy square with a statue in the middle; the statue is of a man who is riding a horse and carrying a whip.

Daddy shows me where he works. It is a tall building with a big, wooden door and shields on the front. There are roaring lions either side of the door, with skeletons walking above the doorway. It says *'Middlesex Guildhall'* on the wall with *'Crown Court'* written underneath. I want to ask Daddy about his job, but I have to be careful in case he gets angry again.

'What do you do here, Daddy?'

'I am a circuit judge.'

'What do circuit judges do?'

My hand is warm in his pocket. We are walking again.

'I decide if people have broken the law or not, and how they should be punished if they have,' he says.

I kick a stone. 'And if they have been bad, what do you do?'

'I make a decision on how long to send them to prison for.'

My daddy sends people to prison.

'Do they have to be really bad to go to prison?' I ask.

'Yes, darling…' he laughs.

'How bad, Daddy?'

Would he ever send me to prison?

'They have to have hurt someone or stolen something of great value, normally.'

'Like what? Who was the last person you sent to prison?'

He hasn't got angry yet, so these questions must be OK.

'Two boys used a knife to break into a Mini and they stole the car. But you don't need to know this my love. These are horrible things. You need only think about happy things,' he says, and strokes my hair.

My heart starts beating fast, so I run away down the street when we turn onto Great Smith Street.

'Don't run on too far ahead!' he shouts.

It is so quiet here. There are tall buildings, which are not open, and there is a whirring fan underground, just under the black bars, and warm air is blowing up from there. A car alarm is going 'whheee whhooo'.

I stop on top of the white-plastic squares with lights underneath, and play hopscotch on them whilst Daddy catches up. Then we turn onto Great Peter Street.

It is even quieter here.

In the window of the Mother's Union gift shop, there are big Easter eggs, which are made of cardboard with crosses on them, and books about God with pictures of Jesus flying over the sea.

I don't like this quiet.

'Can I draw when we get home, Daddy?'

'Yes, my love,' he says.

Good. That will fill the gap between now and dinner time.

'What are we having for dinner, Daddy?'

'Just a cold chicken sandwich…'

Gino's Cafe is closed. There are red seats, and no Coke cans in the glass fridge. I once did a really loud pooh noise in there when I was four. Everyone looked at me. Mummy's face went red.

The Arts Council building is closed too.

Everything is closed.

It's getting dark.

It's just me and Daddy.

Big Ben gongs six times.

This time tomorrow I will be back home with Mummy.

CHAPTER THREE
London, 1989
Lucia is sixteen years old

Lucia sits curled up against the radiator, with her knees clasped to her chest.

A dead woodlouse lies on its back on the carpet. She counts its legs-there are sixteen – and then flicks her glance up at Morten Harket on the wall. LL Cool J's 'I Need Love' plays on her cassette player. Lucia loves this song. She taps her foot energetically to its rhythm and mouths the lyrics.

The phone rings in the sitting room. Its bell is loud and jarring.

Her chest splinters. *I hope it's not for me. Please God, no!* Lucia crosses her fingers and touches her mahogany casket three times. Her pulse thrashes through her wrists. Her upper body feels as if someone is shooting a ball up and down inside there.

Lucia clutches her knees tighter to her chest.

The sitting-room door opens.

Oh God, here we go, that colour sequence; red, yellow, green...

BAM!

She jumps.

Her mother thrusts open her bedroom door, hitting Lucia's shin.

'It's for you. It's Matilda,' her mother barks, and she drops the phone on the floor. She stands in Lucia's doorway squinting, with ruffled hair. 'Don't be too long. I need to use the phone.' Her mother coughs up a ball of tar and leaves.

She always says this.

Lucia's heart hammers. She jams the door shut over the curly phone wire and huddles against the hissing radiator.

'All right, Tilda,' she says, forcing an upbeat tone.

'Yo, Luce, what's up?'

'Not a lot. What you doing?' Lucia asks.

'Sam and Jason are coming over later, and we're going to the King's Head. Do you fancy coming?'

'Can't tonight Til, but can I stay on Friday?'

'Course you can. Come for dinner. It's Mum's lentil stew!'

She loves Friday nights at Tilda's. It's her weekend getaway from her mum. They bus it to Islington for a pub crawl, and then have a late-night kebab at the bus stop. All followed by midnight chats till the early hours over a joint and a cuppa. The hangover is always worth it.

Lucia stretches out her legs to relieve her cramp and listens for her mother's sound.

'Hey Lucia, guess what?' Tilda asks.

'What?'

'Janine Sexton got off with Max Smith at the Heath on Saturday night.'

'Lucia!' her mother calls.

The floorboards creak. She is outside Lucia's door waiting.

Lucia covers the mouth piece with her hand 'Yes, Mum,' she replies, faking a polite tone.

'That's enough now, Lucia, off the phone, please. I need it.'

'Mum, I've only just got on,' she replies.

'I'm waiting for a call, Lucia.'

Liar. 'All right, I'm coming in a minute.'

'No, not in a minute, now!'

She knows Tilda can hear all this. Her eyebrows tighten. There is a throbbing between her legs and she knows pressing herself won't stop it.

'Til, it's my mum. I have to go.'

'Your mum is a right loony, Luce,' Tilda laughs.

'Now Lucia!' her mother screams. 'Get off the phone!'

The radiator scorches Lucia's back, but she continues to press against its burn. The pain pauses time and relieves her anguish. The pulsating between her legs will not stop.

'Lucia, get off!'

She tucks the receiver between her chin and neck. 'OK, Mum, two minutes,' she appeases through the gap in the door.

'No, Lucia, that's enough, now!'

Her mum nudges the door.

Lucia slams it shut.

'Get off that phone now!'

Her shoulders quiver.

Lucia's mum shoves the door open. The brass handle rattles.

Reverberate…

Bounce.

She shudders. Lucia's shin stops her entry.

'I said now!' Her mother thrusts at the door again.

Lucia sits with her back right up against the door. 'Til, I have to go,' Lucia says under her breath.

'You're definitely coming over Friday, yeah?'

'Get off that phone!'

Her mother forces the door hard. It bumps against her spine.

'Mum, get out!' Lucia pushes back, twisting and pressing down on her heels. Her face is hot. Her tears are jammed in her head.

Her mum lunges.

Lucia's neck jerks.

'See you Friday, Til.' Lucia hangs up. She winds the phone wire tight around her hand. Her fingers swell and turn an angry pink.

Thump!

Right, bitch, you are going to get it now. Her teeth grit; her face judders. Lucia stands and opens her bedroom door.

Her mum stumbles sideways as her leaning post is taken away.

'Right, you want your phone; here's your fucking phone,' Lucia yells and lobs the telephone to the other side of the hall.

It crashes with a thud by the bathroom. Its metal body is now detached from its frame.

Its bell whimpers.

'There, are you happy now? Have your fucking phone!' Lucia shuffles back into her bedroom. She closes her door, but faces immediate resistance.

The door thuds.

Lucia leans hard against it, but her mother plunges back. The right door panel loosens.

Lucia holds on to the radiator for support. She pushes back and digs her heels in, using her bottom to drive the door back. Her feet begin to slide. She's not strong enough to win this alone. She turns and thrusts against the door, feeling the veins in her face swell.

A gap emerges in the door.

Lucia leans all her weight onto the door, with one leg bent and the other straight as if she were beginning a 100-metre sprint. Her arms lock. Lucia's feet keep slipping backwards.

The gap in the door widens. She rams back, moaning. Her face is puce and looks like she is constipated.

The gap gets bigger. Lucia does not give up. She gives it one last push.

Thump!

'Get out, you cow. This is my room!' Lucia screams in a tone of desperation. She knows she cannot keep this up. Her arm is dead.

She'll kill me when this door opens.

She rams the door for dear life. Her arms buckle, both elbows lose their lock and a gush of tears spurts from her throat. 'Fuck off, bitch, get out!' she roars.

Sweat trickles down her face and her arms fall. The door flies open and bangs Lucia hard on the forehead.

Seconds of oblivion pass.

Thumping sets in around her temples from where the door hit her. She touches her bump. *Bitch, I'll kill you for this.* Her head stings and a sharp stabbing pain sears across her eye.

Her mum stands in front of her like a gorilla, hunched with her arms hanging down.

Lucia holds the bump on her head and snivels. It swells. *I really do hate you. I want you dead, bitch.*

She hears Aswad belting out from a car outside.

Lucia's vision has crinkly lines in it. Lights flash at the corner of her eye. She looks at her mother, who blocks the doorway, and realises she is trapped. 'What is it you want from me? Why can't you leave me alone, Mum?'

Her mum's lips quiver. 'Yo-yo-yo-you are a vile, selfish person. You have no clue about anything.'

'No, Mum, I'm not vile. You are. You are bitter and jealous because I have a life and you don't. You are a miserable, old cow.'

Her mum tries to reply, but stalls in a muddle of stutter. 'L-L-L…'

'You don't really have a call to make, do you? You just can't stand me having friends and being happy, can you? Bitch,' Lucia shouts.

Her mum's mouth jabbers, 'Y-Y-Y…'

'I hate you!' Lucia shouts.

Whack!

What just happened?

Lucia's face is knocked sideways by a loud clap, like a heavy book hitting the floor. Her mother's hand is cupped perfectly on Lucia's cheek.

Rain starts to drum against the window pane.

The sensation of pins and needles sets in around her eye. *She just slapped me.*

Lucia holds her prickling cheek as the lost seconds catch up with her. She glances at the beads of sweat under her mum's mouth. Her cheek burns. Her eye is sore.

It must have been her ring that hit my eye.

Her mother stoops like a boxer waiting for his hit.

The 6.00pm news blasts out from the sitting room.

Lucia's watering eye flickers. She strains to open it. *Mum's arm launched right back, and then whack.* Fast ticking pulses again between her legs. *I'm going to kill her for real now.*

Lucia grabs her mother by her sweater and shakes her. Her eyes are stretched wide and her body spasms as she shakes her mother. Lucia grits her teeth hard; her face convulses.

'Now, you listen here, bitch,' Lucia says, juddering, 'You hit me like that again and I *will* kill you with my bare hands.'

Her mother's spectacles fly off, her head tilts back and her neck flops from side to side like a rag doll with no core.

'Do you understand me?' Lucia shouts. *Is she conscious?* 'Do you? With my own bare hands, I will kill you!'

Lucia's body shudders. She cannot stop shaking her mum. Blood shoots to her face with every shake. She feels a complete release when it happens. She doesn't know who she is. Fantasies flash in her mind of stabbing her mum in the back three times with the red kitchen knife; deep, hard stabs. Her mum screams for help in her vision, and then falls dead onto the floor.

With wet hair and dank skin, Lucia comes to. *What am I doing?* She catches a glimpse of her mother's white scalp, a reminder of her mortality. Lucia realises she is hurting her. She has a contradictory urge to hold her and make this all better.

Lucia releases her mother from her grip and pushes her to the other side of the hallway, where her mother topples onto the coat rack, but then quickly resumes a semi-upright posture.

Lucia dodges her mum's stare. She knows she is not going to get away with this. She tries to second guess what her mum is about to do.

Pounce!

Her mother launches herself.

Leap...

She marches down the hallway and seizes Lucia by her hair.

'Ow, stop, Mum!'

Her mother yanks Lucia's head down to the floor.

'Help!' Lucia screams.

Her mother tugs Lucia, by her hair, along the hall.

A stinging sensation pierces her head. Bent over and contorted, Lucia has one arm in the air and the other on the floor. 'Let me go! You're hurting me! Please let me go!' she cries.

Her scalp feels like it is on fire. 'You're pulling my hair out, Mum; let me go! I've never done anything to you!'

Tug.

'You're supposed to be my mum!'

Tug.

Lucia writhes and wriggles. Tears stream down her face. She groans and pushes against her mum's waist. 'Let me go, please!'

Her back strains from wrenching. The harder she pulls the harder her mum yanks. She stops heaving herself away because it hurts too much. She stands bent over, holding her mum's knees for balance, and counts the coffee stains on the carpet.

'You never learn do you, you vile creature!' Her mother jerks hard. 'You just never learn.'

Lucia feels a trickle of vomit fizz in her throat. She punches her mother's ribs.

Yank.

She thrashes her fists at her mum's arms, but has no success. And then her survival instinct kicks in. *Stamp!* Hard, on her mother's right foot.

Her mum lets go and stumbles backwards.

The release loosens the strain around her eyes. She grips her lower back for support and stands, looking into her mother's eyes. Mucus drips from Lucia's nose and her hair looks like a wild horse's mane on a windy day.

'I really do hate you,' Lucia says with steeliness in her voice.

Her mum holds in her hand a clump of Lucia's hair, which resembles a brunette Brillo pad.

'You are not my mother,' Lucia says in a controlled tone. 'You are a monster.'

Zema's house flashes in her mind. It is a safe place to go to.

There is a prolonged show of will. Lucia stares the longest and then walks into her room calmly. She puts her bus pass, her two pound coins and her cherry lip balm in her bag. She slips on her coat, slides past her mum and opens the flat door.

'Where are you going, Lucia?'

'As far away as possible from you,' Lucia replies and slams the door.

She leaps down the stairs three at a time and opens the front door. The cold night air soothes her hot face and sore eye.

She looks up at the open sky. Released, she is free.

Lucia jogs in a steady rhythm past the held-up cars. She inhales the smell of exhaust fumes and takes in the lights on the Holiday Inn balconies. Her legs do not tire. She keeps running, with tears cascading down her face.

This night is friendly. Strangers are no threat.

She runs past the Kurumaya restaurant, taking in the smells of steamed fish; past the Hampstead Theatre; and then sprints through the subway up the Finchley Road, finding more stamina with each stride. She concentrates on the sound of her Timberland boots pounding the pavement. Each thud affirms her freedom.

She thinks about Zema's warm flat. Her dad will be reading *The Guardian* with a tooth pick hanging from his mouth. Beethoven will be playing, injera and sega wat (beef stew) will be simmering on the stove. She and Zema will sit outside and smoke Benson and Hedges.

If she's not in, she'll keep running to Golders Green and beyond. It doesn't matter where to. She will run into the night.

The night is hers.

She is free.

CHAPTER FOUR

LONDON, 1980

LUCIA IS SEVEN YEARS OLD

Bang!

Daddy slams the front door shut. We are home now. It is dark, and the carpet smells of clean dust.

'Here, my love, give me your anorak,' Daddy says, 'and wipe your feet.'

I have trodden in dog pooh. It smells horrible.

I give him my coat, and blow into my hands to make them warm. The weather machine on the wall says it is below 5°C.

He bolts the door at the top and bottom. I don't like the sound. I can't get out now.

There is nobody nearby. My heart is beating so hard, it feels like someone is banging a drum inside of me and it won't stop.

How am I going to fill this quiet until tomorrow when I go back home?

Cold air comes from the downstairs loo. My cat, Pearly, died in that loo when I was three. I don't know who killed her. She was cut up into lots of pieces one morning and the bin men took her away.

Daddy hangs his raincoat on the hooks and gives me my Fruit Pastilles.

'You go on up to the sitting room; I'll follow,' he says.

I take my shoes off and jump up the stairs two at a time. My mouth has gone dry. There is no spit when I swallow. *How many hours is it until tomorrow morning, when the door won't be locked anymore and we'll hear people passing by outside?*

It smells of old suitcases in the sitting room. My feet smell of hard Edam cheese, but not as smelly as cheddar cheese. The little carriage clock is ticking, and the rain is dropping on the window. There is no other sound. Daddy is still downstairs, but I know my Caran d'Ache and paper are kept in the second drawer of his desk. He doesn't mind if I open that drawer.

I get them out to draw him a picture.

Daddy likes it when I make pictures. He says they are original. I draw a wonky line with my black pen, and continue the line around the page until it makes a pattern.

Daddy is coming up the stairs. I concentrate hard and look down.

'There's my little love,' he says. 'Are you having a nice time?'

'I'm drawing you a picture,' I say.

He chuckles and pours himself a big glass of whisky in his special glass. It smells so strong that it tickles the hairs in my nose.

He always has a Daniels Whisky when we get home from the park. The ice in his glass clinks, then tings!

Daddy sits next to me, in his green armchair. He taps his hand on the arm of his chair. He hums, like he is bored. I still don't look up because I know he is looking at me. I fill in my pattern with triangles. It looks like Charlotte's web in the book.

A lady with high heels walks by. Her heels go clink clonk. I wish she would stay out there, so I could still hear her noise, but her clink clonk disappears. It's quiet again.

I peep through my fringe. Daddy has fallen asleep. He calls it snoozing. That means he doesn't go to sleep for very long. My breathing comes back again properly. I colour in my black shapes with a lilac pencil and make sure I don't colour over the line.

Daddy snores.

His hands droop off the arms of his chair, and his fat tummy goes up and down. He sounds like a pig grunting when he breathes in and like a kettle whistling when he breathes out.

Now I colour three more squares in grass green and pink.

He grunts three times. His body shakes, and he opens his eyes. They are slits and look like pigs' eyes. My breath is stuck in my throat. His eyes close again.

Big Ben chimes seven times. It's seven o'clock, nearly bath time and bedtime. This time tomorrow, I will be back with Mummy, and watching *Top of The Pops* with Ben and Tim.

I use grey and blue for the circles; it doesn't matter if they don't match.

Raindrops fall on the window at an angle and then slip down. The sky is growling. Thunder is coming soon. I suck my thumb and stroke my cold elbow with the back of my hand. My tummy is rumbling.

Daddy's big toe is very long. His nail is nearly coming through his sock.

Now I colour the last five oblong shapes in orange and yellow.

He grunts and wakes up. He looks confused. 'Hello, my love,' he says, wipes his eyes with his hanky and licks his lips.

'Daddy, I've made you a picture!' I wave it in front of him. The carpet is itchy.

'Isn't that beautiful, darling?' he says, and looks at it far away then close up. 'I'll put that in a frame above my desk,' he says smiling. He likes it.

'Now, my love, how do you fancy a cold chicken sandwich?'

'Yes, please.'

He closes the wooden shutters, puts a metal bar across them and turns on the lamps. He kisses my forehead twice on the way out. His lips are wet; his breath warm.

I eat all the orange Fruit Pastilles while I wait for my sandwich. I try to suck them without chewing, but it's impossible. The photo on the table of Nanny Rosa, wearing a red jumper, reminds me of the Christmas when she bought me a Miss World and an Etch A Sketch.

'Darling!' Daddy calls, 'Your sandwich is ready. Wash your hands and come down.'

*

As I walk downstairs, I hear Daddy roaring like a lion.

I sit on the window seat and suck the end of my hair. I'm frightened.

'Rrrrrrrrrrraaaaaaaaaaaaaaaahhhhhhhhhhhhhhh. Raaaaaaaaaaaaaa. Raaaaaaaaaaaaaa. Rrrrrrrrawwwwwwahh-hhhhhhhhhhhh!'

The front door is still locked. Would he hear if I unlocked it?

'Rrrrrrraaawwww!'

I creep down the rest of the stairs and peek through the crack in the door. Daddy is punching the kitchen counter and shaking his head like a dog that has been in water. His hair is wet. He is growling. On his red polo neck, there are wet circles under his arms.

I wait outside the dining room and cross all of my fingers.

A fork flies off the counter onto the floor.

'Damn you woman!' he curses under his breath.

I think he is talking to Mummy in his head. I count to three.

One…

Two…

Three…

And step inside.

'Hello, my love,' he says, and laughs like he cannot stop.

He knows that I saw him. Sweat is dripping down his face.

It is dark in the dining room, even with the light on. I can see my sandwich on the plate with a gherkin and crisps on the side. There is a wish bone from the chicken on the counter.

'Let's pull the wish bone, Daddy,' I say.

He laughs and holds it up. 'Come on then.'

We pull it and he gets the big bone.

'Make a wish, Daddy.'

'You make one, my love,' he replies and gives the bone to me.

I close my eyes and wish that I don't ever see Daddy shouting like that again.

*

It's bath time, and we are in Daddy's bathroom.

He undresses me. I stand, and he sits on a chair humming 'Do-Re-Mi,' from the film, *The Sound of Music*. He is thinking deep thoughts, but I don't know what they are.

'Lift up your arms, darling, nice and high.'

I put my arms in a straight line up to the sky. When he pulls off my polo-neck jumper, it crackles like electricity. It catches my hair, which sparks too. I get an electric shock when I touch his arm. Daddy says it's called static. He pulls down my trousers and looks at my tummy button for a long time, and then he pulls my knickers down. I take off my socks.

He puts the plug in the bath and runs the hot and cold water together. He says it's important to get the temperature just right. The steam circles up to the ceiling from the water.

Daddy is looking at me in the mirror, watching what I do. I don't know what to do.

I push my tummy button in with my finger, but it pops back out again. I walk on the blue-and-white squares on the floor without treading on the edge of the squares. I count them. There are forty-two squares in total.

He is still looking at me.

'Daddy, can I put some bubble bath in the water?'

'Yes, darling,' he says, so I pour Mr Matey into the hot water. It is bright blue and smells of tangerines. The water changes from white to a magic sea-blue, like in Jersey.

'Where does the steam go, Daddy?' I ask, to stop him looking at me in that scary way.

'It evaporates, darling.'

'What does evaporate mean?'

'It means that it turns to wet air.'

'That's clever.'

There is nothing more I can say to him now. I can only ask questions that are not about him. I throw my wind up fishes into the bath. Daddy tests the water with his hand.

'Can I get in now?'

'Not quite yet. It needs to be lukewarm.'

I walk around on the squares again. This time there are forty-five.

'There you go, my love; in you get,' Daddy says, and rolls up his sleeves like he is about to do a job. My legs tickle inside when he does that and my heart beats fast.

The bath is blue like the rest of the bathroom. It says *'Armitage'* next to the taps. The bubbles cover my body and the water is nice, not like at Mummy's where it makes my skin red. Daddy kneels by the bath with his hands in the water and wiggles his fingers.

I put a big scoop of bubbles on my chin to make a beard.

Daddy laughs at me; his nostrils flutter. 'You splash about, my love, and have a nice time' he says.

I make shapes in the water and count how many seconds the bubbles take to pop. Daddy watches my eyes, smiling.

My plastic fish swim; their wings flap fast. He stands up to go away. I lie back in the warm water and put my foot on the cold tap – it's really cold. Water drips on my foot. It makes the bit between my legs go tingly. I hold my foot there.

Daddy comes back with his camera. I hate when he does this in the bath.

'Now, my love, let's get you washed and scrubbed shall we?'

He rubs Imperial Leather soap into my blue flannel until it becomes frothy. It smells of vanilla. It's his favourite soap. He rubs the flannel under my arms and on my tummy. He tells me to stand up, washes between my legs and then rinses me by splashing water over my body. I close my eyes as the water washes over me.

'Sit down, my love, so we can wash your feet.'

I love this bit.

He puts my leg on the edge of the bath, rubs soap into his hand and washes my foot. He goes in and out of my toes carefully to make sure it is all clean. I don't want him to stop.

Goosebumps go up and down my legs. He does my other foot the same.

'There we go,' he says, 'all done.' He puts my leg back in the water.

I feel sleepy.

The water is getting cold. My fingers are wrinkly.

Daddy is in the corner of the room pointing his camera at me. I don't like it. He is turning his lens backwards and forwards, and bending down to the floor. What do I do?

'Darling!' he says.

I look back at him.

Click!

'Again, my love,'

I try to smile.

Click!

'Give me a really big smile, darling!'

I don't know how to. I suck my cheeks in tight like the ladies do in the films when they are in the bath and a man is watching them. I think that is what he wants.

Click!

'Marvellous. Now let's get you out and get you dry,' he says.

I did it right.

He puts the cap back on his camera lens and sighs like he has caught a fish he was looking for. He lays his camera on the windowsill and lifts me out of the bath, wrapped in a thick warm towel.

*

It is bed time in Daddy's bed, not mine. I sleep with him when I come to stay. I don't know why I don't sleep in my room.

It is warm. Everything is brown, even the walls. The shutters are closed.

If I screamed, no one would hear me.

Daddy lays the towel on the bed for me to sit on. He says, 'It's important to dry yourself properly or else you can get ring worm.'

I think that's a real worm in your skin.

'Sit down, darling,' he says.

He rubs the towel over me and wipes my feet, going in and out of every toe. He says if you don't do it like that you can get athletes' foot. He squirts talcum powder onto his hand and rubs it on my back and arms. It feels silky and smells of flowers.

His hand is smooth. The powder puffs into the air like clouds. I want him to rub my back forever.

I look like Snow White.

'Stand up, darling,' he says and puts my stripy pyjamas on me. They are from Selfridges and smell clean, not of smoke like my purple ones at Mummy's.

'There you go, my love; all ready for bed.'

I don't want to go to bed.

'Can I have a drink and a story first?' I ask. That will make it longer until bedtime.

'Yes, I'll go and make you an Ovaltine, and we'll read *Peter Rabbit*.'

That's the best one. I like the bit when he steals the radishes, gets chased by the big man and escapes under the fence.

'Get into bed. I'll be back in a minute.'

Daddy's bed is huge. The sheets are stiff, and it has lots of fluffy pillows. I am on the left side. He will be on the right side when he comes to bed. It's always the same. His bed is high up like in *The Princess and the Pea*.

Big Ben chimes eight times. It is eight o'clock.

In twelve hours, it will be morning. The shutters will be open, there will be noise, and I will be having my boiled egg and soldiers. Then, in six more hours, I will be back with Mummy, eating white toast with melted butter on and getting my clothes ready for school.

Daddy comes in with my drink. He makes it with lots of frothy milk in my Smarties mug that Shelley Marshall bought me for my birthday.

'Here you go, my love,' he says. He tucks the sheets in, so they are tight around me, and flutters the brown blanket, so that it covers all of the bed.

He sits on the bed and opens the book.

CHAPTER FIVE

LONDON, 1989

LUCIA IS SIXTEEN YEARS OLD

Three days have passed since Lucia ran away to stay with her best friend Zema.

Her last three ten-pence pieces jangle in her pocket, and the residue of Silk Cut cigarette smoke tastes bitter in her mouth. Not even her last cherry Tune can take it away.

She stands outside her flat door and listens to her mother's movements.

Flashbacks of their fight race through her mind like a film reel: the force of her mother's hand hitting her cheek and the hatred in her mother's eye.

Lucia stares at the puddles of dust in each stair corner and wonders why no one cleans it away. The smell of moist rubble gives her a strange sense of comfort. She picks her fingernail in the warm burrow of Twix crumbs and Dentyne wrappers in her pocket. Her heartbeat thumps, whilst she listens to the footsteps of Clara and Mark pottering about upstairs in their happy cocoon. The sound of water rushing through the pipes is close.

She does not want to go in. Her mouth is parched.

She puts her ear to the door, as always, to decipher what mood her mum is in. The deafening sounds of *Countdown* hit her like a hurricane blast.

Thank God for that! Beneath the television sound is the reassuring sound of her mother's hearty cough, bringing up all her phlegm properly. Her mum is not in a mood. A waterfall shoots down from Lucia's throat to her abdomen as the relief sets in. She scratches her head. Flakes of dandruff sprinkle her shoulders.

She turns the key.

'Lucia!' The relief in her mother's cry is stark.

'Hi Mum.' Her mother's need tugs at her.

'How, ho-ho-ho-how was Zema's?' her mother asks.

'OK, thanks,' Lucia replies politely, noticing the shadows under her mum's eyes.

Her mother stands opposite Lucia smelling of fag smoke and crab paste. Her sea-blue tracksuit bottoms are stained with scrambled egg, and around her neck she wears her mother Daphna's egg-white pearls. Lucia's eye catches the bright shade of forest green from the palm tree in the fireplace behind, and the burgundy and lapis blue on the African batik hanging on the wall.

'Did y-y-you ge-ge-ge-get your essay ba-ba-back?' her mum asks.

'Yeah, I got a B,' Lucia lies, blowing air into her cheeks.

'Very good,' her mum replies.

Lucia walks to her bedroom. Her mum follows like a lonely Alsatian.

'Do you want a drink, Lucia?'

'Orange squash, please.'

She wishes she was still at Zema's, smelling the Ethiopian spices simmering on the stove and listening to her brother Mebrete laugh, with his white teeth gleaming in his mouth.

Her bedroom is cold. The smell of damp hits her; that lingering odour, still fresh from the flood of 1979.

*

Flashes of that day shoot through her mind, as she recollects the deep rumble that disturbed that New Year's Day. She looks up at the corner where the first drips of water began. How quickly that drip turned to streaming brown water gushing down every wall, like rivers. She clamps her legs together. She can still hear the sound of her mother howling for help, and can still see her brothers frantically trying to catch the water with saucepans and bowls. But nothing worked.

The maniacal screams from Petunia downstairs echo in her mind, 'My Chesterfield! My Chesterfield!'

Then that unforgettable thud as her bedroom ceiling caved in. Each ceiling fell one by one. With broken pieces of cement everywhere, the flat looked like a wasteland.

The image of the wedges of rubble in the bowls of pickled onions from the night before are still clear in her mind, as is the sorrow, by candlelight, of a lost home. She feels a lump like a hard walnut in her throat, thinking about the sad weeks that followed. Lucia went to live with her father, her mother went to Auntie Dora's, and her brothers moved to their father's whilst their home was restored.

*

Lucia looks down.

She's been in here.

She knows by the lines of dark blue on her carpet. Her felt-backed carpet changes in tone depending on which way it is brushed, and she remembers how it looked before she left.

'Lucia, do you want a Penguin biscuit?' her mother calls.

'Yes, please.'

Lucia flops onto her pink-striped beanbag. She sits, with her knees clutched, and looks at her Coca-Cola collection on the mantlepiece. Her Cherry Coke robot is in centre place, and her centenary bottle next to it reminds Lucia of when she and Tilda went to the Coca-Cola headquarters in Kensington to take their pick of vintage memorabilia. It was like Christmas came early.

China clanks in the kitchen.

'Are you going to come and watch *Blue Peter*?'

'I'll come in a minute, Mum.' She wishes her mother was not so lonely.

Lucia zips open her pink bean bag and waves her bare arm around in the millions of polystyrene balls inside. She loves losing her dancing arm in a deep sea of white balls, which massage her skin. She loves the whistling sounds and their soothing tickle on her flesh.

'Lucia, it's starting…'

The sound of Scottish bagpipes drift from the sitting room; *Blue Peter* is starting. Lucia walks down the hallway and stops by the freezer. She grips the handle and listens to the sound of its non-stop hum. Her mind is captured, out of the blue, by the memory of her recent exchange visit to Paris to stay with Cecile and her family.

*

Two fantastic weeks flood back to her. Smoking Philip Norris cigarettes, she felt so free striding down the Champs de Elysees with Cecile in the evening drizzle.

She can still hear that soft whisper of Cecile's mum waking them up in the morning and can remember those trips to Montmartre. Memories rush back of watching artists chalking portraits along the Seine and fancying Antoine, Cecile's brother, with his mousey, curly hair flopped on his head. She recollects those long evening meals by candlelight, the laughter and the chats. They felt like family.

*

Her attention returns to the hellish sound of TV talking to no one. She screws her fists into tight balls and sighs. That is over. This is reality now.

She peeks through the spyhole in the sitting-room door, which has been there ever since the doors were stripped in 1979, and stares at the back of her mother's nodding head.

Lucia walks in.

Her mother is sitting slouched in her olive-green armchair, gazing out of the window and mumbling to herself, with a Berkeley cigarette between her teeth. Smoke swirls in and around her mouth like it would from a puffing dragon, making her splutter and wheeze. She is surrounded by a sea of newspapers, including the *Daily Mail*; *My Weekly*; and a copy of *Roget's Thesaurus* with the front cover ripped off. Under her foot is an empty plate with a tomato ketchup stain on it. Her wooden coffee table is cluttered with old emery boards, her leather Filofax and her reading specs. It is her mum's world of chaos and comfort.

'Here, Lucia; your sandwich and biscuit.'

'Thanks, Mum.'

On the coffee table, underneath the fronds of the fern plant, is a glass of orange squash in a tumbler, and a sandwich and a Penguin biscuit on a blue-and-white china plate with willows on it.

The sitting room is large, and painted magnolia with a hint of lemon. The curtains are burgundy velvet to match the sofa, and the carpet is French beige. Cigarette smoke spirals in figures of eight from her mother's mouth up to the ceiling, which has lines running from each corner to its centre, where a hexagon labyrinth forms the Grecian ceiling's centre piece.

It stinks of smoke.

Lucia's head is pounding. She sits on the divan covered with an Afghan throw and lined with bright, embroidered cushions. It is a sofa by day, but her mother's bed by night. It has been the way ever since they moved in, in 1978. It is a signature of her mother's sacrifice: having no bedroom when Lucia, Ben and Tim all do. She rarely lets a day go by without reminding them all.

Lucia pulls at the fringe of the Persian rug with her toes.

The blossom branches swing outside. Happy cackles resound from the garden downstairs where Kass bounces on her trampoline. The sky is a crisp cobalt blue. A breeze wafts in and refreshes Lucia's sweaty neck. Lucia watches the blurry TV screen. An old wooden set, it sits lopsided on a metal stand. Grey lines cruise vertically down the screen. Moving the aerial does sweet Fanny Adams so she doesn't bother. She watches the children making origami boats on *Blue Peter* using coloured paper, and floating them in a tank of water.

'Clever those boats are, aren't they?' her mum says, trying to enter into Lucia's world.

She doesn't care about the boats.

Lucia bites into the white, plasticky bread; the tart taste of pickled carrots and onions from the Sandwich Spread spurt a sharp fizz around her mouth. Her gaze is pulled beyond the trees to the red-slated roof tops, under which rich Arabian families live. She wonders about her friend Lyndsey, and thinks how strange it is that her mum is white but wears a hijab.

Her gaze finds its way to the blue glass ornament in the centre of the windowsill.

'Nice sandwich, Lucia?'

'Yes, thanks.'

Lucia turns to her mother, who witters to herself whilst glaring at the oak clock, with no tick, on the wall. The arms always rest at three o'clock. Lucia feels the area around her lungs tighten. She yearns to do something to make her mum happy. She thinks how much better her life would be if her mum wasn't so lonely and didn't need her so much. She wishes she were like Tilda's mum, chopping vegetables when she came home, listening to *Women's Hour* and full of conversation about her fulfilling day at work. Not like Lucia's mum, who goes off to a part-time job as a National Health Service receptionist that she hates, then slumps in front of daytime TV all afternoon. Her contrary feelings of hatred and pity for her mother trap her in a quandary.

She brushes the breadcrumbs off her knees and looks at the TV. The children are painting hard-boiled eggs – fun! She imagines crawling into the screen to be with them.

'Aren't they lovely?' her mum says, still trying to make conversation.

It doesn't work.

Lucia's awareness of her mum hauls her away from *Blue Peter*. She sucks her thumb and curls into the comfort of her inner thoughts, stroking the back of her upper arm with her hand. She closes her eyes, relishing that childhood sensation of her tongue ticking against her thumb.

Her mother mutters incoherent strings of words to herself. 'Yes, yes, mmm, mmm, yes, yes…'

They are both lost in the solace of their own worlds.

'Oh, dear me,' her mother sighs, 'too terrible it all is, Lucia.'

Lucia scrutinises her mum's frown and the furrowed worry lines etched in her forehead. She can see the loneliness in her mum's eyes. Shielded by a hard exterior, they dance a restless story, lost and alone.

It's not her fault, she's had a miserable life, Lucia thinks to herself.

The air purifier by her mother's feet emits a perfumed air.

'Can I have some fruit, Mum?'

'Yes, but no-no-no-not too much. Don't sp-sp-spoil your dinner. We're having chicken pies tonight.'

Lucia reaches for the blue-and-white china fruit bowl, with only a few Coxes apples and three wilting plums left. Everything must get eaten. Nothing goes to waste. It is part of her mother's legacy that she inherited as a war child, from having to survive on rations and bringing home the coal, carried on her back.

If there is no suffering involved, something is not right.

Lucia bites into her apple and enjoys the sweet juice that squirts into her mouth. She gazes into the glass lampshade above. Three dead bluebottles lie in its base. It only gets cleaned out three times a year, which is a ritual where her mother stands screaming on a chair and demands at least three henchmen to assist the operation.

'Are you going to go and do your homework, Lucia?'

'Yeah, in a minute.'

Her eyes shift to the Cezanne print opposite, which is of two old men playing cards in a poorly lit tavern: one thinking and the other smoking a cigar. She dreams of Mediterranean towns where people pass the days easily, whilst she crunches the earthy apple pips. Her mother clears her ear out with her gold pen and smells the pen afterwards.

Blue Peter ends. 'Dud u dud u doo, dud u dud u dud u doo…'

Lucia walks to the door. She stops by her mother's chair, pulled by the comfort of her mum, who chews the biscuit crumbs from her jumper.

'Just go and do half an hour, eh?' her mum suggests.

'All right,' Lucia replies, and walks to her bedroom.

She closes her bedroom door.

CHAPTER SIX
LONDON, 1980
LUCIA IS SEVEN YEARS OLD

The room is dark.

Daddy is having his 'evening drink' downstairs. The bed has lots of space in it and the sheets smell of lemon. My leg is cold. I rub the back of my foot up and down my leg. It helps me to fall asleep. The tap in the bathroom goes drip, drip, drip. The toilet rumbles.

There is a triangle of light in the doorway. Daddy has left the door open and the hall light on because he knows I am scared of the dark. Big Ben strikes on the hour.

I don't like being alone up here. I wish he would come to bed.

Daddy's red tie with gold spots is hanging over the bathroom door. The room smells of his aftershave.

I know I should be asleep.

His glass clinks, and his footsteps downstairs make the floorboards creak.

This time tomorrow I will be back at Mummy's with shouting and noise. On Monday, I will be sitting in the 'quiet bay' for story time, drinking milk, which tastes like sick, from a blue straw.

I suck my thumb. My tongue ticks against it.

My eyes are closing.

I'm falling asleep now.

The village is like nowhere I have ever been. It is tiny, like a miniature dolls' house. I am huge, like a giant snowman towering over everybody. The people look like dwarfs. I am walking along the streets. I am so big that I take up all of the street. There are green fields behind me. It is sunny and the wind is blowing on my face. I am smiling, and the mini people are smiling back at me. The shops sell candyfloss in every colour – red, blue and brown – it's a mini-sized magic world.

I am light when I walk, and the air lifts me when I jump. I am like a puppet with invisible strings on my back. I land gently even from high above. I float higher and higher away from the village and from all the mini matchstick people. I wonder if I am going to fall, but I don't. I flap my arms and start to fly. I glide away into open, blue sky. The green fields below me become tiny. They look like small stripes now. I go faster and faster into the open space. I have no idea how I will land. It's quiet.

Suddenly, there's an escalator. It's horrible. I am running down it really fast and I am hopping three steps at a time, bouncing off each stair. I don't know if I am going to land on a step or slip.

I land in slow motion.

The escalator is going too fast. I know I am going to reach the bottom before I can stop. I am going to crash into the wall ahead. I can't stop! My feet are ahead of me. I am going to crash.

Flash!

The light stings my eyes. My eyes blink fast. *Was that village real?*

I'm awake.

Daddy has come to bed.

That was all a dream. I thought I was flying.

I can hear him taking his clothes off. I keep my eyes closed, so that he thinks I am asleep. I am curled tight in a small ball at the edge of the bed, with the sheet right up to my neck. His belt buckle hits the leg of the chair. His coins jangle in his pocket when he takes his trousers off. I must not look.

But I do.

I can see his white shorts and fat tummy when he goes to the bathroom. He is doing a wee for a long time. The toilet flushes, water runs and then the plug hole clunks.

I want to be flying again. I can't get back to sleep.

It's dark!

The light goes off. Daddy gets into bed next to me. The mattress sinks down and then comes back up like a seesaw. He smells of Imperial Leather soap.

I am far away from him, curled tight on the edge of the bed. I hold my breath. My heart is beating fast and my tummy is fluttering like a butterfly. My throat is scratchy.

I need a drink. I can't swallow.

Big Ben chimes eleven times. That means it is eleven o'clock. It will be morning in seven hours. I want Mummy.

Daddy yawns. He stretches, wipes his eye, and spreads his arms and legs out wide. He is taking up all of the bed. His hand strokes my back. His cold foot touches my leg. His pyjamas are furry and his breath smells of whisky.

'Hello, my love,' he whispers in my ear. Whisky breath is strong.

I do not say anything. I stay curled up in a ball. I want to turn around, but he will know I am awake if I do. My eyes are shut really tight. Brown and blue lines flash in them with yellow stars. My head hurts. Miss Daniels once said if you count sheep, it makes you go to sleep. But I can't see any sheep to count. I don't know how you do it.

My heart is going 'bam, bam' very hard. The blanket is itchy.

Daddy rubs his foot up and down my leg. He knows I am awake. I turn around. He puts his arm around me, and strokes my back. It is warm curled up on Daddy's stomach. My head goes up and down as he breathes. My eyes are closing.

*

It is blurry.

Children are building sandcastles on a big beach. The sea is far out. I am playing with the children. Loud aeroplanes are flying over us. They get louder. It becomes windy. The sky turns stormy. Sand blows all over…

I am turning and tossing. My eyes are closed.

  I'm pushing hard with my hand.

Blank.

I'm kicking.

Stop!

I am kicking Daddy hard.

Go away! I don't like it.

It hurts.

Sweat.

I'm wriggling. The sheets are tangled over my head.

I bump into Daddy's nose. My legs are heavy.

I'm kicking fast.

The wind is blowing hard, and the children are running fast. The sand is sinking.

Bang! My foot is kicking his leg hard. I am trying to breathe, but there is no air.

There is a funny tingling; it's fizzy.

The children start to go down in the sand and then disappear. I am still running fast, faster…

'Sssssshhhhhh,' is whispering in my ear.

Stop.

*

I have woken up.

Big Ben chimes three times. It is three o'clock in the morning.

I open my eyes. Daddy is lying flat with his arms out

and his mouth open. I am hot. My tummy feels sick. I want Mummy.

'Go back to sleep, darling,' Daddy says, 'It is the middle of the night.' He taps my arm three times.

'I feel sick, Daddy,' I say.

'Go back to sleep,' he says again and puts his arm around me. The wooden chair by the bed leg looks like an elephant's foot. My leg hurts. There are tears stuck in my head.

*

'Good morning, my darling,' Daddy says. He is leaning over me stroking my arm. He smells of morning breath and has yellow bits of sleep in the corner of his eyes.

Big Ben chimes seven times.

'Did you sleep well?' he asks.

I don't say anything. My eyes flicker and sting when I open them.

'You had a disrupted night,' Daddy says. 'You were kicking a lot.'

Why was I kicking? The brown blanket was over my face.

'Sorry, Daddy,' I say.

'You kick a lot in the night, my love.' His arm is around me and he licks his lips. He stands up, takes the iron bar off the wooden shutters and opens them. Now it is light in here.

I pull the sheet over my head and close my eyes. I don't want to get out of bed.

Daddy puts on his black dressing gown with white polka dots on. He wipes the sleep out of his eye and sneezes into a handkerchief.

'I'm going downstairs to make your favourite – scrambled eggs on toast,' Daddy says and tickles my feet under the blanket.

It's not my favourite. 'Grandpa's eggs' is my favourite, which is messy scrambled eggs with bread and tomatoes mixed together. I make that with Ben on Saturdays.

I don't say anything. I suck my thumb and pick the skin off my cheek. My legs are stiff.

The sheets were tangled. My foot was hitting his leg hard. Don't think about it!

Tomorrow is school, and I will be making faces out of butter beans and pasta shapes in art with Miss Daniels. It is assembly on Monday morning and we will sing 'All Things Bright and Beautiful' from the orange hymn book, with Mrs Edwards playing the piano. Mr Ellison will wink at me. In the afternoon, it will be rounders. Mummy will be waiting for me after school with my Fruit Pastilles, and when I get home I will have a peanut-butter sandwich and a Penguin biscuit, and watch *Play School* on TV.

'Darling! Please wash your hands and face, and come downstairs,' Daddy calls.

I don't want to go downstairs.

My breath smells of wind under the covers. Daddy is cooking bacon in the kitchen. He always has it on Sundays, with a fried egg, two pieces of toast and juice.

'Darling!' he calls again, 'Please don't make me call you again.'

I get out of bed.

The bathroom floor is cold. I look in the mirror. My face looks funny. One eye is bigger than the other, and my hair is squashed to my cheek. I brush my teeth with my Miss Piggy toothbrush and with the toothpaste that has a blue stripe down the middle.

Daddy's razor blade is on the edge of the sink. His gold cufflinks are on the shelf next to his Givency aftershave bottle with diamond shapes on it. He wears his cufflinks with a smart shirt to The Garrick Club on Sunday. I pick up his aftershave, unscrew the lid and smell it.

'Darling! What are you doing?'

Daddy is standing behind me. I didn't hear him come in. He is looking at me in the mirror. His cheeks are red. His eyes do not move. His nostrils are flickering.

I look at him in the mirror.

'Nothing, Daddy,' I say. 'I was just brushing my teeth.' I put his bottle back on the shelf.

His eyes move from side to side. I look down. I think he might hurt me.

'Don't touch my things again, darling.'

'Sorry, Daddy,' I say, and follow him downstairs.

*

The table is laid with the silver knives and forks with swirls on them, and a napkin is tied in a knot in my glass. There is a big jug of orange juice with bits in on the table. Daddy pours milk on my Rice Krispies. It is creamy from the top of the bottle. Crackle!

Daddy scoops his cornflakes into a bowl and puts *The Observer* newspaper on the table. It makes the tablecloth grey. The magazine next to the paper has a picture of a man in white and it says *'Pope John Paul dies'*. I don't know who John Paul is. On the front of the newspaper it says this in capital letters:

SIR GEOFFREY HOWE DELIVERS FIRST
CONSERVATIVE BUDGET FOR SIX YEARS.

I don't understand. I turn over the page.

Daddy pours his tea into a mug. He is staring at me.

'What's a Conservative budget, Daddy?' I ask.

'It's the money the government decides to spend on the country, my love,' he replies and sips his tea.

'Does it have a lot of money?' I ask to make the quiet go away.

'It depends,' he says, 'on what is happening in the country.'

There is nothing to say now. I kick the chair leg and look down.

'Don't kick the chair, please, darling.' His face looks serious. He is thinking about something, but I don't know what.

'What time are you taking me back to Mummy's?'

'The normal time, but I want to take you to the Turner exhibition first,' he says and blows his nose.

Daddy's tummy was warm.

My scrambled eggs taste creamy, and the butter on my toast is thick. Daddy turns the pepper mill and it sprinkles black raindrops all over my plate.

'Is Turner the one who paints ships, Daddy?'

'Yes, my love, well remembered.'

*

It is busy at the Tate Gallery. I jump into the revolving doors. In the entrance hall, there is a big, white statue, which is of a man and a woman kissing.

'That's a very famous statue, darling,' Daddy says, 'it's called *The Kiss* and it's by Rodin.'

We queue at the cloakroom and give our coats to the Japanese man. It is hot. My tights are itchy. We walk up the stairs, which have a gold rope at the side, to the Turner room. The walls are wooden, and lots of Chinese people are listening to a lady talk, who points a stick at the paintings. All the pictures look the same. They are ships on stormy seas.

'Darling, you must look carefully at the different light,' Daddy says, 'Turner is a master of light.'

They are just white and yellow skies.

I am bored.

Daddy takes me into the next room now and shows me a funny picture of two twin ladies with oblong faces. He says it is called *The Chomley Sisters*.

In the Impressionist gallery is a painting of people lazing in the sun by the water. Some swim and some sunbathe, and the sun sparkles on the water. I like this one best.

'This is by Seurat,' Daddy explains, 'it is called *Les Baigneurs*, which is French for the bathers. If you look closely, you'll see it is made out of little dots. It is a technique called pointillism.'

The abstract room is my favourite – there are big, bright colours like the paintings I do at home and pictures that don't make sense but look fantastic. We stop in front of one with red, blue, green, black and orange squares in the shape of a snail.

'It's called *The Snail* and is by Henri Matisse,' Daddy says. His hand is warm.

'That's not art, Daddy,' I say, 'I could do that myself.'

'Yes, it is, darling,' he laughs, 'because he thought of it and you didn't.'

'Is art what you think of?'

'Yes, art is what you create – what comes out of you. It is your original work.'

'Can anyone make it?'

'If they want to, yes.'

I'll remember that.

Daddy takes me downstairs to the shop to buy a postcard of *The Snail* and then to the cafe for tea. I have a slice of blueberry cheesecake.

He smiles whilst he watches me eat it. 'You enjoy that,' he says.

I was kicking his bony leg hard. I kept doing it again and again.

CHAPTER SEVEN
LONDON, 1989
LUCIA IS SIXTEEN YEARS OLD

Her plum-coloured bedside lamp lights her room with an ambient shade, and the black Habitat spotlight focuses a brighter cone of light onto her desk. The sound of distant traffic goes unnoticed, but the muffled sound of television permeates through her walls, reminding Lucia of her mother's presence.

Lucia's cream-and-pink curtains remain closed.

She slides out the desk tray of her pine bureau, which opens a secret world of her belongings – letters, her seven-sided, combination-lock pencil case and her rubber collection – which are all filed immaculately in each wooden compartment.

A photo is stuck with Blu Tack to the inside frame of the drawer. In it, her father sits relaxed on the doorstep of his mother's home in Southport, wearing a pale-blue shirt and brown sandals. Lucia sits on his lap, sucking her thumb, looking settled and comfy. She is seven years old. A large golden trophy stands in the foreground, owned by Lucia's grandfather, Marti, who won the Horse Racing Championship in 1978 on '*Silver Beauty*'.

She looks at the photo.

Stroking her cold elbow with her hand, she remembers those holidays in Southport: running up the golden sand dunes to her father, who was kneeling at the top with his camera, laughing. She recalls the feel of the warm sand on her bare feet as she slid down towards the grand vista of blue waves.

'Lucia, are you OK?' her mother shouts.

'Yeah…'

She picks her nose. Her homework is boring. She does not want to do it.

She sighs and stares at the image on the front cover of her Catullus poetry book. It has a black background with an oval stained-glass window in the centre, within which a Jesus look-alike figure leans inward, appearing frail and broken hearted.

She looks for the poem that will be the easiest to translate. Opening the book, she reads through 'The Death of Lesbia's Sparrow' on page five. Ms McGowan has translated this poem with them in class, so she remembers the gist of what it is saying, but has not paid close enough attention to the verb construction. It is too long. She is drawn to poem eighty-five on page three: '*Odi et Amo*'.

She can do this one.

Pounce!

She jumps. Her chest cracks like shattered glass.

Her mother whips open the sitting-room door and strides, with a heavy clump, into the kitchen, where drawers slam, cutlery falls and the smell of baking pastry sizzles.

Lucia brings her hands to her legs, but then quickly slides them away. It is a choice whether or not to give flame to this reaction she has to her mother's behaviour. That frantic sound of her mum's hand hitting the brass doorknob, her hazy cough and the banging of pans in the kitchen bring out an energetic friction – that funny twitch between her legs.

Lucia ignores the twitching and with a determined poise, returns to Catullus' broken heart and with her luminous marker, strikes a bright-yellow line through its title. In grey pencil, she scribbles *'I love and I hate.'*

Odi et amo. Quare id faciam, fortasse requires?

Her eye wanders momentarily to her cassette collection behind her. Her Janet Jackson album *Control* pulls her into a reverie as she remembers dancing a slick routine to the punchy soul song with Corrine at Interchange Studios, wearing black jazz shoes and leggings.

Using her Latin dictionary, she translates each word separately and writes its meaning in the text book as a rough draft:

I love and I hate. Why do I do this perhaps I ask?

She glances at the poster of George Michael above her desk, and the lyrics of 'Wake Me Up Before You Go-Go' race through her mind. She takes a deep breath, and looks back down.

Nescio, sed fieri sentio
et excrucior.

'Lucia, is everything OK?' her mum calls again.

She sighs. 'Yes, Mum, fine,' she drones with flared nostrils.

She leans back in her mahogany chair and turns to her wicker basket filled with oddities that she never uses. Sticking out of it is a Mexican leather handbag given to her by her brother's Korean girlfriend. On top of her patchwork quilt is a box of unused oil paints that her brother Tim gave to her at Christmas two years ago. He always buys her gifts of educational value – never leg warmers or chocolates. Her Donkey Kong game and Konica Pop camera, both given to her by her father, also catch her eye through the holes in the wicker. She remembers the day when her dad gave her that camera over a bowl of spinach-and-ricotta gnocchi at the Cosmo restaurant. She was wearing a green-and-red stripy outfit and had a bowl haircut that she hated.

She returns to the second line of the poem and translates:

I don't know, but I feel it happening, and I am tormented.

Lucia rereads her full translation, and rewards herself with a fresh piece of Wrigley's Juicy Fruit gum. She chews on it fiercely to get the best of its juice. Ready to write out her translation onto a new page, she opens her jar of navy ink, takes her fountain pen out of its box and brings her exercise paper into focus. The smell of the ink makes her nose tickle.

Lucia bites the skin inside of her cheek hard and rubs her tongue over the bumpy contours of flesh.

She pumps the cartridge with fresh ink, writes the title of the poem – *'I Love and I Hate'* – in neat handwriting and underlines it with a ruler. She enjoys the sensation of the cool pen against her sticky palm. Turning to the original text for a split second, Lucia looks back at her exercise paper.

What's that?

She looks again and then looks up.

Where did that come from?

On the top right-hand corner of her exercise paper, she notices a large patch of water, in an irregular shape that she had not seen seconds before. It is eleven centimetres wide and ten centimetres deep, in a wavy, *squiggly* outline.

She feels it. It is certainly wet.

When did that appear?

She rubs her middle finger across its moist texture again and looks around the room; her eyes stall at her *Ecoutez Vous* textbook on the shelf behind her.

The room is quiet.

She looks at it again, and studies it.

It was definitely not there before.

She looks up at the ceiling. No water is dripping. She looks around the room; this time more slowly and feels a definite presence of something in the room. She doesn't know what, but she likes it. It takes her away from the boredom of her homework and the after-school routine. Blood shoots around her body. Weird, it just appeared, as if by magic.

Lucia knows that her mother will react to this because she has always had a hysterical response to leaks and water, from the flood of 1979 and the periodic washing-machine spills down into Petunia and Steve's flat.

Studying its shape, Lucia thinks how random it is. She walks to the kitchen, where her mum is peeling potatoes, wearing an Oxo apron and with a cigarette between her teeth. She has her pink transistor radio on London Broadcasting Company (LBC) and turned up loud. It is not properly tuned. Steve Allen's voice crackles.

Lucia stands still in the narrow entrance hall to the kitchen. The brown-and-cream linoleum beneath her feet is ripped, exposing raw floorboards. She gazes at the blackboard hanging on the amber wall with the remnants of yesterday's shopping list written in chalk – *'spuds and leeks'*. Her chest flutters like a trapped bird lives inside it, and she waits like she is standing in the wings of a Broadway stage, about to go on stage to speak a very important line.

'Yes…' her mum mutters.

'Mum, something weird has just happened.'

Her mother looks up like a frightened deer. 'What? What's happened?'

'I was doing my homework, and a patch of water has just appeared on my paper.'

'What do you mean a patch of water? Don't say we've got a leak…'

Dropping the knife on the Formica, her mother throws her fag butt into the sink and marches down the hall into her bedroom. The floorboards shudder under her mother's frenzied stomp. The mirror table rattles.

Lucia follows.

'Where, Lucia? Where is it?'

'Look here,' Lucia says, pointing to the stain of water. 'Here.'

Her mother bends forwards. She squints and touches it with her coarse hand, rubbing the wet patch with her finger, whilst breathing salami-sausage fumes over Lucia.

'Where on earth has that come from?' she asks, looking up at the ceiling. Her mother's mouth is gaping open and she pants loudly. A trickle of phlegm rattles up and down her windpipe.

Cough, you fool.

'There must be water coming through from upstairs, Lucia,' her mum croaks.

Her mother rubs it again and examines it closely. With its chipped nails and thin skin showing tubular, blue veins, Lucia follows the movement of her mother's hand. She fixes her gaze on her mum's ruby wedding ring.

Bitch, it was that ring that whacked me in the eye.

Her buttocks clench together.

Lucia scrunches her face as she watches her mother panic. Her lack of synchronicity with every movement repels Lucia. The arm of her mum's spectacles is not properly hooked around her ear, so they sit wonky on the bridge of her nose. One eye is squinting, which makes the shape of her face irregular. She sweeps the walls with her hands and stumbles from wall to wall, arms outstretched like a sleep walker.

'No, nothing,' she shouts, 'I can't feel a thing. It's bone dry in here.'

'Where, did it come from, then?' Lucia asks, provoking her anxiety further.

'It must have come from somewhere,' her mum says, standing with her feet turned out like a duck. 'And we'll have to find out from where.'

Her mother's eyes dart from corner to corner with a staccato immediacy. Lucia watches. She is more drawn into her mum's reaction than to the mystery of the water. She wants to feed it more.

'I can't feel a thing. Are you sure it wasn't there before, Lucia?'

'I'm sure, Mum. When I took my paper out of the bag, it was dry. I was just translating a poem. I looked away and when I looked back it was there.'

'When did you see it exactly?'

'About five minutes ago.'

'Most puzzling,' her mum says gripping her top lip with her teeth, 'but it must have come from somewhere.'

It didn't. It came from nowhere.

'It's just one of those things,' Lucia says, 'or maybe upstairs have got a leak.'

'W-e-e-e-l-l, it c-a-a-a-n-n-n-t-t have just a-p-p-p-p-p-p-eared,' her mum stutters with a dry mouth. Her mothers' stutter intensifies when she panics.

'Well, if it happens again, Mum, you should go upstairs and ask Clara and Mark.'

'Yes, yes, I will. Bizarre, most bizarre,' her mum mutters and shuffles out of Lucia's room, with her head bowed. She coughs up the ball of phlegm that had been rattling in her pipes and swallows it. It clears her throat for now.

Lucia shuts her door and sits back down.

She sighs and rubs the edges of her scalp with her finger tips. Flakes of white skin fall to her desk, some with red dots in the middle. A siren whizzes by outside, but it quickly quietens.

Her head feels tight; her eyes sore.

Sucking on her last Polo Mint, she strokes her hot cheek with her cold pen and looks around, wondering again, how that water got there and if there is an invisible presence in the room. Maybe there is a spirit trying to talk to her? The thought takes the bite off her loneliness. Maybe it is a spirit whom she could make magic with.

She has often wondered if spirits exist. As a younger girl, she would see shapes in floating cumulus clouds, which would become faces and then disappear. She loved performing magic shows from her Paul Daniel's magic set with her best friend, Megan. Her favourite trick was the coloured cube. She could tell the audience what colour they had chosen. Weekly sleepover parties at Meg's squat often involved doing Ouija boards, and the plate did move to number eight one night! Megan and Lucia invented that psychic walkie-talkie game when they would see if they could hear each other speaking on their imaginary phones from different parts of Haverstock Hill.

Lucia reins in her concentration and writes her translation of the poem on the sheet of exercise paper with the patch of water on it.

I love and I hate. Why do I do this perhaps I ask?
I don't know, but I feel it happening, and I am tormented.

She questions in her mind if she could make other strange occurrences happen.

'Lucia!'

'Yes, Mum?'

'Dinner's ready.'

And she wonders to herself whether *she* could do something, which would precipitate an incident to happen of its own volition.

*

Two blue-and-white china plates with crispy chicken pies, chips and burnt peas sit on the kitchen counter, with steam rising from them. Lucia watches her mum spoon the peas onto the plate. 'It looks delicious, Mum,' she says.

'Here is yours Lucia. Be careful, it's hot.'

Lucia straddles a sea of newspapers to get to her seat at the dining table, which faces the fireplace. Her mum scurries behind and slams the door shut. She slouches in her armchair with the boiling plate on her lap, and leaves Lucia to eat alone at the table.

Her mum never eats at the table.

'This looks delicious, Mum,' Lucia repeats.

'Hmm, hmm,' her mum mutters.

Biting into the hot sheet of chicken-lined pastry, Lucia watches the last shot of Judith Chalmers outside Butlins on *Wish You were Here.*

'Mum, can I turn it down? It's so loud!'

'No, leave it, please.'

'Anyone would think you're deaf.'

'It's how I like it.'

Lucia eats her peas and stares at the mountain of salt on the lace tablecloth, which is there to nurse a stain of Claret wine.

'This is lovely, Mum.' Lucia keeps trying to bridge the gap between them.

Her mum does not respond. She mumbles to herself and gazes blankly at the blossom swaying outside. With only the sound of cutlery dancing on china and the *Coronation Street* theme tune between them, Lucia stares into the chipped tiling on the fireplace and wonders why two tiles are missing on the bottom corner.

Vera Duckworth and Ivy Tilsley sit with curlers in their hair, moaning. The picture is fuzzy as usual.

She catches her mother's eye.

'Everything OK?' her mum asks, with one of her long squints and crumpled eyes.

'Yes, Mum, I'm fine. I'm going to finish my homework.'

'Don't you want a yogurt?'

'No, thanks.'

'I still can't work out where on earth that water came from, Lucia.'

'I know. It's odd.' Lucia stands, pulling the emerald tablecloth by accident as she leaves.

'Be careful, Lucia!'

'Sorry,' Lucia replies and straightens it back out. She picks up her plate and walks past her mum.

Lucia closes the door behind her.

CHAPTER EIGHT
LONDON, 1980
LUCIA IS SEVEN YEARS OLD

I am going back to Mummy's. Daddy and me are at the bus stop.

Wet leaves are stuck to the pavement, and drops of rain spit on my cheek. The cold wind blows in my ears. Daddy puts his umbrella up and holds me close to him. The gold buckle across the top of his shoe sparkles like a star. Gayfayre Street and Cowley Street behind are quiet. No one is around. Mill Bank has busy traffic though, and when the cars splash through the puddles water sprays on my tights.

'Come away from the road, darling,' Daddy says and pulls me back from the road.

Two horns blow loudly from the River Thames, like they are warning of danger. Daddy says it is the tourist boats telling each other they are coming. The bright lights on the bridge twinkle like a white rainbow in the black night.

'That is Chelsea Bridge,' Daddy says. 'The one behind is Albert and then there is Battersea. They spell CAB.'

We have been waiting for the bus for twenty-seven minutes. It takes longer on a Sunday night. My heartbeat inside my chest is going boom, boom, boom, like a drum. It won't stop, even though I keep telling it to. I don't want to go home. I've changed my mind. I want to stay here with Daddy tucked under his arm in the rain.

Two lights are shining through the fog, making the raindrops look like buzzing bees. It says '87' and 'ALDWYCH' on the front in white letters.

'Here we go, my love. Here's our bus,' Daddy says and taps my arm three times.

*

It feels sticky on the top floor of the bus. The windows have steam on, and I draw a triangle with my finger so that I can see out. Daddy puts his arm around me and smiles.

The bus conductor has a gold tooth and long plaits. He gives Daddy and me a ticket, and tells me to, 'Bottle that smile.'

Daddy's eyes look angry.

Someone has written **'DEMON87'** with a penknife on the seat in front. Big Ben and the Houses of Parliament are lit up, and the ice-cream van, where I had my strawberry ice yesterday, is closed. The gates at Westminster Abbey are shut, but the man in the glass box outside is still there, smoking a cigarette.

I want to say something to Daddy, but I don't know what, so I roll up my ticket, pretend it is a cigarette and put it in my mouth. It tastes of cardboard.

'Take it out, darling!' Daddy says, 'It will give you germs.'

His eyes look wobbly. I'm frightened. So, I fold it over four times, until it won't fold anymore, and look down at the Fruitella wrappers on the floor.

This is Whitehall, the road where the serious buildings are. The two soldiers on horses are still outside Downing Street. They must stay there all night! At Trafalgar Square, lots of people are holding up square boards on wooden sticks, which say *'Nuclear Arms – No.'* A man with messy, grey hair and glasses is shouting, 'Say yes to peace,' into a round machine that makes his voice echo loudly. He looks like Worzel Gummidge, but without the carrot nose.

'What are these people doing?' I ask Daddy.

'It's the tail end of a CND rally darling.'

'What's CND?'

'It means "Campaign for Nuclear Disarmament", and is an organisation that tries to eliminate nuclear weapons.'

'Like bombs and gas?'

'Yes, darling,' Daddy says, and pulls me close.

My boom boom goes away.

A circle of pigeons are standing around the edge of the fountain, where people throw pennies in to make a wish. Nobody is feeding them, so they must be hungry.

*

I know we are nearly there now because we are passing Lord's Cricket Ground, with the spiky wire around the edge. My boom boom comes back. It's beating very hard. I try to stop it by swallowing three times, but it moves to my throat. I want to tell Daddy how much I am going to miss him, but I don't know how to.

'Daddy,' I say.

'Yes, my love.'

'Will I see you again soon?'

'You know you will. You'll be coming in two weeks as you always do, and we'll be going to The Garrick for lunch.' He taps my hand three times. That means don't worry.

'Will Captain Ted be there?' I ask him.

'Yes,' he laughs, 'he will.'

Captain Ted always has a tear in his eye, and he can throw a peanut up to the ceiling and catch it in his mouth. He wears a green-and-pink stripy tie like Daddy.

I hate the walk back. My body boom booms fast all over. My throat is blocked by a big lump. We walk past the deaf and dumb school, where people sometimes hide in the bushes and mug you. Daddy holds my hand tight. His heel clicks on the pavement, and his aftershave smells strong when the wind blows. I can still taste the blueberry cheesecake in my mouth from earlier.

The leaves are crinkling in the wind.

Daddy stops outside Mr Stanley's house at number 147. He says he isn't taking me to the door because he 'doesn't want a confrontation with my mother'. He kneels down and kisses me on the cheek. His cheeks feel cold.

'See you in two weeks,' he says. His tongue has cracks on it.

He waits whilst I hopscotch to outside number 139. When I look back he is waving to me, with his hat in his hand, smiling. I want to run back, but I know I can't. A tear nearly comes out of my eye, but I blink fast. A brick in my chest stops any more coming.

I run up the stairs and ring the doorbell. The light goes on. I can see Mummy coming down the stairs through the glass. She looks like a wolf. Boom boom!

She coughs and opens the door. Her eyes look tired. Her hair is sticking up. 'Where's Colin?' she asks.

'He had to go,' I lie.

I don't tell her the truth because it will make her sadder.

*

The bathroom is pink.

The water is hot; it is burning me. Mummy is washing my hair too hard. My head stings when she scrubs it.

'Ow! You're hurting me,' I shout.

'Don't be so silly!' she says.

She still does it too hard. My scalp bleeds a bit.

Mummy soaks my body, and, when she starts to wash my leg with the flannel, the bubbles aren't covering me anymore so she sees the bruises.

'Good God,' she says. 'How on earth did you get these, Lucia?'

'I don't know, Mummy,' I say. 'Daddy says I kick a lot in the night.'

I was kicking. The sheet was twisted. I don't want to remember.

Mummy tuts. She pulls my leg up onto the edge of the bath – it's cold. She presses her finger onto my bruises. They go green and yellow, and then black again when she stops.

'They don't hurt,' I say. I don't want her to worry.

'But I can't understand how you got them.' Her breathing is funny.

The moon outside is white and shaped like a melon slice. The sky is black, and I can see the stars out of the window. Grey water drips into the bath from the washing machine tube.

'Ben! Can you come here? I want you to show you something!' Mummy shouts.

I keep trying to breathe, but there is no breath.

'What, Mum?' Ben, my brother calls.

'Just come here, please.'

The bubbles pop.

When he opens his bedroom door, I hear 'Super Trouper' playing. Justine and Ben are dancing to it again. They always do a routine to that or Bucks Fizz' 'Don't Stop'.

My brother Ben has dyed his hair. It is marmalade colour now, and his t-shirt says *'SPARKS'* and has a picture of a punk on it. I put the soft bubbles over the funny bit between my legs, so he can't see.

The bath water smells of roses.

'Look Ben, look at these,' Mummy says and lifts my leg out of the water. Ben looks at her. They both stare at each other in the eyes for a long time, but don't say anything. Ben's mouth is tight. His eyes are wide open. He doesn't blink.

'How did you get those?' Ben asks me.

'I don't know,' I say because I don't. I splash the water over my tummy and look down.

'I'd take her down to see Dr Edwards first thing,' Ben says, 'Something's not right.'

'Ben, can I come in with you and Justine after my bath?' I ask.

'For a bit,' he says. Then he whispers to Mummy, 'Those need looking at,' and leaves.

Daddy's breath felt warm on my tummy.

The lines on the tiles aren't even. They annoy me. They should be straight.

Mummy wraps the prickly towel around me. It smells damp. She says I can stay in here on my own until I am dry. I sit on the itchy bathmat. I like it with the door locked. There's no sound apart from the pipes rumbling in the airing cupboard. There's a beetle crawling across the carpet. I don't know where it came from.

My feet feel furry. Mummy calls it like a prune. I wish I had feet like Tracey Armstrong, with straight toes, not ones that curve around.

'Lucia, are you nearly dry?' Mummy calls.

'Nearly,' I say.

'There's some clean pyjamas on your bed,' she says.

And I wish I had a tummy button that went in, not out like a chocolate button. If I could change two things, I would have new feet and an inny tummy button.

*

I am allowed fifteen minutes in here with Ben and his friends. Aidan is weird. He doesn't say much. He just smokes cigarettes and wears all black. He has black, spiky hair; black finger nails; and black lipstick! He has three stud earrings in his nose, and wears a skull necklace. Justine is cool. She has white hair, and wears red lipstick and fishnet tights. I want to be like her when I grow up.

Justine and Ben are wrestling on the floor. Aidan and me are watching. It smells of cheesy feet in Ben's room, like Wotsits.

'Dancing Queen', my favourite Abba song, is playing. I pretend to sing into a microphone, but Ben tells me to stop showing off, so I sit down and watch Aidan roll up his cigarette. Ben and Justine are sitting on the floor cushions, eating Rich Tea biscuits. They don't offer me one. I pretend to laugh with them about Quasimodo even though I don't know who Quasimodo is.

I want to join in.

On the red wall is a CND poster. It is next to the postcard of Lenin, and the 'Chagall at the Museum of Modern Art, NYC' painting, with bright colours on it.

'Ben, I saw a CND rally today,' I say, pointing at the poster to impress him.

'Big whoopie doo,' he says.

'Ben! Don't be so cruel! Justine shouts, 'She's your baby sister.'

'So,' he says, 'she's a pain in the dingle berries.' He does a shaky laugh at the back of his throat and pulls his neck in like a tortoise. He feels guilty. It's not a real laugh.

'Go on, bratlet, off you go. Leave us alone now,' he says and shoos me away.

My chest thumps and then tingles. I stand up to leave. I look down.

'You are such a meanie,' Justine says to Ben.

'Good night, Lucia,' Aidan says.

'Good night, Aidan,' I reply.

That's the first time he has ever said anything to me.

*

It's cold in my room. It smells of wee from when my friend from school, Livvy, peed on the floor by accident. I am in bed now. Daddy is probably back home in his big house now.

I wish I were still there with him. Tim is in the sitting room watching football on TV.

Mummy knocks on Ben's door, and opens it. I listen through the wall.

'The washing up still needs doing, Ben,' Mummy says.

'I know. I'll do it in a bit,' Ben replies. I know what's coming.

'But it's getting late. I'd like them to leave please.'

'No, they're not leaving. It's only 8.30pm.'

I want to stick up for Mummy, but I can't. Outside, two men are shouting and throwing a tin can at a car. They sound drunk.

'You still have to do your homework, Ben,' Mummy says. Her voice sounds angry.

'I'll do it later. Now get out, please.'

He shuts his door hard.

Mummy opens it.

'I want them gone, please,' she says. Her voice is shaking.

I cover my ears, but I can still hear it. It just sounds like I am under water. I want to phone Daddy.

'This isn't about homework, or washing up is it? This is about you being jealous of me having a life isn't it?' Ben shouts.

I FEEL SORRY FOR MUMMY.

SLAM!

Mummy pushes the door open.

SLAM!

The light rattles and the floor shakes. I hold my legs together tight and hum to myself. The water in my goldfish bowl is cloudy. I need to change it. Oscar needs feeding soon. I think he is dying.

'I- I -I -I am ask-k-king you to please ask your fr-fr-fr-friends to leave,' she says loudly.

She is stuttering so much, she can't speak. I hate it when she is like this.

I can tell she is scared.

'No, why should they? Just because you are a selfish cow and have no life.'

I hate Ben.

My sheets feel stiff. I pull the ribbon off my teddy's neck and put my head under the covers, so I can't hear, and hum. I want to press my funny bit between my legs, but I don't. I keep humming and close my eyes. Hmm, hmm!

'This is my home, and I am asking them to leave!' she shouts. Her voice wobbles.

'Fuck off!'

SLAM!

The door locks. Mummy punches it.

'Open the door!' she screams. 'Open it now!'

The music goes loud. It's 'Thank You for the Music' by Abba.

I press my funny button hard. It goes fuzzy.

Mummy punches Ben's door harder.

I want it to stop. 'Mummy!' I shout.

'Yes, Lucia, what is it?'

She stands in my doorway. The light is off, so I can only see her shape. Her breathing is odd.

'What is it?' she asks again.

'I love you,' I say to make her feel a bit better.

'Yes,' she says, like she hasn't heard it, 'Uh-huh.'

'Can I call you if I want you, Mummy?'

'You know you can. Stop asking me,' she says and walks out.

I put my three teddies – Zanzibar, Freddie and Tiger – in a row at the end of my bunk, and take my piece of wood out from under my pillow. It is smooth. I hold it tight in my right hand, and, with my left hand, I tap it three times and say out aloud:

'Touch wood, tomorrow everything will be OK.

'Touch wood, tomorrow everything will be OK.

'Touch wood, tomorrow everything will be OK.'

Tomorrow is art with Miss Daniels.

CHAPTER NINE
LONDON, 1989
LUCIA IS SIXTEEN YEARS OLD

Her room is dim.

The light outside is trapped behind a tricoloured – white, grey and blue – speckled sky. Lucia lies on her bed and watches the sky glide leftwards in a continual motion, like a conveyer belt to eternity.

She picks the spot on her nose. Yellow pus shoots out. She squeezes her spot and enjoys the sensation of pain, as more goo dribbles out and deflates its bump.

Her room is still. Nothing moves except the second hand ticking on her alarm clock. Her Chinese doll, Lachie, and her Cabbage Patch doll, Roseanne, sit at the end of her bed staring at her with empty, plastic gazes. She smells burnt toast from the kitchen, and tastes the pickled-onion flavour Monster Munch from earlier, which are still stuck in her teeth. Lucia craves another packet.

She listens to the distant whizz of the traffic on Adelaide Road and the boys passing by shouting, 'Ya mum's a pussy' at each other. *Ah! I know that voice, that's Ron Skinner,* Lucia thinks, and recoils into a tight ball. She holds her stomach to soothe the pinching cramps and feels the wet drip of blood fall onto her sanitary towel between her legs. It is a relief that her periods are regular now, and she is like the other girls at school.

Lucia can hear the closer sound of her mother talking on the phone to her oldest friend, Bridget.

'No, Bri; no! Ah, you are so funny! Is he? Don't be so silly… Uh! But he's out now, yes? Yes, yes…yes, well, he's lucky. Yes, yes. Oh, what an ordeal!'

It gives Lucia a break to have her mother talking to someone else. She does not have to worry about her.

She glares into the shifty eyes of the rabbit on the cover of her *Watership Down* book. They unsettle her. She tucks her neck in and pulls her Benetton jumper tight over her knees. With cold flesh and a fluttering pulse all over her body, Lucia feels queasy. She does not understand her fear. She only knows its rhythm and truth.

She listens.

'Well, Bri, I hope not. No, she just saw it the other day. It seems to have come from nowhere. No, it was bone dry everywhere. Most odd, it was, Bri. God knows if any water is coming through from somewhere… Not since then, no.'

If she's that shocked…

Lucia sits up.

She looks down at her tummy button. Her hands are clasped in a semi-prayer. If she pours water somewhere else, her mum will think it's happened again and go really mental.

A lightning bolt of energy surges through her body like the first rush from an ecstasy pill. She knows this feeling from her occasional weekend binges down at Heaven and sweaty all-nighters at Labyrinth.

She stands.

Lucia tiptoes up and down, and scans the tree tops in the distance. She has the same feeling she gets when she balances on the highest diving board at the Adelaide pool, and looks down 100 metres into the blue water, undecided whether or not to jump.

Without thinking consciously about it, Lucia walks to the kitchen as if she were going to make a cup of tea. She passes the sitting room, where her mum still speaks on the phone.

'Don't be so silly! You are such a hoot, Bri!'

In the south-facing kitchen, Lucia stands in the spotlight of the last of the day's sun, and studies the old Duracell batteries in the fruit bowl on the kitchen table. That old bowl is always used as a dumping ground for disused items. She holds a deep breath, and grabs a red cup from the wooden mug tree on the Formica work surface above the dishwasher.

She turns on the cold tap.

The tap is stiff. She turns it harder. The pipes grumble then shudder, but she coughs to hide any obvious sound and watches the mug fill with ice-cold water.

She shouldn't do this, but she'll only do it once.

Lucia pushes away her conscience and turns off the tap. She walks back to her bedroom with the mug of water in hand, singing Bowie's 'Changes' as she goes.

The light has dropped in her bedroom. The sky is now a frosty blue and is on the cusp of night. She stands in the centre of her room, mug in hand, and looks at the shadow of herself on the floor. It is taller than she is, black and more lanky. It surprises her.

Aware of the sound of her mum still deep in conversation, Lucia is confident she won't be caught. Heartbeat pounding, she kneels down and pours the water on the carpet by her desk, feeling a kind of release.

The water creeps outwards of its own accord, like the edge of a wave meeting sand. The water touches her toe through her faded sock; *cold.*

She watches it expand.

It stops moving and finalises its form in the shape of a jellyfish. Its wetness darkens the carpet from a steel blue to sapphire. She studies it.

Wow, I did that. I can do it again if I want to, she thinks.

She feels alive now, excited, knowing the reaction it will get from her mother. Bringing her attention back to the loneliness of her room, she feels the sweaty itch of clothes worn all day and returns to the kitchen. She puts the mug into the red bowl of soapy dish water.

She can't wait for this bit.

Lucia stands in the hall and peers through the gap in the sitting-room door at the back of her mum's head. The television is on mute. *Grange Hill* is on. Ziggy and Robbie are in Ms McClusky's office, in trouble. She watches their mouths move, whilst her mum shrieks with laughter down the phone.

'Ah! Well I never; what do you know, eh?'

She thinks how nice it is to hear her mum upbeat. Lucia gains comfort from listening to her mum speaking coherently, not in her usual dazed splutter.

Bubbles pop all over her upper body. She steps into the sitting room and stands by the side of the armchair, where her mother sits in her black mohair jumper and loose black trousers, smelling of perfume muffled in wool.

Her mum glances up at her and waves.

As Lucia waits for her mum to finish her conversation, she reads the titles of all of the orange paperbacks in the bookcase: *Animal Farm*, *Aimez Vous Brahms*, *1984*, *Cider with Rosie*, and Lawrence Olivier's biography below.

'I've got to go, Bri,' her mum says, combing her hair with her fingertips.

The air purifier whirrs.

'OK, my dear, lovely to talk to you, bye for now,' her mum says and hangs up.

'Mum?'

'Yes, Lucia?' she replies, gulping her cold coffee.

'Another patch of water has appeared,' Lucia says.

'Don't be so ridiculous. Where for Christ's sake?'

'On my carpet,' Lucia replies.

Her mother pushes herself up by driving her hands down onto her chair's armrests, then bounds down the hall to Lucia's bedroom, where the patch of water waits for them.

Lucia pauses in the doorway, behind her mum, who halts and bends down, her eyes fixated on the water. Her pose resembles a mischievous gnome. She pants like a breathless dog and presses the wet patch with her fingers.

It squelches.

'It's absolutely saturated!' her mum shouts and tilts her head backwards. She moves her head robotically around the room, scrunching her face.

'I just can't understand where on earth it is coming from,' she squeals, brushing her arm across the wall. Her mum stands on her tiptoes and sniffs the wall for damp.

Lucia watches, pulling her top lip.

'No, it's bone dry,' she says, looking back at Lucia with a deep frown.

Now look what I've done...

She steps forwards and stands opposite her mother. The washing machine spins in the background. They examine the shape of the water, unified for a second by its strange, ominous presence. Daylight has disappeared; her room is now pierced by the orange streetlights that shimmer from outside.

'I just can't understand it,' her mother says.

'I know, it's odd,' Lucia replies, and switches on the light.

She has to do it again, just one more time.

Lucia is hooked on her mother's reaction to the water. There is a rush inside her that she cannot understand, which she only knows energetically. It connects her to her mother and fills the void between them. She knows it is wrong, but she is overtaken by a searing energy that propels her to want to do it again.

In the sitting room, she sits on the sofa. Her mum babbles to herself in her armchair, cigarette in hand. The thick atmosphere of smoke clogs Lucia's throat. They watch the news as the headlines roll in – *'Total of 96 Killed at Hillsborough'* – and gawp as pictures flash of a young child being carried out on a stretcher. Images play in slow motion of barriers breaking and people falling on top of each other. A man screams with his eyes closed and a convulsing red face, as his daughter is lifted over the crowds.

Lucia sucks her thumb. She rubs her warm sleeve with her hand, feeling the tight fit of her thumb arched perfectly into the roof of her mouth.

'How did that happen, Mum?' she asks.

'I don't know; too terrible it is. It's a human tragedy,' her mum replies. 'I think there were too many people in the stadium and no one to monitor it.'

Lucia imagines how that man feels, watching both his children being carried out dead, and wonders what he will say to his wife and how they will cope afterwards. *Poor thing,* she thinks and then looks away at the noughts-and-crosses board on the coffee table.

She peeps at her mother who, too, has stopped watching the news and now gazes out of the window, deep in thought, behind her thick-rimmed spectacles.

'I just can't understand where that water is coming from, Lucia,' her mum says with a shake of her head 'I mean, there's no sign whatsoever of a leak.'

'It's weird.' Lucia says taking her thumb out of her mouth.

A surge of energy bursts through her. Lucia goes blank. Her head burns. She stands, glaring at the stone elephant on the windowsill. *I'm going to do it once more, then I'll stop.*

'I'm going to the loo, Mum, back in a sec,' she says and walks out.

Lucia locks the bathroom door and pulls the string of the light switch.

It pings and illuminates the room, exposing the clashing shades of pink. It is a rosy hotchpotch. The walls are a shade of azalea, the carpet is a watermelon colour and the towels are a roseate pink. Nothing matches.

Lucia stares at her worn Burlington sock and inhales a long breath. She savours this moment with herself. She looks up at the light bulb and leans back into her hands, which make a cradle behind her head. She doesn't know why she is doing this, but she pushes away the voice inside that doubts her actions. This new compulsion is alien to her.

She questions how she is going to do this without being heard and flushes the toilet using the sound of cascading water to hide her mischief.

She lifts the mug out of the toothbrush holder, which is peeling away from the wall, and turns on the cold tap. It always confuses her as the hot tap is marked by a blue circle, and the cold tap is marked by a red one. Her mum, Ben and Tim call it 'Heath Robinson'.

The toilet has stopped flushing. It doesn't matter. She would be washing her hands anyway. The pipes burp and grumble.

She fills the cup with cold water.

Her attention is drawn to the balls of dust on the shelf, her mum's Yves Saint Laurent Opium perfume that stinks, and her mum's gold chains tangled in a web.

The cup is now full. Lucia turns the tap off and looks at herself in the mirror. Her face is ashy and grey. Her eyes are puffy, circled by a shade of black, and her expression is sunken. *I used to be pretty,* she thinks, and she runs her tongue across her teeth, trying to force a smile. Her mouth lifts, but her eyes remain sullen.

Cup in hand, she unlocks the door, making sure the key turns with no audible twist.

Why am I doing this?

She opens the bathroom door and, with a galloping heartbeat, takes one giant step into the hall. Her mum could come out at any time, but this element of danger enlivens her. The flip side to her fear is a gushing river inside, rippling over rocks and spreading over land.

She stands outside the sitting room; her body is taut. She listens to the faint garble of her mum under the serious tone of Trevor McDonald on TV.

She pours the water on the carpet.

Like a smoker who has just got her fix of tobacco, she feels released and walks back to the bathroom, puts the toothbrushes back in the cup and places it back in its rightful circular holder – job done.

'Lucia!' her mum calls, 'You OK?'

'Yeah!' she shouts, and walks back into the sitting room, scratching her nose. 'God, it's cold for April,' she says and flops back down on the sofa. She studies the orange and yellow shapes in the abstract painting in the corner, and notices her mum's expressionless face.

On the news, Margaret Thatcher stands in the House of Commons, in a blue dress and with and perfectly styled hair, sending her condolences to the families affected by the Hillsborough tragedy. She speaks with a plum in her mouth.

Lucia watches, scrunching her toes.

'Does spaghetti carbonara sound OK for dinner, Lucia?'

'Mmm,' Lucia hums.

Lucia fixes her gaze on the African wood carvings on the wall, and traces the horizontal lines across them.

'I'll just see tomorrow's weather and then I'll go and make the sauce,' her mum says.

Lucia's breathing is shallow.

She stares into the bowl of potpourri and waits.

CHAPTER TEN

LONDON, 1981

LUCIA IS EIGHT YEARS OLD

No one talks loudly, so I don't.

There is a long wooden table down the middle of the room, with napkins like fans in the wine glasses. There are small tables around the edges. We are at a small table. The walls are green. The floor is wooden with green carpet at the sides. Old-fashioned paintings of smiling babies with wings – cherubs, I think they are called – hang in gold frames on the walls.

Daddy is wearing his pink shirt, with a blazer and tie. The bald bit in the middle of his head is shiny. He brings me to The Garrick on Saturdays when families can come too.

The waitresses look funny. They wear white pinafores and white frilly hats. They walk very fast. The only sounds in the room are the floor squeaking and whispers.

It smells of boiling potatoes and fatty meat.

'Now, darling, you have what you like,' he says in a low voice.

Today, I want to try to say something to Daddy that will make me close to him. 'I'll have lamb cutlets, please,' I say 'and fruit salad afterwards.'

Daddy orders roast beef and then trifle. We both have prawn cocktail to start with.

I get the thoughts and words ready, but when I open my mouth they go away.

He taps his fingernails on the mat like he is playing the piano. I can see myself in his eyes. My nose is flat, and my face is long, like in the magic mirrors at the Science Museum. He has red veins in the whites of his eyes. He does not say anything.

I run my finger around the globe on the place mat and read the writing. It says:

All the world's a stage, and all the men and women merely players. They have their exits and their entrances and one man in his time plays many parts.

'What does this mean, Daddy?'

'It's from Shakespeare's seven ages of man,' he says. 'It is a speech about the different stages of life we go through.'

The whole speech is written on the side of the mat. The last line says 'Second childishness and mere oblivion sans teeth, sans eyes, sans taste, sans everything.' Weird!

'I don't understand this,' I say.

Our prawn cocktails arrive with pink mayonnaise.

'It means that, at the end of our lives, we become like children again, darling,' he says and tucks his napkin into his collar. 'We come full circle.'

'What stage are you at, Daddy?' I shouldn't have said that.

'The middle stage, love,' he says and blushes.

I must be at the beginning stage, so I've got ages before I die.

The waitress takes our glasses away. Daddy brushes the crumbs off his mat and lunges forwards. He leans his elbows on the table. I know it is serious. He presses his fingertips together in a steeple shape. I keep my eyes peeled on the mole on his hand.

'Now, my love, I have a very special surprise for you at home.'

I look up.

He is smiling. His eyes are open so wide that his face gets bigger.

'Is it a new Dash tracksuit?'

'No,' he cackles, 'It is something better than that. You'll see when we get back.'

My lamb chops are small with fat around the edges.

'You tuck in. Start without me,' he says.

A big family walk into the dining room. The young girl is wearing a red-velvet dress. The man nods and waves to Daddy. 'Afternoon, old chap,' he shouts.

'Good day, Jeffrey,' Daddy calls and salutes back to him.

'That's Jeff, an old colleague from Oxford,' he says 'He's a very famous lawyer now.'

I don't care. I want to know what my surprise is.

*

We are back at Daddy's.

The curtain between the dining room and the kitchen is closed. It is normally open.

The room is dull, even with the light on. All the walls are wooden. The windows have net curtains hanging up. I sit on the oak-panelled window seat and bash my leg against it.

'Now, my love,' Daddy says and rubs his hands together like it is cold. 'I want you to meet someone very special.' His shoulders bounce up and down.

There is a warm square of sunlight on my skirt. The round oak dining table has dust on it, even though it polished. Mummy shouldn't have made me wear this dress. It has a stain on it and smells of smoke.

'Who is it, Daddy?' I ask.

'I want you to meet my new girlfriend, who is living here now. Her name is Yvonne.'

Girlfriend?

He draws the flowery curtain back. The curtain rings tinkle. A lady is standing in the kitchen. She is standing straight. She is smart, not like Mummy, in a blue skirt and blue high heels that match. She has a silk scarf around her neck and short hair. She is wearing red lipstick and has red fingernails. She is a real lady.

I keep kicking the wooden window seat with my heel.

'Hello,' she says in a soft voice. She smiles. Her mouth lifts, but her eyes do not move. She links her fingers together and stretches her arms.

'Well, darling, say hello,' Daddy says to me.

'Hello,' I say looking down. She is like a policewoman.

'Why don't I make us a drink?' Daddy says and signals to her to come over. She sits on a dining chair and puts her

Gucci handbag on the table. He brushes his hand across her shoulders and taps her back like he does to me to tell me everything is OK.

Her perfume smells posh. Her gold watch looks expensive. It is a ROLEX.

'Stop kicking the wood, Lucia!' Daddy shouts. His forehead creases.

'Sorry,' I say and slide my hands underneath my bottom, where it's warm.

Yvonne crosses her legs and straightens her skirt.

'Will you be living here all the time?' I ask.

She sniggers. 'Yes, I will,' she replies. 'We've got a cheeky one here, eh, Colin?' she says and nudges her head in my direction.

My chest goes bam.

'Yeeees.' Daddy laughs. He keeps his head down. He seems frightened.

'Two sugars, love?' he asks her.

'Yes, please,' she replies, and swings her leg up and down.

This isn't her house. It was my mummy and daddy's house when they were married.

'So, Lucia, what do you enjoy doing?' Yvonne asks. Her face doesn't move much when she speaks. Spit comes to the edges of her lips and stays there.

'I like dancing and acting,' I say.

'Oh, very good,' she says. She has a funny accent.

'Where are you from?' I ask, looking at the diamond ring on her finger.

'Liverpool,' she says, staring right into my eyes, 'Merseyside. It's up north.'

The bleach from the basement loo smells strong. I stroke my chicken pox scar and then follow my fortune line inside my palm with my finger. I wonder how long I will live for. Daddy hands me strawberry squash in a Wedgwood glass and puts Yvonne's tea on the table. He kisses her head.

She gulps her tea. The lump in her neck goes down then up.

A football goes boing, boing, boing against the wall outside. Two children laugh.

'Why don't we go for a walk after, Colin? It's a nice afternoon,' Yvonne says.

'Yes, good idea, darling,' he replies.

It's not going to be just me and Daddy anymore.

She powders her cheeks with Estée Lauder blusher and combs her hair.

'I'll just go and put something casual on,' Daddy says and walks out.

It's just me and her. It feels like creepy crawlies are running all over my chest. I crunch my ice cube. It shoots pain into my teeth, then up into my head.

Yvonne takes her cup into the kitchen. She puts it into the sink. Her spoon clinks.

I follow her, holding my glass.

The sun is shining through the kitchen window. Trees are rustling in the wind. Their shadows are dancing on the kitchen floor. I stamp on one with my foot, but I can't catch it. It moves away. A bird dives out of the sky and then disappears.

She turns around. She holds the counter and crosses one leg in front of the other one. Her lipstick is a bit smudged at the sides of her lips.

'I won't be taking any nonsense, you know, young lady,' she says.

My head goes fuzzy.

Smash!

I didn't mean to! The glass just slipped out of my hand.

Her toe is pointy. Bits of glass have landed in the shape of a star all over the red tiles. Strawberry squash is splashed on the white cupboard door.

I'm in trouble.

Run.

I can't see properly. I run up the stairs fast.

I slip. I fall on my tummy. Everything is blank. My chin tingles where I bashed it, like a stinging nettle has been rubbed on it. My mouth tastes of disinfectant.

'What are you doing, darling?'

I look up. It smells of hoovered carpet.

I see Daddy's black slipper… his blue trousers…his red jumper…black hairs in his nose.

'I slipped,' I say.

Daddy pulls me up by the hand and brushes down my dress. He rubs my knee better.

The glass…

My heartbeat is banging in my ears. Things sound funny. 'Daddy, please can you take me back to Mummy's?'

'But we are all going for a nice walk, darling.'

'I don't want to. I don't feel well,' I say, holding onto his leg.

He feels my forehead with the back of his hand. I don't want him to take it away.

'You do feel a bit warm, darling.'

Phew – that's lucky.

We walk back down the stairs. He is one step in front, holding my hand. He waits for me to step down before he does. 'Nice and steady,' he says. 'Pay attention to what you do.'

In the dining room, Yvonne is sweeping the glass away with the dustpan and brush.

Daddy stops. He looks at her then at me. 'What's happened here, love?' he asks.

I look down and stand on the sides on my feet.

'Lucia had a bit of an accident, didn't you?' she says.

I look at her.

She hisses with her mouth closed and then smiles. She is nasty under that smile.

'Yes, sorry, Daddy,' I say.

The bell at Westminster Abbey chimes. I can't tell what time it is. People will be playing out on the abbey lawn.

'I'm going to take her back to Valerie's. She's not well,' Daddy says.

'She was fine earlier,' Yvonne replies.

I squeeze Daddy's hand to tell him that I really do want to go home.

'I'm going to take her back anyway.'

Ha! I won.

'I'll just go and get my coat,' he says.

I walk around the table and follow the two gold lines, like train tracks, with my finger.

She bangs the dustpan on the side of the pedal bin. The glass jangles as it falls in.

'Cheeky swine,' she says under breath.

That was about me – swine?

Daddy walks back in. 'Come on, my love' he says and puts his arm around me. 'I won't be long, Yvonne.'

I don't say goodbye.

*

In his Renault Five it smells of tinned barley sweets.

Next to me on the seat is a Dickens and Jones carrier bag. In it is a woollen cardigan with pearl buttons on. That's for her.

Daddy does not talk to me. He looks at me, with one eye, in the mirror that hangs down the middle of the windscreen. I don't look back. I read the *Road Maps of Britain* book. On page 21 are all the roads in Cornwall. Bude is a funny name. It rhymes with my friend Jude.

The car stops. I jolt forwards and bash my head on the back of his seat.

'God-damned fool!' Daddy curses and honks his horn.

I pick at the button on the seat. Whoops.

'Daddy, will I still come and see you every two weeks?' I ask.

'We'll see, my love,' he says.

That means no.

Things won't be the same with Daddy now. Yvonne is going to take him away.

*

I think she is dead.

The curtains are shut, but it is sunny outside. Mummy is lying in bed with the duvet over her head, and there are

105

five bottles of tablets in front of Grandpa Bert's photo on the desk behind her. They are normally on the windowsill.

Grandpa Bert fell asleep from sleeping pills and alcohol, and never woke up.

I look to see if I can see the duvet move, but it is still. I don't know who will look after me if she is dead. I don't think my brothers would.

There is orange peel on the floor. The hi-fi radio is on so loud that I can feel my legs shake from the air coming out of the speaker.

The duvet is moving up and down. Mummy is alive.

'Daddy has got a new girlfriend,' I say.

She sits up quickly. Her eyes are puffy, and her mouth is turned down. She looks ill. Lots of magazines are falling down the side of her bed, and a back scratcher and her address book are on her bed.

'Who? Who is she?'

'Her name is Yvonne. I don't like her,' I say.

She flops back down, turns towards the window and pulls the duvet over her head. 'Go away please, Lucia,' she says from under the cover. 'I am in agony.'

'But I came back to see you.'

'Just go!' she snaps at me.

So, I walk out. My chest feels prickly, like when I eat too fast. It's burning.

I don't know what to do. Ben and Tim are out. Mummy has gone away in her head. Daddy is at home with Yvonne.

I come into the kitchen. It is bright, and the window is open. There are two magpies sitting on the branch of the tree outside, making it bounce. The branch looks like a tiger claw. I salute them twice. You are supposed to or else it is bad luck.

I climb onto the dishwasher so that I can open the big store cupboard. I can sit in there as it is so big; sometimes I do. It has metal mesh at the back where the air comes through. You can see the street if you look out of it. It is where Mummy keeps the cans and jars.

She has been to Bejam's and bought the super-size bag of Hula Hoops for my packed lunches.

I eat one packet after another. I can't stop. It makes my thoughts go blank.

I eat all six and then put the empty packets under the grill, strike a match and turn on the gas. The edges curl up and the packets shrivel into mini-sized ones. Cool.

I'll take them in to school for our museum box on Monday.

CHAPTER ELEVEN
LONDON, 1989
LUCIA IS SIXTEEN YEARS OLD

'For goodness' sake!' her mother wails.

Lucia looks up. Her mum has found the water. Her trousers are creased around her buttocks. She is bent down pounding the carpet. She turns to Lucia and holds up her moist hand in a stop signal with vacant eyes.

'There's another patch here, of water,' she says with a quiver in her throat.

Catherine wheels spin in Lucia's tummy. 'Well, where has it come from?' Lucia replies.

'I-I-I-I don't know. It's a mystery. We've got to find out where on earth this water is coming from.'

Lucia bites her nail and pushes the cuticle back with her forefinger. It bleeds.

'It must be coming from upstairs. I'm going to go up and speak to Clara and Mark, and see if they have a leak,' her mum says.

Lucia feels the biting chill blow into the room when her mother opens the flat door. She listens to her mum stomping up the stairs, coughing in her brittle way. The velvet tones of Wogan on TV float over her.

She walks to the hall doorway and looks up the stairs.

Her mother thumps Clara and Mark's door with an urgent *bam, bam, bam.*

'Hello, hello!' her mum cries, trying to gloss over her panic with a polite finish. It doesn't work. The sound of her pounding fist reverberates around the empty hallway.

Lucia runs her fingers across her lips, waiting for Clara or Mark to answer. She studies the patch of water. It looks like a goat's head with horns from where she stands.

Clara and Mark's door slides open, and then jolts as it jars on a ridge of thick carpet. Lucia listens.

'Hello Valerie,' Clara says in a soft tone. She always sounds subdued.

Lucia bites her hand like a hamster gnawing the bars of its cage.

'Hello Clara. I-I-I-I-I'm s-o-o-o sorry to disturb you both.'

Lucia can tell by the quaver in her mother's voice, that, she is on the verge of tears.

'No, don't be silly, Valerie; how can we help?'

'We seem to have water coming into our flat. We can't see any signs whatsoever of where it is coming from. I'm just wondering if it is coming through from here?'

Shit! I need to pour more water so it looks more serious than it is! What if Clara comes down to look? Quick!

'I don't think so, not that I am aware, but do come in,' Clara says with concern. Their door slides and wedges shut after a sharp push.

Lucia leaps into bathroom. Her hand trembles. She fumbles for the pink cup, in which her brother's razor blades are kept. She takes out the razorblades and turns on the cold tap. She fills the cup with cold water, and pours it into a puddle in the centre of the bathroom carpet.

She stops. Her face burns hot. She can hear the floorboards creaking upstairs and the hushed sound of her mother talking to Clara and Mark. Their voices drone under her mum's erratic babble.

She does not think. Her heart is hammering. She fills the cup with water again and pours it on the wool carpet next to the toilet, only inches from the other one.

That's enough in here. Now, out in the hall, quick!

Lucia is in a frenzy. Her mouth is so dry that her tongue is stuck to the roof of her mouth. When she unsticks it, it sounds like an old plaster being ripped off skin.

She knows she has limited time. She fills the cup with cold water for the third time and creeps out into the hall, lifting her knees up high as she walks. She pours it by the freezer. This will not be visible straight away to anyone walking into the front door.

Lucia hears their door slide over the carpet and voices at the top of the stairs.

She leaps across the hall, and makes it the whole distance in one go. She puts the cup back on the shelf, forgetting

110

to place the razors back in it. They remain scattered on the tumble dryer. She returns to the hall doorway, pulling her hair over her eyes.

She watches her mother's hand slide down the banister. Clara and Mike follow behind.

The Lowry painting on the hall wall, of matchstick children playing in a park covered in snow, reminds Lucia that her life is not normal, like that of other young people. She takes in its busyness, enchanted by how the children look like they are moving even though they are still.

She nods at Clara and Mark. She likes them. They are happy people.

'Hi Lucia,' Clara says. She has fine, blonde hair in a bun, and wears a floral shirt with a bogey-green A-line skirt with moccasins.

Lucia steps back to allow them entry. Her mum pushes Lucia backwards to show Clara and Mark the pool of water, and stumbles.

'Here,' her mother points, 'we found this one a moment ago. The others have been in Lucia's bedroom.'

It is still wet.

Clara and Mark glance down then immediately up, in sync with each other's moves. Mark has a rougher look with messy, grey hair. He is wearing a cord shirt, beige chinos and scuffed Adidas trainers. His expression is pointed; his mouth contorted.

'How odd,' he says in a deep voice.

'Yes, how mysterious,' Clara adds. Her voice is so calm that it makes the hairs on the back of Lucia's neck stand up. She looks at Clara's slender arms and the silver-and-turquoise bracelet around her wrist, and wishes she had such well-manicured hands. Clara looks like she has stepped off a Timotei advert.

Her mother stands close to the freezer, where Lucia has just spilt the new lot of water. Lucia knows it is only seconds before she sees it. Her heart jumps. Joan Collins is arguing with Wogan on TV.

'For God's sake! Another one!' her mum shrieks.

Lucia glances at her mum, who points down with her finger, but looks up with a deep frown and drooping cheeks. Lucia wants to make that vulnerable look go away. She hates to see her mum this helpless. But this hook is too strong.

'That has just appeared, now, as I have been standing here,' her mum says.

Wicked! She thinks she just saw it.

The scent of frankincense from Clara's neck makes Lucia think of church.

'Are you sure?' Clara asks.

'Yes, it wasn't here before, was it, Lucia?'

'No. It wasn't,' Lucia replies nodding.

'Well, I would perhaps contact the landlord and explain what is happening, and see if they can get to the bottom of the problem,' Clara suggests, scanning her mother's face with warmth in her eyes.

'Yes, that would be the best bet,' Mark agrees with a reassuring nod.

Lucia looks at her mother.

'Yes, yes; yes, OK,' she says, 'thank you, both of you, for your help,' her mother says.

Lucia can tell that her mother does not want them to leave, by her lingering glare and gaping mouth.

Mark and Clara walk out. Clara locks eyes with Lucia as she passes her, saying 'Take care.'

Does Clara know it is Lucia?

Her mum pushes the door, but it does not close properly. The lock needs oiling. She charges to the bathroom.

Lucia gets a whiff of Anais Anais perfume as her mum shoots past.

Her mum halts at the bathroom doorway. The silence is thick. Lifting her head in slow motion, she looks back at Lucia, with her brows knotted in worry.

'There's more in here,' her mother murmurs as if there are bubbles of air in her throat.

Lucia tiptoes to look over her mother's shoulder.

'Look, look!' her mum shouts, pointing to the middle of the floor.

Lucia follows her into the bathroom. It smells of soggy washing. Socks and shirts hang on a crowded clothes horse balanced over the bath.

'Two, there are two more!' her mother screams, spitting white drops of saliva and flapping her arms like a bird that cannot take off. 'What are we going to do?'

She watches her mum kneel down by the toilet, rip back the carpet and smack the floorboards with the palm of her hand, feeling for damp. The Vim falls from the shelf above.

'No, there is nothing. Something is happening. Something is not right, Lucia.'

Lucia notices her mum's silver fillings in her rotten yellow-stained teeth. The walls of her throat close in. She glimpses out of the top half of the window, which has no net curtain. She sees the distant twinkle of stars in the midnight-blue sky and traces half a horseshoe shape across the stars with her gaze. The moon is almost full.

Her eye shifts to the razor blades on the dryer that she forgot to put back in the mug.

Her mother has not seen them. Lucia leans on the tumble dryer to obstruct any view of them, and stares back at her mum, whose pupils dart around in the whites of her eyes.

'I've got to go and phone Ben,' her mum says, 'we've got to get him round.'

Her mother shoves Lucia aside and storms past her. Lucia falls onto the edge of the bath and then regains her balance.

He will know it's Lucia. He won't buy this.

She listens to her mother pull the phone over to her armchair and dial.

Lucia peeks through the crack in the sitting-room door. She can only see her mother's bunion wanting to burst through her sock. Lucia stands with parallel feet, careful not to let the floorboards creek and flicks her thumbnail across her middle finger.

'Ben, it's me. Yes, yes. Listen, something is happening, something very odd.'

There is a pause. Lucia can hear her brother's voice coming through the receiver.

'No, Ben. We've got strange appearances of water all over the flat. They are appearing in random places. There is no sign anywhere of a leak,' her mum screeches.

Lucia bites her lip.

'I've been up already; no, there's nothing. They are just appearing from nowhere, Ben. No, I've looked! Nothing, Ben, absolutely nothing!' her mum shouts as if she were trying to convince a jury of her innocence. Lucia hates it when her mum is not heard by Ben.

She lowers her head into her hand and scratches her hairline.

Lucia walks to her bedroom, as if she were sleepwalking, with a calm and vacuous air. In her immediate view, on her special shelf is her display of coloured water in test tubes. She stole these test tubes from the chemistry lab after Ms Hine's boring lesson, along with the wooden stand for them. No one caught her. She could not afford a lava lamp, so, as an alternative, she mixed her oil paints with water, filled the tubes with it (each in a different colour) and placed them in front of a lamp to get a similar effect.

The collection of teal, crimson and amber water grabs her attention. Coloured water! That couldn't be a leak could it? Images of Willy Wonka's chocolate factory fill her mind when she looks at them: twisting slides, chocolate chutes and labyrinths of abracadabra.

'No, Ben, it's not. I saw one appear as I was standing there. She was not there!'

Her mum's yell is close. Lucia knows her brother will be on to her.

She reaches for her box of oil paints and unclips the clasp. Brushing her hand over the neat row of tubes, she chooses cadmium red.

She remembers that she has a bottle of Evian water in her bag and gets that feeling you get when you find the next piece that fits in a painstaking jigsaw. She unscrews the paint lid and squirts a smidge onto her finger. The smell of malt vinegar makes her nose hairs tickle.

She unzips her rucksack and lifts out the bottle of mineral water. She removes its seal, wipes the paint onto the rim of the bottle and shakes it.

The water turns red. She holds the bottle like a magician in a trance. *Quick!*

Lucia squeezes her lips together and pours the red water over her cream-and-pink duvet. Her potion bubbles like froth. Wow.

Shit, now what have I done?

She spins around on her heel and faces the window. A white Peugeot creeps over the speed bumps. The rectangles of light from Taplow and Dorney Towers twinkle. Lucia can see a chink of light where the curtains do not meet at number 103, over the road. She does not feel a part of this night.

'Ben, will you come soon?' Her mum is still on the phone.

Lucia turns. Her eyes linger on the red water, with foaming lather around its edges. Her skin is rushing with hot and cold flushes. *What am I doing?*

I'm not normal like the other kids at school.

Lucia knows something is not right, but cannot get to the bottom of what it is. It is out of her reach, like trying to fish out an object from a deep hole, where the object has fallen too far down.

Her pulse is searing at the sides of her head.

What is happening to me?

CHAPTER TWELVE
LONDON, 1981
LUCIA IS EIGHT YEARS OLD

Yvonne says I should be more ladylike.

'Here, put this on,' she says and puts a black handbag with a gold chain over my shoulder. It makes me look old-fashioned.

'I don't like it,' I say and put it down, 'It's heavy.'

'Tough. You'll have to like it young lady. Your dad has gone to a lot of trouble to book this restaurant tonight, and you can't be looking like a messy pup.'

I am not a messy pup.

She combs my hair. A clump of it comes out in her hand. She hisses through her teeth like it is my fault. I get a lump in my throat, but can't swallow it away.

'It's because of my whooping cough,' I tell her.

'Here, give me your hands,' she barks.

So, I hold them out and she paints them a lady pink with Chanel varnish. Bitten finger nails look wrong painted. I don't like them. She sprays my neck with Loulou perfume. I like that because it covers up the cigarette smell on my dress. She brushes down my corduroy dress with a clothes brush.

'Ragged old thing this is,' she sneers.

My throat goes scratchy. It's not Mummy's fault she's poor.

She puts sparkly blue eyeshadow on me and red lipstick that tastes waxy. Now I look really stupid.

'There,' she says standing behind me in the mirror, 'Much better.'

No, it's not. I was fine before. Mummy says I don't need make up because I have natural beauty anyway.

'Come on,' she says spraying perfume mist on my dress. 'Let's go down and see your father.'

*

The restaurant is opposite The Ritz. It's called La Traviata. The lights are in glass fans on the walls, underneath the pictures of ladies dancing in feather dresses. There is a bowl in the middle of our table with candles floating on water. Jumpy piano music is playing in the background.

Daddy sits next to Yvonne. Her silk dress has no sleeves, so I can see the dimples on her upper arms.

I sit opposite them.

People walk under umbrellas outside, and cars swish through the rain. The handsome waiter with black hair comes to our table. It says *'Call me Marco'* on his badge.

I say, 'Hello Marco.'

He laughs and asks Daddy if he would like to order some drinks.

Daddy orders a bottle of Chirat or something (he says it's one of the best). Marco brings the wine wrapped in a napkin. It glugs as he pours it.

Daddy swivels the wine around, gulps it and then waits for the taste to hit him. 'Spot on,' he says.

Marco tops up Daddy's glass, pours Yvonne some and then me. I don't like wine. It tastes like vinegar.

'Please Can I have Fanta instead?' I ask.

When Marco laughs this time, I can see his lip under his moustache.

'Fanta coming right up for the lady,' he says and makes an O shape with his middle finger and thumb. He kisses his O. '*Bella bambina*,' he says, and pinches my cheek. Daddy laughs so hard his shoulders jig up and down. Yvonne twists her glass around and looks away.

I know what '*bella*' means in Italian. Marco thinks I'm beautiful.

'Now darling,' Daddy says to me, stabbing the tablecloth with the knife, 'Yvonne and I have some *very* exciting news.'

They can't be having a baby; they're too old. My chest feels so tight that I'm finding it hard to breathe. I don't know which one of them to look at.

'We are getting married, darling.'

My ears start burning. I know I should be happy, but I'm not. 'Will I be your bridesmaid?' I ask.

'No, darling,' he snorts, looking at Yvonne 'It's not a hullabaloo wedding, just an informal signing of the marriage register at Chelsea Town Hall. Then off to Venice for a honeymoon.' He taps Yvonne's hand.

That stupid song in that Cornetto advert, goes through my mind when he says Venice, and so does a picture of them together in a gondola, in love.

'When will you be coming back from Venice, Daddy?'

'We're only going for a week,' he replies, 'but, when we come back, we are going to downsize.'

Downsize? I get a picture in my head of Daddy standing in just his underpants when he says 'downsize'. 'You mean you are getting rid of some things?' I ask.

'No, darling,' he says 'we are selling the house in Lord North Street. Yvonne and I are moving to a smaller house near Epsom.'

My mouth is like rubber. I can't speak. I feel tears well up behind my eyes, but I swallow to make them go away so I don't look like a baby.

'When?' I manage to ask quietly.

'When we return from Venice,' he replies. 'You'll like it there, darling. We are going to get a lovely Burmese cat and there is a garden for you to play in.'

Cat? Why would I care about a cat? It's not even my house. I have lots of questions, but I don't know what it is OK to ask.

Marco brings my spaghetti: like a heap of worms with mince on top. He grinds the pepper over it and sprinkles on the Parmesan cheese, which smells like sick. I wind the spaghetti around my fork and suck in the worms. The sauce splashes all over my cheek. Orange dots land on the white tablecloth.

Yvonne pulls out a handkerchief from her handbag and shakes it at me. 'Here, you messy thing, wipe yourself,' she says.

I ignore her and keep sucking in the worms. Mummy never minds if my mouth gets dirty when I eat. She says it's good to enjoy food.

'Here, Lucia,' Yvonne snipes, 'wipe your mouth.'

'No!' I shout, 'I won't. You're not my mum!'

It goes quiet. Then I realise what I have just done. I can't feel anything in my body. I stop eating.

'Are you going to let her speak to me like that, Colin?' Yvonne asks.

Daddy looks down.

I quickly wipe my mouth because he looks afraid.

'Cheeky blighter,' she says, and wriggles into the back of her chair.

I have never seen Daddy look that frightened before. We eat in silence. The only sounds are meat sizzling on the grill and men laughing behind the drinks counter.

'Daddy, will I have a bedroom at your new house?' I ask. I think this question will be OK.

'Yes,' he replies, chewing his salmon. He does not look at me.

'And will I come once a month like now?'

'I don't know,' he snaps. His face goes thin like a deer. 'We haven't worked out the logistics yet, but you won't have our phone number.'

My tummy jumps, like when I miss a step going down or trip on the pavement.

I do not say a word.

Yvonne sips her wine and puts her glass down slowly.

I wish she would get run over.

*

Daddy and Yvonne have moved to Surrey. I visit him, but I cannot phone him.

He phones me. I don't ask why.

I have a fluttering feeling in my chest all the time now because I never know when he will phone.

I like their new house better than the quiet one in London. It is on an estate called Wimpy (though not the hamburger Wimpy), with lots of zigzag roads and red-brick houses on neatly mowed lawns. Kids play out on roller skates, and Casey next door has a massive Sindy house. We play Operation together, the board game.

I have the best room there. It has a gigantic bed in it, with fluffy pillows and a gold head board. I fall asleep straight away. I don't need to touch wood first like I do at Mummy's. Out of the window I can see big, green hills, and in the morning I hear the birds sing.

I came here last night. Mummy handed me over to Daddy at platform 9, Victoria Station. (They were polite to each other this time.) Tomorrow, me, Daddy and Yvonne are going on holiday to Hunstanton in Norfolk for one week. I will miss Mummy.

Daddy is out in the garden talking to Barry from next door. Yvonne is cooking in the kitchen. She doesn't know I am here (in the sitting room next to the kitchen) as I came in quietly. *Blankety Blank* is on TV. Yvonne likes Les Dawson. His fat lip makes her giggle. The kitchen door is a bit open. Water is bubbling away on the stove. The lamb is spitting in the oven.

Yvonne is talking on the phone, which is right by the door. It is odd hearing her sound polite. I pick my fingernail. Too much comes off. My finger swells. I try to make it neater when I hear Yvonne on the phone say, 'Yes, I'll give it to you, do you have a pen ready?'

She must be meaning her and Daddy's number...

'It's 01306 811 902,' she says. 'No, 902, not 903.'

That's it. That's their phone number!

01306 811 902

01306 811 902

01306 811 902

I say it again and again in my head, and slide out of the door, so she does not hear me. I run up the stairs panting.

01306 811 902

I think I've got it now. I know the code anyway.

There is no pen in my bedroom, so I rummage around in the bathroom.

01306 811 902

01306 811 902

That will do. I have found a Rimmel eyeliner in her make-up bag, so I rip off a piece of loo paper and in black letters I write on it:

01306 811 902

There, I've got it! I've got Daddy's phone number.

I fold it into four and hide it at the bottom of my suitcase where nobody can see it.

*

I love it in Hunstanton. It's the best place in the world. Our hotel is called The Burleigh Hotel. It's on the promenade. In front are amber-and-white cliffs that drop down to the sandy beach. Yvonne took me out to sea today in a red pedalo. She did the steering. We went so far out that I could not hear anything except the waves spattering and sloshing, as they sprayed my face. Daddy was pointing his camera lens at us from the shore, taking photos of us. She had to pedal hard coming back because the sea was choppy. After our ride out, she bought me a lollipop that said 'Kiss me quick' on it. She is being nice to me here. I've been holding her hand and laughing with her. We're nearly friends now.

Along the beach, we saw a crowd of people gathering around a dead mammal that stank of wee. Daddy said it was a beached sperm whale, which was very rare. It had no lower teeth and only half a jaw, and, because he was facing the right way, Daddy showed me the whale's blowhole.

After lunch, Daddy and Yvonne drove me to the creek. They sat on a rock, eating a choc ice. I rolled up my dungarees, took my bucket and spade, and went digging for crabs in the water. It was the best fun ever, but I had to tip the crabs out before we came back to the hotel. I'll go back tomorrow and see if they are still there.

*

It's high tea for the children. I am having scampi and chips with Conor and Sandy, who has wonky teeth. They are from Bolton. I've got that super-fast flutter in my tummy.

It's only six o clock. After tea, I will be going to bed so Daddy and Yvonne can have their dinner for grown-ups. That's a lot of hours to be all on my own in a room at the top of the hotel.

*

I am up here alone.

Daddy and Yvonne are four floors down. If something happened to me no one would know. The bumpy bed cover smells of dust. Someone could kidnap me, and Daddy would never know. He would not hear me scream for him. My throat is so tight, I can't breathe. I grip the bed cover.

I'm still frightened, so I turn on the light. That's better. The walls are woodchip, like at Mummy's. I think now I'll go for a walk and see if I can find anyone...

I get out of bed, tiptoe across the room and open the door.

The corridor carpet is brown with red swirls. There is a buzzing noise, and the long light above me is flickering. It smells of croissants out here. It is so quiet, no people, but tomorrow morning, in nine hours, it will be noisy again. The maids with trolleys will be here.

I walk along the corridor past room 401... 406... 409...

I check the plug sockets are off on the hall walls. One isn't, so I switch it so that the red bit isn't showing. I walk to the end of the hall and make sure all the switches are off. There is no red.

My forehead starts to sweat.

I go back to my room. I can't be here on my own. No noise. I wipe the sweat away from my neck, which is dripping water.

Go again. Check one more time…

I walk out again and check the switches are off, firm tight, just in case someone changed them when I wasn't looking. The swirls on the carpet start moving. They get faster.

I knock on the door of 409 to say hello, but there is no answer. I need Daddy.

The plugs are worrying me. They must be off before I can go to sleep.

Now, I'm lost. I turned right at the end of the corridor, and now it's saying the rooms are 507, 508, 509, but my room is 411. I'm in the wrong bit. I run to the end of the corridor, but now it says 452. My feet are cold. I need Daddy. I can't find the lift. It says *FIRE EXIT* above the door with an arrow pointing that way. I run the way the arrow is pointing and see a door with stairs behind it.

Whoops, I trip and bang my toe. It hurts, but I ignore it

I go through the door and run down the stairs fast, jumping two at a time. Ouch! I landed too hard. The floor is freezing under my bare feet. My Minnie Mouse pyjamas are slipping down.

There is the *RECEPTION*, with a man behind a desk tapping his pad with his pencil. 'Evening, love,' he says to me. But I don't know what to say.

A tear creeps down my cheek without telling me it is coming. I wipe it away, but more start pouring out. There are the doors to the bar where Daddy is. I can hear live music and people talking loudly. I stay just outside. It's better here anyway than in my room, because there is noise and people.

A breeze rushes through the front door, which is open. It smells of cockles. Pictures of Princess Diana and Prince Charles are all over the walls, in love hearts with British flags next to them. They just got married.

I think I'll go in now.

I pull the heavy door. The music is so loud that it throws me backwards.

I feel silly when I walk in because people with red faces, drinking beer at the bar, are laughing at me. The jazz band blow saxophones. I can't see Daddy anywhere. There are too many people, so I go up on my tiptoes. Then I see him, just over there! He is sitting on the wooden bench, combing Yvonne's hair with his fingers. She has her leg over him and is licking his face.

He looks up and gapes at me. I know, because his face goes pointed and red, that I am in serious trouble.

'Lucia, what are you doing down here?' he asks is a raspy whisper.

Tears spill through my throat and stream down my face.

'Sorry,' I cry, 'I was frightened.'

He lurches forwards, picks me up and puts me over his shoulder (like a sack of potatoes.) I have to hold on really tight to his shirt because I am slipping down head first. My legs are kicking in the air, but he pounds up the stairs, grunting. I know what's going to happen back at the bedroom. He's going to kill me.

But it shouldn't hurt for long. (The killing, I mean.)

He paces so fast along the corridor that my chin whacks against his back. He is only holding my feet now; I've slipped down. My head is nearly touching the floor. The carpet swirls are making me queasy.

He kicks open the bedroom door.

I hold my breath and grip his back. *Please help*.

Toss.

I bounce, head over heels.

I spring on my back.

Bash.

Ouch!

I somersault backwards, with a twist.

My heels are in the air.

Click. That was my neck cricking.

My head whacks the headboard. *Am I hurt?*

I'm seasick.

He didn't kill me. He threw me on the bed…

I am bouncing on my back.

Daddy is leaning over me grating his teeth, panting. 'What is wrong with you? What is wrong with you?' he roars, rooting his nose into my tummy like a pig looking for food.

I don't answer. I am whimpering.

He rips off his tie and whips it against the bed (not me), shouting, 'What is wrong with you, Lucia?' over and over.

I am so frightened. I crawl off the bed and hide behind the curtain. Everything aches and there is a big bump on my head.

I peep out.

Daddy is standing with his hands on his hips, huffing. 'That was *my* evening with my wife, and you have ruined it,' he growls.

'I'm sorry, Daddy. I needed you because I kept checking the plug sockets.'

'Plug sockets? What has happened to you, Lucia?' He picks me up 'Where is my happy girl? The girl who was full of sunshine?' He puts me on his lap, and bounces me up and down. His face is dripping with sweat. 'Where has this anxiety come from?' he asks, running his fingers through my knotted hair. 'You have become so inward and anxious. Why, Lucia?'

I don't understand what anxiety means. I know I bite my nails. 'I don't know,' I say, sobbing into his shirt. It feels good to not pretend anymore. The sea breeze whistles through the window and brushes my neck.

He grabs my chin. 'Lucia, I want to know what is going on. Has someone hurt you?' he asks, looking into my eyes.

'No,' I reply, wiping the snot away from my nose with my sleeve.

'Has your mother or your evil brothers turned you against me and my wife?'

'No.' I am trying to catch my breath. 'Why would they?'

'Well, why this change in your behaviour?'

I say nothing.

'I want to get to the bottom of whatever is troubling you.' He brings out his pen from inside his blazer and reaches for his notebook on the cabinet. He clicks his pen and begins his interview. 'Tell me about your mother.' he says.

'She's sad,' I tell him, 'and it's my fault.'

He puts his pen down and frowns. 'Lucia, it is not your fault. You must not carry that responsibility. You are a child.'

'But I want to make her better and I can't.'

'You must just be happy,' he says ruffling my hair, 'be a child and smile.'

My tummy sinks. I think of the girls at school who have happy mummies.

'I want to know about your brothers. Tim? How is Tim?' he asks.

'I love Tim. He takes me to the park and to the arcades to play racing.'

'What about Benedict?'

I don't say anything. He flicks my chin upwards. 'Benedict?' he asks.

'He gives me Chinese burns.'

'Chinese burns? Where?'

'Here,' I say, pointing to my arm.

He writes that down. 'And Auntie Dora, do you see her and her husband Ernst?'

'We go for Friday Shabbat sometimes. I like eating their egg and onion, and seeing their dog, but he smells,' I reply.

I am tired from crying so much. My eyes close.

'Get into bed, darling,' he says, 'we can talk more tomorrow.'

It's warm under the sheets.

Daddy tucks me in and kisses my head. 'Now go to sleep and don't worry about a thing,' he says and walks away.

'Daddy!' I shout.

'What?'

'Your phone number,' I say 'Why can't I have your phone number?'

It just came out, what I *really* wanted to say just came out.

He sighs. 'It's your mother, Lucia.' Then his face goes like a beetroot. 'I *hate* your mother. She never leaves me alone. My wife and I want some peace.'

'Will I ever have your phone number?'

'When you are older, yes, and when we can have a relationship independent of her. Now get some sleep.'

Older: that's me in a suit, driving to a posh restaurant.

'Daddy?

'What, darling?

'Do you still love me now that you are married to Yvonne?'

He goes quiet. 'Of course I do,' he says, 'you can love more than one person, you know.' He shuts the door.

I get up, open it and put my shoe as a door stop to keep it a bit open, in case I get locked in. I check the loo paper is still in my suitcase with his number on. Yes, it's there: *'01306 811 902'*.

I am back in bed now, listening to the waves rushing then slowing. I can smell the fish-and-chip air. Tomorrow, we may go out in a red boat again. Maybe I'll find those crabs that I left at the creek.

CHAPTER THIRTEEN

LONDON, 1989

LUCIA IS SIXTEEN YEARS OLD

'Muuuuum!' Lucia screams from her bedroom doorway.

Her mother pokes her head out of the sitting room. 'Yes, wh-wh-wh-what is it?'

'Look! Quick come, more red water has just appeared on my bed!'

Her mother's face goes seasick green and then ash grey. She clutches her transistor radio close to her breast and does not move. Lucia thinks how like a pathetic child she looks, standing there with jabbering lips and red-and-white mottled thighs.

'Look, Mum! Come here!'

Her mum walks towards Lucia and peers around her bedroom door.

The red water looks stark against the cream shade of the

duvet cover. She has poured it in greater quantity over the entire duvet this time.

'When, when did you see that, Lu-Lu-Lucia?'

'Just now.'

Her mother drops her radio. The batteries fall out. She kneels down by the bed as if preparing for holy prayer. Rubbing her finger over the red stain, her mum sniffs the red water, coughing.

'That's paint,' she says decidedly. 'Paint. It smells of paint.'

She knows...

'No, it doesn't,' Lucia replies. 'It smells of alcohol.'

Her mother takes another whiff and then steps away, sniffing the air like a dog on the prowl. 'It definitely smells of paint, Lucia; I'm sure.'

Lucia looks her mother up and down, fixing her stare on the chicken- skin-like patch on her thigh where her skin has creased and gathered. She thinks how old she is getting; she is sixty in three years' time.

Lucia's eyes move up to her mum's neck, where her flesh is puckered, then to her face where the brunette stain of Loving Care hair dye is marked around her hairline. She takes in the smell of baby lotion that drifts off her mum's body.

'We'll ask Ben. He'll be here in a minute,' her mum says sliding her feet across the floor as if walking through slush.

He'll know. She'll have to do something to follow on from the paint to make it look like a natural development.

Lucia runs her hand over her greasy hair. She thinks how flat it has become with length. It needs layering.

Turpentine! Turps! That smells like paint! Lucia thinks, as though she has just found the answer to a difficult algebra equation. *I'll pour turpentine on the floor. That will throw them off course and take the attention away from me.*

The front door key turns.

She jumps.

It's him. Quick, look busy. Lucia sits at her desk and opens *As You Like It*, at act two, scene three.

'Hiya', Ben calls.

'Ben!' her mother shrieks.

She bites her nail and listens to them talking in the hallway.

'What's been happening since the last update?' Ben asks.

'Red water,' her mum quivers. 'There's another stain of red water on Lucia's bed.'

'Show me.'

The hall floorboards squeak then spring.

Her mother walks in. Her brother Ben towers above her from behind.

'Hi Luce,' he says flicking his head towards her.

'Hi Ben.' Lucia looks down.

The text blurs, and letters swim into one another.

'We found it about ten minutes ago,' her mum says, pointing to the bed.

Ben sniggers and then grins. He stands straight, with his hands in his pocket. He wears a loose Gap shirt and Nike trainers with no socks. The hair on his shins is fair, and he is holding an old edition of *Titus Andronicus*, which is the play he is directing at The Lyric Theatre. 'Who found it?' he asks, turning to Lucia.

'Lucia found it. She called me, ve-ve-very alarmed' her mother replies.

'I saw it appear,' Lucia declares. 'I looked up and it was just there.'

He raises his left eyebrow. 'You saw it appear? Pigs might fly.'

'I did,' she hollers, wiping her sweaty palm against her trouser. 'I did!'

Ben's eyes shift from side to side as he retreats into his own thoughts. Her mum tries to catch his eye. Lucia watches them both contemplate the story from their different angles.

'Odd,' he says, coming back from his wanderings. 'How, very strange.' The tone of his words is sarcastic; his gaze is distant.

Two flies flit around the lightbulb making a rapid tapping sound as they bump against it. Lucia follows their chase, and wonders if flies have feelings like humans. Her glare darts to the window and she catches sight of the frosty-blue evening sky with a topaz glow streaked across.

'Smell it, Ben', her mum insists. 'It smells like paint.'

Her brother bends over and sniffs it several times. 'Yes, paint; that is definitely paint,' he says with assurance. 'Do we have any paint, Mum?'

Her mother lets out a long breath. 'Well, not red paint, no. We only have the magnolia paint left over from when Michael decorated.'

Ben's eyes scan the empty space and then meet Lucia's eyes. Her head fills with blood. She drops her gaze, aware of her brother observing her, and claws the carpet with her toes.

She knows that he knows.

And he knows that she knows that he knows.

What can he do? He can't prove it. She'll show him. She *will*.

The carpet feels prickly under her feet. That dream last night flashes back to her in strange segments. She lost her mum in the fairground. There were blue Smurfs everywhere.

'Mum, show me where the paint is,' Ben says.

'Well, it's under the sink, where it always is; here...' her mum leads Ben out to the kitchen.

Lucia will prove him wrong, but she's got to do something else fast.

Her bedroom door is ajar. She tiptoes over to where the crack is and listens to them search the kitchen cupboards for red paint.

Tins crash and fall.

Thud! The door under the kitchen sink often falls if you don't pull it first, and then slide it – Heath Robinson, they call it, as a running joke. Most doors in this flat fall off if you don't manoeuvre them first.

She frowns at her foot and stretches out her toes. Her feet resemble Marcie Grayson's feet now, with proper arches and long frog-like toes, but when she releases them they fall back to their irregular shape.

She hears more banging in the kitchen. Her throat constricts.

Sue is shouting at Ali on *EastEnders*. It turns into a piercing, pained scream. Lucia covers her ears with her hands to block out the sound.

The rowing takes her back to standing at the top of the stairs in the dark, aged five, at Lord North Street, hearing her mum howl as her dad whacked her, saying, 'Insane you are, Valerie; insane. I want you and your foul boys out of my house!' She shouldn't have been listening. The slap was quick, a lash, then it went silent. Those memories of hearing her father hitting her mother are still very much present.

Lucia drops her hands. Everything sounds muffled, just like when you hold a shell up to your ear.

Sue is wailing like a mad woman now, like she is opening and closing her mouth as she screams.

'Mum, this is Lucia having us on!' Ben shouts.

Lucia pulls back so they cannot see her through the crack in the door as they walk back to the sitting room. She waits for them to close the sitting-room door.

Her mouth tastes metallic, like when she had flu. Her mind is jumbled. More fragments from last night's dream return. She could not find her mum. She was alone. The man at the waltzers was horrid. He didn't help when she asked him if he had seen her. He smoked a cigarette and carried on spinning the carriages, saying, 'No, love'; his arm was covered in a tattoo of a dragon breathing fire.

Lucia walks down the hallway, pressing her toe down first at each step, to check the floorboards do not creak, and stands outside the sitting room, listening.

'Mum, it's so obvious; this is her trying to get your attention,' Ben insists.

'No, B-B-Ben, it's not; it's not.'

'Oh, come on, Mum, wake up and smell the coffee. Who else is it then?'

'I don't know.'

Creak.

Shit!

Lucia lifts her right foot and stands on one leg.

'Ben, it's not her. I saw the water appear in the hall the other day, when Clara and Mark were here. I saw it with my ow-ow-own eyes.'

'You're so gullible, Mum. It's her! I'm telling you it is.'

'No, Ben. I thought it was at first, but now I don't. It's too strange.'

Her brother's tone lowers. Barely audible, it changes to a steely whisper. 'This is all to do with *Colin*, Mum,' he says, his weird behaviour, cutting off from her like this. This is about her father.'

'Uh-huh, maybe,' her mum slurs.

'This is similar to the blusher patches, Mum. Remember how far she took that?'

Lucia catches her angular jaw in the gold-plated mirror. She twists her face to catch herself in a different light. Her cheeks are sunken, her skin is off yellow and look at all those blackheads on her nose!

'No, Ben, that was different.'

'How? How was that different? It was still attention seeking.'

Lucia squeezes the bridge of her nose hard. A grey worm oozes out of her skin. She wipes it against her trouser.

'I'm going to speak to her, Mum.'

'No, don't, Ben; don't.'

'No, I'm going to. She needs confronting.'

Lucia's stomach leaps to her chest. It's worth the risk even if she gets caught. *Go!*

Straddling the central floorboard in the hall to avoid any trace of a sound, she gets to the kitchen without any squeak. It's easier to not to be audible in the kitchen, because the boards don't dent when you walk on them.

Her mum has left the kitchen cupboard under the sink open.

Lucia bends down and runs her eyes over the bottles of Brasso, Mr Sheen and Parazone bleach. *There it is!* At the back, right at the back, she has found it: a two-litre bottle of white spirit next to the Dulux emulsion. She pulls it out. It is heavy. Hugging it close to her chest, she follows her tracks back along the hall and turns into her brothers' old bedroom.

It feels airy in here, because it is unused, but it is still heavy in atmosphere, and painted in carmine red. It has not been decorated since her brothers left home; the curtains are a rich maroon, and the carpet is still a raspberry shade. It is a mystery to Lucia why her mother has never claimed this empty room as her bedroom. She still chooses the single divan in the sitting room.

Her brothers' combined record collection remains stacked against the boarded-up fireplace, their unwanted books are still in the bookcase and there, on the wall, is Ben's A-level masterpiece. Lucia gazes at it, still able to get lost in its beauty; a naked Chinese woman leans against a wall, her fingers touching her neck, and she is wearing 'fuck me', red high heels. *'Put on your red shoes and dance the blues'*, it says in black writing against a pale-blue backdrop. That writing took Ben ages, she remembers; he was squinting to get it right.

Everything in Lucia's life is becoming remote. She is sucked into this frenzy, hugging a bottle of turpentine for dear life and looking around like a lost tourist.

She cannot get out of this now. If she stops, it will look weirder.

Lucia squeezes the cap as it instructs, follows the arrows and turns it anticlockwise.

Whoa! She takes in a lungful. It chokes her.

Bringing her hand to her neck, she fights for breath, only just managing to get past the next inhale. She splays her fingers across the pine chest. Keeping her gaze fixed on her fingers, Lucia breathes methodically to get her normal rhythm back.

Her breathing settles. Her lungs remain tight.

She looks at the bottle.

At the bottom, it has a red cross in a black box with **'INFLAMMABLE'** written there.

'INFLAMMABLE' she reads. *I could drink that and die, and then this wouldn't be happening. We'd all be better off.* She runs her fingers over the label. *They'd find me dead and wish they'd been kinder to me. They'd ring Dad, tell him I was dead and he'd regret marrying that bitch. They'd realise how I really felt.*

She can't do it. Dying is too frightening.

Lucia walks to the centre of the room and pours the white spirit on to the carpet. This is the game she enjoys. *That's not enough! More!* The potent stench of turpentine fills the room.

She gags.

Hiding the half-full bottle of turpentine behind the left wardrobe, she jumps back to her bedroom and closes her door.

It goes quiet for a moment. Huddled up by her bed, Lucia bangs her teeth hard against her knee. The edge of her teeth cut into her flesh leaving a bite mark.

The sitting-room door flies open.

'FUCK OFF' she writes with her finger in the dust on her bedside table.

'Ben! What's that smell?' her mother cries.

Lucia jumps up as they sniffle their way down the hall.

'What smell?' Lucia asks, opening her door.

Her mum barges in to her bedroom. 'No, it's not in here,' she barks.

'It's in here, Mum,' Ben says pointing into his old bedroom. 'In here.'

Her mother turns and walks out.

Lucia follows.

There it is – the puddle of turpentine on the carpet.

'Good God!' her mum yells, running her gold necklace over her teeth. 'It's turpentine Ben. It's turps!'

They all stand looking at the unexplained pool.

Ben's purses his lips. Lucia watches him. He does not appear to be breathing. His eyebrows move downwards, and his eyes turn into thin slits. 'Sinister, this is; sinister. I don't like it one bit,' he says.

'Look, Ben!' her mum yells. 'Look, it's all over the bed!'

'Open the window, Mum, or we'll pass out,' he orders.

Her mother stands on the bed and pushes upwards on the window several times, but it is jammed.

'Push harder!' Ben shouts.

She shoves it open and a stream of cool air flows in.

'That's better,' Ben says.

Lucia wedges her heels into the cheap carpet, feeling Ben's breath fan the side of her neck. 'How could this have happened?' she asks him.

'That's what we have to establish. Someone is doing this,' he says.

'D-d-d-d-do you th-th-think someone is hiding in this flat, Ben?' her mums asks, clutching her bosom.

'No, I think the answer is closer to home,' he answers, wiping his nose with the back of his hand, 'and we need to get to the bottom of it.'

Lucia gulps.

She studies his flaky scalp, caused by psoriasis, and then looks through the bars of her empty hamster cage. She never knew how her hamster, Roscoe, had escaped.

The ending of that dream comes back to her. She found her mum. She was walking away with another woman. They were both young and Lucia kept calling her, 'Mum! Mum!' Her mum couldn't hear. She kept walking away.

'Ben, will you stay?' asks her mother.

'No, I've got to go. I've got rehearsal early in the morning. It's press night tomorrow.'

'Oh God, yes, I forgot.'

'Call me first thing,' Ben says, 'if anything else happens.'

'OK,' her mum replies, 'I will.'

CHAPTER FOURTEEN

LONDON, 1982: BROKEN CHINA

LUCIA IS NINE YEARS OLD

Mr Simms called me into his office today. I thought I was in trouble. It was my stealing review. I had forgotten.

He pulled up his trouser leg and coughed into his fist. 'Do sit down,' he said.

I sat in front of him.

'Have you managed not to steal since we last met, Lucia?'

I nodded and said, 'Yes.'

It was a lie.

He handed me a book called *Tom's Midnight Garden*, with a yellow ribbon tied around it, and said, 'Well done! Congratulations for stopping stealing, Lucia.' He doesn't know that me and Zema stole a bag of milk teeth from Woolworths and got caught. The lady tapped Zema on the shoulder and asked her to empty her handbag. She had seen us stealing on the camera. I was supposed to be on look-out, but I didn't see the camera at the back of the shop. When Zema tipped the sweets out onto the counter, I thought we were going to prison.

The manager said it was, 'Just a warning.'

Next time they *will* call the police.

I stole a Strawberry Shortcake doll from Toys Toys Toys the day after. It was £4.99. I just put it in my bag and walked out when the lady was helping someone else. My heart was thumping against my ribs, but no one came after me.

I didn't tell Mr Simms. He said he was very pleased with me because 'compulsive disorders' are very hard to beat. I didn't know I had a compulsive disorder. Compulsive disorder sounds complicated, like an illness.

It is a bit true that I haven't stolen since my last review, because I haven't stolen from school. The last thing I stole from school was an orange from Mary Stone's lunch box. I didn't even want it, but I took it anyway. I feel I have to steal because I have done it so many times before. He knew about the orange anyway. I told him.

I must never do it again or I will have to give the book back to Mr Simms.

'Let's make this the start of a new chapter, Lucia,' he said.

I nodded so hard that my chin bashed my chest and hurt my teeth. 'Yes, Mr Simms,' I replied.

'Well done again,' he said and shook my hand so hard that my wrist ached. I took the book and untied the yellow ribbon. The cover has a picture of a young girl wearing a long, flowing dress. She is walking along a garden path with rose bushes at the side.

I still have the make-up bag that I stole from Tim's friend Crystal. It is full of eyeshadows and lipsticks. I need to give it back because there is a thing in there that people use when they can't breathe. It is an L-shaped plastic thing that you click and medicine puffs out of it. I have seen people use it in the waiting room at the doctors when their chest is wheezy. I didn't know it was in there when I stole it. I found out afterwards.

If I don't give it back, Crystal could die.

Once I have given that back to Crystal, I will tell Fanny and Zema that I am not playing 'Steal Deal' anymore. That is when one person chats up the shop assistant (normally me) to distract them whilst the other person steals as much as they can. We divide up the things between us when we get home (that's the fun bit.) I am not even going to steal the sugars or jams from the trays outside of the rooms at the Holiday Inn with Mary anymore.

Mr Simms has been very kind giving me this book.

'This is turning over a new leaf now,' he said.

I must never do it again.

*

'Lucia, help me. I'm in agony!' Mummy screams.

I run out of my room. She is crawling out of the sitting room, roaring, with her back looking like a camel's, going up, down, up, down.

I don't know what to do. I stand and watch her scrambling along; I'm useless like she tells me I am.

'Don't just stand there, do something!' she growls. 'Useless child.'

I follow her into the bathroom. 'How can I help?' I ask, jiggling up and down.

'I need the loo!' she screams. 'I can't get up, help me!' She raises her arm.

I hold it and when she gets closer to the toilet, I pull her hard.

'No, you stupid child,' she yells. 'Not like that.'

I don't know what to do. I put my hands on her waist and pull her up to the loo. She holds the toilet seat and groans. She is nearly all the way up to the seat, but as she twists herself around, she falls to the floor and lands on her side.

'Wwwaaahhh,' she wails, clawing the carpet.

I watch from behind as she wriggles on the floor. I should stroke her hair, but I feel like ice inside when I look at her.

'Lucia, my back has gone! I'm paralysed; call an ambulance, quick!'

'What, 999?'

'Yes, 999, you stupid child! Quick.'

My hand shakes as I dial 999.

'Hello, ambulance, fire or police?' a man says.

'Ambulance; my mum is paralysed,' I say, fast.

'Hello, hello,' he says like he can't hear me, 'Are you there?' I think he hears Mummy screaming in the background. 'Are you all right, love?'

I feel woozy. 'No,' I say 'My mum just fell off the loo. She is paralysed. I think it may be my fault. Can you come and help because I don't know how to.'

'Can't she move at all?' he asks.

146

'No, she can't. Listen,' I say and drag the phone to the hall, holding the receiver to the bathroom.

'Aaaaaahhhhhhhhhhhhh!'

'See, she is in pain, so please come,' I say to him.

'Don't worry. We'll be there right away.'

'What shall I do?' I ask him. I am crying a bit. I make my mouth go really tight because I must be strong for her.

'Just reassure her everything will be OK. We'll be there by the time you click your fingers,' he says, laughing.

When I put the phone down, I click my fingers. But he hasn't come.

I don't reassure her. I stay in the kitchen and eat Dairylea. Ben is back from his dad's house. The ambulance arrives, and two men come up the stairs with a long, steel bed. I wait in the kitchen and close my ears because I don't like to hear her screaming.

They carry Mummy out on the bed, under a green blanket. I stand with Ben at the top of the stairs and watch her go down to the ambulance, grunting. It's horrible. I don't know when I'll see her again. I hope she doesn't die because I haven't told her I love her.

I feel blank.

'Don't worry, Luce, she'll be back soon,' Ben says and rubs my shoulder.

*

Mummy has to stay in hospital for two weeks to have an operation because she has a slipped disk in her back. I am going to school as normal. Tim and Ben are looking after me.

Auntie Joyce has been to see me and brought me smoked salmon from Selfridges, and I have been staying at Auntie Dora's at the weekend. Mummy will be home on Tuesday.

*

It's supper time.

Me, Ben and Tim are in our usual places around the dinner table: me by the sofa, Ben in the corner and Tim by the fireplace. I know Mum's in a mood, because she is silent in the kitchen. I can only hear cupboard doors slamming.

Ben wipes his nose with his hand, smiles at me with angry eyes and then lets out a noise as if he has just eaten a refreshing lolly. Tim looks down at his hands. A belch sound comes from his throat. I pick the candle wax off the lace tablecloth and crunch it into little pieces in the palm of my hand.

A big row is on the way. I've got that horrid, tight feeling between my legs.

The news is on TV. A reporter is saying that a British helicopter has been attacked by ships in the Falklands and that, 'Mr Pymm thinks we will invade to protect British territory.'

'Will that mean there will be a war in England?' I ask.

Tim smirks and pushes his knuckles so they click. 'No, it will be in Argentina.'

That sounds far away, so that's OK.

'Ready,' Mum calls in a husky voice.

Me and Ben go to the kitchen to collect the plates. Mum's chest is so crackly she can barely breathe. She has two cigarettes burning in different ashtrays. Baking trays are strewn across the counter.

Ben impersonates her stringy smile that she does when she is in a mood, when her eyes raise and her teeth show. We laugh as we carry in the plates of bangers and mash. Mum scampers behind, short of breath.

We eat in silence. Mum squints at us from her armchair.

'So, looks like its war in the Falklands, eh?' Tim says in a jolly way.

Mum says nothing back. She just stares at us. It is dark outside now.

Ben's mouth goes tight and his nostrils flare. Tim ducks his head, so his nose touches his food. He chews like he hasn't eaten for days.

'Not a clue, any of you have , as to wh-wh-what goes in-in-into running this home single-handed have you?' Mum says like her throat is blocked.

'Here we go. Change the broken record, will you?' Ben says, rolling his eyes.

Tim scoops potatoes onto his fork fast.

'Not a clue!' she yells, spitting out a bit of sausage. 'Totally unaware, the lot of you!'

Ben slams down his cutlery. He's got big nostrils. 'Why are you incapable of getting through a day without your venomous anger ruining everyone else's life?' he shouts.

Mummy throws her plate onto the floor. Mashed potato goes splat on the carpet. Her plate cracks into five pieces.

She stands. She is hunched over. Her teeth are chattering. 'Are-are-are any of you aware of how serious an op-op-op-operation I have had, and how much pain I have been in?'

She has steamy glasses. I think she's about to cry.

'Yes!' Tim says trying to make things better. 'Of course we are, but you won't ever let us help.' He is always the one to try to make things better for her.

Ben makes it worse again. 'You're just a martyr, Mum!'

She stomps over to us, gnashing her teeth. The walls shake. Her glasses hang off her nose. I see her hand shaking.

'Yo-yo-you are all just a bu-bu-bunch of lazy sloths!' she splutters.

Ben laughs. It's an angry laugh.

'That's unfair!' Tim says, and shows his crooked teeth.

'Unfair! Do you know how long I have been running this home single-handed?' Her voice is so high it's about to crack.

'It's your choice, Mum!' Ben shouts.

'Choice!' she screams, 'Choice? Let's see how you do without me? You can do it alone.'

The tablecloth slips away from me.

Whoosh.

Plates fly in the air.

Splat! Mashed potato flies through the air and lands on my face.

There are peas everywhere. One after another, plates smash against the walls. There is broken china all over the carpet and ketchup stains the wall.

Mummy is standing in the middle of the room, huffing and puffing. Ketchup is all over her face. My sausages are on her bed, with my fork still in one of them. Tim is laughing into his hand with a twisted face.

'Do it alone the lot of you. Do it without me!' she croaks.

Mummy leaves sniffling.

The door slams shut.

I think she's going to kill herself in the canal.

*

Tim is swaying from side to side, looking out of the window and cracking his knuckles. Ben is sweeping up the food. The sausage with a fork in it reminds me of the one in the titles at the beginning of *Grange Hill*.

Ben's t-shirt says 'Hungry Like the Wolf'. I'm staring at it and it all comes back to me. Mummy's face started to shake, she was spitting and then she pulled the tablecloth off. There were plates flying around the room.

Now she's gone. It's just us.

'Complicated soul,' Tim mumbles.

'She's a bag of contradictions,' Ben says.

'Well,' Tim says, swinging his arm as if he is batting with a cricket bat, 'that definitely goes down as her best strop to date, yes?'

I can't get rid of the thought of Mummy floating in Regents Park Canal. 'What's wrong with her?' I ask, picking my toenail.

'She's a negative person, Luce,' Ben replies, holding the dustpan. 'She's self-preoccupied and she blames the world for her problems.' He goes to the kitchen and empties the pan in the bin.

'Why?' I call out.

'Because she doesn't know any different,' Ben replies.

'Well,' Tim says, turning around with his hands on his hips and rubbing his lips together, 'I think the answer lies with her mother and father.' He turns away again.

'What do you mean?' I ask.

'Her father was a violent man,' Ben says coming back into the room. 'Mum used to see him beating up Grandma Daphna a lot. He was abusive.'

Bloody nose – I make that picture go out of my head by thinking of *Sesames Street*'s Big Bird.

Tim picks up his book, *The Collector*, and walks out. 'I'll get the hoover,' he says.

Ben follows, and they laugh in the kitchen. 'This will go down in history as "bangers-and-mash-gate"!' Tim says.

It's not funny.

I go into the kitchen. 'Why is she like that though?' I ask. 'Funny sometimes, not normal?'

'She drinks, Luce,' Ben says shaking a tea towel.

'What do you mean, she drinks?'

'She drinks whisky and wine secretly, and that makes her mood change. It's a chemical change.'

'What do you mean, Ben?'

'She's a secretive alcoholic, Luce. That's way more dangerous than an honest one.'

He's wrong. 'Will she come back?' I ask.

'Course she will. It's all for effect,' Ben replies. 'You watch, it will be business as usual tomorrow morning.'

I'm going to find her. I put on my anorak over my pyjamas, put on my sticky trainers and go downstairs. When I open the front door, the air smells of sugary cherries. I sit on the step and wait for her.

Mr Abrahams walks past with his dog. 'Good evening,' he says. He doesn't know what just happened. No one does. Everyone thinks we are normal.

That picture of Mummy dead in the canal keeps floating through my head, but I watch the cat behind the dustbins instead. She's jumping, and her collar chain is jingling.

Mummy will come back. She has to make my packed lunch for tomorrow.

CHAPTER FIFTEEN

LONDON, 1989

LUCIA IS SIXTEEN YEARS OLD

It is a sticky evening. The air outside is close and smells of freshly laid tarmac. A distant roll of thunder shakes the sky. Lucia listens as she twists her Rubik's Cube. She has nearly done it; there are only two more sides to match the coloured lines on.

Her brass doorknob turns with a definite twist.

She glances up.

Ben enters. He shuts her door behind him and slides his hands into his back pockets. He snickers through sealed lips. Lucia tries to swallow, but the spit won't go down.

'We need to get to the bottom of this,' he says.

'Bottom of what?'

'You know what.'

'I don't,' she says, flicking her gaze down to his trainer. The purple tick across it makes her think of the bougainvillea in southern Spain; old, glass-eyed women in black; whitewashed houses, and dingy bars where old men play draughts and drink San Miguel.

'You do, Luce.' Ben's face is stern; his poise is determined. He towers above Lucia. His wide shoulders block any chance of her escaping. His jaw is pulsing. 'I've got all night,' he says, walking towards her. 'If that is what it takes.'

Lucia steps backwards. She is trapped in the corner.

Ben rests his hand on her pine dresser. She notices his uneven fingernails. His vile Polytar shampoo smells like rat pooh. Yuk!

'Luce, I know this is you doing these things; just admit it.'

'It's not, Ben. You've got it wrong!'

'Look at me, Luce; look at me in the eyes,' he says scanning her face.

She peers up and establishes contact, then immediately breaks it.

'Go on, look at me and tell me honestly this is not you,' he demands. 'You can't, can you?'

She looks into his light brown eyes, and then drops her gaze to his chest, where his open shirt exposes his muscles. 'It's not me, Ben,' she says, nodding.

'It must be, Lucia. There is no other explanation for how coloured water and turpentine are appearing around the flat. Has Zema put you up to this?'

'No.'

'Is this a game that you started playing and feel you have to keep up?'

'No!' she pleads. 'I've got better things to do.'

'Well, how else do we explain water and turpentine appearing all over the place, eh? Cos ghosts don't exist; not in my book, anyway.'

'I don't know,' she says, clicking her lip-balm tin open with her thumb.

There is an ominous silence. A warm breeze blows in, smelling of honeysuckle.

'You can tell me, you know, Luce; I won't be angry.' His tone softens.

Should she tell him the truth? Should she?

'There's nothing to tell. It's not me,' she insists.

He lunges forwards. His face is only centimetres from hers. 'I know how dishonest you can be, Lucia,' he says. 'You can, can't you?'

She fixes her gaze on her dresser. It has a crooked crack down its middle. She pulls the front piece of pine forwards, exposing the rotting wood underneath.

'No, that's not true,' she says.

'Remember all the stealing and the blusher patches. Look how far you took that.'

The blusher patches, yes. That episode streams back to her: she caked her arms and legs in Miss World blusher and ended up in a Harley Street consulting room to be told she was allergic to penicillin. It was a lie.

'That was when I was nine, Ben,' Lucia replies.

'So, so what? You still did it. Your age is irrelevant. You still took us for a ride. If you did it then, you could do it now, as far as I'm concerned.'

Lucia tries to speak, but her top lip is stuck. Her heartbeat is flashing around her chest like the neon lights that surround the Coca-Cola sign at Piccadilly Circus.

She clenches her fist.

BAM! She thumps her fist on the chest of drawers. Two Body Shop bath pearls jump onto the carpet and then roll across the floor.

'Look, Ben, I don't give a toss what you think of me, OK? But I am not doing these things. I don't know what the fuck is going on. I can't explain it either.'

Ben lets out a wry laugh and gazes at the wall. 'Well, let's hope we find out who is doing it then,' he says and storms out.

The scent of Ben's Right Guard deodorant lingers over her. She burps. The taste of omelette repeats in her throat. In the mirror, Lucia looks at her furry tongue covered in red spots. The willy-shaped thing between her tonsils jiggles.

She regrets not telling Ben the truth.

Lucia walks over to the window and leans out into the dewy evening. A pigeon stands on the ledge, with its grey underbelly bulging. It gawps at her and then waddles to the front of the ledge before flying away over the roofs of Birch Close.

She tilts back her head and lets the sprinkle of hot rain cleanse her blushing face. A rainbow arches perfectly in the sky; its pastel colours shimmer, but only lilac and yellow are clearly defined. The colours disappear as quickly as the pigeon left.

Lucia bobs her head and turns.

What does she care anyway?

She hates her life. She hates them.

What has she got to lose?

Lucia reaches under her bed and pulls out the bottle of turpentine she hid there.

It is now only a quarter full. *Shall I drink this or pour it over me?* She unscrews the lid. *It doesn't matter which, I've blown it anyway.*

She goes blank…

Lucia closes her eyes and pours the turpentine over her head.

She shoves the empty bottle under her bed and shudders.

Crashing to her knees, she feels nothing for a second, and then screams, 'Muuuuuuuuuuuuuuuuuum!'

Searing and tingling, it feels as if hundreds of beetles are scrambling around her head. The burning on her scalp creeps down to her eyes and her lips. The side of her face becomes numb.

'Muuuuuuuuuuuuuuuuuuuuuuuuuuuuuuuuuuuuuuuum!'

Brain damage?

She hears her mum panting in front of her.

'Good heavens!' her mum howls, 'Good heavens on earth. Lucia! Lucia!' Her mother stands over her daughter, who is kneeling on the floor with her head cocked, fumbling at the air with her hands. 'What on earth has happened to you?'

'Mum, help me! It's my scalp; my scalp is burning!'

'Good God, for heaven's sake. Ben! Ben!' her mum screams. 'Come quick, Lucia's head is burning with, with, with,' she runs her fingers through Lucia's hair and sniffs her hands. 'Ben, there's turpentine in her hair! *Turpentine… in… her… hair!*

'Can you open your eyes, Luce?' Ben asks, controlled in tone.

'No. They sting.'

It feels as if someone is jabbing a knife from behind her eyes. The agony pierces down to her cheek and neck.

'Ben, let's, let's, let's take her to A&E [Accident and Emergency],' her mum splutters.

'No, let's wash it out first,' Ben insists, 'and then see how she is.'

They raise her. Ben links arms with Lucia. Her mother locks fingers with her, and they guide her, like a blind man, to the bathroom.

'I'll get a cushion for her to kneel on,' her mum twitters and scuttles out.

Lucia kneels by the side of the bath and rests her forehead on the rim. Her cheek is stinging; her head is throbbing.

Her mum returns with a cushion. 'Quick, Ben, get some water on her head, for goodness' sake. Quick!' she flaps.

'Mum, calm down!' Ben snarls. 'It doesn't help to panic.' Ben hands Lucia a towel. 'Here, put this on your eyes.' He presses it against her swollen eyes. The pressure relieves the stinging. He attaches the plastic shower to the taps. 'Tell me if this is OK, Luce?' he asks, sprinkling the lukewarm water over her head.

Ah! The relief. 'Its fine, thanks,' Lucia replies. The sensation of Ben's hand moving from her neck over her head and wringing her hair out on the other side is hypnotic. The tepid water tickling her scalp feels wonderful. Maybe he does love her after all.

'Here, Ben, use the baby shampoo. It's softer. Good God, look, Ben, her-her-her hair is singed!'

'Well, turps does burn, Mum!' he snaps, rubbing the shampoo into Lucia's scalp.

'Look how red it is!'

'Go away, Mum,' Lucia flinches.

'Mum, go and sit down. You're making things worse,' Ben orders and wraps a towel in a tight turban around Lucia's hair.

'My eyes hurt, Ben,' Lucia gripes.

'Here, hold this up against them.' He hands her a cold, wrung-out towel.

Lucia presses it up to her eyes.

Ben leads her into the sitting room. 'Be careful of the phone wire, Luce; don't trip,' he warns, and guides her to the divan, where she sits with her head in the wet towel.

Lucia savours this fleeting moment of affection from Ben; this soothing spark of brotherly love.

'I'll make us all a drink,' he chirps.

Her mother sighs.

Wavy horizontal lines float in her blackened vision. They turn to stars the harder she presses the towel against them. *Am I blind?*

'Lucia, Lucia, what an earth happened to you?' her mum whispers.

'I don't know, Mum. I was filing paper. I felt my hair go wet and then scorching hot, so I screamed for you,' Lucia replies.

'What, just suddenly, you felt it?'

'Yes.'

She hears the clinking of spoons in the kitchen and Ben's heavy footsteps approaching.

'Here you go, Luce; your tea is by your foot,' Ben says and rubs her knee, before flopping on the sofa.

They sit in silence; it is an amicable silence, not one of hostility or hate.

A warm breeze brushes against Lucia's neck and she listens to the tinkling of glasses from the gathering going on in the garden downstairs. She takes the towel away from her eyes and blinks fast. They water. She can see the marble eggs on the coffee table, but her vision is misty. She closes them again.

'Why don't you lie down, baby boodle, eh?' her mum suggests.

Lucia grabs the pink cushion from her mum's divan and curls up in a ball. The spider plant dangling above prickles her cheek. A dull ache looms across her skull, but she dozes off into a light sleep against the backdrop of banter downstairs.

The murky voices of her mum and brother float over her, leaving her undisturbed.

'Look at her, Ben; pathetic, she looks. The sight of her when I found her was ghastly. Shall we take her to A&E?'

'And say what?'

'Well, that it was an accident.'

'Don't be ridiculous. They'll be onto social services immediately. Leave it.'

'Too awful, this all is Ben.'

'I know, it's sad. But I still think it's her needing attention.'

*

'Listen!'

Lucia wakes from her hazy slumber. She sits up. Her eyes open more easily.

'Listen!' Ben exclaims.

Her mother perches on the edge of her chair.

'Can you hear?' Ben asks, pointing to his stomach. His gaze flips back and forth between Lucia and their mother. '*Sssshh!*' he whispers, beckoning to them both.

Lucia leans forwards.

She hears an electric whirring sound coming from where Ben sits. It is a churning sound, like a metal machine trying to get started on a cold day.

Lucia looks into Ben's eyes. They are eyes of childlike wonder. His mouth is gaping open, and it stretches even wider as she skims his expression.

'Can you hear, Luce?' he asks.

The whirring sound builds momentum, like propellers warming up for take-off.

'The noise! It's coming from my stomach!' Ben yells 'I can feel it. Fuck!' He jumps up and shakes his legs, as if trying to shoo off insects.

The sound of metal blades swirling becomes louder, like there is a helicopter in the room.

Lucia's hand flies to her throat. 'Oh my God!' she smiles. 'Where's it coming from?'

'It's coming from me,' Ben shouts.

It is a non-human sound coming from her brother's stomach – fucking weird!

Ben cradles his stomach and looks with a stony intensity out of the window. The helicopter noise becomes thunderous: *brrrrrrr, brrrrrrr, brrrrrrr.*

Lucia locks eyes with Ben and her mum in a triangular gaze.

Bbbbbbbbbbbbbbbbbbbbbrrrrrrrrrrrrrrrrrrrrrrrrrrr.

She drops her eyes. The diamond patterns on the rug expand and contract. The noise stops. Suddenly, just like that, it stops.

Ben sits forwards. He looks at Lucia and lets out a monotone laugh. 'Freaky,' he says.

Lucia's mum sits with her legs spread apart and her face resting in her palms.

'I have *never* experienced anything like that in my life,' Ben says, fanning his face, 'ever. That was totally incredible. I felt it here.' He jabs his navel. 'My tummy was vibrating like a machine was in there. I thought I was dreaming.' He grins at Lucia.

'I told you, Ben!' her mother shouts, arms flailing. 'There is something going on. Something is happening!'

'Maybe you are right,' Ben replies. 'Maybe there is.'

Now he believes it.

Lucia breaks eye contact with them. Her eye pain has dimmed. Her gaze skims the book shelves opposite; there's Simone De Beauvoir's *Nature of the Second Sex* and Sarah Maitland's *Daughter of Jerusalem*.

What was that? I didn't make that happen. Or did I? she wonders.

'I think we need help, Ben,' her mother burbles. 'I really do. It's like there's a-a presence here; someone hiding in the walls.'

'I still can't believe that just happened. Who will believe this?'

There is a stoic silence in the room.

'People will think we are deranged when we tell them all this,' he continues, 'I mean someone would have to have been in here to believe that.'

Lucia cannot believe that has just happened. She can do anything now. Her playground is bigger and deeper. She has free rein.

'What do we do Ben, eh?' her mother shrugs.

Lucia looks up and tries to join in.

'We need to confide in someone,' Ben replies, twisting his sleeve.

'You know, Ben, I spoke with Maeve last night and she has given me a number for some people,' her mum says.

'What people?' he asks.

'I th-th-think she sa-sa-said it was the London School of Psychic Studies. It is based in Central London somewhere. She said it is excellent.'

Lucia stands.

'Where are you going, Lucia?' her mum asks.

'I need a bath, Mum. I stink of turpentine,' Lucia replies, sniffing her t-shirt.

'Do you think she should, Ben?'

'She'll be fine, but keep the temperature mild Luce, OK?' he urges.

'OK.' She walks out.

Her body feels heavy; her head is tight like she is wearing a helmet of bricks. Weary, Lucia closes the sitting-room door behind her.

*

They catch her eye, just like that. Lined up neatly under the coat rack are her stupid, blue, Barratt's wellington boots, next to her mum's Fireman-Sam-style yellow ones.

She hates her thermal-lined boots. When it snows, her mum makes her wear them to school, but Lucia puts her pumps in her bag and changes into them half way down the road. All the other girls at school have colourful moon boots.

Look at them, sticking out from under the raincoats. She picks one up, and puts it in the middle of the hall. Blood rushes to her cheeks. *Why did you just do that? Weirdo...* It's the oddness that compels her; the randomness of a wellington boot in the middle of the hall. *Look at it, standing there on its own! Tee hee.*

Lucia moves the other one and places it opposite the first, so their toes are facing each other.

She chuckles. They look like they have personalities; like they could walk off on their own, and scare someone.

She puts her hands inside them. They are toasty warm. With her hands still inside the boots, she slides them from side to side, like windscreen wipers moving.

Lucia catches herself. *What are you doing?* They look so odd! In the middle of the hall, two wellington boots stand slanting left, inches apart from one another. *Leave them there.*

She walks into the bathroom and runs a hot bath full of Radox bath salts.

CHAPTER SIXTEEN
LONDON, 1984
LUCIA IS ELEVEN YEARS OLD

I've started secondary school now. I'm in class 1C. My new best friend is Maisie. She has a lovely house in Hampstead, and she wears cowboy boots *and* a real flying jacket. Her mum is really pretty, and she teaches Masie to play the cello.

I've been going to Masie's after school. We hang out with her friend Dane. I don't like him. He's got goofy teeth and dribbles when he speaks. Masie is different when she is with him. Her laugh goes funny and she doesn't speak as posh. They sniff lighter fuel together, but it makes me dizzy and the veins in my head swell.

Yesterday, we threw eggs at cars on the Finchley Road with Dane.

Masie doesn't know, but I go once a week now to speak to Dr Donavan at the surgery. Mum is worried about me because of how much I touch wood. I know it is not right, but when I touch wood it makes sure that nothing bad will happen. I have to take a piece of wood to school now. I take the slat from the end of my bed in my bag, and when I get frightened I hold it.

I have to touch wood eight times before my bath every night. I say aloud all the things that are worrying me. Dr Donavan says it is anxiety. I don't know what that means, but I think I have always had it whatever it is.

I like Dr Donavan. He wears round glasses and talks in a quiet Irish voice. He listens to me like no one else does. I tell him about Dad not phoning me anymore. He says that Dad's behaviour is 'irresponsible'.

Dad forgot my birthday. He has never done that before. His card always arrives two days before everyone else's. I knew that he had not sent me a card before I got down to the bottom of the stairs because I could not see his squiggly handwriting on the mat. I know his writing so well, the way his *y*'s join, but no other letter. His cards also always come in a vanilla-coloured envelope. There was no vanilla one on the mat. Cousin Alexis sent me a card with £5 inside, and Auntie Dora sent me an Our Price voucher. Dad forgot. He said he was going to buy me a new carpet for my new pink bedroom, but Mum said not to worry; she will buy me one from the cheap shop in Kilburn.

He doesn't phone once a week anymore. I haven't been to stay with them in Reigate for nine months. Dad writes me a note with a time to meet him at Green Park. We have lunch without Yvonne and then he goes back. He says it is because Yvonne does not want to see me since my 'appalling' behaviour in Hunstanton. I did go to their house in Reigate once, but she did not speak to me. I don't think he is allowed to see me much. Either that or he doesn't love me anymore.

I've still got his phone number on the toilet tissue. It's in my piggy bank. If I phoned him, though, he'd kill me. He said he is going to take me on holiday to Brittany soon, just me and him (without bitch face.)

Mum has bought me my own black-and-white TV for my birthday anyway. A bomb exploded today at a hotel in Brighton. Margaret Thatcher nearly got killed. I don't understand who would try to kill her, and I don't understand why, if everyone hates Margaret Thatcher so much, they are so relieved that she is still alive.

It's 6.30pm. Ben is playing Frankie Goes to Hollywood loud in his room.

Mum bursts in there. 'Turn it down please, Ben,' she snaps.

I sit by my bedroom door.

'No, why should I?' he replies. 'It's not that loud.'

Here we go…

'I ca-ca-can't hear a thing in there,' Mum stutters.

'Well, get a hearing aid then,' Ben shouts. He turns it up really loud.

Relax, don't do it when you want to go to it…

Oh no…

Mum stomps across the room and turns his music off. The lampshade rattles.

'What are you doing, bitch?' Ben says.

'This is my, my, my home,' Mum replies. It sounds like there is air trapped in the back of her throat. 'I want it off!'

I grab my piece of wood and hold it tight. I wish things were normal.

'And I happen to live here,' Ben shouts. 'God, weren't you happy enough kicking my friends out earlier? Is it your hobby to make everyone miserable?'

I'm on her side.

'I have no be-be-bedroom, Benedict, if you have forgotten...'

'So, big deal, people are dying of hunger in Ethiopia. Not my problem,' he shouts.

'It is your-your-your problem, actually,' Mum gabbles. She is about to break. 'Are you going to wash up all of the mugs and ashtrays?'

'No, you can do it, Mum; you kicked them out.'

That's not fair. He should clean them.

'This-this-this, is the fourth time I have come home from work to find your dirty dishes le-le-left for me to wash up.'

'So, big deal.'

It goes quiet.

'It is a big deal to me, actually,' Mum says.

'Everything is a big deal to you. That's your life, Mum.'

The walls shake.

I peek through his door. They are pushing each other, like in a wrestling match.

'Get off me, Mum!' Ben shouts.

'That's it! I've had enough of your insolence. Get out of my home!' she screams.

'It's my home too!' he whinges.

I go back to my room. It's horrid to watch.

'I don't want you here anymore. I've had enough. Now get out!'

I press myself between my legs to make the anger away.

The bookcase bangs against the wall.

'Get off me, Mum!' Ben screams.

'I said get out of my house!'

I hear a punch, then panting. The room feels like it is rocking. I go and watch again. Ben is bent over, pushing Mum's arms away. She is punching his head. They bash against the mirror table. The dried flowers fall off.

Snot drips from Ben's nose. 'You never wanted me did you?' he snivels.

Mum pushes him towards the door. 'Get out of my home!'

'I'm not going!' He grinds his body against the front door.

Ben is bent over in the doorway, whimpering. Mum is pushing his head away. I have only seen him cry once before, after he was knifed outside Ladbrokes. He is half way between the flat and the outside hall. His grip slides and then he falls down the top section of the stairs. Mum slams the door shut.

'Bitch, let me in!' Ben punches the door hard. 'I'm your son!'

'Go!' Mum shouts, with gritted teeth. 'Go to your father. He'll have you.'

Ben thumps down the stairs. I run to my window. He jumps to the bottom and looks up. I wave, but he just wipes his nose and walks towards the Holiday Inn.

Mum is sobbing in the hallway with her mouth open, so it sounds like a howl. I don't know what to do with myself.

I sit on my bed with my wood. I think about what Brown Owl, (at Brownies) said last night in our closing circle, that everything has a beginning and an end.

If she is right, then all of these problems will end one day.

I don't know if Ben will come back. I should go and comfort Mum, but I don't know how to, so I just hold onto my wood.

Touch wood, this stops soon.

Touch wood, this stops soon.

Touch wood, this stops soon.

I do it one more time for luck.

Dr Donavan told me to think of something positive before I touch wood, but I can't think of anything. I want to cry, but my throat is blocked, and my tummy has pins and needles inside. I hate the sound of Mum sniffling.

I try to make it go away by blocking my ears and saying my favourite poem aloud.

John had Great Big
Waterproof Boots on.
John had a Great Big
Waterproof Hat;
John had a
Great Big
Waterproof
Mackintosh
And that (said John)
Is that!

I hope Ben will be OK…

*

The key turns in the front door. 'Hi!' Tim calls, expecting a sea of hellos.

No one answers.

'Hello,' he says again, this time more cautiously.

I open my door. He is standing in the hall in his leather jacket and black cap.

The sitting-room doorknob rattles.

'Hi Tim,' Mum says, holding onto the door frame for balance. I don't know why.

'What's wrong?' Tim asks. 'You look peculiar.'

'Nothing,' Mum nods.

Tim walks to his room. 'Where's Ben?' he asks.

Mum looks down. 'He's gone.'

'What? What do you mean "he's gone"?' His funny teeth are biting his top lip.

'I-I-I-I've thrown him out.'

Tim storms into the kitchen. 'I don't fucking believe this!' he shouts. Tim doesn't get angry very often. He is quiet and does everything Mum wants. Sometimes though, he explodes.

Mum keeps her grip of the door frame.

'What the fuck did you throw him out for?' Tim yells from the kitchen. His voice gets louder. 'He's just in the middle of his mocks. He needs stability!'

Mum is still in the hallway, running her necklace along her lip. 'I-I-I-I-I've ju-ju-just had e-e-enough, Tim.'

'Enough of what? What's he done wrong?'

I stay quiet and hold on to my Snoopy.

'I-I-I've had enough of ru-ru-ru-running a home, single-handed. He's better off with your father.'

Jesus!

There is a loud smash. I don't see anything for a second. Then the mirror above the coat rack cracks. Shattered glass falls towards the bathroom. Milk splatters all over the walls.

'Well, I've had enough too!' Tim shouts. 'I've had a fucking enough of it all, Mum.'

Tim charges out of the kitchen, along the hall. Broken glass crunches under his Doc Martens. Mum follows him into his room. He opens his drawers, and starts throwing underpants and socks into his sausage bag. 'This craziness has got to end,' he seethes.

'Wh-wh-wh-what are you doing?' Mum asks.

'I'm going to go and stay with Scott,' he replies, in a quieter tone, 'until my teaching job in Malta begins. I can't stay here anymore.'

Scott lives next door.

'You don't have to do that,' Mum mumbles. She looks afraid.

'I do. I'll stay there until Ben comes home.' He slings his bag across his shoulder and marches to the bathroom. He chucks his razors and toothbrush into his bag, and opens the hall door.

'Tim!' Mum shouts.

'You're on your own with this one. I'm gone,' he replies and slams the door.

It goes quiet for a few minutes.

I don't know what to say. Can I phone Meg?' I ask.

'Do what you like,' she replies, and shuffles into the sitting room. The drinks cabinet door squeaks and the glasses rattle.

I walk to the kitchen, stepping over the broken glass. I look for an apple, but the fruit in the bowl is mouldy. I sweep up the glass with the dustpan and brush, and wash away all of the milk from the floor. I can't believe Tim lobbed that milk bottle. It could have hit Mum in the eye, and she could have gone blind.

It's dark outside. I take the telephone into my room.

There is no one I can tell. My heart is beating fast. I think about dialling that number for Dad. In the olden days, before he married bitch face, I could have called him. He would have come and taken me away from this madness.

I dial Meg.

'She is out,' her mum says.

We are supposed to be practising our dance for her mum's squat party next week. We have made up a routine to Dead or Alive's 'You Spin Me Round', and are going to wear yellow jumpsuits and jellies.

I hug my teddy, Goldie. He growls when you punch his stomach.

'*Grrrrr!*'

That feels better.

'*Grrrrr!*'

I cry into Goldie's fur.

I hope they come home soon. I don't want to be alone with her.

CHAPTER SEVENTEEN

LONDON, 1989

LUCIA IS SIXTEEN YEARS OLD

Lucia cups her hand and guides the hot water over her breasts and neck. She runs her hand up and down her calf, and lies back into the hive of frothy bubbles.

Pop, pop, pop; an orchestra of crackling bubbles tickles her ear.

'Mum!' Ben calls.

She listens to their voices outside.

'Mum! Look, the boots. They've moved!' Ben titters.

Her mum is silent.

Lucia wraps the towel around her. She opens the bathroom door, looks down at the wellington boots and meets their gawping faces head on. The boots look so funny – odd funny – standing there in isolation. Observing them as if she was seeing them for the first time, she pouts to avoid guffawing. It looks as if they have walked across the hall on their own.

Her mother lets out a croaky laugh.

Ben chuckles and then becomes stern 'Mum!' he says. '*Give those people a ring.*'

'What people?'

'The ones Maeve told you about. Phone them! We need help.'

'I think… I think… I think I left the number in my diary.' Her mother shuffles into the sitting room, tripping on the phone wire.

'Weird, eh? Moving boots,' Ben snickers.

Lucia cannot control her quaking laugh. 'Moving boots, I know,' she replies, running her teeth over her bottom lip. 'Odd.'

'Odd? You can say that again.'

*

A week has now passed. Ben has arrived. The sky is a mass of slate-grey cloud. Lucia sits on her mum's divan, running her finger along the bumpy lines on the cover. Her mother is in her armchair, cross-legged, humming to her internal rhythm of worry.

The doorbell rings.

Ben jumps up, slapping his thighs, 'I'll get it,' he says and dashes out.

His footsteps thumping down the stairs make the wine glasses rattle in the drinks cabinet. Lucia can hear a collection of men's voices at the bottom of the stairs. She looks at her mother who sits just like you do when you are taking off in a plane.

The male murmur comes closer.

The men enter the room behind Ben. It quickly feels full in here, and smells of fresh air and rain. The three men sit on the sofa.

Ben shakes all of their hands. 'Hi, Benedict Clarke, pleasure to meet you all,' he says.

'Hi, Gary Reinbaum,' the one on the left says and stands, 'London School of Psychic Studies.' He shows Ben his identity card and shakes his hand. Gary introduces his colleagues: Doug on the right and Terence in the middle.

Doug looks like Suggs from Madness, only stodgier. He has grisly stubble and a tough demeanour in his faded jeans, bomber jacket and steel-toe-capped Doc Martens. This isn't what a psychic should look like. Lucia thought that psychics all had wobbly eyes and did tarot readings in Carnaby Street!

Gary looks like Doug's twin, only thinner. He is bald, has a more defined chin, and is smartly dressed in a white shirt and brogues. His words take longer to finish and are said perfectly.

Terence looks like a real psychic. He's the wizard. Lucia likes him. She is drawn to his numinous aura. His big eyes look like they have magic strings behind them that lead to Narnian worlds or magical places that only Doctor Who might inhabit. Terence can see the invisible.

He has wild, grey hair, and long lines that run down his face from his eyes to his mouth. Veins gleam in his face; the purple ones in his neck pop out. He is lanky and has a drip of mucus hanging from his nose. He wears a black cape, and looks down whilst his colleagues do all the talking.

Lucia notices his spindly fingers and the spiky ring on his middle one. A piece of tree bark hangs around his neck. He is the real psychic healer. The other two look like his bodyguards.

'I'll get us some tea,' Ben smiles and skips out.

Her mother leans forwards and extends her hand. Doug meets it with a hearty shake. 'Douglas, Doug McAlister; pleasure to meet you.'

Her mother flashes a fake smile. 'Valerie, Valerie Goldman. This is my daughter, Lucia,' she mother says, withdrawing her hand quickly.

Lucia whizzes her eyes across the men's faces. She notices the wizard in the middle trying to catch her eye. She looks down and hangs on to the creasing sounds of Doug's leather jacket and the chinking of teaspoons from the kitchen.

Ben enters carrying the red, seventies tray with her mother's best Denby china tea set stacked on it. This only comes out for special people. He pours the tea and puts the plate of Jammie Dodgers on the coffee table. 'Help yourself,' Ben says and hands them each a cup of tea.

Lucia watches Doug bite into his biscuit. His crunch is loud and like a kid, he bites out the jam centre out first. He brushes the crumbs away, and coughs into his fist.

'So, Mrs Goldman, you and I spoke last week about what has been happening,' he begins, wiggling his finger back and forth, 'but it would be helpful for my colleagues here if you could summarise the events.'

Her mother rolls her eyes and clutches her pearl necklace. 'Well, it all began with water,' she drones, 'Puddles, everywhere.'

'No, Mum!' Ben snarls, 'It didn't. Be specific.' He turns to Doug, pointing his hand out as if directing someone straight on. 'It *began*, back in April, when my *sister* found a patch of water on her paper when doing her Latin homework.' All three men hang onto Ben's every word. 'And then a phase developed of random water puddles appearing everywhere.'

'Everywhere,' her mum screeches, 'absolutely everywhere!'

'Mum!' Ben scowls as if rebuking a young child. 'I'll speak. And then, about three weeks after that' he says, resuming a normal pitch, 'we started to discover red and blue water all over the place, on beds and carpets. And that went on for about, for about—'

'A week,' her mum interrupts, tapping her foot on the carpet.

The wizard goggles at Lucia. She scrunches her hair into a bun.

'Yeah, about a week,' Ben continues. 'And then we started to discover large patches of turpentine on beds and on the carpets, and that went on for a couple of weeks. And then *I... I...*' he repeats '*I* thought it was my *sister* playing tricks on us, so I confronted her one evening.'

He knows.

Lucia glances up. The wizard is staring into her eyes. It is a penetrating stare, one that sees all. He is not easily deceived. He can see everything: her pain and her hostility towards her mum. He gets her. He is no fool.

'So, what happened after you confronted her?' Gary asks, dropping his eyes.

'Well,' Ben titters, 'it was quite a night. Firstly, we found her screaming in her room with turpentine in her hair – terrible it was – and then we were all sitting here, where we are now, and suddenly,' he gropes at his stomach, 'suddenly, this noise came from *me*. It was like a helicopter was in the room. It was one of the most incredible things I have ever experienced.'

'And then?' Gary asks.

'And then, the recent phase has been *boots*.'

Lucia tightens her bun and sucks in her cheeks. The wizard is watching her every move. She tries to meet his stare, but fixes her gaze on the diamante glimmer on Ben's shirt.

'Boots?' Doug asks with a puckered brow.

'Yes, for about two weeks now, we have been finding wellington boots in funny arrangements; specific arrangements,' he asserts, cutting the air with both hands.

'Like what? Can you describe it?' Doug asks.

'Yes,' Ben replies, grinning at Lucia, 'symmetrical patterns that look planned.'

What if the wizard makes Lucia's crime public?

Her tongue is thick. Her ears become hot.

Doug looks to his colleagues for reassurance and then resumes a posture of authority.

'This all sounds like common psychokinetic activity, which can arise in households,' he blows air into his cupped hands. 'What we can do today is a channelling process, which my colleague, Terence will perform to ascertain whether there is any kind of misplaced energy here causing these disruptions.'

Her mother toots and nods. Ben scowls at her with a glare of disapproval.

'Of course, that is if that is something you will consent to?' Doug asks. 'It normally does help to identify where these problems can be stemming from.'

Lucia is convinced they are going to find her out.

'Yes,' Ben says politely, 'anything you can do to help.'

Lucia watches the wizard lift his black briefcase up from under the table. He presses the two gold buttons either side. The clasp releases. The lid flips up.

He lifts out a Dairy Milk purple coloured cloth and shakes it. The sound of it rippling cuts the air.

'Sorry, I'll clear some space,' Ben says, and lifts the fern plant and the tray of coloured marble eggs off the table onto the floor.

Lucia follows Terence's every move as he prepares for his magical séance.

How cool is this? Lucia thinks.

There are no words from the wizard, just a terse head shake. He lays the satin cloth on the table and straightens the corners. He brings out three slim brass candlesticks and places them in a neat horizontal line with a narrow gap between each pair.

'Hmmm,' he puzzles and scratches his head. Something is not right. He moves the end one further to the right, and then adjusts the other two to reach parallel perfection. He fiddles in the side pocket of his briefcase. It sounds like clothes pegs grinding against each other. He pulls out three white candles and places one in each candlestick.

The middle one does not fit.

He twists it until it slots in. Wax shavings scatter.

There is a brooding silence. All eyes are on him. Terence sits back and looks at his display, rubbing his hands together.

'OK,' Doug announces, 'Terence is ready to begin his channelling. It is important that you please remain as quiet as possible as any noise, even white noise, can disturb his process.'

Lucia's heart jumps. This is make or break.

The wizard strikes a match. He lights each wick and scans the flames. Three carroty-orange flames each elongate into a pointy triangle and then find stillness. He bows his head and closes his eyes. His hand hovers over the flames.

The middle flame kicks and spits.

What's it doing?

'Yeees, yeees.' It is a confirming *yes* that the wizard rumbles.

Lucia feels a lurch in her stomach. *What if he channels the truth?*

The wizard raises his arms, as if calling on the spirits. He holds them there patting the air as if he is moulding a sculpture. Lucia is lost in his spell. His hands descend. They stop and embrace an invisible balloon of water.

Lucia steals a glimpse at her mother. The flames shine with an amber glow, which falls across her mother's face. Her cheeks droop like a bulldog's. Her eyes are sad. There are stories in her mum's eyes that she will never know.

The wizard's arms now gyrate in a harmonic motion. His hands waltz and his fingers twinkle. The hairs on the back of Lucia's neck stand up. She always looks at a person's hands. She can tell if they have a hard or a soft personality by the architecture of their hands, and their movements.

Mum is hard.

Ben is a bit hard and a bit soft.

Doug is hard and soft, like Ben; Gary is soft; and the wizard is super soft.

Here he goes again…

With hands outstretched, up go his arms. This time, the wizard lets out a deep baritone hum. 'Hmmmmmmmmmmmmmmmmmmmmm.' He holds it without stopping for breath and then, *vroom,* he revs it up.

The pitch of his drone shifts from first to second gear. The sound moves to the back of his throat. Tremolo, vibrato; a tremble in his hum creates a buzzing ring, like when you press down on a spinning top.

His tone starts to ring and trill and gets louder.

'Hmmmwwhhaaaaaahmmmmmaaaaaaaaaaaaaaaaa-aaaaaaaaa.'

The brass teapot on the bookcase clatters.

Clang! The baby photo of Lucia crashes down. Lucia thinks of Lucky, the silent slave in *Waiting for Godot,* who bursts out into a bleating rant that only he understands.

Look at that middle flame! It flickers as if wind is blowing.

Lucia stares at it willing it to flicker faster. *Show them!* It does. The orange flame ducks, sizzles, splutters and then leaps, cutting the air with a *whoosh.* She doesn't know if it has picked up that *she* is the trickster, or if 'something' is happening, but she loves this excitement and the mesmerised glint in all of their eyes.

Ben's eyes swivel towards Lucia. His pupils are huge and the mole above his lip twitches. She does not know how to respond to his need for connection.

The wizard brings his hands onto his lap. His spell settles to a purr. His eyes remain closed. The flame has tamed, and is now just wavering.

They wait.

He opens his eyes. 'Ah,' he sighs as if he has just finished a satisfying pooh.

The séance has ended. They await the verdict.

Terence stares blankly out of the window.

The sky has now cleared. A speckled froth of blue and grey cloud with a carnation-pink shimmer around it resembles a classic Pre-Raphaelite picture.

Doug and Gary gather in close under the wizard's cape. Lucia watches Terence witter to his sidekicks. The two men nod in unison to Terence's instruction and then slide away. Doug's eyes flit from east to west. 'My colleague here,' he says gesturing to Terence with his thumb, 'has definitely picked up on some malignant energy here, in this flat.'

'Malignant energy? What exactly do you mean?' her mum asks, blinking repetitively.

'Well, Mrs Goldman, energy is hard to diagnose or explain,' he replies in his thick East End tone. 'It is possible that a ley-line grid is running under a point at this property.' The wizard nods knowingly. 'Or it *could* be connected to a person who once lived here and is now deceased. More likely though,' he coughs, 'is that my colleague is picking up on distressed energy given off by a disturbed person, here present. This could be causing the psychokinetic activity you are experiencing.'

Lucia looks into the wizard's eyes. He knows as well as she does that the latter is correct. His glare pierces through her, but she doesn't understand. Is there something weird happening, or is this malignant energy making her do these odd things?

'I see,' her mother mumbles, 'so where do we go from here?'

'First and foremost, it is critical that you all remain as calm as possible,' Doug says. 'We do appreciate how difficult this is for all of you, but you will help yourselves if you remain as relaxed as possible.'

'Calm? Ca ca ca calm?' her mother squeals. Steam coats her mother's spectacles. 'How do we remain calm? Our lives arc in chaos. My-my-my-my-my dau-dau-daughter,' she gestures to Lucia, her stutter stuck in her throat, 'has GCSEs to co-co-complete, and I have a *job* as a receptionist to hold down.'

Lucia raises her hands to her face and holds them there. How can she do this to her mum?

Doug holds his hand up in a stop signal to her mum. 'Mrs Goldman, I do understand.' He moves his hands towards her as if trying to stop a wave from getting through. 'What you must try to understand is that energy breeds energy. The more agitated you become, the more you will feed the activity.'

'He's right, Mum,' Ben says.

Her mother holds her head in her hands. Her ashtray falls. A knoll of snake-like butts rest on a bed of ash.

'You will help to calm things if you get on with your lives as normal,' he affirms.

'Normal?' her mum squeaks.

'Mum!' Ben bellows. 'Listen to them!'

Doug pulls out a business card from a silver box and hands it to her mother. 'Do take this. It is a healing clinic that is open to the public.'

Her mother snatches it.

'It is to enhance the individual, to assist them to find their own point of balance,' Doug adds. 'I can assure you it is not brainwashing. The intention is that the healer acts as a channel for the healing energies to bring this about.'

'I see,' her mum mumbles.

'Thank you,' Ben says as if speaking for a young child who has no manners.

'May I ask if it is just the three of you in this family?' Doug asks.

'No,' her mum replies. 'My eldest son lives abroad. He is coming home next week.'

'Right then,' Gary interjects, slapping his knees 'I think that is all for today. Do come along to our clinic.'

Lucia watches the wizard disassemble his magic display, listening to the chinking of his candlesticks. Ben shakes hands with Doug and Gary. 'Thank you very much for coming,' he says, and stands to assist them out.

The wizard clicks his briefcase shut.

Lucia stands and then sits. Mistake!

No. It wasn't a mistake. *Go!*

She stands and walks up to the wizard. His cape smells of burnt kindling. His eyes are kind. After years of being misunderstood, she has finally found someone who gets her. She shakes his hand, which feels as soft as it looks.

'Flow,' he says to her in earnest. 'Flow with life, my child, not against it.'

Flow with life? What does that mean? Images flurry in her mind of being trapped in a cyclone. *You wouldn't flow with that, would you? You'd try to get away. Crap.*

The two psychics nod at her and follow Ben out. Lucia imagines the wizard going home to a thatched cottage with a hearty open fire and mystical books in every bookcase.

She follows the sound of the men's voices to the bottom of the stairs and turns to her mother, who looks lost and is flicking her nail.

CHAPTER EIGHTEEN

LONDON, 1985

LUCIA IS TWELVE YEARS OLD

Ben did come home after Mum kicked him out, but for four months only. He passed his A levels and has gone to Durham University to read English. Tim stayed with Scott for eight months, before beginning the job he had already been offered in Malta, teaching English. He has now moved there to start a new life.

It's just me now, alone with her.

Their bedroom is dusty and smells stale. Tim's Talking Heads records are on the left side of the fireplace and Ben's remaining Bowie records are on the right side. The plant in the middle is dead. Ben's Bowie memorabilia is still under his bed, in the brown suitcase. I have nothing to do. Mum is in the sitting room being weird, with the TV on loud, so I pull the suitcase out. It is too heavy to lift. I get on my hands and knees, and slide it into my room.

It's amazing inside. There are Bowie books, records, scarves, calendars, you name it: everything. There's even a tin with Bowie on it. I pick up the *Bowie Years* book that's on top.

I flick through and look at the pictures. Oh my God! I can't believe it. On page 159 it says *'I took him home and neatly fucked him on my bed.'* That is so rude! I read it again and again because I don't understand how a man can fuck another man 'neatly'. It sounds gross. I can't see it in my head, but I keep trying.

I fold over page 159, so I can read it again tomorrow, and close the book.

Mum opens my door.

I look up. She is chewing the last of her pork pie. Pastry crumbs are all over her jumper. She can't stand up straight.

Blood starts to race in my arms and neck.

Her eyes keep closing. I get that tight feeling in my fanny.

'Wh-wh-wh-what are you doing, Lucia?'

I clip Ben's case shut. 'I'm looking through Ben's Bowie collection. I miss him,' I reply. I want to run out, but she is blocking the door. 'Is he coming home soon?' I ask.

'What do you mean, you stupid child? No, of course he's not. He's at university.'

She tumbles onto the wardrobe.

I push Ben's suitcase away.

'Ar-ar-aren't you do-do-doing your ho-ho-ho-homework?' she stammers.

'No, not today.' I am still kneeling on the floor.

'Why not, you useless child? Why are you wasting your time like this?' Her teeth grit so hard that her face judders.

There is no one here to help me. The burglar alarm over the road won't shut up.

'I haven't got any to do. I'm not wasting my time,' I reply.

'All you do is waste your time, you useless creature,' she says.

The dried white spit at the corner of her lips makes me want to puke. 'I'm sorting through Ben's collection for him.'

'What about the cleaning you said yo-yo-you would to do for me?' She always stutters like this when she is on one of her funny moods.

'What cleaning?'

'You-you-you-you were supposed to dust. As usual, you are selfish and only think o-o-o-of yourself.'

'I'll do it tomorrow,' I reply.

'Tomorrow? Tomorrow?' She stomps towards me, pointing. 'It's always tomorrow with you; why can't you ever do anything now?'

She staggers over to my bed.

The stench of meat on her breath makes me gag. 'Go away!' I say, pushing her shoe away from me.

She kicks my knee hard.

'Ow!' I squeal, rubbing my knee. 'What was that for?'

She squints. Her mouth is screwed up tight. She kicks me again. 'You vile child,' she hisses.

This time it really hurts because the point of her shoe hits my knee bone.

'Ow! Stop kicking me!' I shuffle on my knees towards my TV. The freezer hums in the hall. I rub my hands up and down my arms. 'What are you looking at me like that for, you weirdo?' I say.

She stands and looks down at me. I push her leg away. She loses her balance and topples onto the desk. The photo frames crash down. The chair falls over.

Mum regains her balance. 'You vile creature!' She slaps me around the back of my head.

My scalp tingles. I turn away and hold my face in my hands, listening to her huff and puff behind me.

'You really are a monstrosity of a person. Do-do-do yo-yo-you know that?'

I don't say anything back. My head is pounding.

'You've caused me no-no-nothing but-but misery since the day you were born,' she says.

I look up at her repulsive face. 'I hate you,' I say. 'You are so ugly to me. I'd like to watch you be killed.'

'Ho-ho-how dare… how *dare* you sp-sp-sp-speak to me like that?' She staggers again. 'Bend over!' she roars. Her face shudders.

I don't move.

'Bend over I said!'

I am backed into a corner. If I try to get away, she'll kick me again, so I crawl into the middle of my room and lower my head to the ground. Giving in is the easiest thing to do.

'I said bend over properly, you rotten child!'

I burrow my head into my arms and stick my bottom in the air.

She kneels down and holds my neck down with her hand. I can't breathe or move my head. She slaps me hard on my buttocks. I clench my cheeks, but it doesn't hurt too much because my cords are thick.

Then she lifts up my jumper and wallops me on my naked flesh 'Don't you *dare* speak to me like that ever again!' She spanks me over and over in the same place.

My skin burns where she has hit me. I've got that rushing between my legs. The carpet is itchy on my ear. 'I'm choking, Mum!' I cry.

She lets go of my neck. I feel as if I have water in my ears.

'Have you finished?' I ask.

She stands and looks at me with eyes of hatred.

'Well, have you?' I ask, sitting up. 'Do you want to hurt me anymore, you evil woman?'

Clout!

I go blank. I don't feel anything at first. My eyes whiz round. I hear the fluttering of pages. Then a book falls, on its spine, into my lap. It is my poetry book, which she just threw at me.

My cheek is scratched. I try to stand, but my legs give out and I fall to the floor.

My face is all flushed, but my hands are freezing cold. That piercing alarm sound over the road is jarring. Its rotating, amber light flickers on my walls.

She stumbles out.

I try to stand again and make it to my bed. My temples are thumping from where the book hit me. My knees hurt the most from her shoe. It's a shooting pain down my leg, which is hard to describe. There is already a big, black bruise on my knee.

I've got to tell someone about this. I reach for my piggy bank and peel off the plastic stopper. I pull out the tissue paper with Dad's number on it.

01306 811 902

What would happen if I called him and told him what she just did? He may love me again, but he'll kill me for finding out his number. I rip the tissue into shreds. There is no point. He doesn't love me anymore. No one does. Ben has gone. Tim is away, and I have no phone number for him in Malta.

I could go and sleep in the armchairs over at the Holiday Inn like I did last Thursday night. I told them I was locked out and the night porter brought me hot chocolate and told me stupid jokes. They didn't charge me.

Then I remember about Cody and Janet at drama club. They both live in a foster home and go horse riding every summer on the beach in Cornwall. They have a great life and sometimes go to Lapland at Christmas. That is better than my life.

I don't know how to get into a foster home.

I don't think I'd get in anyway, because my mum is posh, so people think she is a good mother. I lay my head on my soft pillows and pull the duvet over my head. I pick my nails and try to come up with a plan.

Dr Donavan. What would he say?

He'd tell me to think happy thoughts. He says people's negativity should never destroy you. So, I make a plan in my head of all the happy things I can do this week:

1. I've got craft, design and technology on Tuesday with Mr McDonough.
2. I'm going to Maisie's house after school on Wednesday. (But that's not all positive because she only likes me when I am happy. I'll have to pretend.)
3. I could go now over to Meg's. It's Friday, and her mum has band practice, so we can do dance contests with Pema and Mei, and have a midnight feast.
4. I will ask Cody next Saturday at improv class how to get into his foster home.
5. One day, I am going to make something brilliant of my life and prove to that evil cow that I am not useless.

I relax my bottom. My buttocks are still clenched. That feels a bit better. It's hard to move. I ache all over.

I think again about that 'neatly' fucked thing.

I still can't see it.

*

Dad phoned me after eight months. I am going to stay with him and Yvonne for the weekend. I get the train on my own now.

It is windy when I come out of Reigate station. They drive up in their new Toyota. Yvonne has sunglasses on even though it is overcast. She is in a red-and-white polka-dot blouse with a navy jacket over it. She runs her fingers through her hair.

Dad pulls over and gets out of the car. I run into his arms and rest my head on his stomach.

'Come on, little one, in you get,' he says, stroking my hair. 'We're going for lunch at a lovely pub in Escher.' He pulls back the front seat for me.

I climb in.

Yvonne doesn't look at me. 'Scruffy as usual,' she mutters under her breath and puts on her lipstick.

We pull out of the station towards town. I start to feel sick. I don't know how to fill the silence in the car. They don't talk to me, so I play I spy with myself as we drive past the green fields. I find three things beginning with C – a crow, a cart and a can of Lilt.

I spent all those months wanting to come. Now I'm here, I'd rather be back at home.

The Star is an olde worlde pub, with low ceilings and wooden beams. There are brass mugs hanging above the bar. It smells of cider, and the barman is joking with two women when we walk in. We sit at a table by the window.

'Right,' Yvonne says, putting her handbag down, 'I'll go and order some lunch. Colin, what are you having?'

'I'll have the Ploughman's, please, darling,' he says, 'And a whisky.'

'And you, Skippy?' Yvonne asks.

'Skippy?'

'I asked you what you are having for lunch, Lucia.'

'Scampi and chips please,' I say.

Yvonne goes to the bar. I nestle up close to Dad. This is my chance to find out why he doesn't phone me anymore.

'Dad?' I say. My heart is racing.

'Yes,' he replies.

'Are we still going to Brittany, on holiday, just you and me?'

'Yes, darling,' he says. He is looking at the hanging flower baskets outside, and he is tapping his knee.

'Definitely, Dad?'

'I said yes!' he scowls.

I run my finger along the drinks mat.

'We'll go, I promise,' he says, holding my hand.

'You don't phone me much anymore, Dad.'

Yvonne walks over with the drinks and puts them on the table. I go back to my seat, sip my Coke and try to figure out what Dad is thinking. I shouldn't have said the last thing.

'How did you get those scratches, Lucia?' Yvonne asks, swigging her lager. 'You look like something the cat brought home.'

Dad looks at me.

I look down. 'Oh, it's nothing,' I say.

Dad grabs my face. He presses his fingers into my cheeks and narrows his eyes. 'How did you get those scratches on your cheek, darling?' he asks.

'I just had a fight with a girl at school,' I lie.

'No guesses who won then,' Yvonne mocks.

Dad's face is serious. 'Are you having problems at school?' he asks.

'No,' I reply, rearranging my knife and fork. 'It was just a silly row with someone in my class.'

Our food arrives. The scampi stink of batter. The chips are the fat, crinkly ones that we don't have at home. Yvonne puts a Cliff Richard song on the jukebox. There is lots of chatter in the pub now, so it doesn't matter that we don't speak much.

Dad doesn't look up once all through lunch.

I eat my last chip.

Yvonne nudges me. 'Come on, Lucia. Let's have a go on the fruit machine and leave your dad to daydream.'

I hope he's OK.

At the fruit machine, Yvonne hands me 50p. 'Put it in there,' she says, pointing to the coin slot.

The red squares flash at me. A silly piano tune plays, like at a fairground. I press the red buttons one after the other. I don't know what I'm doing. The bananas and cherries are flashing.

'Go on, Lucia!' Yvonne cajoles.

I press the middle button over and over. I like the bleeping noise. The music is on loud in the background. Everyone is laughing. I forget where I am. The machine starts going crazy. A trilling trumpet sound blasts out, grating in my ear. The cherries, grapes and apples flash like mad.

Clunk.

Clunk.

Clunk.

Oh my God! Loads of fifty pence pieces shoot down into the coin box. They don't stop.

'She's only gone and won jackpot, Colin!' Yvonne cheers.

Dad doesn't register what she says. He is looking down, rubbing his knee. I scoop up the coins. It's like Christmas come early.

'Err, excuse me, young lady,' Yvonne says. She pushes me. 'I think you'll find that's my money. It was my 50p.'

I carry on picking up the coins from the floor because the coin tray is overflowing. I've never had money like this before. I can give some to Mum.

I stand with the heap of change in my hand.

Ow!

I glance down. A crescent-shaped nail mark dents my arm. I drop the change and run to the ladies loo. I lock the cubicle door and sit on the seat. The lady next door is doing a wee. I can see her feet. I can't hold in these tears. I push my arm hard against my eyes, so she can't hear me cry. When she flushes the loo, I blow my nose and blub into my sleeve.

The graffiti on the back of the door says:

Katy is a slag.

I bet the girl who wrote that had shaggy, permed hair and wore nasty trackies.

It is swollen where Yvonne pinched me. I press some toilet paper against it to stop it bleeding, and wait for the lady to walk out. I go and wash my face with cold water. My eyes won't stop watering.

Positive thoughts…

Think positive thoughts…

1. I will stay in the lovely big bed at Dad's house tonight.
2. Tomorrow, we will have Frosties with creamy milk for breakfast.
3. I may be able to stay until late tomorrow (Sunday).

I can't think.

I hate my life.

Think positive! Remember what Dr Donavan says.

4. Monday is Maisie's birthday. I am going to her house for dinner.

That cold water feels refreshing on my face. I splash it over again and pull back my cheeks with my hands to stop the tears coming.

5. One day this won't happen anymore.

CHAPTER NINETEEN

LONDON, 1989

LUCIA IS SIXTEEN YEARS OLD

Lucia picks up her black eyeliner.

She removes the lid. It pops.

The pencil point is sharp.

Lucia draws thick, black lines across her face in diagonal patterns.

She looks at herself in the mirror. She resembles Spiderman, with her face covered in a web of black lines. Lucia is haunted; her vacant glare is staring back at her.

She is a stranger to herself.

Beads of sweat rise to the surface of the black paint. Her scalp itches; her nose burns. Frightened by herself, she knows she will scare her mother, whom she hears in the kitchen. Lucia lurches forwards and stares closely at herself. *What is making me do these things?*

Lucia hides her eyeliner under her pillow and walks out of her room, with her mouth open and her stare catatonic. Her mother marches out of the kitchen holding a bowl of pickled onions.

Lucia halts.

Her mother drops the bowl and gasps. 'Good God, Lucia, what has happened to you?'

'What do you mean?' Lucia asks.

'Look at your face, Lucia! It's covered in-in-in bla-bla-black lines.' Her mother's tone becomes uncharacteristically quiet. She walks towards her daughter and lifts Lucia's chin with her hand. 'Look at you,' she says, 'just look at you!'

Together they turn and look in the mirror on the wall.

There she is again, hidden under a mask of thick, black lines. At least her Mum is paying attention to her. The contact between them feels closer than normal, but that impenetrable wall exists. This would be the time to tell her mum the truth, but she does don't know how.

'What's happening to you, Lucia?'

'I don't know, Mum. I don't know what's happening to me.'

'You look possessed!'

'I think I am.'

It is true. Lucia does feel possessed. She does not understand what is making her do these things now. She does not consciously decide to do them before she acts.

'I'm going to call Ben. Leave them on. He must see.'

Lucia huddles on the hall floor and picks her nail whilst her mother phones Ben. She wants to wipe the paint off. It itches, but her mask must stay on for now.

*

Ben now lives in a flat in Kentish Town, with his friend Matt. He has been there since he left university a year ago. He is running his own theatre company from home.

Ben walks into the flat wearing washed out 501s and a Lacoste t-shirt. Lucia feels flushes of cold sweat run up and down her back as she looks up at his flaring nostrils. She feels remote and unable to connect with him in any way.

'When did this happen?' he asks.

'Ha-ha-ha-half an h-h-hour ago,' her mum replies.

Ben squats and cups Lucia's face with his hand. She pulls away, sobbing.

'It's OK. We are going to get you help,' he says, running his fingers through her matted hair.

'You must get her to that healing clinic, Mum,' Ben orders.

'I don't know Ben,' her mother replies, 'it all sounds so wishy washy.'

'Mum!' Ben shouts. 'There is no room for your negativity. Lucia needs help. We must get her it fast.'

'OK,' her mum nods, 'I'll take her tomorrow.'

*

It is a big, maroon door. Above, in a gold plate, black writing reads '**_LONDON SCHOOL OF PSYCHIC STUDIES_**'. A uniformed security guard stands outside, with his hands behind his back. He moves aside to let Lucia and her mother walk into the building.

'Is this the healing clinic?' her mum asks.

'Straight through the double doors,' he replies, pointing ahead.

Lucia walks ahead through the foyer, past the drinks machine. Her mother shuffles behind gripping her Tate Gallery bag. Lucia pouts her annoyance, by forming her lips into a frozen beak, and paces ahead. She can feel her mum's resignation to all this.

In the main hall, rows of classroom-like tables are spaced apart like dominoes. Introverted-looking people sit behind them, in orange-plastic chairs, talking to members of the public. The sounds of clanking heels and whispering, tickles Lucia's ear drums.

It is cold and smells of nag champa incense in here, which is the stuff Tula's mum used to burn. Lucia and her mother stand by the door. A petite woman walks towards them and extends her hand. She is wearing a brown pencil skirt and a frilly blouse.

'Hello, you must be Lucia,' she says in a welcoming tone. 'I'm Brenda.'

Lucia notices her spindly fingers as she shakes Brenda's hand and wonders to herself if this woman will suss out her game. She looks into her eyes. The thin lines at the corners look like whiskers. Her neat bob haircut and plain attire give her the look of a spinster.

'Do follow me,' Brenda says.

Lucia looks at her mother.

'I'll wait in the hall for you,' her mum says to Lucia, who follows Brenda through a labyrinth of tables to a separate part of the hall marked off by a silk screen with green dragons and a Tibetan tonglen printed on it. She hopes her mum will be OK.

'Please, sit,' Brenda says, pointing to the chair.

Lucia perches on the edge. Her shoulders tense.

Soft music plays the sounds of waves hitting the shoreline with a flute melody over it. She turns her feet inwards and looks at the table in front with coloured rocks and crystals on it. A lump of rose quartz catches her eye.

'Now, just relax, dear child,' Brenda whispers and places her hands on Lucia's shoulders. Her fingers feel cold on Lucia's neck.

'Just focus on your breath,' Brenda says, 'It is safe here.'

Is it?

'I am not going to hurt you.'

Lucia closes her eyes; her shoulders drop. She feels heat quickly rise to the surface of her skin and she unleashes her clenched fingers. Thoughts race in her mind: Will she go to prison if this woman finds her out? Why didn't Zema call her back last night?

'Think of a time, Lucia, when you felt calm,' Brenda says softly.

Calm?

She calls on memories of happy holidays in Umbria with Tilda and her family, roaming hilly streets before the sun got too hot, visiting churches and then diving into that icy-cold pool. That was calm, as was settling down to dinner to the sound of chirping cicadas, allowing the laughter of Matilda's family to carry her.

Brenda's hands feel like putty as they mould into Lucia's shoulders. She feels Brenda's breath fanning her neck. It makes her shiver.

'That's it. Wherever you are, stay there.'

A single tear rolls down her sweaty cheek. She tries to stay there under that stripy canopy, eating pizza. That balmy summer's night never darkened, but the closer memory of the black lines on her face comes racing to the forefront of her mind. Why did she do it?

Brenda holds Lucia's pulsing head, and then brushes her fingertips up and down Lucia's spine. Her body tingles.

'You have a lot of anxious energy, Lucia. Try to calm your thoughts.'

But she can't. She is haunted by what she did last night, covering her face in those lines. Brenda's hands land diagonally across Lucia's lungs.

'This is where negative emotions are often stored,' Brenda whispers. 'And I am going to release them for you.'

Brenda pinches Lucia's back with a nip and then takes her hands away, rustling her fingers. She repeats this several times. Goosebumps appear on Lucia's arms. Her eyes close and her thoughts quieten. Now only the sound of rippling water and Peruvian horn pipes fill her mind. She does not want Brenda to take her hands away.

'All is well, Lucia,' Brenda says, 'Now I want you to visualise a big, bright light shining out from the centre of *your* world.'

Lucia thinks of an oblong fluorescent light radiating out from the middle of her tummy, an image that comes to her from seeing Christ on the cross on the stained glass at St Mary's Church.

'Hold it there,' Brenda says, 'It is yours. Own it.'

She likes the thought of that light being hers. Very little is hers. She hears footsteps pass by. Her headache lifts. A brick that has been stuck there vanishes. Her head now feels light, like bubbles popping, one by one, inside her brain. Brenda runs her fingers across Lucia's neck and then removes her hands.

Lucia's muscles quiver.

Brenda walks to Lucia's side and hands her a cup of water. 'Please drink this to rehydrate,' she says and rubs her arm. 'You did very well, Lucia. Take your time getting up.'

Light-headed, Lucia sips the water and stands. She follows Brenda to the table over there. Brenda holds out a basket of coloured stones. 'Take the one that stands out to you,' she says. Lucia picks up the lump of rose quartz and asks if she can take it.

'Yes, do. It will help to heal the unaligned chakras in you.'

Lucia does not understand what chakras are, but puts it in her pocket, pleased with what she has taken.

'Now,' says Brenda holding out a splayed pack of cards, 'These will help you. Pick one out.'

Lucia picks out the one in the middle and turns it around. It has a picture of a rainbow in primary colours on along with a smiling matchstick girl. It says in bold print:

HOPE

Hope, she thinks, *what does that mean?* The picture makes her chest expand, and she pictures herself in years to come walking in green fields, away from her mum, feeling free.

'Refer to it,' Brenda says, 'When you feel alone or vulnerable.'

'Thank you,' Lucia says, and follows Brenda back out through the hall where others are being healed by different practitioners. Feeling airy inside, Lucia's body constricts when she sees her mum in the foyer reading the *Daily Mail*. That vacuum between them is still there, and she freezes inside, knowing she has to hold herself back again.

'Everything OK?' her mum asks, tight lipped.

'Yeah, it was actually,' Lucia replies.

Headlines in the paper show protests in Tiananmen Square. Her mum folds the paper and puts it in her bag with the pile of McDonald's napkins she pinched on the way over here.

'What happened?' her mum asks.

'She just did a healing on me,' Lucia shrugs, holding on to her lump of rose quartz. She can't say more. Her mum won't understand.

'Do you feel better?'

'A bit,' Lucia replies, but instantly feels that heavy glaze resettle in her head again.

Nothing has really changed. It will take more than hornpipes and crystals to make this go away.

'Come on, let's get back before rush hour,' her mum says and stands.

The kind man opens the door for them both. They leave; this time Lucia trails behind.

*

The tube carriage sways. The light flickers off. It comes on again. They sit side by side. Lucia grips the arm rest and pulls out Brenda's blessing card.

'**HOPE**' she reads, and flicks the card with her thumbnail.

Her cheeks prickle, and a river of tears streams down her face unexpectedly. She twists her torso away from her mother and runs her hand down her cheek.

Lucia catches her long face in the black glass. She flicks her gaze up at the Rastafarian man opposite. His dreadlocks hang out of a Trilby hat and his gold tooth glistens. He looks into her eyes and smiles. A gush of tears spring from her eyes again, making her sniffle.

'You OK?' her mum asks, looking at her daughter in the black glass.

'Yeah, fine,' Lucia replies.

At Swiss Cottage, the train slows. The Rastafarian salutes Lucia. It's as if he is saying good luck. She nods back at him and waits behind her mother for the train to stop.

Walking up the rickety escalator, Lucia reads the adverts on the wall, *'Me and My Girl'*, *'Cats'* and *'Miss Saigon'*. She's seen them all before, but focusing on the colours helps her fight back this surge of sorrow that she does not want her mum to see.

She trips as she steps off the escalator too late. A Nigerian station assistant holds out his arm for her as she regains her balance. She steps aside before the ticket barrier. Her mum stops behind. The air is smoky, and Lucia hears the rumbling of trains approaching the tunnel below, followed by screeching brakes.

'What is it?' her mum asks.

Lucia turns and looks at her mother, whom she can see is trying to comfort her, and wipes her snotty nose.

'I don't know, Mum,' she says blubbing, 'I don't know.'

'Come on tell me, what's wrong?' her mum asks, touching Lucia's hand.

Lucia flinches and pulls her hand back. 'Nothing!' she shouts. 'Go away!'

Her mother rubs Lucia's shoulder. Her attempt at intimacy repulses Lucia. She bursts out into a guttural sob.

'Here,' her mum dangles a used tissue. 'Has something happened?'

'No,' Lucia bawls. She can't hide these tears now. 'I just don't know what's happening to me, Mum!'

'Well, nor do I, but we'll get through; we always do.'

'I'm sorry, Mum,' she snivels, and wipes away the line of snot that dangles from her nose like a yo-yo.

'Sorry for what?'

'For everything,' Lucia sobs, 'That your life is so hard and that I make it harder.'

Her mum holds her hand. The brittle coarseness of her mum's skin repels Lucia, so she shrugs it off.

'No, you don't!' her mum screeches. 'Where has all this come from?'

'I just feel so bad that you have no one.'

'Don't be silly. I have the boys. I have you.'

'But you have no money.'

'Listen,' her mum says looking into her eyes, 'We are fine. We eat, don't we? We have good holidays. We never go short of anything, do we?'

The station assistants laugh. The plump one throws a coin in the air and lets it fall. 'Heads, you win!' he shouts.

She wants to tell her mum the truth about what she is doing, but that wall between them won't allow for any more intimacy.

'Mum, do you hate me?'

'Don't be silly.' Her mum winces. 'Course I don't.'

'Why do you never tell me you love me?'

'Be-be-because th-th-those things don't need saying!'

Rush hour crowds stream past. Lucia watches a giggling toddler, on his dad's shoulders, pass by.

'Come on, let's get home in time for *Brookside*, eh?' her mother says.

They shuffle through the ticket barrier together in a familiar zone of distance but comfort.

CHAPTER TWENTY

LONDON 1987

LUCIA IS FOURTEEN YEARS OLD

Looking out on the morning rain
I used to feel so uninspired.

I extend my arm out in front and roll my head around in a full circle to the sound of the piano. Aretha Franklin's soulful voice opens me up inside and allows me to forget my troubles. We sway from side to side as the drum beat kicks in. We are standing in two rows, all wearing our pink catsuits, rehearsing for our annual festival at the Salle Pleyel in Paris, next month.

The violin begins to play.

And when I knew I had to face another day
Lord, it made me feel so tired.

My head collapses onto my chest in sync with Trisha and Penelope's movements.

Before the day I met you

We take three steps forwards and spin on the spot as the violin notes quicken.

Life was so unkind

We each sweep one of our feet to the side and our upper bodies drop, so we are hunched, with our heads hanging down.

But you're the key to my piece of mind,
'Cause you make me feel...

We rise, bringing our arms up like the sun coming up at daybreak. My hair slips away from my face. I feel beautiful for just one second.

You make me feel...

My leg kicks. I plié and grand jeté. I leap through the air like a gazelle. My arms become wings.

You make me feel
Like a natural woman.

We spring across the floor, with our arms extended out and our heads leaning right back so our chests are wide open.

I land with a thud. Sophie's foot lands in unison with mine – nice feet. We pose with our hips thrust to one side. I have permission to be sexy. It feels nice.

'Beautiful, Lucia,' Fran, our teacher, says, smiling from where she stands at the side of the church hall. 'That's it, keep your regard nice and open.' She places her cold hands around my chin and lifts my head slightly.

I didn't know just what was wrong with me,

We flow across the space with elongated arms, our heads following as if being guided on leads.

I walk, rolling my head and rotating my hips. The dust is gritty beneath my foot.

Till your kiss helped me name it

I stand still and arch my body to the side, like I am sunbathing whilst standing. I stay there for a few seconds, enjoying the stretch. We repeat the chorus again. This time, we are staggered, with two groups moving across the floor, one a few beats behind the other. I lose myself in the movement. I feel free and wild. This is the only time in the week when I feel joy like this.

Oh, baby, what you've done to me
You make me feel so good inside

I bend my knee forwards and lean backwards. My back is stretched; my neck is long.

I pause there and breathe.

'Beautiful, girls,' Fran says, again, this time walking around us, looking at our postures.

And I just want to be, close to you
You make me feel so alive

I love this bit. I lean my body sideways into Casie's. She lifts me from my hips, so my legs leave the ground. I am in a C shape in the air. Everyone else is partnered up. We repeat the chorus, doing grand jeté after grand jeté across the floor. I feel part of this group, like I belong.

You make me feel

The music begins to quieten.

You make me feel

The music stops.

We sit in a circle on the dusty floor. Fran gives us notes and tells us how much we have improved since she first taught us the choreography, six months ago. She is happy for us all to dance in Paris.

*

I walk back from dance class, with Francesca, along Abbey Road. It's rush hour. I feel so alive, and I am able to see the world better. It's like I have better vision. Everything seems brighter and closer. I can look at people as they pass me by, and I notice the sounds around me more. I feel less afraid. I try to walk like Francesca, upright and confident. Even though she is spotty, I would like to have her life – A grades all year round. I know that her mum is dead, poor thing, but she still has a happy life. She goes home to a cosy house and a dad who encourages her with her homework. I go home to the ogre who doesn't want me and who is always spoiling for a fight.

The pelican crossing nears on Adelaide Road. I feel that horrid jitter in my chest come back. I wish I could keep walking with Francesca and never go home again, but I say goodbye at the corner of Winchester Road.

My time out is over.

*

It's pizza and chips for dinner.

The Krypton Factor is on. Five men struggle through netting, splashing through mud. Mum sits in her armchair. She squints at me through her squared specs, with her dinner on her lap.

'You h-h-haven't go-go-go-got a clue about responsibility, have you?' she stammers.

I drop my knife and fork, and look at the bare branches outside. I haven't got the energy for this tonight. I wonder when the cherry blossoms will start to appear.

Her face is screwed up. I can see her chomping on her thoughts. A hurricane is brewing inside.

'You don't do you, not a clue?'

I leave a quarter of my pizza and walk to the door.

She gets up and blocks the door with her arms splayed against it. 'You d-d-don't know what it's like to really suffer do you?' Her fingers are gnarled; her forehead is crinkled.

I try to think of tomorrow. 'No, not like you,' I reply. If I go along with her, she will tame quicker. I know the drill.

'D-d-d-do do you know what I was doing at your age?'

I slump onto the sofa and hug the flowery cushion.

'I was bringing home coal on my back and running a home. I-I-I…' she taps her chest. 'I was running a home single-handed. Y-y-y-you-you-you couldn't run a pantry let alone a home could you, you useless creature?'

I stare at the tawny-brown lining between her teeth. 'No, Mum, I couldn't; you're right. No one has suffered like you.'

'I mean w-w-what planet do you live on, child?' Her mouth is arid. 'Most pe-pe-people your age have serious responsibilities.'

At 14?

I get up, thrust past her and turn the door handle.

Mum slams it shut and pushes me onto the sofa. She grabs and wrenches my hair.

I squeal.

She muffles my cry by pushing my face into the sofa. 'When will you learn? You will never make anything of your life if you don't learn,' she grimaces.

Learn what?

I try to rise. She pushes me down as if I were a ball in water. I turn and look up at her withered skin. A feeling of emptiness washes over me; there is nothing to live for tomorrow and no fight left.

She yanks my hair again and punches my head.

My top teeth hit my bottom lip. My lip bleeds.

Keeping my glance fixed straight ahead, I rise, still under her grip. I elbow her in the face and feel an immediate release.

I hear her glasses fall onto the telephone. I glance up at her.

She is leant over the armchair, catching her breath. Before she has a chance to pounce on me again, I grab her hair and yank it hard. Her hair smells like a burning hairdryer. I want to spit on her. 'You see you don't like it, do you?' I shout, clenching my teeth. 'The day you die,' I say with burning cheeks, 'is the day I will be free.'

She is stooped and looks at me 'You really are an evil person,' she says. 'Having you was the biggest mistake.'

I push her. She falls against the bookcase. The Penguin books slide down the back. The wooden xylophone that she bought on her honeymoon with Dad in Tanzania falls to the floor. I step over it and open the door. I put on my anorak and turn the door latch.

'Where are you going?' she calls. Her cry is like a young child calling its mum.

Her need always pulls on my heartstrings even after a fight.

'I don't know,' I reply, 'but I do know that if you keep this up for much longer, you will lose me forever.'

I run down the stairs without closing the door. The evening air is fresh. I don't know where I am going. I just walk towards Wadham Gardens. I don't normally go there in the dark. It is a quiet, rich street, where rapists could lurk in the bushes.

I don't care. I just walk, and collect the conkers on my way.

*

I love this place. I'm sure I've been here before.

It's the mini village in Saxon times. Yes, I've come back in time. The roads are so precise. The shops and houses look like cardboard-cut-out ones, the kind you see in a glass display box at the Science Museum. I have this ability to bounce everywhere. I love it. It gives me so much freedom. The sky is bright blue. The air is so lovely and fresh.

I bounce down these tiny, narrow streets.

I have no responsibility, and there's nowhere I have to be. I am happy and free.

The women are wearing frilly bonnets and matching smocks; the men are wearing breeches and shirts. They are all smiling too. Everyone, absolutely everyone, is smiling.

These streets are magical. You can take any turning and you end up in a different world, but they are linked. It's like walking through a labyrinth.

I'm on a new street now, where all the houses are green brick. I can hear people chiselling and hammering. People are waving at me.

My heart thunders. I am caked in sweat.

It's dark. I see my woodchip wall. My feet are freezing cold.

That great village was a dream. I loved it so much. I need to get back there.

I hear Mum groaning.

My eyes are crusty; my throat is dry. I curl up into a ball and bring the duvet over my head. This new episode has been bad. The waves of her attacks can go on for hours.

I look at my radio alarm clock. It says 3.47am.

Her groans get louder. Each groan undulates into the next one. She sounds like a woman in labour; there are five or six moans, and then a violent wail. I press my hands against my ears to block out her sounds. I feel so helpless. There is nothing anyone can do to help her when she has one of her headaches. She has been having five attacks a night lately. Dr Jeffries has put her on lithium and steroids, but they are not working. They just make her overweight.

Cluster headaches are difficult to cure. Dr Jeffries thinks they will stop after her mother (Grandma Daphna) dies, because he thinks that her relationship with her mother is causing the headaches. It could be ages before her mum dies!

She paces up and down the hall, howling. She bangs her head on the hall wall to stop the pain. My walls tremble. The sound is hollow because our walls are so thin.

I get up and open my door. 'Mum?'

'Ahhhhhh! Please, Lucia, don't speak to me!'

She is curled up against the wall, holding a flannel to her temple. 'Here, Lucia.' She dangles her flannel at me. 'Get me a cold one, quick.' She gags as she speaks.

I snatch her boiling-hot flannel, take it to the bathroom and run it under the cold tap, and hand it back to her, dripping wet.

She gasps as she holds the flannel to her temple. Her face is scarlet; her eye is swollen. There is a bump on her head from all the pounding. 'Please make this pain stop, Lucia!'

My mouth fills with saliva. My tummy churns. 'It will go soon,' I whisper. 'I promise, Mum.'

'No, this flannel is no good! It's gone hot already.' She dashes to the bathroom, kneels on the carpet and sticks her head under the cold running water.

That doesn't work. Her hair soaking wet, Mum thrashes past me into the boys' old bedroom, where she now sleeps. She heads straight for her oxygen, which they delivered last week. She sits in the wicker chair and stretches her mask around her head, inhaling deep lugs of air.

The oxygen cylinder hisses as it vaporises. The sound of her heavy breathing and grunting is easier to hear than her wailing. Confident that Mum is settling, I go back to my room.

The red candle on my mantelpiece catches my eye. It's the one I have never used, and is in the carved-gourd bowl from Tanzania. Mum bought it on her honeymoon with Dad. It sits there as décor. I light it for the first time, and find a fragment of peace as I watch the flame waver. I stretch my forehead to release the tension and, for the first time ever, I think about God. I don't know if I believe in him, but maybe he can help. For some reason, I think about Mr Robson, in his rainbow boots and leggings. He teaches me religious education. Fuck knows why he comes to mind, but

I remember him saying that if you pray, the Lord will hear you.

As the wax accumulates close to the wick, I reach for a piece of paper and lean it on my *Beano* album. Mum's whining is now less urgent.

I drip the hot wax onto my paper and, with my finger, smudge it into the shape of a cross. I hear a car chug past so daylight must be coming soon. I become engrossed with what I am doing and pour more wax onto my paper. Running my finger tip through it, I mould the wet wax into letters. I write a message to God underneath my cross:

DEAR GOD,
I CAN'T CARRY THIS PAIN ON MY OWN ANYMORE. PLEASE FIND ME A FRIEND TO HELP ME WITH THIS.
LOVE, LUCIA

It goes quiet. Too quiet.

I run into the boys' bedroom. Mum has fallen asleep. She is lying in bed, with her head cocked sideways, and she is propped up by dozens of cushions. Her mouth hangs open and the flannel rests over her head. Circles of sweat are visible on her nightdress, and her damp hair is pressed against her face. The shell lamp behind her shines brightly onto her face. I turn the light away.

She looks so fragile.

I run to the kitchen to make her a cup of tea in case she wakes up. I leave the teabag in. She always likes a cup of strong tea after an attack. I put it on her table by her bed and sit on the chair next to her. The sound of her snoring is a relief. She has fought so hard to achieve this slumber. Saliva dribbles from the side of her mouth. I wipe it away with a tissue and take the flannel away from her face.

I must stay with her. She could die because of a shortage of oxygen to her brain. I need to be nicer to her. I mean, these headaches she gets, I could be the cause of them. She tells me I make her life a misery. Maybe she is right.

I hold her hand whilst she sleeps and watch the sky light up through the slit in the curtain. Only last week, I told her I wanted her to die. Now she could. There would be no one there for me if she died. I must be a better daughter.

I kiss her forehead. My tummy lurches. 'Sleep well,' I say.

It's 5.05am. She has to get up for work in two hours. She always goes to work after an attack to make sure she gets enough money to feed *me*. See, it *is* my fault!

I can't face double maths with Mrs Bronson today.

I'll bunk off again. I'll get the bus to Oxford Street, and go to that cafe in Carnaby Street. I've been doing this a lot recently, missing classes, but no one has said anything yet.

CHAPTER TWENTY-ONE

London, 1989

Lucia is sixteen years old

Lucia's mother is in the sitting room, polishing her beloved brass. LBC radio blasts out. Ben is on his way round.

Alone in her room, Lucia holds her lump of rose quartz from Brenda close to her chest and tries to draw on Brenda's help, but it is too far away. It is like trying to reach a hanging branch through a slit in the fence.

A sinking sensation belts her between her lungs as she thinks of her father, living in Alicante with Yvonne. No word from him for ten months, and no birthday or Christmas card this year. He could be dead for all she knows.

It's all Yvonne's fault, the bitch – I wish she was dead.

She walks like a ghost to the bathroom and locks the door.

It is quiet in here save for the dripping tap and burping immersion heater. Her eyes stall at her mum's antique jewels on the chipped bathroom shelf. She opens her mother's paisley tin and picks out her grandmother's garnet ring. One garnet is missing, and the gold underneath is black with dirt. She can just see her Grandma Daphna's venomous face, shaking her walking stick and shouting hateful words at Lucia and her cousin Katie. They did throw banana skins back at her, but she deserved it. Most people love their grandmother. Lucia hated hers.

She is bored. Lucia picks up the can of BIC shaving cream without knowing why she has. Even though her brothers have long since left home, it still resides at the end of the shelf next to the cotton-wool holder. She shakes it and squirts a lump onto her thumb – it's creamy and nice.

The white blob falls to the floor. It reeks of tart lime.

She stares at it and dips her big toe in. It is frothy. What could she do with it now?

Lucia kneels down and squirts another blob onto the carpet, but this time dips her finger into the cold cream. The outside world falls out of focus.

Without conscious thought, Lucia writes big bold letters on the carpet with the shaving cream as if she were icing a big cream cake.

She writes:

To You,
Kill or I will.

Fuck!

Lucia flinches. She stands, looks up at the ceiling and then glances back down at what she has just written. She rubs her arms as if she is standing in a blizzard.

I didn't write that. Those words didn't come from me.

Lucia reads the menacing message again: 'Kill or I will.'

Kill who?

She does not understand. She doesn't want to kill anyone, not that she knows of.

Lucia is caught by surprise by what she has done, by who she is becoming, yet this adrenalin rush is so addictive. Lucia feels a hunger inside to write more, to see what words come out this time.

Lucia unlocks the door and returns to her room, passing her mother, who is muttering, still engrossed in polishing her brass teapot.

She closes her bedroom door and realises she is still holding the shaving cream. She drops it and grips hold of the radiator, yanking it hard like a prisoner trapped by chains.

She wants to understand more about those words.

Lucia paces up and down her room. It is grey outside. Taplow and Dorney Towers look even more depressing than usual.

She sits on her bed and wraps her patchwork quilt around her shoulders. Lucia wonders if there is something at work here; after all, where did the helicopter noise come from and why did those psychics say they picked up on something? Where did those words come from? They were not planned.

Lucia stands.

She looks up at the corners of each wall and speaks with intention, as if she were talking to a person.

'Who are you?' she asks, 'Talk to me; who are you and what are you doing?'

She waits for an answer, but hears nothing.

'Please tell me who you are,' her tone is quiet. 'Where do you come from?'

Lucia feels a chill wash over her. The hairs at the back of her neck stand.

She walks over to the door and picks up the can of shaving cream that is lying on the carpet. She shakes it. If anyone saw her now they would lock her up. She knows that, but she is being pulled by this invisible force inside her.

Crouching down, Lucia presses the nozzle and writes another message in big letters on her carpet. This time, she writes:

Hello,

My name is

GINGER

Oh my God!

Lucia walks back towards the door gawping at the words she has written.

She looks around the room, waiting for someone to appear. She imagines a spindly rag-doll figure with gollywog eyes, coming through the walls and floating down towards her.

That's how she imagines Ginger. Her cheeks burn as she stands.

There is something going on; she knew it. This isn't normal. Something is happening to her. She peels her polo neck away from her sweaty neck.

Lucia picks up the shaving cream and lobs it at the wall in a shot of rage.

The nozzle dents the woodchip wallpaper and sawdust spurts out from the hole it has made. The can of shaving cream crashes onto the mantelpiece.

Flashing yellow circles appear in her vision and her posters of Morten Harket flash at her. She bends down and cups her face in her hands.

'Lucia! What on earth was that noise?' her mum yaps.

She stands, and shakes her arms and legs as if swamped by flies. 'What noise?'

'I heard a bang!' her mum calls.

Lucia picks up the can and buries it under her duvet cover. 'I didn't hear a noise,' she replies, walking into the sitting room.

Her mum pokes her head up like an ostrich. 'I definitely heard a bang, Lucia,' her mum says, and she stands up.

Her mum's brass teapot falls to the floor. Her mother's fingers are black from the Brasso polish and reek of vinegar. Her mum whips open the sitting-room door, looks from left to right as if crossing a busy road, and then turns left towards the bathroom. 'I definitely heard something,' she paces into Lucia's bedroom. 'For goodness' sake Lucia, look!' Her mum stands aside. 'Look!'

Lucia notices her mother's hands are trembling, and leans into the bathroom doorway. The message looks more haunting than it did ten minutes ago. The shaving cream has melted, and the words are more ingrained into the carpet.

'Writing,' her mother pants. 'It's a message.'

Lucia watches her mum pat the wording and run her finger under her nose, leaving a blob of cream on her nostrils.

'In shaving cream!' her mum yells, repeating, 'Shaving cream, shaving cream,' over and over, like a broken record.

'Yes, Mum! You've said that; it's shaving cream,' Lucia replies.

'W-w-w-ell, how did th-th-th-that get there?'

'I don't know,' Lucia says, looking away.

Footsteps thump up the stairwell.

The key slowly turns in the front door. Lucia looks up.

'Hi,' Ben says as if expecting a surprise. He peers around the door.

'Look, Ben!' Lucia's mother shrieks, 'Come here!'

Ben brushes past Lucia and pushes her mum aside. Keith Sweat blares from his headphones. He looks down at the floor. His breathing is audible.

'This is a nasty message,' he says in a gruff tone, 'Angry. Are there any more?'

'N-N-Not that I kn-kn-know of, no,' her mum stammers.

Ben puts his hands into his pockets and flashes his teeth. 'What are we going to do?' His eyes stretch open so wide that his face expands. 'This is the most insane story we are immersed in. Who will believe this?'

Lucia walks to her room. 'Mum!' she calls. 'Look!' Lucia points to the message on her carpet and walks into her bedroom.

Her mother strides down the hallway.

Ben follows. They stand in a semicircle looking down at the carpet.

A silence pervades her room.

'Hello, my name is Ginger,' Ben reads. 'Ginger.' He resumes a sober face. 'That's a spooky name.'

'Ginger? That could be a man. I-I-I-I definitely th-th-th-think someone, a male, is hiding in the flat, Ben,' her mum insists. She stamps her foot on the floor. 'There must be.'

'Mum,' he says. 'We've been through this. Something is going on. We need to accept that.'

'B-B-B-But, I c-ca-ca-can't. This is stuff you read about in horror books, not something that happens in real lives.'

'I know,' Ben agrees, looking out of the window. He then comes to suddenly. 'Look, why don't you both go out and see a film or something, and I'll clean this up. It will do the pair of you good to get out.'

'No, Ben. I don't want to.' Her mum recoils. 'I need to be here on watch.'

'Go on, I think *Dead Poets Society* has opened at Screen on the Hill. Go, and I'll clean away the messages,' he says, grinning into his sleeve, and follows her mother out of the room.

Lucia shuts her bedroom door. She takes her anorak off the coat hook and puts it on.

She wants to talk to Ginger, find out who he is and what he has to say to her. This is exciting! Lucia takes the shaving cream from her under her duvet cover and shakes it.

She kneels down.

'What are you doing here?' Lucia whispers to the floor. 'Why are you here?'

Like a burglar on borrowed time, she writes this in capital letters on her bed:

DO NOT FEAR, FOR I AM HERE

*

The table is laid with shiny silverware and burgundy plates. The plaited bread sits under a white cloth next to the Menorah. Three candle flames dance the tango. Ernst stares into the flames with a sombre frown; his long nose points like an arrow. He wears his velvet kippah for the evening prayer, which Lucia notices has a beautiful golden spiral design on its trim.

'Baruch ata Adonai Eloheinu melech ha'olam, boreh pri hagefen. Amen.'

Ernst cuts the challah bread after saying the blessing and hands them each a piece. Her mother declines. It's her way of rejecting Judaism, and claiming her independence from her stifling sister and brother-in-law.

Ernst passes round the golden cup of sweet wine.

Lucia swallows it with a grimace. Her mother speeds through the prayer and swigs the wine. The feast begins with minced egg and onion with matzah.

Lucia spoons it into her mouth as if she has never been fed. She adores Dora's Shabbat special, but its taste is spoilt by the pungent smell of wet fur. Dora and Ernst's sheepdog, Desmond, is the true chieftain of their Highgate home. His odour, tainted with the scent of full grain leather from their pouf in the sitting room, permeates the air in every room.

Dora slices the chicken, and dishes out the roast potatoes and peas. She is in her stripy Benetton dress, with gold chains hanging around her neck.

'Here, Val, have some more; you've only got enough to feed a pigeon. Here, have some breast meat,' Dora says.

'No, thank you. I'm fine, honestly,' her mum replies.

'How are the boys, Val?' asks Ernst.

'They're well...' her mum replies, tapping her fork on her plate. 'Be-Be-Ben's production of *The Marriage of Figaro* starts on tour next month, opening in Cardiff. It's had rave reviews.'

'Really...' Dora replies, 'Isn't he a clever boy, eh?'

'Wonderful the previews are,' her mum eulogises.

'Yes, Val, you've said. Lucia, do you want any more spuds, my darling?'

'No thanks,' Lucia replies.

'Oh, go on, finish the potatoes, baby queen...'

'She's had enough. That's enough now,' her mother scorns.

'She may still be hungry,' Dora intervenes. 'She can have more if she likes.'

Lucia's mum nods disapprovingly. She never lets up about Lucia's food habits; she either eats too little or too much. Lucia holds out her plate as Dora spoons more potatoes onto it.

'And how is Tim?' Ernst asks.

'He-he- he's coming ba-ba-ba-back from Malta on Tuesday.'

'Because of all this nonsense?' he leers, raising one eyebrow.

'He wants to be-be-be here with us at this time,' her mum insists. 'Yes, he's coming home!'

'And his teaching job?' asks Ernst.

'He-he-he's being tr-tr-tr-transferred to a post in Chelsea,' her mum replies.

Auntie Dora rolls her eyes and runs her hand through her hair. 'So, what's happening now with it all, Val?' she asks, grinning at Ernst.

Lucia kicks the chair leg.

'Well,' her mum coughs, 'Th-th-things have been mo-mo-moving around: kitchen things mainly, and shoes.'

Ernst sneers at Dora.

'Now messages are appearing in shaving cream on the carpet, Val adds'

Dora's face creases and she rolls her eyes again. 'What a load of *narishkeit*,' she says, 'I've never heard so much rot in all my days, have you, Ernst?'

'It's not rot!' her mum flaps. 'It's real. This is happening in our lives!'

Lucia watches the flame waver.

'Well, so much for the healing schmealing!' Dora mocks.

Lucia wishes this would stop. She hates watching them bullying her mother.

'I-I-I've g-g-got on to the chair for psychic research at Birmingham University, actually, a man called Richard Menzies; very well-known he is in the field,' her mum says.

'And what's he going to do?' Ernst asks, running his finger around his spoon.

'Help, I hope!' her mum belts out.

'I see.' Dora beams.

Lucia doesn't know how to protect her mum from the bullying. She can't stand by and watch, so she gets up and walks to the toilet. The kitsch wallpaper gives her a headache. She locks the door and sits with her head in her hands, listening to the clattering of plates and raised voices. She hears Ernst's hand slap the table followed by her mum's desperate plea as he continues to interrogate her.

'How Val? How on earth do shoes move?'

'W-w-w-well…'

'How?'

Lucia presses her hands against her ears. *What are you doing you stupid girl?* She thinks.

'Explain it, Val. Rationally, explain it!'

Look what you're doing to her!

CHAPTER
TWENTY-TWO

LONDON, 1988

LUCIA IS FIFTEEN YEARS OLD

From His Honour Judge Colin Goldman:

4 November 1988

Dear Lucia,

Just a very quick note to say Saturday, at Green Park Tube station, 12.30pm

Love,

Dad xxx

It has been a year since I have seen him.

I need to look my best, so I go for my new Gap outfit: a ccrise crossover top with matching trousers. I add my blue pumps from Du-Du's.

Green Park station is bustling as usual. A busker plays 'Imagine' on his guitar, whilst tourists race by, laden with Hamley's carrier bags. The bright-orange tiles with images of Sherlock Holmes on always cheer me up.

I step on the rickety escalator. It chugs monotonously. I wonder if Dad will be there. The smell of burning soot is potent. The *Me and My Girl* poster draws me in: a blue man and his daughter tap dance under a ruby-red umbrella. It was only two years ago that I saw that with Dad; Cornettos and cosiness in the front row of the stalls. A woman walks past me in high heels and wide shoulder pads. Her pink fingernails are striking against her black skin, as is her scent of Poison.

I step off the escalator. There he is! He raises his top hat and smiles.

I inhale a gust of sooty wind and put my ticket into the barrier. It beeps. I walk through with a tight kink in my stomach.

'Hello, my darling one,' Dad says, and embraces me with a kiss on the cheek.

He is carrying an Army and Navy bag with something heavy inside. I am not sure what to say or how to behave. I pull away from his embrace and tuck my hair behind my ears. 'Nice to see you again, Dad,' I say politely.

It is not the usual posh restaurant. We are at Overton's restaurant in Victoria. The green carpet is tatty, the wallpaper is peeling and the menu is bog-standard English grub.

We sit at a table by the window overlooking Victoria Station. It is draughty.

I order fish and chips with mushy peas. He orders a steak sandwich with onion rings and a pint of Guinness. There is an awkward silence between us. Dad's brow is puckered. He runs his tongue along his teeth and grumbles under his breath.

I am terrified to say the wrong thing. 'How are the cats?' I ask.

'Very well, thank you,' he replies. 'Zoe is getting on in years now.'

His Guinness arrives. He takes a large gulp and licks the white head off his lips. 'Darling, I have called you here today because there is something I need to tell you.'

My heart beat pounds through the side of my neck. 'What, Dad?'

'You know, darling, that I am retiring in two months, don't you?'

'I had an idea, yes.'

He undoes the button on his cuff and winds up his shirt sleeve. 'I have been feeling very tired lately,' he says. 'I have been getting ringing in my ears, so the court has advised that I take retirement early.'

'That will be good for you, Dad.' I know more is coming.

Our food arrives, but I am not hungry. The chips look greasy. I look out of the window. *Cats* is still on at the Apollo. There must be a Saturday matinee as people are queuing up to get in.

He bites into his sandwich. The ciabatta smells freshly baked. 'That's not all, darling,' he says, wiping his mouth. *I knew it.* 'Yvonne and I have decided to go and live in Spain.'

'Spain?' I choke on a piece of batter.

'Yes, my darling. We have found a lovely place in a small town near Alicante. It will be a much slower pace of life for me. My doctor has encouraged me to make this move.'

I feel my face grow pale as pans bang in the kitchen behind the bar. It stinks of stale ale here. A waitress takes the orders from the two men sitting behind us.

'So, when are you going?' I ask.

'Very soon,' he replies. 'Our belongings are being shipped over there in three weeks. We will be following by air after that.'

I come over all dizzy. The wallpaper looks wavy. I hold my head in my hands.

'There is nothing to worry about,' he says, tapping my arm. 'You will enjoy coming to visit us.'

I glance up. 'Will I be allowed your phone number this time?'

'No,' he says, nodding. 'I am afraid not. Nor will you be allowed my address.'

I gulp. I am unable to swallow. I try again, but my tonsils swell. This feels like the end: his way of saying goodbye. 'No address at all?' I ask, tears brimming in my eyes.

'I will give you a "care of" address to which letters can be sent.'

'A "care of" address?'

'Yes, you can write to me care of our housing management agency. They will pass the letters on to me.' He hands me a business card with 'Martin Maguire' written on it in bold.

A wave of bravery rolls over me. 'Why?' I ask.

I wait.

He rubs his hands together, and stares right into my pupils. 'You know, darling, you know very well,' his voice deepens. Spit brims at the sides of his lips. 'I don't like you asking me questions. It is what my wife wants. We want peace.'

I sit back and say no more. I knew it was all to do with bitch face.

'Now, darling,' he says, in calmer tone, 'I want to give you these.' He places the Army and Navy carrier bag on the table, and pulls out the photo albums of my childhood.

I stare at them. I can't believe he is giving these back to me. 'Why don't you want these photos, Dad?' I ask. 'You took them.'

'Because they are for you, darling,' his face flushes purple. 'They are of you and your life.'

They smell stale, as if they have just come out of a sealed box opened after many years. I find it hard to breathe. I try to climb over the next breath with a deep inhale, but I feel winded, like I have just jumped into freezing-cold water.

This is the ultimate rejection: only a 'care of' address, no phone number and a return of my past. My cheeks prickle. I struggle to find any words.

I flick through the red album and spot the photos of Mum dancing in the sea on their honeymoon in Tanzania. I'd forgotten those ones of me running along the beach in St Brelade's Bay, but I remember these, pose upon pose of me lying naked on a bed in that mansion owned by Miles Crayson. I recall all of those moments spent agonising over the right light.

I shut the album. 'Thanks,' I shrug.

'You are welcome,' Dad replies, and pats my hand.

He leaves two fresh banknotes on the black tray and stands, signalling that we are leaving. He puts my jacket around my shoulders. I take the Army and Navy bag and follow him down the stairs.

We walk towards Grosvenor Gardens. He has his arm around me.

'Why don't you come back to the hotel for coffee?' he suggests.

I can't. My skin feels as if ants are crawling all over it. If I go back for a cosy coffee, I will prolong the agony of our final farewell. If I walk away now, I can face the pain. 'I need to get back, Dad,' I reply. 'Thanks anyway.'

'I'll walk you to the bus stop, darling, but I need to go to the cash machine first. I want to give you some money to buy yourself something nice.'

We stop at Barclays Bank next to The Shakespeare Arms. He slides his card in where the green light flashes. The machine beeps.

He punches his forehead.

'What is it, Dad?'

He strikes the air with his fist and paces up and down.

'Dad?'

He looks at me with hollow cheeks. His face is ashen. 'I have forgotten my pin number.' Dad kicks the wall and thumps the screen. 'I can't remember it!' he thunders.

'Maybe it's your birth date?' I suggest.

He looks at me with a dropped jaw. 'What, love?'

'I often use my date of birth as a pin number,' I say.

He scratches his head. It is clear he can't remember his birth date.

I count the years back on my fingers. 'It's 10th May 1925!' I shout.

He presses the four digits on the keyboard. The machine churns out crisp new notes. 'Ah!' He cocks his head back and grunts. 'Well done, darling.'

He hands me a folded wad of notes. I put them straight in my pocket; I peer through a broken plank in the fence and stare at the workmen digging deep, clay ditches. The piercing sound of the pneumatic drill hurts my ears.

'Come on,' he says, and drags me away.

We walk towards the number eighty-two bus stop.

'My memory; I'm losing my memory,' he confides, looking at his shoe.

'It is probably just a phase, Dad.' I say.

'No, Lucia. It's not.' He shakes his head. 'Last week, I left some milk heating on the stove and burnt the pan. I completely forgot I had put it there.'

I stare at his bushy eyebrows and those widely spaced eyes. I have never understood my father. His thoughts and feelings have always been impenetrable. I have always had to second guess him. Right now, I understand something about him. I just saw how terrified he was at the prospect of losing his mind.

His mind is his identity. Who would he be without his intelligence? Some people with mental weakness have an endearing vulnerability. I see it in the deaf-and-dumb kids outside John Barnes School. They have a compelling innocence, but he doesn't have that. If his mind goes, who will he be?

The number eighty-two bus turns around from the terminus.

'Are you sure you will not come back for coffee, darling?'

'No, Dad, I must get back.'

He turns to me and runs his fingers through my hair. 'I forgot to tell you, darling, how beautiful you look.'

I look down at the cracked pavement and turn my foot on its side. 'Thank you,' I reply. I am glad he noticed the effort I'd made.

He lifts my chin up and runs his finger along my bottom lip. It tickles. It feels nice. I know it shouldn't. A gush of cold wind cools my flushing cheeks. His face moves towards mine at a diagonal angle.

I am about to pull away, but his salty lips touch mine. I feel his tongue in my mouth.

I recoil.

'Dad!' I gasp, and wipe my lips with my sleeve.

For fuck's sake, he just kissed me! I forgot for a second he was my Dad. I could have kissed him some more. 'I need to get that bus, Dad.'

He kisses my forehead, steak smelling kisses. 'Be the best you can be,' he says with watery eyes. 'Be happy.'

I step onto the bus and flash my pass at the driver, whose eyes stare dully at me. I sit next to a lady doing a crossword and wave at Dad. I can still taste him on my lips.

The bus pulls away. He smiles and waves back, hat in hand.

I clench my fist and press it against my forehead. As we turn down Wilton Street, my eyes fill with tears. I watch people hurrying on the street and feel as if I am watching a film of ordinary lives, which I am not part of. Jewelled ladies walk up the steps of The Dorchester Hotel. They are part of this film too.

'I don't need a dad!' I tell myself. I remember Sharon Johnson from primary school. Her dad dropped dead in his cab, aged fifty-four, from a heart attack. She was fine and still came to school looking beautiful in her knickerbockers.

As I try to convince myself that I don't need a dad, something within me cracks. A feeling of desolation catches in my throat, so I cannot swallow down any saliva. I realise I am completely alone in this world. I watch the clouds waft across the stormy, blue sky; they look like fish fins.

That kiss was forbidden. No one will ever know.

I get off the bus outside Comet on Finchley Road. The autumn trees are turning gold. I walk home carrying the photo albums.

Mum is standing at the top of the stairs waiting for me, as usual. 'What happened?' she asks, with gerbil-like eyes.

'He's fucked me off!' I reply.

'What do you mean, Lucia?' She follows me into my room.

I throw the albums onto my bed and scrunch my hair. 'He's moving to Spain with Yvonne.'

'For good?' Mum asks.

'As far as I know,' I reply. 'That's the impression he gave me. I am not allowed his address this time.'

'No address at all?'

'Just a "care of" address, for some dick head, who owns his house.'

'What a strange man he is,' Mum murmurs and stretches her mouth with her hand. 'What are you going to do?'

'What the fuck can I do?' I reply. 'He doesn't want me in his life anymore, Mum. I don't give a toss about him and his cunt of a wife anyway.' My head throbs behind my eyebrows. I feel sick. 'Please, Mum,' I say. Will you leave me alone? I need some space.'

Mum leaves.

I sit on my bed and open the album of Mum at forty before she had me. She looks so beautiful leaning against the tree trunk with sultry eyes in her Kente shirt. In this one, she is wearing a cream suit with brown shoes, and her hair is beautifully styled. She is standing next to Dad, who is in his robes. They are outside Middlesex Guildhall. That must have been the day he was appointed as a judge. Years of being a single mum with no money have taken their toll on her.

I flick through shots of her with me as a baby. I look adorable, with rosy cheeks and bulging, blue eyes, holding my furry rabbit. And there is Mum, looking at me with doting eyes as I do my jigsaw puzzle next to her. When did her hatred for me set in?

I open the red leather album of my life after they had divorced. There is uncertainty in my eyes now. My poses become more forced. Look at those shots of me naked by the pool in Jersey, skipping rope in hand. I am aware of the camera. I am doing what he wants.

I can remember him taking these ones of me lying in the bath. My feet rest on the bath rim and I am pouting with my finger on my lips. It is the expression of a grown woman in a young girl's body – creepy. My coy expression is put on; my eyes are not smiling. They are slits – lonely slits. I am surly and uncomfortable with where I am.

Here are the ones of Dad, Yvonne and me in Hunstanton. There I am, sitting next to her in that red pedalo, holding a big, orange lolly with *Kiss me Quick* written on it. I am laughing with a suntanned face.

I spit on them. 'I hate you!' I shout.

It is a self-adhesive album, with plastic film over the photographs, so my saliva just dribbles down the page. I stamp my foot on the album and grind my heel into the page, but it is made from a fibre-based board so my heel makes no indent.

'Fucking bitch!' I scream, and hurl the album at the wall. It's over. She has got him all to herself now.

Mum scurries in. 'What on earth are you doing, Lucia?'

'It's these albums, Mum,' I snivel. 'Dad doesn't want them. He's given them back to me.'

'How aw-aw-aw-awful of him,' she stammers.

I clip my bum bag around my waist, and throw in my lip balm and fags.

'Where are you going, L-L-Lucia?'

'I need to get out, Mum. I'm going to Tilda's for the night.'

'Will you be back first thing tomorrow?' she asks.

'Yeah, I will.'

'Here.' She hands me a crumpled tenner.

'No, Mum, it's fine. Dad gave me £100.'

'No, here,' she says, 'take it anyway, for your fare. Keep his money for emergencies.'

I hate taking her money. I can see she's got no more notes in her purse. 'Are you sure?'

'Here! Take it!' she insists.

I stuff it in my pocket, 'Thanks Mum. See you tomorrow morning,' I say, and walk out.

*

It's midnight. We park along the canal-side at Hackney Marsh. The air is fresh, and muffled beats break free from the warehouse in front. Green and red strobes flicker through the glass roof. It smells illegal. I think of Mum asleep, alone, as we queue behind hooded ragamuffins and girls in Wallabies.

'Open your hand, Luce,' Natalia says.

I do so, and she drops an ecstasy pill into my palm, whilst sliding her hand into my pocket.

'It's just half a green burger,' she says, handing me the Evian.

I swallow it and gag. It tastes sour as it sticks to the back of my tongue.

The massive warehouse is cold. It smells of poppers. Sweating men, in cycling shorts and glowing bracelets, dance on blocks. I wait for the pill to kick in. We stand huddled together. No one talks. We just side step and window wash with our hands to the beat.

Tilda hands me a spliff. I take a long drag and bounce to the trebly tones. I worry about Mum again, and then a wave of energy rushes up my arms. It comes again, up the back of my neck.

I feel weightless. To the baseline beats and shooting strobe lights, I close my eyes and jog on the spot.

A man next to me in a hat blows his whistle and nuts the air with his head. He smiles. Horns blast as I make shapes with my body. I punch my hands to the piano harmonies. My body rushes.

There is no sense of time. My face starts to burn; my clothes are dripping wet. Queasy, I slow down next to Tilda, who pushes the air with her hands, stepping back and forth.

'Where are the others?' I ask.

'Outside,' she says.

I don't care. Reality has gone. My visions of Mum are eclipsed; my guilt about her life are shrouded. I remember Dad is leaving. I still feel the cut, but it is distant, a thing of yesterday.

I'm rushing, safe here amongst this colourful tribe of strangers.

'We are not part-timers, we are only hardcore,' they chant, sucking ice pops.

*

It's a relief to see morning light. Dawn is hazy, and sweaty people mill about, hoods up, still lost in the beat. I sit on the wall and stare into the litter-coated canal. I smell like an elephant. Tilda sits next to me and rolls a joint. It's 6.10am. My hands glow and my mouth tastes metallic.

I'll ask Sensei to drop me at Camden and I'll walk home. If I go back to Tilda's, Mum will start calling at 8.00am to find out when I am coming home.

'Good night, Lucia?' Tilda asks, licking a Rizla.

'Yeah,' I reply, bowing my head.

She hands me the spliff. I draw on it hard to bring back my buzz.

'Who was that bloke?' she asks.

'What bloke?'

'The one I saw giving you a massage?'

I just remember holding his hand and feeling his sweat drip down my neck.

'You dirty raver,' Tilda laughs, 'E marriage, eh?'

I think his name was Aiden from Walthamstow.

The gravel crunches under my trainers as we walk to the car. I put on my cardigan, as it's chilly.

A woman in dungarees runs up to me and taps me on the shoulder. 'Hiya,' she says as if she's known me years.

I'm embarrassed. I don't recognise her.

'Good buzz, eh?' she beams, handing me two flyers. One says *'SUPERSTITION'*, and the other says *'Biology – Clapham Common next Friday'*, 'Maybe see you there,' she says and walks off.

My jaw is grinding. 'Yeah, maybe,' I shout, 'Cheers!'

CHAPTER TWENTY-THREE

LONDON, 1989

LUCIA IS SIXTEEN YEARS OLD

Lucia sneaks out of her room. Her mother is preparing supper in the kitchen. Tim is watching the cricket in the sitting room.

The sitting-room door is closed.

She stands in the hallway, with a black marker in her hand. She removes the lid as quietly as possible and in large bold letters, writes on the magnolia hall wall:

Welcome Home Tim,
Your feet smell.

I am Ginger. I am the anger given off by Colin Goldman.

He's fucked off to Spain.

WELCOME TO THE MAD HOUSE!

The sitting-room door opens.

Lucia flies back into her room. Her cheeks are blotched red, and there are beads of sweat under her nose. She stands behind her door, which is ajar, and watches through the crack.

Tim stands in the hall in his slippers. He bursts out into a high pitched guffaw.

He has just come home, having been teaching English language in Malta for the past four years. Lucia's mother asked him to return. He is focusing on completing his novel and has moved back into the flat. Lucia likes having him around because of his electric laugh and how he sees the funny side of everything. He and Lucia had bonded, whilst both she and her mum visited him in Silemma. They had spent many afternoons together in the games arcade playing Pylons. (That is a game where you dodge the electric pylons or you get blown up.)

'Mum!' Tim calls, giggling, 'There are four new messages in the hall!'

Her mother shoots out of the kitchen. 'Go-go-good God, what on earth is this now?'

They both go quiet and stare at the wall.

'Awful this is, awful,' her mother says with a tremor in her voice, 'I-I-I st-st-st-still think someone is here hiding within the walls.'

Lucia watches.

Tim runs his finger over his lips. 'They are strange messages,' he says pensively. 'This one here, about Colin, is poignant,' he points at the wall. 'As for my feet smelling…!' He lets out a crazed laugh with a screwed-up face. When his face goes all mangled like that, it makes Lucia think of a Hitchcock character.

'I think this, about my feet, is very witty actually,' he cackles.

Her mother convulses with laughter too, and then steadies herself as she looks up at the wall. 'I-I-I'm go-go-go-going to call that Richard Menzies at Birmingham University back. I can't go on like this, Tim.' Her mother dashes into the sitting room.

Tim stares at the hall wall with a sullen glare. Her mother pops her head out of the sitting-room door and hands him a fiver. 'Here, could you run to Bejam's and buy some mince? We've run out.'

'Sure,' he replies, 'no problem.' He nips to his bedroom to put on his shoes. Whilst Tim is in there, Lucia creeps out of her room on tiptoes, pen in hand, and writes on the wall:

Be jams doesn't sell mince, stupid.

*

Lucia's mother has again telephoned Richard Menzies, chair of psychology at Birmingham University. He has put her on to two well-known parapsychologists, whom he thinks will be able to help. They are about to arrive. Ben has come along to the meeting with Tim, Lucia and her mother.

It is a hot mid-summer's afternoon. Both windows are open in the sitting room. A harmonic orchestra of birds tweet outside. The tree outside is in full bloom, and the scent of freesias blows in from the garden below. Happy sounds radiate upwards from a family barbequing sausages and children splashing in the paddling pool.

Tim wears his chinos and black t-shirt, and sits in the bespoke chair. Ben sits on a dining chair, in a white shirt and long shorts, and looks tanned after his recent trip to Barbados with his father. He stinks of Brylcreem. Her mother is in the armchair.

Lucia sits on the divan with her head in her hands. She has just placed one of the marble eggs from the coffee table behind her foot, behind the Afghan cover. When it's safe, she will kick it out to the centre of the room, so it looks like it has rolled out on its own.

Both experts are in their late fifties and sit side by side on the sofa. Eugene Holtz is stocky, and wears a pinstripe suit and tie. He is balding, with a thick moustache that curls up at both ends. He wears brown spectacles, and is an assertive, well-spoken Cockney – a working-class Jew from Highgate, to be precise. He is not your typical ghostbuster.

John-Bradley Beaumont is a different beast: a tall, stooping figure, who is pale faced and timid in manner. He, too wears a suit, but one that looks as if it has been worn all week. He wears a grave expression and considers his words carefully.

'I'll explain a little of our background,' Eugene Holtz begins. 'I am president of the Society for Psychical Research. I have been investigating paranormal activity over fifteen years.' He coughs into his fist and gestures to John-Bradley. 'My colleague here is also an experienced parapsychologist and paranormal investigator. We investigated a famous case together in Stanmore, three years ago, and lived with the family during a very long episode of paranormal activity. Both of us have publications here and in the United States.' Eugene's velvety tone is soothing on the ear. Lucia listens as if he were telling a bedtime story.

'I am very sorry to hear of the distressing events here,' John-Bradley interjects, 'and I do hope we will be able to help you to at least come to terms with what is happening.'

'Come to terms with?' her mother blurts out in a shrill tone.

'I'm afraid we don't have a magic cure, but we do bring many years of experience with us.' He hitches up his trousers. 'Would you kindly update us on recent developments since we spoke last Monday?'

'Well,' Tim says, 'as you can see, messages are now appearing all over the walls.'

'Yes, I can see,' Eugene replies, 'some rather humorous, may I say,' he smirks.

'Well,' Tim announces in a formal manner. 'Things are now disappearing and reappearing in odd places. This seems to be the new phase, shall we say.'

'Like what?' Eugene asks.

'Things we need; for example, my credit card was not in my wallet before I went out, and when I came home it was in the bottom of the loo.'

'The loo?' Eugene laughs.

'Yes,' Tim replies, clearing his throat, 'and our keys keep going missing. I couldn't find mine as I was leaving here yesterday, and, when I got to the bottom of the stairs, they were lying on the pavement outside.'

'I see,' Eugene says, making notes on an A4 pad, 'anything else?'

'Yes,' Ben butts in. 'patterns, lots of patterns,' he disappears into his own thoughts. 'Strange things keep appearing in patterns.'

'Like what?' asks John-Bradley.

'There was a long line of Ladybird books all placed meticulously along the hall floor the other day,' Ben chortles. 'On the centre one was the jar of dried flowers from the hall table. That was one incident. The other,' he starts to laugh more vigorously, 'was a cucumber wearing a condom, on a plate. Underneath, in shaving cream, was a message that said *"You are a gay boy."*'

Tim bursts out into a shriek of laughter.

'I see,' Eugene says, grinning from ear to ear, 'This sounds like a very mischievous spirit.' Eugene sits back and crosses his legs. 'What you are experiencing here is a classic poltergeist phenomenon,' he announces like someone announcing the departure of a train.

'Poltergeist what?' her mother screeches.

'Everything you describe happening here is symptomatic of poltergeist activity, which is more common than you think. It often focuses around a distressed teenager, who is normally at the epicentre.'

Lucia places her foot over the marble egg and jiggles it. Should she?

Eugene's eye drops to her leg.

She feels a thud in her chest and pushes the egg back under the cover.

'I see,' her mother replies. She scratches her nose.

John-Bradley leans forwards. 'Often paranormal activity is connected to misplaced sexual energy.'

Misplaced what?

'May I ask if there been any sexual abuse in this family?'

'No, no, no!' her mother screeches in triplicate, 'absolutely not.'

Those early days in her father's bed flash back to Lucia. The kicking and the bruises the day after, but she can't get further than that kicking in her mind. Is it a memory that she has barred from her mind or a memory that is not there at all?

'Well, actually,' she says, looking up.

Eugene and John-Bradley flick their eyes up in unison. 'Yes, Lucia, go on,' John-Bradley says, encouraging her to speak more.

'I just remember …' Lucia looks at her mother.

'Don't be so ridiculous!' Her mother scorns. 'Your father never…'

'Oh, it was nothing,' Lucia shrugs. 'It was just a silly thought, sorry.'

Eugene scribbles down more notes on his pad and glances up with one eye. 'Has there been any other abuse?' he asks.

'Absolutely not!' Her mother thunders.

Tim interrupts with a calm demeanour. 'There have been some rather serious complications with Lucia's father though,' he says.

Lucia feels her cheeks become hot and her breath getting out of step with itself. She clasps and unclasps her hands.

'Will you elucidate?' Eugene asks.

'Well,' Tim jiggles his foot against the chair. 'There's been a gradual distancing over many years. He is absent now and lives abroad.'

'No contact at all?' Eugene asks.

'Barely,' her mother says.

'And this is your father too?' John-Bradley asks Tim.

'No,' Ben replies. 'Tim and I come from my mother's first marriage. We are in regular contact with our father. Lucia came from my mother's second marriage, which is a completely different story.'

There is a chilling silence in the room. Lucia looks up at the ceiling, where there is a rope of rainbow-coloured light from the sun's reflection, lying still. That purple is the lovely colour of lupins.

'The first thing to reassure you,' Eugene says, 'is that poltergeists are rarely harmful. They won't hurt you. They are mischievous spirits – disruptive, yes – but they do eventually burn out. You see, "poltergeist" was originally a German word. It means noisy spirit.'

'I see,' her mum says, rolling her eyes. '*Eventually* is a rather whimsical time frame.'

'I can't give you a time frame, I'm afraid,' Eugene replies. 'Paranormal activity is unpredictable.'

Lucia stares at Eugene's bulging Adam's apple. She can't help but wonder if this man is a bona fide ghostbuster or just a con man who needs a good cause.

'The very famous Stanmore case, which we were involved in,' Eugene says, beaming, 'lasted for over sixteen months.'

'Sixteen months?' her mother and Ben reply simultaneously.

'Yep,' Eugene replies in his Bermondsey-cum-Highgate accent. 'Stella was the sixteen-year-old at the epicentre of that. She had eight different male voices coming through her at points.'

Male voices? That gets Lucia thinking…

'Where was this?' her mum asks.

'It was the Stanmore poltergeist case. Both John-Bradley and I were witness to beds crashing about, spoons bending, and Stella was seen flying through the air and levitating on two occasions.'

Levitating?

'Furniture regularly hurtled around, and the male voices that came through Stella were incredible. We could not find or replicate them from anywhere. We even offered a £1,000 reward to see if anyone could copy them, but no one could.'

Tim taps his foot on the floor, whilst Ben looks at Lucia with stern eyes.

'So, what on earth are we supposed to do?' her mother asks in a matter of fact way.

'I want to ask you to please keep an accurate log of everything that happens,' Eugene says.

'Certainly,' Tim obliges. 'I'll do that.'

'Please call me day or night when activity intensifies, and I will come straight away,' Eugene says. 'I can talk to spirits and am often able to calm things down.' Eugene looks at all of them with alert eyes. 'Do try to get on with things as best you can. I know it is hard, but the less impact you allow it to have on you, the better.'

Her mother takes a deep breath. 'Good heavens on earth,' she sighs. 'Who would have thought it, eh, a North London poltergeist? This is what novels are made of.'

'Indeed,' John-Bradley agrees knowingly. 'These experiences can change lives. People often come through paranormal activity transformed, and often become closer as a family.'

Lucia's heartbeat quickens as images of a girl flying through the air race through her mind. What kind of things can she get up to now? All mischief is hers. Questions jostle around in her head at quite a pace. What she doesn't understand is whether there is really a poltergeist here making her do these things or if *she* is the poltergeist?

'So we will be in touch very soon, Mrs Goldman,' Eugene says, adjusting his tie.

'Yes, we will,' her mother replies.

Both men stand. Lucia keeps her head tucked down.

'I'll see you both out,' Ben says and leads the men to the door.

Tim waves to them. 'Thanks for your time; I'll keep that diary,' he says and reaches for an orange from the fruit bowl.

As Tim's back is turned, Lucia kicks the marble egg. It rolls out into the centre of the room.

'Tim, look!' Her mother jumps up, pointing at it. 'The egg, it just moved.'

Tim turns and stares at the egg. 'For fuck's sake,' he vituperates. 'Just fuck off and do one!'

Lucia walks to her room, leaving Tim and her mother in a darkened daydream. Ben returns from seeing the ghostbusters out and closes the sitting-room door.

Lucia creeps out of her bedroom, pen in hand. She removes the lid and on the hall wall, she writes:

EUGENE HOLTZ IS A FUCKING WANKER.

CHAPTER
TWENTY-FOUR
LONDON, 1989
LUCIA IS SIXTEEN YEARS OLD

Lucia sits curled up on her bedroom floor with her hands over her knees. She looks up at the white trail of cloud in the sky and feels pressure building inside her.

People think it's a real poltergeist now. She has to keep this up.

She can't think straight. Her entire mindset is now geared to thinking of the next thing she can do. She has not done any homework for weeks and lies to her maths teacher about why she has not done any assignments. She does not sleep, but gets up at 3.00am and leaves weird arrangements on the hall floor, and then often falls asleep on the bus home.

Her face is ashen. She has no appetite, and she just plays with her food at meal times. Her weight has dropped to six stone, and she is becoming more and more socially excluded as friends find out about what is happening. Neither Meg nor Maisie call her much these days.

There is an expectation on her to keep it up, and if she were to stop, they would know it was her. Lucia is convinced that if she gets caught, then she would be sent to prison.

Heat rises up her neck. She imagines what life will be like inside, stuck in a cell, listening to the sound of keys jangling and wardens spitting. She'll be beaten black and blue after the lights go out and she'll never see anyone again. They'll kill her.

But, no matter how afraid she feels, she cannot stop these impulses. Lucia wishes she had never started this stupid thing. Why wasn't she an anorexic or something less complicated? Why a poltergeist?

There is no way back now. Everything closes in on her. Desperate for a friend to tell her secret to, she sobs into her knee. 'Somebody please help me,' she whispers. 'I am sorry for all of this. I never meant for it to happen.'

A surge of energy rips through her body. She stands.

Lucia grabs her black marker from her desk and writes on her bedroom wall:

I am your friend, Lucia. I will look after you. I am your guardian angel, Love Ginger.

She does not know what a guardian angel is, but images of a floating fairy hover in her mind. As Lucia writes these words, she feels a release, all of this pent-up anger she feels about her absent father; her alienation from her depressed mother is given an outlet. She loves this freedom to write all over the walls, and, when she does it, her worries go away.

She writes more:

Don't be afraid of me. I have come to help you.

She drops the pen on the floor. Its nib smells of vinegar. *Who is writing these messages? Is it me or the poltergeist? Who is Ginger?* She picks at the Fruit Pastille stuck in her tooth. 'Who the fuck are you?' she asks, spinning around on her heels. She writes:

I am your spirit, the one who has not yet lived. I am here to help you. Trust in me. I will bring you happiness. Love from Ginger.

*

Tim is working on his novel at his desk in his bedroom. He has given up teaching English language now because writing is what he really wants to do. Her mother sits, as usual, in her armchair and watches the Wimbledon ladies semi-finals on TV.

The sitting-room door is ajar.

Lucia feels a new bolt of energy soar through her. She creeps on her tiptoes to the kitchen, picks up the remaining four eggs in the stand and skulks back to the hall.

She stands outside the sitting room and lobs one egg through the gap in the door.

It smashes against the tiled fireplace. Like an emotional orgasm, sparks of electricity race through her arms. The force she threw that with gave her anger a vent. She lobs the second one, then the third and darts to the bathroom like a frightened rat.

'Tim!' her mum shrieks.

Lucia pushes the bathroom door to.

'Yes, Mum?' Tim replies.

'Three eggs have just flown in at full force!'

Tim does not answer.

Lucia's heart thuds in her wrists. She slinks back out and lobs the other one.

Splash!

Crash!

Splat!

'Tim!'

'Oh, for fuck's sake, what is it, Mum? I'm trying to write!'

Lucia is back in the bathroom.

'Another egg has just come hurtling in. There's yolk everywhere, and Maeve's painting is...' Her mother's voice cracks. 'It's completely ruined.'

Lucia flushes the loo and walks out into the hall, where she meets Tim. She stares down at his blue boating shoes. His toes look square in them. Tim and Lucia walk into the sitting room together, where her mother stands clutching her bosom.

'Look,' her mother says, pointing to the mirror, 'Four of them flew in one after the other at rocket speed. No human could have thrown them like that.'

Yolk drips down the fireplace. Eggshell sticks to the mirror with a mucus-like gel smeared around it. Lucia looks at Maeve's painting. The glass is shattered in the left corner.

'Look,' her mother quavers, 'Maeve's painting is cracked.'

Lucia feels a punch right in the middle of her solar plexus. These paintings by Maeve are pieces of art that her mum treasures. Now, she has ruined it. Lucia stamps her foot, the way a horse stamps to get rid of flies, and then quickly realises she has revealed her annoyance with herself to them.

'We can get that reframed, Mum, don't worry,' Tim says, patting her mother on the shoulder. 'I must write this down for Eugene. What was the exact time this happened?' he asks, jotting down notes.

'The first th-th-th-three flew in at 3.05pm,' her mother stammers looking at her watch, 'and then the other one came hurtling in a few minutes later.'

'And where was Lucia?' Tim asks, stroking his pencil against his lip.

'I was on the loo,' Lucia replies.

'I think you should call Eugene, Mum, and get him round,' Tim says.

'Yes; yes, I will,' her mother mutters.

*

Crash!

Bang!

Wallop!

The hall walls jolt and shudder.

'Good God! What on earth was that?' her mother runs out into the hall.

Lucia edges out of her room. Tim runs out of the kitchen into the hall. The mirror table is lying on its side. The vase of dried flowers lies smashed to smithereens next to it. The desk chair from Lucia's room stands on its head by the bathroom door.

It only has three legs. The fourth one has snapped off.

'Ho-ho-how on ea-ea-earth did that chair get there?' her mum stutters.

Tim's eyes scan the chaos in the hallway. He rubs his lips together and gazes up at the ceiling as if there are answers up there. 'I don't know,' he says, 'I was thinking about my novel.'

'That chair,' her mother says, 'is from your room, Lucia!'

'I know,' Lucia replies, 'it just flew out of my room.'

'What, you just saw that *fly* out of your room?' Tim asks. His eyes widen. 'Are you certain?'

'Yeah, I saw it. It just flew,' she replies. Lucia avoids eye contact with either of them and twists her ringlets with her finger. 'I was reading a magazine on my bed. It all happened so quickly.'

'I better jot these events down in my notebook,' Tim says, walking into his room. As he turns, his eye catches the new graffiti on the freezer door:

GINGER RULES
YOU SILLY BUNCH
OF CUNTS

Tim pounds the freezer door with his fist. Its whirring stops. 'Who are you calling a cunt?'

Her mother is bent over in hysterics, whilst Lucia stands behind, giggling. She always finds Tim's explosions comical.

'I'll show you who the fucking cunt is!' Tim bellows. 'Go on then, Ginger! Show us your fisticuffs. Show us who you really are!' He walks into his room and slams the door. 'Do one, Polty! Fuck off and leave me alone.'

'I'm going to call Eugene,' her mother says.

Lucia waits outside the sitting-room door, whilst her mother speaks to Eugene Holtz. She bites her nail and listens to it crunch in her mouth.

*

Eugene Holtz has arrived, following her mother's call. There is an opaque cloud of cigarette smoke hovering in the sitting room. Tim sits, barefoot, in his aertex t-shirt and shorts. He is holding his collection of notes on the last week's activity. Lucia's mother sits in her armchair, sucking on a Berkeley fag as if it were a dummy.

Lucia walks into the room having just poured water on her trousers. Her heart is beating so fast, it is as if she has just sprinted a mile without stopping.

'So,' Eugene says, 'when we spoke a chair had flown across the hallway and eggs had been hurtling about. Activity appears to be intensifying...'

'Yes, most certainly,' Tim replies.

Eugene brings out his Dictaphone and presses the record button. 'May I?' he asks.

'Yes, of course,' Tim replies, 'recording this is fine.'

Eugene takes a deep breath and speaks clearly into his machine. 'It is Saturday afternoon. It is 4.00pm. I am at the Goldman's house. I have been called by Valerie after a week of constant activity. Lucia, her mother and eldest brother are present. The family do not appear to be coping well.' He places the recorder on the coffee table and rubs his hands together as if he has just won a lucrative deal involving lots of money. 'So, please update me.'

'Well,' Tim says. He coughs into his fist and straightens his back, as if he is just about to present a seminar to thousands of people. 'Furniture has been flying around the flat.'

'Would you just read me your notes?' Eugene asks. 'I need to get a sense of the frequency of the activity.'

'Certainly,' Tim replies obediently. 'This was just yesterday evening. At 7.45pm, a plant in the kitchen swayed with the window closed. First, it was an almost imperceptible moment, then two minutes later it swayed back and forth several inches. Lucia was in the kitchen with me. At 7.55pm, Lucia found a cushion from the chair by the phone table on the hall floor. At 7.58pm, there was a noise in the sitting room as if a champagne cork had hit the ceiling. It transpired to have been Mum's contact lenses from the bathroom. They were found at 8.02pm on top of bookshelves nearest sitting-room door. Lucia was not in the sitting room at the time.' Tim turns his notebook to a new page. 'At 8.04pm, there was an apport; the green lighter that was normally on the small table by the armchair was suddenly on the floor by the bed. Lucia was in the sitting room, alone. At 8.11pm...' he draws a breath as if tired, 'a rubber from the sitting-room dining table appeared on the hall floor. This was found by me alone; Lucia and Mum were in the kitchen. At 9.00pm, a twig flew into the sitting room through the window and landed on the dining-room table. This was *just* last night's activity.'

'I see,' Eugene says, pulling up his sock. 'And this has been the daily level of activity?'

'Yes, pretty much,' her mother replies. 'We didn't mention the new messages.'

'I saw those on entering,' Eugene says, grinning. 'May I ask if anybody has been physically hurt?'

'No, we have not been hurt by any moving objects,' Tim replies.

Eugene looks around the room. 'Right,' he says, standing. 'Let's see if we can have a word with Ginger and see what he has to say from himself.'

'You talk to poltergeists?' her mother asks.

'Oh yes,' Eugene replies. 'I'm well versed in talking to spirits.'

They follow Eugene out into the hall. Lucia's shoulders are hunched. Tim and her mum look like lost children.

'Hello Ginger; Eugene here,' he calls. 'I know about mischievous spirits like you. You seem very angry at the minute. Is there anything you would like to tell me?'

It goes quiet. They wait.

Lucia thinks about the male voices that came through Stella in the Stanmore case. Could she magic a male voice to come through her? She opens her mouth to speak, but doesn't dare.

'Come on, Ginger, it's me, Eugene. Can you tell me where you have come from?'

Eugene walks into her bedroom. They follow in a line.

'What is it you have come to say?' Eugene asks, spinning around. He turns to the three of them. 'He's obviously hibernating. They do choose their time, these poltergeists,' he says.

'Is that so?' her mum replies.

'What is it you are so angry about, Ginger?' he calls.

She's angry about everything. They wait for several minutes.

'No, I don't think we are going to get any dialogue today.'

They follow Eugene back into the sitting room and resume their seats. Eugene turns his tape over and leans forwards. 'And how are you, Lucia?'

Lucia looks up at his hairy moustache. She feels apart from the conversation, like an onlooker watching pedestrians crossing the road. 'I'm OK; a bit confused.'

'This is an unsettling time,' Eugene says in a paternal tone. 'Do you have any pastoral support?'

Lucia looks at her mother as if unable to answer the question on her own.

'No, she doesn't,' her mother replies for her.

Eugene runs his finger over his eyebrow and flicks his eyes up. 'I think it would be wise to send Lucia for some further healing, as this activity *is* focusing around her. Poltergeists cling on to disturbed energy in teenagers. If things calm down within the teenager, then the poltergeist will have less to feed off.'

'I think that is a good idea,' Tim says.

'I will contact someone I know who can help. They are based in Malvern. Is this OK?'

Her mother sighs and rolls her eyes.

Lucia buries her head in her hands. That angel card that Brenda gave her, which said '**HOPE**' on it, comes back to her. The thought of someone helping her out of this awful place gives her a glimmer of that hope. 'I would like that, thank you', she says to Eugene.

'How on earth do you recommend that we live our lives?' her mother asks, gesticulating with her hands.

'The more you carry on as normal, the less you will feed the activity,' Eugene replies.

'Not as easy as it sounds,' Tim says.

'This link I have *will* assist you,' Eugene affirms. 'I will phone you tomorrow with a contact, but *please*, rest assured this will pass.'

Eugene leaves.

Lucia waits for Tim to return to his room. An arctic chill comes down her spine.

Quick! She grabs the hundreds of two-pence pieces that she took from her brother's savings tin earlier and throws them down the hallway. It sounds like someone breaking in as they crash against the bathroom door.

'Good God!' her mother screams. 'Not another bloody thing!' She sprints out of the kitchen to find Lucia standing in the hall surrounded by a sea of coins.

Lucia looks down, with that echoing scream of her mother's still rippling through her. 'I just found them when I opened my door,' she says.

'Those coins are from in here, Tim says, emerging from his room.

'Di-di-did you s-s-see them fly out of your room?'

'No, I didn't, Mum. But, mind you, I was writing, with my back to the door.'

'Shall I call Eugene back?' her mum asks.

'No, leave it, I'll record it in the diary,' Tim replies, and returns to his room.

CHAPTER TWENTY-FIVE

LONDON, 1989

LUCIA IS SIXTEEN YEARS OLD

There is a pitter-patter noise as Lucia and her mum exit Malvern station.

The lawns are neatly cut, and the cottages are quaint. As Lucia waits for her mother to finish her fag, her eyes dance across the medley of dahlias and chrysanthemums planted in the gardens. The display of bumblebee, chartreuse and crimson petals lifts her mood.

Lucia's skin feels freezing, even though the air is mild. She holds a Coke can full of water in her pocket. She filled the can in the train toilet before they got off. She plans to pour it down her leg before they arrive, to leave no room for doubt that this is real.

A mini cab pulls up. Lucia and her mother get in.

Belinda Carlisle's 'Heaven Is a Place on Earth' is playing on the radio. Three glass bobbles in the shape of traffic lights hang from the cabby's mirror and stink of cheap cologne. Lucia and her mum sit at opposite ends of the back seat, gazing out of their windows. Her mouth tastes of rusty steel and her breath smells of antiseptic.

'Nice day for a visit,' the cabby says.

'Yes, indeed,' her mother replies, sucking her teeth.

The time is right. Lucia pours the cold water down her trouser, as they turn onto the High Street. The cold makes her wince. She looks down at the black sea monster stained on her leg. It looks weird, even to her. 'Mum! Look!' she points.

'Good God, Lucia! Look at your trouser. It's soaked!' her mother cries.

The cabby frowns at Lucia in his mirror.

'I saw that appear with my very own eyes,' her mum says.

Ha!

The water creeps along her leg. Now it looks like a wonky tiger paw.

'It's freezing,' Lucia moans.

Her mum touches Lucia's thigh.

'Leave it,' she barks and pushes her mother's arm away.

The taxi pulls up on a leafy street. 'That's £6.00, please, love.'

Her mother hands him a crumpled fiver and some loose change. They get out.

They see a sign:

Welcome to Maslow Cottages

It is like something out of a Roald Dahl book. They can barely see the house from where they stand. A cottage sits at the top of hundreds of cobbled steps, carved between two steep hills sprinkled with daises. Gnome statues are plonked in between the flowers, with messages on wooden placards stuck to them: *'Prevail in peace. Follow the way.'*

Lucia leads the walk up. Her mother drags behind, panting and struggling to keep up. She clenches her teeth at her brewing irritation with her mother. A blue Smurf catches Lucia's eye. He has a pipe in his mouth and a wicked smile. 'Creep,' she shouts and stops to gather her breath by the bird feed next to it. Her mum coughs up a ball of mucus and spits it into a used tissue.

Leila and Hans wait outside their rustic cottage to greet them. They look like they have been in marital bliss for years. Lucia cringes at their gooey smiles. She hates the patronising authority they emanate. They both wear brown, lace-up shoes and loose, amber clothing. Leila has a Celtic medallion around her neck. Both are skinny and look like they live off mung-bean soup.

'Hello, you must be Lucia. Welcome,' says Leila. Her voice is quiet yet confident.

'Hi,' Lucia replies, and looks down at the gravel.

'Hello,' her mother hails from behind.

'Come on in,' Hans says, beckoning them inside. 'If you wouldn't mind taking off your shoes,' he says, closing the door.

Leila takes their coats and asks Lucia to wait in the sitting room, whilst they have a chat with her mother. Hans leads

Lucia into the front room. It is airy, and a purple butterfly rests on the curtain.

'Please, just sit and be at peace,' Hans says. 'I will come and collect you shortly. Is there anything I can get you?' he asks.

'Err, I'll have a glass of water, please,' Lucia replies.

Hans returns with her water. Lucia hears the kitchen door close. She wonders if her mum will be OK in there. Val hates these kinds of people. 'Phonies' she calls them.

This sitting room is basic, with thick, beige carpet that soaks up your feet. There is no furniture, only a chair, and bookshelves filled with books on Zen, Taoism and 'being here now'.

Lucia sits on the wooden chair. It creaks. She lets it take her weight as she feels her neck muscles loosen. She hears the stream outside. Her eyelids feel heavy. She takes deliberate breaths in and out. Maybe she can let these people help her. She looks down at her wet leg. Who is she kidding anyway? How long can this go on for?

This room reminds her of Tula's house. Tula had been one of Lucia's friends from primary school. She and her mother, Padmaya, were Bhagwan Osho followers, who wore the colours of sunset and black beads around their necks. Not dissimilar to these guys.

They lived in a spacious ground-floor flat off Regent's Park Road with huge rooms, shiny parquet floors and plants hanging from every available space. Large patio doors opened out onto a south-facing garden, from which the sun would stream in. There was a blend of aromas of patchouli oil and Body Shop jojoba products. In the evening, the smell of spaghetti cooked in butter and garlic was potent, as was the earthy taste of Padmaya's tahini dressing.

Tula's mum would often walk around naked, humming out of tune or making love to her boyfriend, Dharm, on the floor cushions. Padmaya's screams of ecstasy were audible from the sitting room, and Dharm's head bobbing up and down between her thighs was visible to anyone passing.

Lucia would stay and go to sleep with Tula, up on her shelf. Yes, Tula slept on a shelf. It went along the entire width of the hall ceiling. You climbed up a spiral staircase into a cocooned world lit by lamps and plastered with shelves full of books. Tula's home was a free space for Lucia, where she would enjoy drinking honey water and painting murals on the walls.

Lucia comes back to the sound of the stream rippling outside. The calm in this room makes her flesh tingle. She remembers how that sense of space felt at Tula's, away from the harsh criticism of her mother. As she looks at the painting on the wall, a thought comes to her. *Maybe this is not my fault. Maybe I am OK.*

A film reel of the recent months plays in her mind. There she is throwing beds around, smashing wardrobes and hiding, always hiding. Why the fuck is she doing this? Who has she become?

Hans opens the door and walks in with another man, whom he introduces as Christopher. Christopher is more conservative looking than Hans, with a thick, black moustache, and dressed in a white shirt and navy trousers. He looks like a German banker.

'We're ready for you now,' Hans says softly.

Lucia stands. 'Where's my mum?'

'She's with Leila in the kitchen. She's fine.'

Lucia sweats as she follows the men up the stairs. They guide her into a small room at the top of the house with pale-green walls and a faint smell of rose water. There is a chenille sofa and nothing else except a picture on the wall of a lotus pond. The room is at the back of the house, far away from everything, even the birdsong outside.

'What happens now?' Lucia asks, biting the inside of her cheek.

'Please sit down,' Hans replies. 'We'll guide you as we go.'

Lucia sits on the sofa. Its scratchy texture makes her teeth go funny. Hans sits next to her. The smell of his pineapple shampoo and the fresh aroma in the room make a stark contrast to the stench of cigarette smoke on her clothes. Lucia notices it when she is in a different environment.

Hans puts his hand on her wet knee. 'Lucia, we are aware of what has been happening to you. It sounds very frightening. We are going to try to help you today.'

She jumps inside. 'What are you going to do?' she asks.

'My colleague and I are going to do a shamanic cleansing to release this negative energy ruling your life.'

That sounds like something out of *Carrie*. 'What's that?' she asks.

'It's a form if exorcism.'

'Exorcism?'

'Please don't be alarmed,' he reassures. 'It will be a release for you. It sounds like you are carrying a lot of confusion at the minute.'

Lucia looks into Hans' eyes. His skin is weathered. He looks older close up. A tear drops from her eye onto her arm. She wants to let this man help, but she is like her own policeman, standing guard with a truncheon. She is trapped by her secret. 'I need help,' she says. 'I don't know what is happening to me.'

'It's OK. Let us assist you, Lucia,' he says, 'to look towards a better life.'

A better life? She can't imagine what that would look like, but maybe this could be the start of something new.

'You look tired,' Hans says.

'I am,' she replies. 'I can barely walk. I feel like I'm carrying rocks on my back.'

He exhales audibly. 'We will leave the room now. I want you to remove your clothes, put on the gown hanging on the door and lie comfortably on the sofa.'

It is a silk gown with a sash, like a kimono. She lies face down on the sofa and drapes the sheet next to her over her body. The silk feels cools against her clammy skin.

The exorcists knock and enter. She feels a pair of hands hold her feet and another pair of hands rest across her back.

'Is this contact OK?' Hans asks.

She nods and closes her eyes.

'Just relax, Lucia,' he continues.

Lucia feels a twister-like hotchpotch of hands moving across her back. She does not know whose hands are whose, but feels the swash and jangle of a tickle shoot up her neck. They lift her suddenly in the air. She is elevated in the shape of a star. The feeling of them taking her weight is wonderful. She can let go.

I can stop this. I can stop this.

They bring her down onto the sofa, and pull her arms and her legs, so she is stretched out to the max.

I can.

They release their hold and then repeat this action over and over.

I can have a better life. It is possible. Her body loosens with each tug, as if heavy rocks are being removed from her arms and legs.

The men walk around her dashing their hands across her body, chanting a Hiawatha-like song. Their tone is deep. At the end of each word they exhale a loud 'oomph'.

They stop.

A pair of hands lands on the back of her head. Their warm touch and the stillness in the room make her feel sleepy. Her eyes close. Her thoughts slow. Their fists knead into her back. The men then make a bass humming sound, which carries on into the next whirr. The sound becomes so loud it vibrates like an aeroplane engine just before take-off. Waves of shivers wash over her body.

'*Ccccraaaa! Ccccraaaa!*' they shout as they snatch at her back and then throw away handfuls of energy. She hears the brushing sound of their feet as they walk around her conducting this symphony of sound. '*Ccccraaaa!*'

They grind their fists into her back, kneading and twisting them into her muscles. She hears her ligaments click into place. Something rebalances. They slap their hands up and down her spine. The sensation stings, but it massages her tissue at the same time. Her head goes dizzy. She drifts off into a calm sleep.

She wakes to the feeling of them brushing their hands across her back as if they were smoothing the last layer of icing on a cake.

She turns her head to the side. Saliva dribbles from her mouth. 'Is it over?' she asks.

'Yes, we've finished our cleansing. When you're ready, you can get dressed. We will be back in about ten minutes.'

Lucia's head feels light and wispy. That heaviness in her back has lifted. She feels a buzz inside, as if an electricity cable were running through her. As Lucia clips on her bra, she remembers the confidence she felt when they held her in the air, that her life could be different.

Hans knocks and enters.

Lucia rests on the sofa with the sheet over her knees. He hands her a glass of water and sits next to her.

'How are you feeling?' he asks.

Lucia gulps down a mouthful of water. 'Lighter,' she replies. 'How long was I asleep for?'

'About half an hour. You were very tense,' he says, twisting his beard hair. 'I could feel how closed you were.'

Closed?

This is an opportunity for her to open up to someone she trusts, but not too much or she will admit the truth. She takes a deep breath. 'Hans, there is something wrong with me. I don't know what it is.'

'It can feel like that when we are in dark places.'

She gets a whiff of his stale librarian-like breath. 'I'm trapped in this place.'

'It feels like that right now, but, when you have come through it, you will be much stronger.'

'I don't want to be strong. I want to be normal.'

'And what is normal?' he asks.

She shrugs and wipes her eyes with her sleeve. 'My friends are normal. They have happy families who love each other. I don't...' She trips on her words.

'I understand, but you can still navigate *your* own way, even in difficult circumstances. You must protect yourself, Lucia.'

'How do I do that?'

He puts his hands in a prayer position. 'Be mindful of the situations you gravitate towards. You are very vulnerable, Lucia.' He reaches for the wicker basket on the windowsill and places it on his lap.

She looks inside. There are hundreds of semi-precious stones gleaming at her: agate, cat's eye, onyx and a beautiful lump of rose quartz on the top. It's twinkling glitter make her want to grab it.

'Here, put your hand in and chose a stone,' he says, 'one that stands out to you.'

Lucia looks at him like a child in a sweetie shop. She dips her hand into the sea of stones and waves it about. The stones sound like seashells hitting the shore as they wash against her arm. She pulls out a big, green gemstone with red dots inside it.

'That's bloodstone,' Hans says.

She doesn't like it. Lucia puts it back and picks out a smaller stone. It is seahorse green and feels smooth.

'That's a piece of jadeite,' Hans says.

'I want this one,' she replies, and wraps her hand around it.

'Let it protect you. Keep hold of it at all times and ask it for guidance.'

'Thank you.' As Lucia slips it into her pocket, she feels a commitment to herself, and makes a pact that this stone and this visit will help her move on. Things will be different from now on.

'When we are going through hard times,' he says, 'we need to call on help from invisible sources.' He puts his hand on her shoulder. 'Tap into these sources. Help is there.'

Lucia stands. She has goosebumps all over her arms.

'I'll take you back downstairs,' Hans says, and leads her out.

Hans opens the door to a pristine green-and-white kitchen. Her mother is bent over, sitting on a high stool like she has been counting the seconds. Her Tate Gallery bag is still hung over her wrist. Her anorak is still on.

Leila hands Lucia her jacket and smiles.

'Are you ready?' her mum asks.

No exorcist can change this dynamic. She cannot be who she is in this relationship.

Leila and Hans walk them to the door. Her gut twists and wrenches. Lucia wishes she could stay here and wake up tomorrow with the sun streaming through the window.

'Do take care,' Hans says, brushing her back with his hand.

'Bye bye,' Leila says with concerned eyes.

'Thank you,' her mother replies.

Her mum walks ahead of Lucia, making short yelps as she treads down each step. Lucia can hear her mum mutter an imaginary phone call to herself that has not happened. 'Yes; yes, absolutely. Malvern, yes; it was, yes.'

It's back to lonely.

Lucia slides her hand inside her pocket and holds her stone. It feels cold. *Ask it for guidance.* She throws the stone past her mum. It bounces down the steps and lands by a rock.

'What an earth was that?' Her mum turns around.

'It was my stone!'

'What stone?'

'They gave it to me. It just flew out of my pocket.'

Lucia has broken her pact with herself.

Her mother bends down and picks it up.

'No! Don't touch it!' Lucia shouts and grabs the piece of jadeite from her mother.

'Why?'

'It's my magic stone.'

It will take more than gnomes and pixies to stop her doing this.

Her mother looks at Lucia and sucks her teeth. 'I think this has made things much worse,' she says, hobbling down the stairs.

CHAPTER TWENTY-SIX

LONDON, 1989

LUCIA IS SIXTEEN YEARS OLD

'No, Mum, I've been thinking about it for days. I'm convinced now; it is Lucia doing this,' Ben insists.

Lucia grips the door frame outside the sitting room and listens.

'Oh, come on, Ben,' Tim sighs. 'We've established it can't be. There have been so many incidents in the last week that couldn't have possibly been her.'

'He's right, Ben,' her mother adds.

'I mean, the rapping we heard yesterday couldn't have possibly been Lucia,' Tim rambles. 'The German dictionary that flew in here could only have come from my room. Lucia was in the bathroom at the time.'

Lucia's thorax shudders.

'No,' Ben bellows. 'I've been going over it in my mind. Poltergeists don't exist. I'm going to watch her every move for the next twenty-four hours.'

She swallows. Her mouth feels like rubber.

'Oh, come on, Ben, that's a bit extreme. If you're that certain, why don't we have a tape recorder running for the next few hours?' Tim suggests.

'OK. But I'm staying here to watch her.'

Tim ejects the old tape and inserts a new one. 'Right, I'll place this in the hall.'

Lucia sneaks back to her room and closes her door. A high-pitched ringing starts in her ears. She has to carry on. It's gone too far.

*

She creeps out and lobs the letter rack from the glass table across the hall. It lands with a thud near the boots. She streaks back to her room.

The sitting-room door opens.

'It was the letter rack,' her mum shouts. 'It flew across the hall.'

'I heard the floorboards creak,' Ben says.

'I didn't,' Tim replies.

'Nor did I,' her mum says, and closes the sitting-room door.

Lucia presses her big toe on the floorboard to see where it hollows. She has everything to play for now. She tiptoes to the bathroom.

'Where is she?' Ben whispers as she passes.

'She's in her room, I think,' her mum answers.

Lucia opens the bathroom door. She picks up the soap dish, four soap bars and a packet of sanitary towels. Crouching, Lucia skulks back to her room, with her goodies stuffed under her tank top. She takes one giant step over the tape recorder.

'Is she outside? I think I heard a noise.'

'No. She's still in her room.'

Lucia clutches the two parts of the glass dish. She lobs one half at the bathroom door and star jumps sideways back to her room.

It hits the door with a loud clunk.

A hand pounces onto the sitting-room doorknob. Ben lunges down the hallway to her room. She throws the other section of the dish onto her bed.

Ben enters. 'That was you, wasn't it?'

'No. I was just coming out to see what that was.' Her face sweats. She flicks her eyes over to her bed. The other half of the soap dish landed behind her furry toy bunny rabbit.

Ben pushes his tongue against the inside of his cheek. 'Why are you out of breath then?'

'I'm not.' She looks down at the Pierre Cardin elastic peeping out of his jeans.

'Yes, you are? You threw that didn't you?'

'Don't be stupid,' she laughs.

'I'm watching you, Sonny Jim,' Ben warns and leaves

The tomato ketchup is still in her room. She undoes the lid and pours it on the sanitary towel. It looks gross, like real blood. She creeps into her brother's bedroom and leaves it on his floor. En route back, she throws the four soaps at the sitting-room door.

The sitting-room door flies open.

'It's more stuff from the bathroom,' Tim calls. He presses the eject button and turns the tape over.

*

The tape recorder is still running. It has been on for the last week, non-stop. During that time, none of them, including Ben, have been able to catch Lucia out. He is still unsure whether this is his sister doing this or whether some paranormal activity is happening, and has now asked a friend, Drew Foggin, to come and help. He has just arrived to speak to her mum and Tim about it.

Lucia listens from the hall.

'Look,' Ben whispers. 'Drew is a crystal healer. I think it would good for him to look at all of this from another perspective.'

Confident that she has time, she skulks to the sitting room. If they don't believe it's a poltergeist, now they will. She hurls the coffee table onto its side. It's wooden slats crash to the floor. The brass tray flies across the room. Twang.

She hears their footsteps.

Energy surges through her veins like the first rush of ecstasy. She flings the marble eggs at the wall. One by one, they dent the wallpaper and crash to the floor. Lucia chucks the bowl of potpourri at the mirror and pelts backwards out of the room, as if being fast forwarded in time.

She bashes into Ben in the hall. 'What was that?' she asks.

Ben glances into the sitting room. 'The coffee table has flown across the room,' he says. 'I saw it.'

The mirror is splintered down the middle. Potpourri sprinkles the carpet, and the china bowl is shattered in the fireplace.

'My favourite bowl is smashed to smithereens,' her mother howls, pulling her hair.

Lucia watches her mother kneel down, choking on her tears. She pushes away her creeping conscience. All of this destruction she is causing…

This isn't her fault, she tells herself. This isn't her fault.

*

Drew Foggin is lanky. He has mousy-brown, spiky hair. He is shabbily dressed in black tracksuit bottoms and a pair of battered Dunlop trainers. He smells like he has just walked out of a smoky room. His eyes are bloodshot.

They gather around him like lost tourists.

'I just want to walk around and see if I can feel where the main energy points in this flat are.' He saunters into her brother's bedroom.

They follow.

Drew holds his hands out, as if checking to see if it were raining. 'Yeah, there's definitely an energy point in here.' He bends down. 'The energy is coming off my crystal here. There is a ley-line grid running under here.' He points to the fireplace and lays two crystals on the tiles. 'Leave them there. They will tame volatile energy.'

Her mother rolls her eyes.

Drew walks into Lucia's bedroom. He looks around and lays his last crystal down under the window. 'This could be another point.'

'I see,' her mother says, raising her eyebrows.

'Mum,' Ben says. 'Drew says he'd be willing to move in for a week or so to help calm things down. He thinks another presence here would help.'

'No way.' Her mother slices the air with her hand. 'I don't want anyone else here, not at this time.'

'Why not?' Ben shouts.

'Be-bee-because th-th-th-things are hard enough.' Her stutter worsens. 'I can't cope with a-a-a-any more pr-pr-pr-pressure.'

'But it wouldn't be pressure. Drew would be here to help. Something needs to change round here, Mum.'

'Absolutely not!'

Ben puts his hands in his pockets and shakes his head. 'This is the underlying cause of all of this chaos, you know. This is all to do with *your* negativity.'

'That's a bit unfair, Ben,' Tim mutters from behind.

'How can you blame this on me?' her mum pleads.

'I'm not blaming this on you, Mum,' Ben replies. 'I am saying that your negativity is making this whole situation much worse.' His voice gets bigger. 'Why can't you ever be open to anything positive?'

Her mother looks into Ben's eyes. 'I-I-I-I am doing my best to cope with this devastation. I am trying to ke-ke-ke-keep my family together.' The conviction in her mother's tone weakens.

Lucia can't bear to watch her mother grovelling in her defence.

'I am doing everything I can. I don't want anyone here who is not family.'

Ben flings his suede jacket over his shoulders. 'Suit yourself, but until *you* change, nothing here will ever change. If you won't try to help yourself, then I'm not going to help anymore. Don't say I didn't try.' He thrusts past her. 'You've had your chance.'

Lucia gets a lump in her throat.

Drew follows Ben to the door. They leave. Tim cracks his knuckles. Her mother coughs and trundles out.

'Can I make you a cup of tea, Mum?' Lucia asks.

'No thanks,' her mum replies, sniffling her way to the kitchen.

*

Lucia waits.

She stands with a box of matches in her hand.

The only way to overcome any last suspicions is to throw caution to the wind. The sound of the washing machine on spin is close. The smell of homemade ragu simmering on the stove drifts out of the kitchen, where her mother loads the dishwasher. Her brothers talk quietly in what was their room, behind a closed door.

She walks into the sitting room and over to her mother's bed. The matches rattle in the box. She takes one out.

What the fuck am I doing?

She strikes it. The match ignites.

Lucia watches the flame bounce along the matchstick. It scorches her thumb. She drops the match on the divan.

The flame burns a hole in the cover and then sprawls outwards. The tassels of the pink cushion singe. The flame bursts upwards as it gathers momentum, and it sounds like a plastic sheet being shaken in the air. A flash of sweltering heat punches her in the face.

'Fire!' she screams. 'Fire!'

Ben runs into the sitting room. Tim and her mother scamper behind.

'For fuck's sake!' Ben shouts.

Her mother's hand flies to her mouth. 'Good God! Water! Get water!'

A rush of flames shoots up in front of the window. The world outside is occluded by a mountain of orange heat. Tim and Ben rush to the kitchen. The sound of crockery banging is close. They bolt back, buckets of water in hand.

'Get out of the way, Mum!' Ben shouts and throws the water onto the divan. It exterminates most of the flames, but small ones still dance along the cushion edges.

Tim sloshes water onto the cushions. There is a sizzling sound. The flames die.

Ben returns with two more buckets and pours them one by one over the divan. The smell of burnt charcoal after a bonfire permeates the room.

Her mother kneels down and splutters. There is black soot all over her nose. Tim helps her mother up and sits her in her chair, as she heaves over the empty bucket. 'I can't do this anymore. I just can't!' her mother cries. A dribble of vomit spills from her mother's mouth.

Ben pulls the bedding off the divan. 'Here, Tim, can you take these?'

There is a hole in the mattress, where the filling is popping through. He opens the windows and fans the air with his hand, whilst Tim dumps the bedding outside the flat.

'So, who saw the fire first?' Tim asks, entering.

'I did,' Lucia replies. 'I came in and the bed was on fire.'

'This is the first manifestation that could have hurt us or even killed us,' Ben says, sitting on the sofa. 'That must have been what they call spontaneous combustion.'

Tim sits on a dining chair, 'This can't go on,' he says, looking down at his navel.

'I agree,' replies Ben. He wipes his nose with the back of his hand. 'Something needs to happen urgently.'

'What are we going to do? My home is in ruins!' her mother screams.

'It is not you or your home I am worried about, Mum,' Ben says. 'It's Lucia I'm worried about.'

A shooting pain whizzes across Lucia's diaphragm.

Her mother breaks out into a wailing cry. Her glasses fly off her nose and she bends over, jerking with sobs. 'So, none of you care about me?'

The piercing sound of her mother's howl sends shivers up Lucia's neck. She has never heard her mum cry like this before. She cannot bear to see her mother bawling with her shoulders hunched. She just wants to hold her. Lucia has always known that her mother had a short stint in a psychiatric hospital, after Tim and Ben's father had an affair with another woman. That thought of her mum strapped to a metal bed being stunned with electricity is too unbearable to even contemplate. She pushes the thought away.

'How can you not care about me?' her mother asks. Her face is screwed up, stained with tears. 'I am doing everything I can to help this family. I can't take a minute more!'

'I know,' Ben replies. 'I'm not denying that. But this isn't about you, Mum. It's about Lucia. She needs your help.'

Her mum tries to catch her breath.

Ben kneads his eyebrows with his fingers. 'I think you should move out for a bit, Mum.'

Her mother looks at Ben. 'What do you mean?'

'I think yours and Lucia's dynamic is feeding this problem and making it much worse. Let's see what happens if you were to move out.'

'Ben's right,' Tim adds. 'We can look after Lucia.'

Lucia gulps.

'Look, Mum,' Ben says in a soft tone. 'I think you should go and stay with Bridget for a couple of weeks to see if things calm down. Meanwhile, we'll get you a new bed sorted.'

Her mother sits back. Her shoulders drop. 'Maybe you're right. I can't stay here.'

This is it. She could lose her mother – for good.

'Listen, Mum, why don't you go and pack some things. I'll call Bridget and explain the situation,' Tim says.

Her mother walks out of the room.

Lucia follows. 'I'll help you pack, Mum.'

In the bathroom, her mum unzips her wash bag and gathers her cosmetics.

Lucia smells that familiar scent of overdried hair that she could recognise as her mother's smell in a crowd of a million. It is from that old-fashioned hairdryer she uses. She stares at her mum's wrinkled knuckles moving from the shelf to the cupboard. *Please don't go, Mum.* How could she do this to her own mother?

She must stop.

Lucia now realises she is driving her mother away. Who will she have now? Ben and Tim won't care if she gets her bra size right or has the right cheese on her sandwiches for lunch. She will be completely on her own now.

'Here, Lucia, would you go and get me my brush from the sitting room, please? It's on the windowsill,' her mother asks.

'Can I come and see you at Bridget's, Mum?'

'Of course you can. I am only going for a while.'

Lucia's heart clobbers. 'I love you, Mum,' she says.

Her mum looks right into her daughter's eyes. 'Do you?'

'Of course I do.'

Lucia walks to the sitting room to get her mother's roller brush. Her skin has gone stone cold. This has gone too far now. She will stop this; somehow, she will stop.

Lucia picks up her mother's brush and walks back to the bathroom. But, as much as Lucia wants to stop, she knows that the force driving her to do these things is way bigger than she is.

'Here, Mum. Here's your brush,' she says, and puts it on top of the washing machine.

CHAPTER TWENTY-SEVEN

LONDON, 1989

LUCIA IS SIXTEEN YEARS OLD

Lucia's mum has been away for two weeks, with her friend Bridget, and is now home.

'We are now taking the recorder into the sitting room,' Tim speaks into the cassette recorder. 'This is Lucia on Thursday afternoon, July 30, at 4.00pm.' He puts the player on the dining table, where Lucia is doing her coursework. Tim sits on the sofa pretending to read the TV guide. Her mother is sitting cross-legged in her chair, with a fag between her teeth.

'Remember when Mum used to take us away, Michael?' asks Lucia.

'No, I don't remember actually,' Tim replies.

'I was just telling Jennifer about when Mum used to take me to the theatre before she died. Do you remember, Michael?'

'I'm not Michael. I'm Tim.'

'Do you remember Tim and Ben?' she blurts out.

'What do you mean, "Do you remember Tim and Ben?"?'

'They used to take me swimming and to the championships. Mum, can you get me some orange juice, please.'

'Who?' her mother asks, standing.

'Mum,' Lucia replies.

'Who's Mum?'

'You're Mum.'

'Am I, good,' she says grinning, and goes to the kitchen to get Lucia's juice.

'Margaret Thatcher was my best friend,' Lucia gabbles in a cockney accent.

Tim looks down with his finger resting above his lip.

'Michael, do you remember when we went to see Van Gogh?'

'My name isn't Michael, its Tim.'

'Don't try and cover it up,' Lucia laughs, knowing Tim is annoyed. 'Tim died when he was six.'

'Here, Lucia, is your juice' her mum says, putting a tumbler full of orange juice in front of her.

'Thanks Jennifer,' Lucia says, and gulps it. 'Ah, refreshing,' she pronounces, and sits back. She throws off her t-shirt, and sits there in just her bra and trousers.

'Why did you do that?' asks Tim.

'I'm hot; clothes are stupid.' She sips more juice. 'Peter and Jane were political activists you know, vying against me;

vying against me. They were *vying*! They were condemning me.'

'I see,' her mum replies and inhales a long tail of smoke.

Lucia bangs the salt holder on the table. 'Daphna is after you,' she burbles. 'Daphna is after you.' She looks down at the tape recorder. 'Are you going to send this to the Royal Barbican Centre?'

'I might do, as your acting is so good.' Tim replies.

Lucia pounds her chest like Tarzan. 'I'm a prostitute you know, I have been on the game since I was four. Daphna! Daphna!' she bleats and twitches. 'Pickheads! The rats! The rats! The rats! The rats!'

'Tim she's gone completely this time,' her mother mutters.

'I know,' he laughs.

'The rat bit into my nose. I thought it was the end of the day,' she whispers. 'Jennifer just stood there crying.'

'Who's Jennifer?' her mother asks.

'You're Jennifer.'

'Am I?'

'You know, Godot once said to me, "Beckett is your darling". He said, "Look…" He said, "Look, if you want to marry Beckett, then you eat him." Well, that contains a lot of ambiguity,' Lucia gabbles, still in an East London accent.

'Why don't you put your top back on, Lucia? It is silly sitting there in your bra.' her mum asks.

Lucia's trances are a new development. They began two weeks ago, with twitching and wincing, and then maniacal dancing and talking in different voices, as if she is channelling different characters through her. She is broken in two, and in the midst of a horrific psychic breakdown.

'She was a nun, you see,' Lucia replies. 'We are going to fight!' she shouts, and then sits down rubbing her head. 'I wish I could see properly.'

'What can you see?' her mum asks, worried.

'Red and white, I told you.' Lucia unfastens her bra and throws it on the floor. 'I must look up how you spell "infatuated",' she continues, twiddling with the Blu Tack. 'I was infatuated by Jeffrey Finsburg; we had an affair, and he tried to lick me. Infatuated... infatuated!' she witters.

'Oh dear, Tim,' her mum sighs.

'Pacman! Pacman! *Bad man*,' she shouts, slapping the table. 'I remember when Ben and Tim told me that, when they were alive – well, Ben was killed in the First World War, well, Second World War, when Hitler paved the way,' she snorts loudly. 'Ben is a Jew, a heavy Jew. He has a kippah; a kippah. But he's not as *frum* as Tim. Tim really was *frum*,' she laughs hysterically.

Tim titters. 'Was he?'

'They didn't kill me because I was anti-Semitic, but – you see, Jennifer – when my mum went to Hitler and said, "Don't get feisty, ya fascist; ya National Frontist," he spat in her face. I was just a foetus, an amoeba umbilical cord.'

She sips the last of her juice. Her tone now becomes animated. 'So, anyway, I was born into a gas chamber – into fucking Auschwitz, but I escaped. I said, "Mum, I am very sorry, but I have to go." She said...' Lucia now wails, '"Don't go, don't leave me!" I said, "Mum, Hitler and Mussolini are coming; they are on their way." She said, "All right, love. Ben's been pushed out; you must purge my life out of your head. Purge it." So, I went to the restoration of Charles

II and then I went to the Battle of Hastings where I was reincarnated.'

Lucia starts to whimper. 'There was Tim; all alone, all alone. I said, "You've really been mistaken this time; you've been on those Camels," but he didn't say anything. So, there I was, on my own with no family, so I said, "Look, Hitler, look…" I said, "you and I are great sparing" I said I'm going to kill my mum well she's not quite dead because I don't get her.' Her accent becomes Germanic. 'Hitler said, "You stay there." "All right," I said, and there I was with a swastika on mum's forehead, a pink triangle, the lot, and then came Eugene Holtz. Mum was alive; she was resplendent. How do you spell "resplendent"?' Lucia snorts. 'So, there it goes… My name is Jackie. It is a tedious life I told you; you have already warned me, but I can't bring her back today.' She spits phlegm into a napkin.

'Oh, don't spit into a napkin; it is quite vile,' her mum says.

'Fucker! Fucker!' screams Lucia.

'That's not very polite,' Tim says, flicking through the TV pages.

'And then I found Mum lying on the road in front of a tree,' Lucia slurs. 'She was just there dead; lying all alone.'

'Just try and ignore her,' her mum mutters to Tim.

'Did you remember that Antony Burgess is coming for lunch?' Lucia squeezes her nose with her fingers, making her voice sound tinny. 'He's bringing smoked salmon and lettuce.'

'Is that right?' Tim smirks.

'Yes, but don't tell anyone because it's a secret; sssshhhhh!' she says. They don't respond. Lucia looks down at her file papers. 'We must see *Ocean Apart* at eleven o'clock Tim,' Lucia shouts.

Tim does not acknowledge her.

'*Tim!*'

'Yes, yes, I know; quite right,' he replies.

'Do you like it?' her mum asks trying to bring her back to the present.

Her mother is lost as to how to relate to her daughter. She has taken Lucia to see a neurologist who did an electroencephalogram (EEG). Lucia had to sit with metal disks stuck to her scalp, with wires attached to them and watch a screen with electrical waves dancing across it. It was like something from *D.A.R.Y.L.* The result was normal.

'Is it a sequel, Tim?' Lucia asks inquisitively.

'It is not a sequel; it is the next episode,' he replies, in a patronising tone.

'Does it include the League of Nations?' Lucia asks.

'I should imagine so, yes; it is the end of the First World War.'

It is unclear sometimes whether Lucia has come to or is still in a trance.

'How is your eyesight now?' her mum asks.

'It's gone green and white now.'

'Green and white?' her mum asks lighting another fag. 'Do-do-do you mean everything is gr-gr-green and white?'

'Yes,' Lucia replies and erases a sentence of her work with the rubber on the end of her pencil. 'I'm meeting T.S. Eliot in the park later. Can you give me a lift, Mum?'

'Yes, I can.'

'Does "science fiction" mean it is true, Mum?'

'No, course not,' her mum replies, 'How can fiction be true?'

'What is it when it is a true story?' Lucia asks.

'Non-fiction,' her mum replies. 'I think she is normal now; I think the trance has finished,' her mum whispers to Tim.

'It's not over yet,' Tim replies, barely moving his lips.

'Shall we go and kill ourselves tomorrow?' Lucia asks.

'Why do you say that?' her mum replies.

'I feel like there is no tomorrow,' Lucia replies. Her head falls onto the table.

The tape recorder clicks. It is the end of the tape. Tim turns over the cassette. 'This is Lucia, still in a trance; it's now 6.20pm on Thursday evening.'

'Blah, blah, blah,' Lucia shouts. She gets up and stomps up and down the hallway laughing and doing karate kicks. 'Laa deee daaa deee daaaaa.'

'What are you doing now, Lucia?' Tim calls from the sitting room.

Lucia jogs back in and takes off her trousers.

'Oh no, here we go,' Tim mumbles. 'Why are you on the floor on your hands and knees like that?' he asks Lucia.

'Here comes a wee! Weee! Pissss! Pissss!' Lucia blurts and urinates on the carpet.

'Oh, Lucia, you are naughty,' her mum says.

'I can't stop it!' Lucia says, laughing uncontrollably.

'Why?'

'Cos it just comes out!'

'Oh, it's too bad!' her mum sighs, 'Honestly!'

'That was quite a big one,' says Tim.

'This is too terrible,' her mother trembles. 'I wonder if Dr Jeffries is still at the surgery?'

'I can't! I can't!' Lucia cries and runs out to the bathroom. Tim gets up and heads out after her. She stands by the basin and wets herself again. 'Pooh pooh coming now.'

'Better not,' Tim says. He fills the bucket with hot water and detergent and begins scrubbing the carpet.

'Ping-pong!' Lucia shouts in a Chinese accent. 'My son used to do that,' she says standing over him.

'Really? Who's your son?' Tim asks.

'Stan Cooper.'

Her mother comes into the bathroom, panting. 'I couldn't get hold of Dr Jeffries,' she says, and she hands Lucia some tracksuit bottoms. 'Here Lucia, you must control yourself now.'

'I can't stop it! It just comes out.' Lucia stands in the bath tub, washing herself with a sponge.

Lucia gets out and puts on her Adidas bottoms.

'What are you thinking about, Lucia?' her mother asks holding her daughter by the chin. She looks uncharacteristically into the whites of Lucia's eyes.

'Miaow! Pooh-land,' she witters, and opens the bathroom cupboard.

Lucia takes down the bottle of aspirin and turns the lid.

'Come on now!' her mother says, 'I think Mary is going to come round in a minute, will you go down?'

Lucia tips three aspirin into her hand and turns on the cold water.

Tim stands, with scrubbing brush in hand and his feet turned inwards. The bathroom stinks of Ajax. 'What on earth are you doing?' he shouts.

'I'm taking an aspirin.'

'Ho-ho-ho-how many have you got?' her mum asks, unclasping Lucia's hand.

'Just two,' Lucia replies and swallows them down.

'Have you got a headache?' her mum asks.

'No.'

The tap is still running. Lucia is drinking like she hasn't drunk for days.

'You are stupid taking an aspirin when you haven't got a pain,' her mum shouts.

'Fuck off! I've got a pain in my heart.'

'Have you?'

'I wish I could see.'

'Can you still not see, Lucia?' her mum asks.

'A bit.'

'What can you see?'

'Plums.'

'Plums?'

Tim pours the dirty water down the loo. 'Right,' he says, putting the bucket under the sink. 'I think that's enough urine for one day. Are you normal now?' he asks Lucia.

'I'm fine!'

'You haven't been fine,' he says, 'you've been in a trance all afternoon. Do you know what day it is?'

'Yah- rule me say, yah-rule me say, rip off her pantie,' she chants in a Jamaican accent. 'Sharul! Sharul! Sharul! You fucking tinker! We went to Babylon, Babylon!'

'Why don't you go and lie down?' her mum suggests.

Lucia follows her mother to her room and curls into a ball on her bed.

'Look at her, Tim; she's pathetic,' her mum mutters. 'What are we going to do?'

'I don't know, Mum,' Tim replies.

'The flock moved from dressage to Pink Floyd,' Lucia slurs, holding her teddy. 'The chooka-chooka train. Chooo. Chooo. Chooo. Go away, go away.'

Whilst one part of Lucia is lost in chaos, the other part knows what is happening. Lucia is aware of what she is doing in these trances, but she cannot control this untamed expression coming from within her.

'We must get this room redecorated from top to bottom,' her mother whispers to Tim at the door. 'I think all this graffiti from Ginger is having a terrible effect on her.'

'Yes, I agree,' Tim mumbles and shuffles out behind her mother.

They leave Lucia on her bed, talking to herself.

*

Lucia is resting on her bed, recovering from her trance. Tim has gone out for a pint with his friend Mark. Maeve, Valerie's friend, has come over to see her. Val called her in a state of desperate worry. Lucia can hear every word coming from the sitting room, as she drops in and out of light sleep.

'I-I-I -I just don't kn-kn-know what to do,' her mother quavers. 'She's in a most desperate state, Maeve: wetting herself, talking about spies and gas chambers. She calls me Jennifer half the time. I mean she's ill. I have been calling Dr Jeffries at the surgery.'

'And what does he recommend?' Maeve's voice is so calming, like a lavender-scented breeze wafting in.

'Well, he-he-he re-re-re-referred her to neurology. The EEG and brain scan were normal. He thinks she should see a psychiatrist for an opinion.'

'Val, you must find the right help. Your daughter is clearly having some kind of serious breakdown.'

'Yes,' her mum agrees. 'I'm sure redecorating her room will help her state of mind, just getting all that menacing graffiti off the walls. They're coming tomorrow, the two decorators.'

'I'm glad, but *all* of you need help. This is too much strain for you to carry, Val. You will get ill if you don't get professional help from someone who specialises in this kind of disease.'

'But we-we-we don't know wh-wh-wh-what it is?'

'Well, something hasn't been right for many years, since the complications with Colin began. He has a lot to answer for if you ask me, Val.'

'Yes.'

'How on earth do I find the right kind of help for her? Poor child!'

'You need experienced psychological help. Look, here Val.' Paper rustles. 'I've found the name of a very established psychologist called Charles Bagnall. He's a fellow at King's College Cambridge and has done a lot of work for Channel Four. He is charming and accessible. I urge you to contact him. You must stop with all these parapsychologists. They are not helping. You must find someone who can tackle the root cause.'

'Yes; yes, thank you, Maeve.'

'Why don't you come and stay for a couple of nights for some respite?'

'I've just been away, Maeve. I must stay with her. Sh-sh-she was talking about killing herself the other night.'

Maeve sighs. 'What a truly awful time for you, Val. You look exhausted.'

'I-I-I just don't kn-kn-know who she is anymore.'

Lucia listens to her mother sob.

She sits up. Lucia realises this could make her mother ill, like she was before Lucia was born. Her mum could be back in hospital, being tortured with electric waves because of her.

'What i-i-i-is so bizarre,' her mum continues, 'is the way she can be in a trance, talking about having lunch with T.S. Eliot, and then seconds later she can be completely normal. It's like she is two people.'

Maeve exhales a long breath. 'Perhaps, she is suffering with some kind of personality disorder, but whatever is causing this poltergeist activity can be healed with the right help, Val. I have every confidence that Lucia will return to live a fully functional life.'

'I'm not sure, but I will contact this chap.'

'Please do. I'm very worried about you all.'

CHAPTER TWENTY-EIGHT

LONDON, 1989

LUCIA IS SIXTEEN YEARS OLD

'I am an alien from Peru!' she shouts boisterously. 'Mary of Magdalene doesn't agree.' Lucia crosses her eyes. She brings her hands up to her chin in a prayer pose and blows air into her cheeks.

'Oh, no, Tim, she's off again,' her mum says.

Lucia looks around the room squinting, and shields her eyes as if boiling sun were beating down. She points at her mum and brother, and rants in a German accent. 'They are vying for us; you know, vying! If we ignore them, they will come knocking.'

Tim presses his knuckles against his lips. 'Is that right, Lucia?' he sneers.

Lucia's mouth drops open. She begins to shake.

'Oh no, Tim, look,' her mum whines.

She falls to the floor. 'Mrs Rinehart is coming!'

'What, Lucia? Come on now, stop this!' Her mum slaps her cheek.

The slap stings, but she ignores the pain. 'Mrs Reinhart has a message from the Queen,' Lucia's voice is high pitched and posh. 'It's an important message. The spies are coming.'

Lucia rolls onto her knees and stands. She pounds down the hallway to her bedroom. Her mother and brother follow. In her room, her eyes roll into the back of her head. She convulses and makes a strange sound: a grumbling bark.

'Lucia! Lucia!' her mum shouts, slapping her face again. 'Come on, now!'

Lucia crawls onto her bed. She turns on her side to face her mother, who is kneeling on the floor. She moves her finger slowly towards her mother's nose, just like ET does the first time he sees Elliott. 'Who are you?' she asks, as if sleep talking. 'What is your name?'

'Lucia, it's me. It's your mother,' she replies, pinching her arm.

Lucia feels vomit fizz in her throat. She retches. Purple and black dots swim in front of her eyes. She turns onto her back and she stares up at the ceiling, with a catatonic glare.

'Take a picture to show, Eugene, Tim!' her mum says. 'Quick.'

Tim stands over Lucia pointing his Polaroid at her face and clicks. It makes the sound a photocopier makes when paper comes through.

'Here,' Tim says. 'I got it.'

'Look at her,' her mum mutters. 'She looks so pathetic. I don't know what to do!'

Lucia can hear every word they are saying. She bites her bottom lip fast and twitches, with one eye open.

'Look,' her mum whispers. 'She's twitching again.'

Lucia's arms spasm.

'Lucia!' her mother shouts.

Lucia sticks out her tongue. 'Bad!' She jabs the air curiously. 'They will come, you know; the spies, to get us all.' She rolls into a foetal position, and rocks back and forth, mumbling to herself.

Her mother gently pulls her shoulder. 'Lucia…'

She flinches and pushes her mum away. Lucia flails her arms in the air to keep her mum out of reach. 'No. Go!' she shouts, 'Freddie and Ginger are coming. Go!' She punches the bed with her fists and thrashes her body from side to side.

'Lucia! Stop this please.' Her mum pins Lucia's arms back behind her head to try to calm her, but Lucia thrusts her hips up so hard that she knocks her mum sideways.

The clock radio falls to the floor.

'Call Eugene, Tim, quick,' her mum says.

Lucia listens to Tim shuffle out. She slides her legs down and lies horizontal. Her breathing is so shallow she can barely feel her lungs working. Lucia lays her arms out by her side and sings the song she has been singing for days to a nursery rhyme melody:

One, two, Freddie's gonna get you.
Three, four, he's knocking at your door.

Five, six, get a crucifix.
Seven, eight, now it's too late.

As she sings, Lucia gets an image in her mind of a girl jumping through a skipping rope, on her own. Other children play a long way off, but their voices are all muffled. A man stares at her from behind a tree. He has long, greasy hair, and is wearing an old rugby sweater and cords. The image of the girl becomes more and more blurred until she has disappeared.

Tim walks in. 'Eugene is on his way.'

'She just sang the song again,' her mum mutters under her breath, 'the one about Freddie and Ginger.'

Lucia sits up, as if suddenly waking from a nightmare. Sweat drips from her temples. She yanks her t-shirt away from her body. 'He took her!' she screams at the top of her lungs. 'The man took her!'

'Lucia, it's OK!' her mum says, stroking her leg. 'It must have been a dream.'

Lucia grabs her pillow and brings it to her face. It feels cool. 'No, no. The man, he took her,' she says, trembling. 'I saw him.'

'What did you see, Lucia?' her mum asks.

Lucia flops back down. Her face burns. 'I saw the man looking at her,' she pants. 'He was coming.'

The doorbell rings.

'Tim, you go. I'll stay here with her. Come on,' her mum says, stroking Lucia's brow. 'You're scorching hot, child. Let's get you up.'

As Lucia sits up, her mum holds her hand on her back to keep Lucia upright, just like a mother does to a newborn baby. Lucia's wet hair hangs down, prickling her arm.

'Here, sip some of this,' her mum says, holding a glass of yesterday's water to her lips.

Lucia takes a sip. She can feel the cool water slide down her hot throat. She hears Eugene's voice coming up the stairs and nestles her face into her mother's neck. 'Please, Mum, make this all stop!'

*

Eugene guides Lucia down the hallway, holding her hand. 'Come on, let's go and calm down,' he says.

Lucia follows him like a small child. She smells her mum's Anais Anais perfume and hears her brother shuffling behind. She twitches like a person with Tourette's syndrome.

'Here we are; now let's sit you down,' Eugene says.

Lucia collapses onto the sofa. Eugene pulls her legs up and rests them on a pile of cushions. He kneels down beside her and puts the remaining cushions under her head. She looks frail, like a damaged animal.

'I just want you to relax,' he says, feeling her pulse. 'Well, that all feels normal.'

Lucia's arms drop down. Her spine relaxes; her muscles loosen.

Eugene grips Lucia's hand. His hand feels snug and weathered. The way he runs the tip of his thumb across her palm is just like how her father did when they used to walk through St James' Park together.

'Now, Lucia. I want you to close your eyes. I am going to count to twenty. As I count, I want you to feel yourself falling into a nice, deep sleep, OK?'

She nods. Her eyelids shut.

'Good girl.' He clutches her hand tight. 'I want you to bring your attention to the sensations in your body.'

She mustn't let herself go completely.

'One. That's it. Now focus on your breathing; just feel the air going in and out. Two and three.'

Lucia feels a prickling sensation across her back. The hairs on her arms stand up.

'Six. Now you are feeling nice and light, Lucia. There is no weight in your body.'

Her face softens.

'Eight.'

She feels the pull of deep asleep.

But…

'Ten.'

She is still here. One eye is watching.

He squeezes her hand. 'Now feel yourself becoming nice and drowsy, Lucia.'

Lucia feels the itchy, velvety fabric beneath her. She releases her grip of the cushion she holds. She trusts Eugene now. She wants to surrender to his spell, but knows she cannot.

'Twelve.' His voice becomes closer. 'Thirteen. The only noise you can hear now is my voice.'

Lucia thinks of the tall grandfather clock at her Auntie Dora's house. It always chimes on the hour, even through the night.

'Fifteen.'

She likes going to stay at Auntie Dora's, playing in the garden with Katie, catching the frogs from the pond and exploring Ernst's greenhouse.

'Sixteen. Seventeen,' he continues.

Lucia does feel sleepy, but she is aware of her mother and brother's presence in the room.

'Twenty. Now, Lucia, all you should be aware of is your breathing.'

Lucia lies still; her tummy rising up and sinking down with each breath. Her fingers loosely clasp Eugene's hand, which radiates warmth.

The room is as still as a film set before the action.

'Hello, Lucia. It's me, Eugene. Nod if you can hear me.'

How can you nod if you are supposed to be asleep?

'Can you hear me?' He squeezes her hand three times.

She nods.

'These are very hard times for you, Lucia. Will you tell me what is going through your mind at the minute?'

Her mouth feels like it has been sucked dry by one of those high-powered suction devices that dentists use. She pushes her tongue up to try to induce some moisture, but it feels like sandpaper. 'I have no mind,' she says. 'I'm dead.'

'You're dead?'

'I want to be,' she says, curling her toes.

'Why is that, Lucia?'

'It's all heavy on top of me.'

'What's heavy?'

'Everything; it's confusing,' she drones.

Lucia smells Eugene's sickly cologne as he moves closer to her.

'What is confusing, Lucia?'

'I am two people.'

She fidgets a bit. 'I am not me.'

'Who are you, then?'

Lucia's voice becomes slurred, like her words are trapped in her throat. 'I don't know.'

The air purifier chugs. It sounds as though something is clogging it.

'Who is this other person?'

'It's Ginger. It's Ginger.'

'*Who is* Ginger, Lucia?'

'He's my friend.' Her words drawl. 'He makes me do these things.'

'Ginger does?'

'Yes, he tells me to do them.'

'What does he say to you, Lucia?'

'He says that he is here to help me.'

Lucia is aware of her mind relaxing. She must not let go of the reins.

'Help you?'

'Yes, to save me from these bad people.'

Eugene coughs several times and then begins again. 'Who are these bad people?'

Lucia turns her head the other way. 'You don't know them.' Saliva dribbles down the side of her mouth. 'There are bad people, everywhere.'

'What are their names?'

She shakes her head. 'He says not to say.'

'Who says not to?'

She opens her mouth, but no words come. Although drowsy, she is still conscious.

'Take your time,' Eugene assures. His breath smells stale.

'Ginger is telling me to be careful.'

'Careful of what?' Eugene asks.

Lucia's eyes sting. A tear slides down her cheek. Eugene wipes it away with his hand.

'I must be careful of all of you.'

'Why, Lucia?'

'You don't love me. No one does.' Her throat relaxes. She is forgetting herself. 'I only have Ginger.'

'But your family love you.'

'They don't.' These words slip out without thought, but she falters, aware of what she is saying. 'My dad, he's gone forever. The rest of them don't care.'

'Your father?'

She cries without sound, other than the snagging rhythm of her breath. 'He is never coming back.'

'Have you felt like this a long time, Lucia?'

Lucia nods. 'I am in a war,' she says. 'I must get out of here.'

'It's OK.' Eugene strokes her forehead. 'Tell me about this war, Lucia.'

She shakes her head.

'You must get out of here, you say?'

'Yes, to somewhere happy.'

'What does happy look like, Lucia?'

Her voice becomes squeaky, as if she has just inhaled a slug of balloon air. 'Smarties and gingerbread men.' She opens her eyes and glares through Eugene's spectacles. The glass on them is so thick, his eyes seem miles away. 'Happy is safe.'

'Is this place not safe, Lucia?'

'No,' she shakes her head. 'I am always scared.'

'Of what?'

Lucia says nothing.

'What are you scared of, Lucia?'

'I'm afraid of the pain.'

'What pain, Lucia?'

Her mother coughs and then begins to choke.

Lucia flinches. 'No more!' she cries.

'It's OK, Lucia. That's enough for now.' He pats her hand. 'I'm going to count to ten. As I count, I want you to slowly open your eyes.'

The first thing Lucia sees when she sits up is her brother's legs. They stretch out across the rug. He is slouched on the divan, glaring at her with pursed lips. Lucia looks at her mother, who pulls at her top lip with her teeth and nods disapprovingly. Lucia runs over the interview in her mind. Has she said something that could have got her into trouble? 'I don't feel well,' she moans quietly.

'Why don't you go and lie down?' her mother suggests.

'Come on, Lucia,' Eugene says, standing. 'I'll come and settle you.'

The black graffiti on her bedroom walls makes Lucia's chest jump in spasms. This room is a shit heap of angry messages from Ginger. She crawls into bed and pulls the duvet over her. It feels as if money spiders are crawling under her skin.

Eugene sits on her bed.

'Please stay with me,' Lucia says, gripping his hand. 'I'm afraid.'

'What are you afraid of, Lucia?'

Lucia bites her pillow to stop her tears from gushing out. 'I'm always afraid, but I don't know what of.'

'Has someone hurt you, Lucia?' he asks in a hushed tone.

She shakes her head and groans. 'No, they haven't. It's the song in my head again: the Freddie and Ginger song.'

'It's OK, Lucia, I'll stay with you,' Eugene says, patting her back. 'Everything is going to be just fine. That's just a silly, stupid song. Whenever you hear it, I want you to think about something else. Now you are going to enjoy a nice, peaceful sleep, Lucia and when you wake up you will feel right as rain.'

CHAPTER
TWENTY-NINE

LONDON, 1989

LUCIA IS SIXTEEN YEARS OLD

Lucia has just come out of another trance and is washing up in the kitchen.

The hot water tap runs.

Aloe-vera-scented washing-up liquid bubbles away in the red bowl. She can hear her mum and Tim talking over the sound of Anneka Rice on the television.

I wish I could fly, so it would look like I'd levitated like the girl in Stanmore.

She scrubs the base of the saucepan with the Brillo pad and balances the saucepan on the draining board.

Lucia leaves the tap running and lies down on the kitchen floor.

She waits.

The tap still runs.

'Mum!' Tim shrieks. 'Come here. Lucia is spark out on the floor.'

Lucia's eyes are closed and her breathing is shallow. She lies in a pool of hot water from where the sink has overflowed. The water scorches her flesh, but she fights against the pain.

'Lucia! Lucia wake up!' her Mother shouts, shaking her by the arm.

Lucia focuses on the sound of running water and the smell of cabbage in stagnant water.

'Quick, Tim, let's get her up. She must have passed out.'

They pull her up by her hands.

She opens her eyes and feigns a look of surprise. 'Where am I?'

They sit her on the red stool. Tim pulls off her drenched t-shirt. 'You must have gone into another trance, Lucia,' he says and turns off the tap.

Her mother dashes to the bathroom. She returns with four towels, which she piles on the flooded linoleum. 'Do you remember anything, Lucia?' she asks her daughter.

'A tiger jumped out of the sink and then I floated up to the light. The light was very close to my face.'

'She must have levitated, Tim,' her Mum murmurs.

'Yes, she must have,' Tim replies.

'Quick, Tim, get her jeans off. They are soaking wet.'

Tim unbuttons Lucia's 501s. He kneels down and pulls off her jeans, one leg at a time. Her legs are pink with goosebumps all over them.

Lucia stands and urinates on the floor.

'Oh no, Tim,' her Mother cries. 'She is wetting herself again!'

Tim brushes down his trousers where her urine sprayed him. They guide Lucia by the hands into the sitting room. 'Get a clean sheet, Tim, quick!' her mother orders.

Tim runs to the bathroom. He scuffles back in and lays a cotton sheet over the sofa. They lie Lucia down.

Her teeth gnash as she hums the Freddie and Ginger song. 'I am possessed by Freddie and Ginger,' she slurs. 'I am possessed.'

'Who are Freddie and Ginger, Tim? This is not my daughter. I wish I could help her.'

Lucia's eyes are closed. Their voices sound to her as the outside world sounds when sinking underwater.

'Have you phoned that fellow of psychology yet, whom Maeve recommended, Mum?' Tim asks. 'Charles Bagnall, wasn't he called?'

'I've left three messages, but he hasn't called me back, yet,' her mother replies.

'Try him again,' Tim urges. 'Try him now.'

Lucia twitches.

Her tongue hangs out, as she drifts in and out of sleep. She can hear the manic tones of her mother on the phone. 'Yes, please. Please, if you can come now, yes.'

'Lucia?' Tim nudges her shoulder.

She flinches.

'Lucia, are you awake?'

Her mum enters. 'He's on his way, with a co-co-colleague of his, Walter Mathews.'

'She's completely out of it,' Tim says.

Lucia smells the lemon sherbet on his breath.

'Just leave her. Let them see her when they arrive.'

Half an hour has passed.

The doorbell rings. Lucia jumps inside. As she hears the men's voices in the stairwell, she begins to spasm for effect. After all, these men have come out to see her. They need some kind of show.

They enter the room. She can smell burnt tarmac on their coats.

She convulses. Her shoulders jerk.

Lucia can feel a presence standing over her. She keeps her eyes closed.

'How long has this been going on for?' one of them asks.

'A-a-a-a-all afternoon,' her mother replies.

'Well,' Tim interjects. 'This trance started at about 2.00pm. I actually found her on the floor, unconscious in a pool of scalding water. She had levitated, so it seems.'

'From where?' one of the men asks. His tone is soothing and calm.

'We are not clear from where. She said the light was close to her face,' Tim replies.

'I see.'

They don't sound convinced.

Lucia's body undulates. She looks like she is body popping. 'Uggh. Uggh!' she wails, pointing at the ceiling. The left side of her mouth drops down. 'Oooooh.'

'And this is normal for her?'

'Well, this is her usual behaviour when she is in trance, yes,' Tim replies.

Lucia hears the cushions waft out air as the men sit on the sofa.

'She is completely disconnected from everything when she is like this,' her mother says.

'Yes, I can see. She is clearly very disturbed.'

'Sh-sh-sh-she hears this so-so-song, about Freddie and Ginger. She says people are coming to hurt her,' her mother babbles.

Lucia's frenzied movements stop. She listens.

'Freddie and Ginger?'

'Yes, they occur a lot in her trance monologues,' Tim replies.

The two men sound identical in their tone: posh and intelligent sounding. She cannot differentiate one from the other.

'Has Lucia had any psychological help?' one asks.

'No, she hasn't,' Tim replies.

'I have reviewed the incidents that you told me about the other night,' one of the men says, 'and it seems more than likely that your daughter's problem is a psychosexual one.'

Psychosexual? What the fuck? Lucia turns onto her side, and feels the draught from under the window tickle her neck.

"A what?' her mum asks. 'Will you explain what you mean by that exactly?'

'Yes, certainly,' the same man replies. Lucia wants to open her eyes to see what he looks like.

She imagines he is middle-aged, thin and intellectual-looking with specs across the bridge of his nose.

'It is well recognised that adolescents, more often girls than boys, are sometimes the focus of psychic phenomena of a poltergeist type, like this, if there is some malalignment of their sexual energies.'

Malalignment of sexual energies? Lucia's mind spins. *Is this to do with masturbation or sex?* She has only had sex once with Desmond. It was shit and hurt.

'I'm not clear what you mean by that at all,' her mother states.

'I'll elucidate. Such individuals nearly always come from unhappy backgrounds where there has been less affection than there might have been, and sometimes there is a frank family breakdown. How much this all applies to your situation, you alone can judge, Mrs Goldman.'

Lucia clenches her thighs together.

'Well, I don't think i-i-it does at all,' her mother replies with a wobble in her voice. 'There has been no breakdown here, apart from the crisis we are enduring at the minute.'

'Well,' Tim says clearing his throat. 'There has been a serious breakdown of communication between Lucia and her father. She has no contact with him at all at present.'

'I see. This could well be a contributory factor. A sudden breaking of contact can cause major psychic disturbances,' the same man continues. He sounds like he has a sweet trapped in the back of his throat and needs to cough. 'Indeed, how emotional energy of a sexual type can be transformed into psychic energy sufficient to produce physical manifestations like those you are experiencing is still quite obscure, as is so much of the psychic field. But, no matter what sceptics may say, I know these manifestations are quite real and not fraudulent.'

'Yes! They certainly are,' her mother says punching her armrest. 'Well, how do you advise we proceed, particularly with my daughter's current state of mind? I have had to take her out of school this last month, and she has GCSEs to complete.'

'I think your decision to remove Lucia from school at the minute is a fruitful one. You would be well advised to avoid psychic and spiritualistic groups,' the quieter man says. 'You should get counselling, both for your daughter and for your family, as that will be the only way through. There is a plethora of counsellors in Hampstead, but here is a number for the Westminster Pastoral Foundation, which will direct you along the appropriate channels.'

'Thank you,' her mother says. Her armchair creaks as she leans forwards to take the contact details. 'I'll get in touch with them.'

'As regards your daughter's immediate emotional needs, my advice would be to be as gentle as possible with her. Her psychological state seems acutely frail.'

Gentle?

'If the wrong kind of intervention were to happen, she could have a complete psychic breakdown.'

'I see,' her mum says, coughing. 'Well, I will get in touch with this foundation.'

'Things will settle down if you pursue this route. I've seen it happen before.'

'Have you?' her mother asks, with a squeaky voice.

'Oh, yes. You are not alone in experiencing poltergeist activity of this type. It is more common than people believe.'

'Right,' her mother sighs, 'that's at least some comfort to hear.'

Lucia can hear the relief in her mother's voice. Something in Lucia settles too. The explanation, 'malalignment of sexual energies', makes her feel less alone. This still doesn't make sense, but if there are other girls like her, who are going through a poltergeist experience, then she is not as weird as she thinks. As she listens to the men leave, a realisation washes over her that this *could* all change one day. It *could* all change, and one day she could be normal again.

*

She stands in the hall. The walls turn into the bars of an animal cage.

I am worthless.

The world looks empty to her. No one sees her or knows how she feels inside.

She would be better off on the moon.

These people are shit. Her wrists sweat. The wallpaper blurs. She feels trapped in this cage, with only a wheel to go around on. She feels dead, as she listens to the sound of her mum mumbling to herself and the freezer whirring.

Lucia walks into her brother's bedroom. She is her hamster Rosco: wild and untamed. She can roam where she chooses. She stands in the middle of the fireplace.

She pulls down her jeans and knickers, and crouches down. The nippy air coming through the ventilation slats feels cold against her naked buttocks. She pushes.

She excretes in the fireplace.

Lucia feels the heat beneath her as her shit lands.

She stands and looks at what she has done. There, a large, twisty turd; *her* twisty turd.

That's not mine. I didn't do that.

She did. She did do that.

Tears brim in her eyes. Lucia walks over to the window and looks at the world through the net curtain. It's too late. She's done it now.

The smell is more potent from afar. Her chest tightens. She cannot believe what she has just done. What compelled her to do that?

It wasn't me, she thinks.

Lucia walks out of the room. She shuts her door and waits.

*

'That is definitely a human shit,' Ben says. 'Lucia did that. Poltergeists don't crap in fireplaces.'

'Oh, don't be ridiculous,' her mum says. 'That's not human excreta.'

'Smell it! Someone has come in and dumped there.'

'Oh, come on, Ben,' Tim says with a smirk in his voice. 'She couldn't have done that!'

'Why? Why couldn't she have done that? It's not hard to pull your pants down and crap.'

Her mum bursts out into a hysterical laugh. It is a deep laugh that comes right from her tummy.

'I hope this isn't a new phase,' Tim says. 'That all we need, Harry Shittingtons.'

'Which one of us lucky ones is going to clear it up?' Ben asks.

Lucia sits behind her bedroom door, listening.

'Shall we draw straws?' Tim asks, and breaks out into a high-pitched cackle.

'Well, I'm not doing it,' Ben replies, and struts out.

'Here, I'll do it,' her mum says. 'Go and get me the rubber gloves and the dustpan.'

'Dustpan?' Tim shrieks. 'That's not meant for faeces. I'll get a carrier bag.'

'Ah, the stench,' her mum howls.

Tim runs to the kitchen and returns with rubber gloves and a carrier bag.

'Utterly vile, this is, cleaning up shit in my own home. Here take it, Tim, out of the flat. Get it out!'

Lucia hears the front door slam shut.

'Ben, will you bring me in a bucket of disinfectant and a scrubbing brush?' her mum calls. 'This fireplace needs a scrub.'

*

The phone rings.

Lucia is crouched on top of her brother's wardrobe with her underwear down. She is surrounded by the old carrier bags that live up there, which are full of unused coat hangers and unwanted clothes that no one can be bothered to take to the charity shop.

'Yes, speaking?' her mother says, in her exaggerated posh voice. Her mother closes the sitting-room door, so that Lucia cannot hear any more of the conversation. Ben and Tim are in the kitchen, imitating a friend, Bev Stanner, who dribbles and has a weird stare. It seems like ages that Lucia is poised on top of the wardrobe, crapping again. She thinks that she is bird now, surrounded by her nest of feathers, safe and cocooned from the rest of the world.

The sitting-room door flies open. 'Ben! Tim!' her mum calls, scampering into the kitchen. 'That was a lady from ITV. They want to make a documentary about us, and about the poltergeist.' Her mum's voice sounds jerky and energised.

'You're kidding?' Tim replies.

'No, I'm not. It was a female researcher, Florence Williams. She wants to meet to me to find o-o-o-out what has been going on. It's for a s-s-s-series about the paranormal.'

'What else did she say?' Ben asks.

'Just that she wants to meet me to get some more details on what has been happening.'

'How did she find out about us?'

'I don't know; maybe through Eugene Holtz.'

Lucia looks down at the floor. It's a long way down. She forgets how she got up here. The maroon carpet swirls around in her eyes. Her pulse pounds in her temples and her ears start to ring.

Did she hear that right? ITV want to make a programme about this?

CHAPTER THIRTY

LONDON, 1989

LUCIA IS SIXTEEN YEARS OLD

Lucia and her mother attended a posh tea with triangular sandwiches and baked scones with clotted cream at Claridge's yesterday. They met with Florence Williams, a documentary researcher from ITV, who interviewed them about the poltergeist activity. She invited the family to attend a televised panel discussion about the events in their home as part of a series called *Tales After Dark*.

Lucia sits on a kitchen stool.

She stares out of the window fiddling with a Duracell battery. The taste of curried haddock repeats in her mouth as the smell of burnt rice from today's lunch wafts over her. Her brothers and mother are in the sitting room, discussing the prospect of going on TV.

'No way am I doing it! It's completely exploitative and playing on our vulnerability,' Ben shouts.

There is a long silence.

'Not necessarily,' Tim mumbles. 'Not if you look at it from a different angle.'

'Fuck the angle!' You can't put Lucia through that. It will terrify her, completely expose us all and make things much worse.'

Lucia scratches her head as she listens. She is comforted by Ben's love and protection. It surprises her when he sticks up for her, because it reveals affection that he never expresses. He is right. It would terrify her, but, as she has gone this far, she has to go all the way.

'Honestly, Mum. It would be the worst thing you could do to put Lucia through that. All her school friends will see, which will expose her to bullying. I am not making a fool of myself and appearing on no TV show for no one!'

'Sh-sh-sh-she will be prote-te-te-tected, Ben. She will have a pseudonym and will be wearing a wig,' her mum replies in a hushed tone.

'The airing time is late anyway Ben,' Tim adds. 'It goes out at 11.00pm. That would limit the audience.'

'She was very nice, that researcher,' her Mum adds. 'Eugene would be there on the panel, as well as a well-known canon from Chichester Cathedral.'

'I don't give a toss who will be there!' Ben shouts. 'You really are off your rockers even contemplating this. It will completely undermine us and achieve nothing.'

Lucia bites into a banana, thinking about the fame this could bring her. She can see her name in glitzy lights – *the girl who had a poltergeist*. However, that rush of adrenalin soon turns to a thudding heartbeat about what this really means. She will be exposed to the nation and have to keep up this story. How will she do it?

'On the contrary, Ben,' Tim murmurs. 'Exposing our experience will help us'

'Help us? How?'

'Well,' Tim replies with a dip in his tone. 'If it's a series, we will presumably be part of a group of people who have had similar experiences. Maybe it will put the sceptics in their place.'

'I agree,' her Mum adds.

Lucia hears Ben's shin thud against the table as he stands.

'Well, if you two want to look like total fools, then do it, but don't come crying to me when it all backfires. You'll regret it,' Ben shouts and leaves.

The front door slams shut.

The poltergeist is who Lucia has become. Ginger is whom Lucia communicates through now. She wonders how she will look on television. They say her name would be 'Sophie'. Tim will be called 'Hugo'. They would both wear wigs and black glasses as a disguise.

She didn't see this coming at all.

*

Her mum waits in the green room.

Lucia follows Tim, Eugene and Canon Julian Walkley into the studio. The floor is blue. The walls are red. Five leather chairs are arranged in a semicircle, with a glass table in front of them with a jug of water and five glasses on it. There is a funny smell of Pritt Stick on set.

Lucia sits next to Tim. She is dressed in her burgundy crossover top and matching trousers. She is wearing a blonde, Marilyn Monroe style wig and dark glasses. Tim is in a black suit and tie. He too wears a wig of dark-brown hair, and shades. He looks like Dustin Hoffman in a bad mood.

Eugene Holtz sits at the end, in a satin suit and looking smug. Next to him is Canon Julian Walkley in his white collar and black robe. The canon has a quiet manner and small, brown eyes. He sits upright with his hands placed on his lap. Lucia trusts him. There is something he understands about her.

Paul Samms, the presenter, sits centre stage in his pinstripe suit and red tie. He has a North London accent and a swanky manner.

Lucia doesn't like him. She doesn't trust his smirk or the insincere look in his eyes.

Sweat trickles down her cleavage. Her wig pinches at the sides of her scalp. She does not know where to look, with so many cameras pointing at her from the studio floor.

The lights dim.

It is dark.

The sound of a beating drum echoes around them. It sounds like a heartbeat inside a womb.

A male voice shouts from behind camera two. 'Places please.' He counts down from ten to one. 'Lights!'

She can't feel her breathing or her pulse.

'Action!'

The amber lights shine. The drum sound fades.

Two cameras zoom up to Paul Samms, whose face is under a spotlight. He reads from an autocue. 'For the past twelve months, Sophie and her family have had their lives ruined by extreme poltergeist activity. It started back in April with pools of water appearing on the carpets. Manifestations have since ranged from beds flying around the flat to spontaneous fires erupting and Sophie herself levitating.' Camera one moves to the left. The camera man pulls the back lever and re positions it. 'We are joined today by Sophie herself, and her brother Hugo who has experienced the poltergeist activity first hand.' A third camera whizzes up to Tim, showing a stoic side shot of him. 'We are also joined by British paranormal investigator, Eugene Holtz, alongside Canon Julian Walkley, who is here to share his views on the paranormal. Welcome to you all.'

All three cameras roll backwards.

The lights shine so brightly, Lucia's cheeks burn.

'So, let's start with you Sophie. Tell us what's been happening?' Paul Samms asks.

She opens her mouth to speak, but her mouth is so dry her lips won't part. She leans forwards to take a sip of her water, but her hand trembles so much she dare not pick up the glass. 'It started with water,' she babbles.

'What, random pools of water?'

'Yes,' she replies, clenching her fist. 'Then patches of turpentine appeared on the beds and things started to move around the flat.'

'Like what?' Paul pouts at her with wide eyes.

She gets rushes of shivers up her arms. Her mind goes blank. Camera one creeps right up to her. She sees a triple reflection of her face in the lens. *Is this really happening?*

'It started with wellington boots moving around,' she replies. 'And then it developed into things like ashtrays, cans of food and eggs flying around, followed by heavy furniture.' She can hear the sound of herself speaking in a monotone gabble. 'Then these creepy messages started to appear on the walls, from Ginger.'

'And did that frighten you?'

She runs her tongue across the top of her teeth. Her mouth feels furry. 'Yes, it was creepy at first, but then we got used to it.'

Paul Samms picks up the messages and holds them up to camera one, like he is feeding a billy goat. Cameras two and three rush in and focus on the pages of writing.

'Here we can see some of the messages from Ginger,' he says, grinning. 'As you can see, the writing is undefined and squiggly.' He puts the papers down and turns to Lucia. All three cameras slide backwards. 'And then things escalated?' he prompts.

'Yes, things just went crazy,' she replies. 'Furniture was flying everywhere.'

'And you levitated into the air, is that right?' His ears rise up as he grins.

She looks down at the tiling on the floor. 'Yes, I did.' Her heartbeat is jumping, in spasms, through her top, and it feels like water is stuck in her ears. 'I woke up in a pool of boiling hot water. I don't know how I got there.'

'And have you been scared by all of this activity?'

'To begin with,' she replies, 'but we've got used to it now. It's become part of our lives.'

'OK,' Paul says, rubbing his hands together. 'Let's come to you, Hugo. So, you have been living in the flat whilst all this has been going on?'

Tim sits upright, with his feet parallel on the floor. 'Well, I came home from Malta three months into the activity, actually.'

'And have you experienced any of these manifestations first hand?' Paul asks.

'Yes; yes, I have.'

'Will you tell us about them?'

'Well,' Tim replies, coughing into his fist. 'There have been countless incidents to report. The most recent example was only three days ago, when we had a whole night of activity. It started at about 10.00pm, with very loud rapping coming from the hall. This was then followed by heavy objects flying into my room, hitting the wardrobe.'

'Like what?'

'Well, a dining-room chair came thrashing in and smashed the mirror on my wardrobe. Later that night, I experienced pins pricking in my feet and legs, and my duvet was being tugged off me.

'And was Sophie in the room with you?'

She scratches her arm.

'She was asleep in my room, but could not have possibly thrown any of the objects as we were both in bed when they came hurtling in.'

Paul holds his hand up to camera two. 'These are the pins that pricked Hugo that night.' Camera two focuses in on Paul's hand. 'They look like Czech pins,' Paul Samms says inquisitively. 'And have you never seen these before?'

'No,' Tim replies. 'None of us had seen them before.'

But Lucia had. They had belonged to Zema's granddad. Lucia had gone to stay with him during the summer holiday, at their home in Worthing-by-Sea. He gave them to her as a memento and she had kept them hidden at the bottom of her wicker basket.

'And this is a typical night of activity then, Hugo?' Paul asks.

'Fairly typical,' Tim replies. 'Things have peaked, most definitely, in the last two to three weeks.'

'And you think this is a real poltergeist?'

Tim brushes his finger across his lip. Camera one moves close to his face and then points at Lucia. It keeps looking at her for her reaction. She catches her reflection in the camera again. She does not recognise herself with blonde hair. Lucia notices a clock in the corner of the camera, racing down from sixty to one, and there is a snapping sound above, as the lights change direction.

'Well,' Tim replies. 'To begin with, I wasn't sure, but, eleven months on, we have all been transformed. What you think you believe in and what experience teaches you to believe in are often two very different things.' Tim cackles wisely as he speaks.

'So, you do believe in poltergeists?'

'Yes. I do now.'

'So, Eugene, you've been investigating poltergeists for over twenty years now. Is that correct?' Paul Samms asks.

'Yes,' Eugene replies, nodding. 'I have.' Eugene sits back in his chair. His shoulders broaden, and he rolls back his cuff. Lucia can tell that he loves the exposure. This is about his ego trip. 'I was very involved with Stella and her family during the Stanmore poltergeist case. I have also been involved with Sophie and her family.'

Even though Eugene is being questioned, camera one moves around Lucia. It's like a fly that won't go away, but at least she doesn't have to speak now.

She listens.

'So, Eugene, what have you actually witnessed at Sophie's house?'

Eugene clears his throat and loosens his tie. 'I have normally arrived after an episode of activity,' he replies in a thicker cockney accent than usual. 'I have, however, heard a lot of activity whilst speaking with Mrs Levinson, Sophie's mother, on the phone. I've seen the writing on the walls, and Sophie in a trance state. I hypnotised her one day after she had levitated.'

Paul Samms wears a patronising grin and purses his lips. 'But nothing has actually happened when you have physically been there?' he asks.

'Other than seeing Sophie in an altered state, no.'

'Did you witness events first hand during the Stanmore poltergeist?'

'Oh, yes; oh, yes,' Eugene replies, edging to the front of his seat. Lucia can see he is using this programme as airtime to show off about the Stanmore poltergeist. 'I saw Stella fly through the air on a number of occasions,' Eugene says. His front two teeth hit his lip when he speaks. 'I was also witness to eight different male voices coming through Stella in the course of a one-hour period. We had a reward open to anyone who could replicate those voices, and no one could.' He sits back and crosses his legs.

Paul Samms takes a sip of water. 'Do you think there is a similarity between these two poltergeist cases?'

Eugene clasps his fingers. 'I do, yes.' Lucia is relieved he has said that, as she is obviously not his favourite – Stella is. 'Poltergeist activity has a very similar quality across the board. They have their own personalities, but in both these instances they are male. Ginger is definitely a male spirit.'

'And it is your belief, is it Eugene, that poltergeists come from outside the person, and that the paranormal really does exist?'

Lucia's thumb bleeds from where she has picked her nail. The heat on her skin makes her feel queasy.

'Oh, without doubt,' Eugene replies. 'Psychokinetic activity is real, but can be triggered, most definitely, by psychic or emotional disturbance. This is why, in most cases, poltergeists hook onto teenagers, because of their inner turbulence.'

'Let's come to Canon Julian Walkley. Do you agree with Eugene?' Paul asks.

Two cameras rush towards the canon. The cameraman pulls back the lever and wheels the camera backwards.

Canon Julian Walkley takes his time to respond. He is a quiet man, understated, and different from Eugene. He looks directly into the camera. 'Psychological or psychic breakdown can often manifest itself in ways like this,' he replies, tapping his fingers on his knee. 'Poltergeists are not the only manifestations of psychic breakdown. Psychokinetic activity can be wide ranging,' he concludes.

'So, you don't think poltergeists come from outside of the person?'

'No, I don't.' His tone is soft. 'I think all paranormal activity is caused by psychic disturbance or a split inside.

I very much think poltergeists come from within and are part of a person. Our inner and outer worlds are inextricably linked.' He locks his fingers in the shape of a steeple. 'It is often when our inner and outer worlds become separated that psychokinetic activity occurs.'

A long discussion breaks out between Eugene and Julian Walkley about the different kinds of poltergeist activity. Eugene rants on for ages about his involvement in the Stanmore case, bragging about what he did to help Stella. Lucia watches. She is annoyed that Eugene is using this air time for self-publicity.

'And what do you think about this, Sophie?' Paul asks. 'Do you think this poltergeist is part of you?'

Lucia starts to speak, but falters, as images streak through her mind. They'll take her from here in handcuffs into one of those vans with black windows, and drive her to Holloway Prison. She'll have to wear a tracksuit with a yellow band around her waist. She'll be alone in her cell at night. After lights go out, she'll hear mad women wailing, and it will stink of boiled cabbage and yesterday's piss.

'Do you want me to repeat the question, Sophie?'

She sips some water. 'Yes, please.'

'Do you think this poltergeist is part of you?'

She looks at Canon Julian Walkley. He does not judge her.

'I've been told I am the epicentre of this activity,' she replies in a composed manner. 'So, yes, I guess this poltergeist is part of me.'

Paul Samms adjusts his earpiece. 'How does that feel, Sophie, to know that this poltergeist is part of you?'

She shrugs and wipes the sweat away from under her nose. 'Well, it's odd, but, like anything, in time you have to accept things as they are no matter how tough, so, yes, I have to accept it.'

The lights dim. Camera three homes in on Paul. 'Thank you to you all,' he says opening out his hands. 'This has been an interesting insight into poltergeist activity.' He turns to Lucia. 'Thank you, Sophie and Hugo, for sharing your experiences.' And then he gestures to Eugene. 'Thank you to Eugene Holtz and Canon Julian Walkley for your insights on the subject. Next week, we are looking at out-of-body experiences, as part of our look at the supernatural and things that go "bump" in the night. Thank you and good night.'

The lights fade.

The beating drum sounds.

Black out.

*

Tim and Lucia walk into the green room. There are TV screens on every wall.

Her mother sits on the sofa with her head in her hands. She looks up. 'Too terrible that was. B-B-B-Ben was right. It was an awful mistake.'

Lucia feels a thump in her chest.

'I don't think it was that bad,' Tim replies in an upbeat tone.

'It was,' her mother replies. 'They made a total mockery of us.'

CHAPTER
THIRTY-ONE

LONDON, 1990

LUCIA IS SEVENTEEN YEARS OLD

Lucia wakes. She wipes the crust away from under her eyes. The thumping in her chest has not stopped since the filming at ITV studios. Lucia has made a fool of herself. She has lied to the British public. Now it will be televised to the nation, and everyone will see her wearing that stupid, blonde wig, with that idiotic presenter smirking at her. How could things have gone this far?

Today is the start of a new life. She is going to stop this now.

Lucia thinks back to the help she received from Hans in Malvern. 'You can still navigate your own way, even in difficult circumstances.' Her mum is washing up in the kitchen. LBC blasts out from the sitting room. Only she can put an end to this. No amount of healers or ghostbusters can do it for her. She must take responsibility for her life.

Lucia bounces out of bed and opens her curtains. Sun streams in to her room. She throws on her Whistles top from yesterday and her jeans. There, on her desk is the **'HOPE'** card Brenda gave her and her green piece of jadeite. She puts them in her pocket. There is no need for breakfast or even to wash. She must do this now. She laces up her Timberland boots, puts on her jacket and walks out into the hall.

Her mother scuttles out in her nightdress. 'Where are you going?'

Lucia's mouth tastes fusty. 'I've got to go somewhere.'

'Where? It's only seven o'clock. You haven't even had any breakfast.'

'I'll have some when I get back.' She opens the door and runs down the stairs.

It's a crisp morning. Mr Abrahams walks past with his poodle, and waves. She starts to jog towards Primrose Hill. The breeze whistles in her ear. The early morning birdsong comforts her. Her lungs burn as her pace quickens, but she does not stop. She focuses on the sound of her boot slapping the pavement, and decides to head down to the canal.

This has gone too far now. It stops today.

Lucia races past her old primary school. The same climbing frame is still in the playground. The vision of Mrs Wallace blowing her whistle shouting, 'Get off of that wall,' comes back to her, as if it was yesterday. How did things go from playing hopscotch to this?

Her calf muscles tighten as she sprints up Primrose Hill. Lucia spits on the ground and grits her teeth. She is going to become someone different from now on.

She is out of breath and has a sharp pain below her ribs. She runs.

Feeling the stiffness in her legs, she focuses on her breathing and chants to herself as she sprints over the hill.

'I will stop this today. I will never do this again.

'I will stop this today. I will never do this again.

'I will stop this today. I will never do this again.'

She does believe she will stop, even though she cannot imagine what will life will be like afterwards. Lucia crosses the road and races over the bridge down to the canal path, and thinks about eating a thick slice of granary toast with marmite on when she gets home.

She stops opposite the Pirates Club where a line of canoes is chained up along the water's edge. Lucia locks her legs and holds onto her knees as she catches her breath. It is desolate along this canal path. '***KAZ LOVES DAVE***' is sprayed in red paint across the bridge, and a dead cat floats on the water. She gags. Fucking gross!

Her skin itches from the sting of the cold air. It is chilly, and it stinks of mould down here. A cyclist darts past; his wheels crunch on the gravel. There is no one else around. Anything could happen to her. She could be raped and dumped in the canal with the cat, and no one would know where she went, *and* on the day when she was turning her life around.

She looks left towards Camden Lock. There are people around if she needs help.

Lucia pulls her green stone from her pocket. She twists it around in the palm of her hand. *Ask it for guidance.* She brings it up to her lips and kisses it. 'This stops today,' she whispers. 'I am going to throw you away. I want you to help me to stop doing this.'

Lucia takes a deep breath and steps close to the edge.

She counts, 'One… two… three,' and throws the stone into the water.

It splashes.

A circle of ripples creeps outwards.

She looks for her stone, hoping it will resurface, but it doesn't. It has gone. Should she have done that?

Yes! She should. Her sinking stone represents the end of this episode and the beginning of something new. Her pulse pounds in her ears. What will she do now? Ginger, her poltergeist, has been part of her life for a year. She draws on that moment when Hans and Christopher lifted her in the air. She felt a real confidence then, that her life could be better.

Tears brim at the corners of her eyes. She will keep this secret forever. No one will ever know this was her and she will never do it again. She is *not* a poltergeist anymore.

Lucia jogs towards the park. She has a stitch, but she concentrates on the sound of the wind brushing in her ear and settles into her rhythm. As her speed increases, Lucia's worries wash over her.

The morning sun beams down on her forehead. It focuses her on right now, where everything is just OK. She feels free as she runs – untouchable. Sprinting over Primrose Hill, she chants aloud again, 'Today is a new start. I will never ever do this again. I have dreams that can be real. I can be happy.'

*

It is five days later.

She's got to… Just this one more time and then that will be it.

Lucia's blood jets with energy. The feeling throughout her body is so intense that the top of her head feels as though it is about to fly off. She shakes her legs to try to still this gush of electricity bursting through her, hoping it will pass.

It doesn't.

She walks to the kitchen. Lucia opens the kitchen drawer quietly, so there is no rattle of cutlery. She takes out the three teaspoons in the front compartment, and creeps back down the hallway.

She bends the spoons, one by one. That feels good!

Lucia kneels down and arranges them on the hall carpet in a circle. It doesn't look complete. What else can she do? She picks up the bowl of potpourri on the mirror table and tips the dried flowers onto the carpet in the middle of the spoons. She stands.

She looks at the circle of spoons with the flowers in the middle. It is decorative, like a manmade mandala. The sound of her mother is close. Whilst Lucia knows that she has let herself down, she feels that release wash over her. She has fed her craving.

This really is the last time.

She walks to her room.

*

It can't just end, she thinks. *What will people think? Why did the poltergeist just stop? There needs to be a conclusion. If it just stops, it will look odd.*

It is now one week since Lucia's relapse, when she left the three bent spoons in the hallway. She feels a need to round things off with a definite statement and then that will be it. She paces up and down her room, pulling her hair. What can she do to mark the end of this?

I know… I'll write something…

Getting a feeling like the one you get when you find the last piece to a jigsaw puzzle, Lucia grabs her pad of writing paper and a black pen. She kneels. She leans her pad on her *Beano* album and writes a letter to her mother.

As she writes, the frantic energy racing through her veins slows.

DEAR VALERIE,

MADMEN FLOAT ON STARS.

WELL, THIS YEAR IS COMING TO AN END! HAVE YOU COME TO ANY SORT OF CONCLUSION? OR NOT? YOUR DAUGHTER IS IN NEED OF LOVE YOU MUST LET HER OFF THAT LEAD THAT YOU HOLD; LET HER GO WHERE SHE WANTS TO GO.

CAN YOU NOT SEE OR ARE YOU BLIND? THESE LAST TWELVE MONTHS HAVE TAUGHT YOU NOTHING; YOU ARE STILL THE SAME.

YOUR CHILD IS FULLY GROWN, SO LET HER BE FULLY GROWN UP.

I'M NOT GOING TO CONTINUE MANIFESTING MYSELF; IT DOES NO GOOD. THESE LAST MONTHS, I HAVE NOT HARMED HER, BUT HAVE STRENGTHENED HER. I HAVE GIVEN HER LOVE, IN A FUNNY WAY. YOU DON'T TRUST HER LIKE I DO. I KNOW HER WELL; I AM PART OF HER. I POSSESS HER TO MAKE HER DO THE THINGS SHE DOES.

MR HOLTZ CAN'T GET RID OF ME, NO ONE CAN. I AM A SPIRIT AND WILL DIE WHEN SHE DIES. I WILL HIDE MYSELF NOW, AND LET YOU ALL

LIVE HAPPILY IN 1990 AND FROM THEN ON. BUT I WILL ALWAYS HELP LUCE, FOR I LOVE HER VERY MUCH, AND SHE LOVES ME. I'VE TRIED TO SET HER FREE, BUT NOW YOU MUST LET HER GO; SHE'S RESPONSIBLE AND VERY CAPABLE. LET LUCIA BE THE PERSON SHE WANTS TO BE!

LET HER GO.

SPACEMEN FLY AT NIGHT.

YOURS LOVINGLY,

GINGER

PS I SHALL NOW REVEAL MY NAME. MY NAME IS...

COLIN GOLDMAN.

I AM THE ANGER GIVEN OFF BY HIM.

Lucia rereads the letter. She does not know where these words have come from. They just flowed through her.

Tim washes up in the kitchen, listening to the radio. The volume is loud enough to drown out the sound of Lucia's footsteps.

She creeps down the hallway, letter in hand.

The sitting-room door is half open. Her mother stares blankly at the TV.

Lucia stands on her tiptoes and throws the letter over the top of the sitting-room door. It flutters down onto the carpet and lands by her mother's feet. She pelts back to her room, and positions herself behind her door.

'Good God! Tim! There's a letter from Ginger!'

Tim rushes into the sitting room. He knocks the wood carving off the wall by accident. It crashes to the floor.

'Look! It just flew in!' her mother shrieks.

'What does it say, Mum?'

'Well, it's hard to decipher. Look at the handwriting!'

'Here, give it to me. It's typical Ginger writing.' Tim snatches it.

Lucia listens to Tim reading the letter aloud to her mother. He sounds like a priest delivering a sermon to its congregation.

'Now you must let her go. Let her be the person she wants to be.'

She cannot identify these words as her own and cannot believe *she* wrote it. Well, she didn't, did she? Ginger, her poltergeist, wrote it.

Will her mother change and learn from this? Or will things stay the same?

'Well, that's a poignant letter,' Tim murmurs. 'Possibly Ginger's best one to date.'

Lucia sits on her bed and runs her fingers through her greasy hair.

'Very poignant,' her mother replies. 'It's hard to believe a poltergeist wrote this.'

Can this really be the end now? Can she find a way forward? She bites her fingernail.

She doesn't know, but it has to be.

If she gets the urge to do it again, she must do something else; go for a run or something – anything to re-channel this poltergeist energy.

It's almost impossible for Lucia to imagine not doing these strange things anymore, but she needs to find something new.

*

It is two months later.

It is a grey afternoon.

She feels that familiar energy pulsing through her veins. She sucks in her cheeks as she gets the urge to write a message on the wall or lob a brick through the window. She looks out at Dorney Towers in the grim light – it looks lonely.

Quick, it's time to split.

She rips off her clothes, puts on her tracksuit bottoms and Puma trainers, and races out of the door without saying goodbye.

She jogs past the Holiday Inn. Not knowing where she is headed excites her. She could go anywhere. Blood rushes to her cheeks. Cold air ripples through her hair. She feels that manic energy inside her body settle as her pace picks up. *This is behind you now. Come on!*

Sprinting down Avenue Road, she passes gated mansions and one Rolls Royce after another. There is something about this road that makes her feel unsafe, and musters thoughts in her mind of late-night burglaries. Being careful not to slip on the damp ground, she heads up Acacia Road towards St John's Wood, passing the chic deli and the Oxfam shop. Ah! The smell of woodland spice along here is medicinal.

Lucia's running is taking the place of her poltergeist. Every time she gets a compulsion, she runs for miles across London until the urge has gone. Lucia has joined an athletic club now, where she trains in track and cross-country three evenings a week.

She is making new friends and finding a new outlet. Lucia spends Sunday mornings with her trainer, Harry, doing long circuits across Hampstead Heath. She prefers the steady rhythm of cross-country running over the fast pace of track sprinting. She loves the stamina she is finding and the space it gives her to work through her thoughts. Harry has entered Lucia for several cross-country races, and she came third last week in an inter-borough run.

Her legs move without her. Her body feels so light, she can barely feel herself run.

She dashes past the crematorium where Grandpa Bert was burnt, opposite Lords Cricket Ground. Her strides get wider as she races towards Baker Street. No direction. No rules. She can run forever. The smoky smell of shish kebabs tickles her nose as she passes a Lebanese restaurant. The owner salutes.

The street lights come on, and an amber line of dots shine against a deepening blue sky.

This is Lucia's new beautiful.

CHAPTER THIRTY-TWO

LONDON, 1990

LUCIA IS SEVENTEEN YEARS OLD

It has been ten weeks since Lucia wrote the final letter from Ginger to her mum. She has not done another thing since, but she misses Ginger. Her life seems empty without her spirit friend. The flat has been redecorated. No more messages on the walls. Her room is now painted pale grey with a blue mount, with new wooden floorboards and a grey futon, the one she wanted from Habitat. No one would think a poltergeist had resided here. Everything looks just fine and dandy: normal.

Lucia sits on her sofa bed and listens to her mum talking on the phone. Her inner world is a sword fight of thoughts brandished against one another. *I haven't done enough revision. I'm going to fail my GCSEs and won't be able to get a job.* She wants to creep out and lob an egg along the hallway. The itch eats away at her like a swathe of carpenter ants gnawing through an apple. What does life mean now Ginger has gone? She pulls out the crumpled piece of paper from under her pillow with her list of affirmations on: 'I can navigate my own way even in difficult circumstances.'

One more time and that would be it? *No!* she thinks. *I am not a poltergeist. I am a person.* Lucia throws her swimming costume into a bag, along with her goggles and a towel, which is still damp from yesterday.

She bursts out of her room, opens the front door and jogs to Winchester Road and through the square to the swimming pool. She pays the cashier her £1.00 entry fee and sprints down to the changing rooms, which are filthy and packed with a group of school kids changing. She notices how her breasts have grown as she pulls her swimming costume up and over her neck. They feel more swollen, but her legs are still stick thin.

Lucia scrunches up her feet as she walks over balls of hair. A wave of self doubt creeps in. *I'm useless. Nothing I ever do works out. I'll never be anybody.* The stench of chlorine sticks in her throat. A lifeguard with huge biceps sits on a high platform and plays with his wristwatch. Children splash and jump on floats in the shallow end, and a row of kids with wet hair sit on the spectator seats eating Curly Wurlys. The nippy air brings up goosebumps on her arms. She shivers.

The Adelaide pool has three lanes. She stands at the head of the fast lane. This is where she stood when she won her race in the swimming gala at primary school. She chanted, 'Adrian Moorhouse,' to herself that day as she thrashed down the pool on her back.

Lucia bends her knees, pulls her goggles over her eyes and notices the lifeguard look at her. She coyly brings her hand to her neck and stares back. He winks.

The sounds of screaming kids wash over her.

She focuses on the blue lines at the bottom of the pool, which is a place she knows she can swim down to and hear no noise. Lucia swings her arms back and forth, gathering momentum. She rises onto her tiptoes and dives into the pool, her arms a sleek arrow, as she gracefully hits the water. The cold splash on her skin is bliss. Her thoughts stop. Lucia comes up for air and pulls back the water with her arms, gliding past the line of spectators.

Her ears pop as she increases her speed. She feels the strength in her arms as they pull through the water; her legs move in sync like a frog. At the shallow end, she does a somersault under water, kicks off from the side and finds her rhythm in her steady breathing. Her energy grows as she heaves through the water.

The freezing water lifts that deadening energy stuck in her head.

After another length, her negative thoughts creep back: her father hasn't phoned for nine months, the dread of her mum bored at home and her pending GCSEs, which she is going to fail. Turning onto her back, she kicks her legs as fast as she can and stretches out her arms, feeling the grace with which they rotate down and through the water. Focusing on the rows of orange lights on the ceiling, she affirms positive things to herself: *I do have a future. I can be happy. I don't need a dad.* She hears the muffled sound of laughter. Her lungs start to expand, as she pounds down the pool doing front crawl. Lucia concentrates on the sound of her hand slapping the water, as her head tilts to the side to take in gasps of air. No one can get her here.

She can swim.

She has control.

Lucia stops and coughs up a stream of mucous. She holds the bar at the side of the pool and brings her knees up to her chest, whilst catching her breath. She looks out of the long windows, and sees the bright-green trees and blue sky.

The lifeguard blows his whistle at a boy dive bombing into the water, and shakes his head.

'Not allowed in here,' he hails.

Lucia has the energy for five more lengths. She will push on until she tires. The water is one place where she has a break from her self-defeating thoughts. She takes her time, now coasting along in breaststroke, taking in the action of the pool. The feeling of tears trapped behind her eyebrows loosens and that deadening energy that weighs her down starts to lift.

After seven more lengths, she climbs up the steps. Water falls from her costume and splats on the floor. She looks back at the lifeguard. He waves. She walks back to the changing rooms, which is now less crowded, and looks at her blue lips and pale skin in the mirror.

On her way through the foyer, she buys a bag of penny sweets and browses the notice board for diving classes. She has better attention and is able to take in the outside world now after her swim. She may try the beginners class on Tuesday evenings. She has always wanted to do back flips into the water, like her cousin, Katie.

The cool air hits her as the doors slide open. Lucia puts on her cardigan and smells the chlorine on her skin. She sits on the bench outside the community centre and bites into a sour cola bottle. She enjoys the feeling of being part of the world without all that fear. It has gone, for now.

A lady walks past pushing a pram. Lucia imagines her name is Isabel, who is a housewife from Hampstead, and she watches her talking to her baby, who gargles and points to the sky. She sucks on a fireball, and sees how long she can keep it in her mouth before it gets too hot. Just about to bite into it, she sees Mary and her brother, Sam, cruising towards her. She has known them since year two in primary school.

'Hi Lucia,' Mary calls.

Lucia tenses. Her peace has been interrupted. 'Hi,' she replies.

They sit next to her. Mary offers her a crisp. 'Do you want to come and watch the football match?' Mary asks.

'What, now?'

'Yeah, go on; it will be a laugh.'

Lucia realises her mum will be worrying about her. She's been gone over an hour. 'Yeah, all right,' she replies. 'I just need to call my mum.'

Lucia leaves her bag with Mary and runs up the stairs to the phone box. She slides in her last ten pence, dials and waits for it to ring. Her heart thunders. She doesn't know what mood her mum will be in.

'Hello,' her mother croaks.

'Hi Mum, it's me.'

'Lu-Lu-Lucia, where on earth are you? I've been worried sick.'

'I've been swimming.'

'You didn't say wh-wh-where yo-yo-you were going.'

'Sorry. Look, I'm fine. I'm going to watch a football match. I'll be back later.'

'Is-is-is-is everything all right?'

'Yes, Mum, it's fine.'

'Has anything happened?'

'What do you mean?'

'You know, wi-wi-wi-with Ginger?'

'No, don't be daft. Look, I'll be back in an hour.'

The pips beep.

'I'm making oxtail for supper…'

'OK, Mum.'

She hears a click and then the dial tone. Lucia hates being cut off from her mum like that. What if her mum dies suddenly? That would have been her last goodbye. Lucia has the urge to call her back, but she pushes the worry away and goes back outside, where Mary and Sam are dribbling a football back and forth.

'Are you coming, Luce?' Mary asks.

'Yeah, I am,' Lucia replies, jumping down the stairs.

As they walk towards the football pitch, Lucia feels the lightness she felt when she came out of the pool slip away. The need in her mother's voice has clawed away her calm.

Her anxiety edges back in. She only has one hour of freedom left.

Then she remembers that diving class on Tuesday night *and* her cross-country race in Ruislip on Saturday. She will be running then, and she *will* find that quiet inside again.

*

The bus is packed with kids from the Jewish Free School. It pulls up at the stop by the church. She jumps off and feels a stabbing pain in her stomach. Today is Lucia's first GCSE exam. It's history. She becomes dizzy and sees red stars in her vision. She sits on the wall in front of the hedge and takes deep breaths. Her tummy churns. Pools of saliva gather under her tongue. Lucia knows she is about to vomit, so she stands and turns away from the road. She bends over and gags. She swallows over and over to stop herself from being sick, but retches and burps, spurting out a wash of yellow liquid with peas in it.

'Lucia!'

She feels a gentle hand on her back. Lucia looks up. It is Tammy and Philomena from class 5M. She doesn't know them very well, only from seeing them around. They're the fifth-year beauties.

'Oh my God, are you OK?' Tammy asks.

Lucia wipes her mouth with her sleeve. 'I've just chucked up.'

They sit her on the wall. 'Here, I'll go to the garage and get you some water,' Tammy says and runs off, whilst Philomena sits with her arm around Lucia.

'Have you revised?' Philomena asks.

'Yeah,' Lucia replies. 'I was up cramming until 2.00am.'

'You shouldn't push so hard. It's only school.'

Lucia sips the water Tammy brings her and sucks on a Trebor mint, refreshing the taste in her mouth. The girls help Lucia up and walk with her to the school gates. A long line of girls wait outside the assembly hall.

'Thanks, guys,' Lucia says, and goes back outside.

Lucia paces up and down, taking in big lungfuls of cold air. She feels her pulse racing in her neck and tells herself she will *not* fail. She sees the assembly doors open and people filing in one by one. As she nears the hall, Ms McKenzie, her class teacher, approaches her.

'Miss, I've just thrown up,' Lucia moans. 'I don't feel well.'

'Yes, I've heard, Lucia,' Ms McKenzie replies. 'I'll sit you next to where I am invigilating, and if you feel unwell at any point, just let me know, OK?'

Lucia nods, and walks with her teacher into the hall. She sits at a desk next to the stage and bites on another mint. She takes out her fountain pen and Tippex from her pencil case and looks up at the clock. *You're useless. You'll never be anybody.* She sees her mother's venomous eyes, as images flash back, of her, trapped in her bedroom, being beaten by her mum.

Her shoulders shudder.

'Turn over your sheets, please, and write your name and candidate number,' the deputy headmaster says calmly.

Lucia turns over her exam paper, and writes '**5162**' in the left-hand box. *'You rotten child.'* A tear drops from her eye and lands on her paper, smudging the number '**5**'. She brushes her face with her hand and glances up at Ms McKenzie, who sticks her thumb up at Lucia and blinks deliberately at her. She understands Lucia's problems, as it was Ms McKenzie her mother came to see when Lucia had to take time off school during her trances. 'Do your best,' her teacher mouths. 'Trust yourself.'

'You have 1 hour 45 minutes to complete this exam,' Mr Daley says. 'If, at any point, you need the toilet, please raise your hand, and an invigilator will assist you out. You may begin.'

Lucia looks down at her paper. *'The maximum mark for this section is 64'* it says. She reads through the first question. She bites the inside of her cheek hard. She doesn't understand it. It asks whether aid from USA enabled the Weimar Republic to recover after 1923. But she does know a lot about Germany. She turns to the next page and reads the other question option: *'It was the economic Depression that enabled Hitler to become chancellor of Germany in January 1923. How far do you agree with this interpretation of the importance of the Depression in bringing the Nazis to power?'*

She knows this! She practised this question last night. Lucia rolls up her sleeves. She takes the lid off her pen and taps it on the table, staring at Ms McKenzie's sparkling white Reeboks.

Like lightning bolting through her, energy sears through her arms, and her hands start to sweat. *'The interpretation is valid up to a point'* she writes. Her fingers tingle as her hand brushes across the page, and her thoughts tumble to the forefront of her mind. *'Hitler was able to exploit the effects of the Depression and his popularity soared as a consequence.'* Lucia gets lost in her writing. *'The Depression made people willing to listen to*

Hitler's ideas. However, it was the intrigues of President Von Hindenburg and Von Papen that directly led to Hitler's appointment.'

Her hand aches. She bends back her fingers and hears her knuckles crack. She takes a sip of cold water and looks back at Minnie Shultz, who wears a red bow in her hair and has a mascot on her desk. Minnie will get straight A's. Lucia turns to the next section, which is worth thirty-six marks. This is easier, studying different sources and saying what they suggest about Nazi attitudes to women. Lucia reads the snippets and confidently writes her answer.

She does know the answers, she does…

'You have ten minutes left,' Mr Daley says, standing.

Lucia gazes out into the courtyard and watches the spitting rain dropping into the fountain. She gazes at the statue of Francis Mary Buss, their school founder, and feels a tingling buzz settle over her body. She is happy with the answers that she has written.

Lucia finishes the last question about German society under the Nazis, and then rereads her paper, before putting her pen down.

'That is time. Please stop writing,' Mr Daley says.

Ms McKenzie winks at her. Lucia sits back as the invigilators collect the exam papers. She puts on her bomber jacket and slings her bag over her shoulder. As she walks out, Fanny taps her on the shoulder. 'Did you do OK, Lucia?

'I did it!' Lucia shouts, punching the air.

Fanny throws her arms around Lucia. 'Well done, girl!' she says, slapping her back. 'Do you want to come out for some lunch?'

'Yeah, I will,' Lucia replies, following Fanny and her tribe of beautiful babes up the steps.

She did it! She isn't as confident about Latin on Tuesday, but she got though today. The poltergeist experts said she may need to defer her exams because of the activity, but, with the help of her running and swimming, she is pulling through.

Lucia walks with the girls up Camden Road towards Cantelowes Park, smiling.

They told her she wouldn't do it, but she just did.

She's pulling through…

CHAPTER THIRTY-THREE

LONDON, 1990

LUCIA IS SEVENTEEN YEARS OLD

Today is Lucia's fifth cross-country race this season. As she walks out of Ruislip station, Lucia feels that Sunday loneliness exaggerated by the busy dual carriageway and all of the shops being shut. She sees the corner shop is open, so goes in to buy a mint Aero and a carton of Ribena for after her race.

Lucia follows signs to the 'National Women's Race', and walks along a quiet street. The air is frosty, and the ground is slippery, covered in yellow leaves, so she puts on her spikes early. She approaches an open, green area where crowds gather. Lucia feels a lump appear in her throat. She needs to do well today. She came tenth last time, and that isn't good enough to qualify for the championships this summer.

Over by the Nestlé marquee, Lucia sees her running buddy, Sally doing squats with their trainer, Harry. She changes into her racing gear, pins her number across her vest and saunters over to them. Lucia begins doing stretches before their pep talk with Harry.

'I feel knackered already,' Sally says, pulling a stretch band across her foot.

'Me too,' Lucia agrees. 'I've had no sleep.'

Raising her knee up to her groin, Lucia gets flashbacks of her mum howling in pain last night. Her mother had three of her headaches and was pacing around the flat, banging her head on walls, until 5.00am. The guilt eats away at her. She cowers and walks away towards an oak tree, taking deep breaths.

'OK, girls,' Harry says, blowing into his hands. 'Right, Sally, you need to focus and stay focused, and, Lucia, remember to keep you pace steady for the first couple of miles. Find your rhythm, and nice and easy does it. You pick up speed half way.'

Sally and Lucia walk towards the start line, where hundreds of girls gather. She takes a last sip from her water bottle and punches the air, telling her thoughts to go away. This is her day, her race. She can worry about her mum's pain after, but right now she must focus. She closes her eyes to erase the pictures of her agonised mum, and gives her peroneal muscle one last stretch. No matter how hard she tries, she still hears her mother's piercing scream echoing down her eardrums, 'Lu-cccc-iiiii-aaaaaaaa!'

She swallows and slips through the crowd to the front. Sally is on her right side and a six-foot girl towers over her on the left, but it's not about height. It's about stamina. Lucia remembers her first ever race, where she learnt to push through the first wave of exhaustion, after which a new wave of energy arrives. Scanning the line of Adidas spikes with her eyes, she looks ahead at the open space in front. She can do this…

'Take your marks…' a uniformed man says into the tannoy. 'Get set…'

She lurches.

'Go.'

A horn blasts. The crowd surge forwards. Lucia allows a stream of girls to pass her and jogs at a steady pace behind the group up front. Mud splashes over her legs and the chilling breeze washes over her. Quickly, her worries dissolve, as she uses her arms to pull herself up the first hill on the course. The freezing air she inhales feels like ice cream in her lungs, but the more she runs, the more she gets used to the cold burn on her skin.

She brings her knees up higher as she hastens her jog. She must not lose sight of the core group up front. She'll dribble behind and take them over mid-way. Her calf muscles stiffen as she hauls herself up the first hill. It's a long stint upward, and a thick fog lingers.

Now, steaming down the other side, she spreads out her arms and lets her legs move with no effort. Free, she feels that beautiful wind blow under her vest. Intoxicated by this icy air, Lucia treasures this free-wheel downwards.

A trickle of runners cruise past her, but she lets them pass. Now on even ground, she slows to catch her breath and push through her creeping fatigue. She must keep going. If she stops, it will be harder to start again.

Lucia follows a single file of girls through a muddy trail in the woods, where the air smells orangey. Her ankle buckles as she runs over a ditch. It feels like a sprain, but she carries on. Images of her mum, bent over in agony, creep back, but she grits her teeth and spits on the ground. *Fuck off. This is my time.*

Her pace speeds up.

She runs through her thoughts until she brings herself to a place where there is nothing except the sensation of her breath. Out of the woods, she follows the course around a sharp bend and on through a field with a lake in the middle. Sally has trailed behind, but the two girls alongside her, numbers fifty-two and thirty-one, help keep her tempo steady. As she runs, her eyes settle on a white swan gliding on the water and a robin hopping about near a silver birch.

Lucia finds solace for a moment. She feels at one with this wide, open parkland, and thinks about how different these trees will look in six months' time, when they are in bloom. Catching sight of another hill ahead, she changes gear and finds a swell of new energy as the gradient steepens. She runs past a table with bottles of water on, and picks one up; she swigs it as she runs.

Muddy, freezing, she is fully in the present, lost in her speed.

The circuit twice passes through a forest in a figure of eight. Lucia runs with little sensation in her legs. Her skin is anaesthetised by the freezing air. Questions come to mind, again, about Ginger and the chaos that she caused, but the rushing breeze and the friction of her spikes beating the grass wash away her questions. That's over. Her movement is now her control. Running through this woodland is all that counts.

This is her now.

The course steers around a playground and then onto open road. The surface changing to concrete hurts her foot, but she becomes accustomed to its hollow feel and keeps her eyes in front. This last bit seems to go on forever, but the chinking sound of her spike hitting the gravel gives her something to focus on, as her stamina wavers. After ten minutes of straight road, the circuit leads them through a thicket and back onto open fields.

The heavy fog has lifted. Now only two girls are in front of her: number twenty-two with the orange-and-black vest, and the lanky woman who started off next to her. Finding the last of her reserves, she clenches her jaw and sprints. The veins in her face swell. Letting out a heaving sound as she runs, she catches the girls up and sprints alongside them.

The end is in sight.

With wind lashing in her ears, she overtakes both women, and a force comes through her that she did not know she had. She runs alone into the empty green in front, hearing only the sound of her grating breath. There are no runners in front of her; she can now see the black-and-white flags at the finish line.

Crowds cheer and clap.

She drives her arms through the air with each stride.

Their cheers amplify.

One more stomp, a leap…

Her foot hits the black line.

She's done it. She's won.

Lucia collapses onto the tarpaulin, presses her knees up to her chest and feels her burning cheeks. She has no breath.

A volunteer rushes up to Lucia and wraps her in a black bin liner for insulation. 'Well done, you got first place – gold.'

Lucia rolls over onto her side to ease her stitch. She reaches for a bottle of water, and listens to the shrieking crowds, as the other racers come through the finish line.

*

Her mum and brothers are getting used to life after the poltergeist, although they are still on edge, and jump at any creak or bump, suspecting Ginger is back. Ben still lives in his flat in Kentish Town and is directing plays. Tim continues to teach English language and is still staying at the flat, which helps pacify Lucia and her mother's relationship.

They have been attending family therapy once a week for the last month.

Lucia hates the sessions because Seth, their therapist, is against her.

It's in a dilapidated, three-storey building, opposite the White Rose pub, just off Portobello Road. It is a small, carpeted room, with five comfy chairs positioned in a circle and a small window. It smells of old newspapers. Seth Price, their therapist, wears his usual shabby shirt, blue tie and trousers. He has boils on his neck; messy, grey hair; and looks like a schoolmaster who needs to retire.

Tim is in his smart blazer, and Ben is slouched in his 501s and bomber jacket. They both sit slightly apart from Lucia and her mother.

'So, how have things been this week?' Seth asks.

'Well, calmer,' her mother replies. 'Th-th-th-things are still quiet. There has been no further activity, poltergeist wise, but my headaches ha-ha-have been very bad this week.'

'I'm sorry to hear that,' Seth replies. There is a long silence. Seth taps his pencil against his knee. 'How do you all feel about your mother's headaches?' he asks.

'Well,' Tim sighs and gazes up at the ceiling. 'They seem to have got more frequent since the poltergeist activity has ended, strangely enough.'

'Is this accurate, Mrs Goldman?'

'Yes. Yes, it is.'

Lucia looks down.

'I think they are to do with her unhappiness,' Ben says.

'They are cluster headaches!' her mum shrieks. 'Many people my age have them for all kinds of reasons.'

'And Lucia?' Seth probes.

Lucia scratches her knee. 'I hate seeing her in so much pain. I hate that I can't help her.'

'Do you feel responsible for your mum's pain?' Seth asks.

'Yes,' Lucia replies, plainly. 'I do.'

'It does seem poignant that you say they have worsened since the psychic activity ended,' Seth comments. 'Do you see any pattern here at all?'

No one answers.

'And have you done anything about seeking new employment, Mrs Goldman?' Seth asks, as he slides his wedding ring off and then back on his finger.

'No. No, I haven't,' her mum replies.

'See, this is the problem and, I think, the root of her

headaches,' Ben interrupts. 'Mum won't take responsibility for her life and make any changes.'

'That's ever so accusatory,' Seth replies. 'Is this the usual tone of your dynamic?

'Yes. Yes, it is,' her mum replies.

'That's not entirely true,' Tim adds, straightening his tie. 'I wouldn't say Ben is accusatory. His observations are certainly correct at times.'

Lucia picks at the stitching on her seat and stares at Seth's weathered hands. She guesses he must be around sixty-two and is married to an old-fashioned woman, who bakes bread and listens to Radio 4.

It goes quiet again. A milk float passes by outside, breaking the silence. Lucia thinks how strange it is that a milkman is working at 5.30pm.

Seth squints and then writes notes in his file. 'It seems you all gang up on your mother a lot and blame her for everything. Would that be a fair assessment?'

'Not at all,' Ben replies, firmly. 'It's the other way round. She blames us for her problems.'

'Mrs Goldman?'

Her mother crosses her legs and folds her arms. 'Well, at times, I fe-fe-fe-feel they do, yes, but not all of the time; certainly not.'

'Do you get any time to yourself, Mrs Goldman?' Seth asks, looking directly at her.

'Well, yes; yes, I do in the afternoons, after work. And I did go to the theatre, but less so recently.'

'It seems that, from where I am sitting, you still do a lot for them all and still relate to them as children. Would I be right?'

Lucia catches Ben's attention. He raises one eyebrow and smiles. It's like this every week, with Seth taking her mum's side.

'Well, they are my children!' her mother's voice quivers.

'But, your sons are adults now, and your daughter is seventeen.'

'But she still needs me,' her mother asserts. 'She's been very frail.'

'True,' he agrees, 'but the more you do for yourself, the better your dynamic will be with your daughter. She will feel less responsible for you if you are leading a fuller life.'

The session continues for another half hour, with Seth giving her mum all of the attention. Tim opens up at the end about the love he feels for his mother, which he never expresses, and the gratitude he feels for what she did for him as a child. Seth also recommends that Lucia has therapy alone, with an adolescent therapist, to deal with her anger.

After their session, the family go for their debrief cuppa at the coffee shop next to Notting Hill Tube station. The song, 'Always On My Mind,' by The Pet Shop Boys is playing on the radio, and the sounds of hissing steam and clattering plates resound throughout the cafe.

Her mother orders a pot of tea with assorted biscuits. 'Well, that wasn't too bad, I suppose,' her mother sighs, tucking in her chair.

'He was very confrontational today, I thought,' Ben replies.

'Yes, I agree,' Tim adds. 'He was. His suggestions are good though, about new employment, eh, Mum?'

There is a silence between them.

'I don't know. I'm not sure what the point is, to be honest.'

'Well, what's the point of us all coming, if you won't make any changes? This is supposed to be about us moving forwards. You've got to do your bit too,' Ben snaps and dunks his custard cream into his tea. 'Seth's right. It is time you got out of that place. You'd be much happier somewhere else, Mum.'

'Well, where?'

'Anywhere. There'll be loads of receptionist jobs in schools or hospitals. Anything would be better than working for that monster. You *do* have choice, Mum.'

Her mother clicks a sweetener into her tea. 'I'll have a look in the *Ham & High* tomorrow and see what's in there.'

'That would be a good idea,' Tim mumbles.

Lucia counts the number of dots on her digestive biscuit. The walls feel like they are closing in on her. 'Mum, will you take my bag home with you in the car?' she asks, standing.

'Wh-wh-wh-why? Where are you go-go-going?'

'I'm going to run home. I need to run,' she says, taking off her jacket.

'Run home? It's miles. Don't be ridiculous child!'

'I'm not being ridiculous. It will be good practice.'

'Nonsense this ru-ru-running thing is. It's obsessive.'

'Don't be so critical of her, Mum! If she wants to run home, let her.' Ben shouts. 'You go, Luce.'

Lucia pushes the chair in front forwards and squeezes through without saying goodbye. The misty air outside is a relief. She looks left and then right, but she hasn't a clue which is the way home, so she runs past the Tube station towards Westbourne Grove.

Lucia listens to the heavy flow of traffic passing. As she settles into her moving rhythm, the dull pain in her head fades and the feeling of being trapped dissipates.

One day, she will be an adult, and free from all of this. She won't need to go to these therapy sessions to justify herself. She will have her own life, and she will be able to make all her own decisions.

TWO
YEARS
LATER...

CHAPTER THIRTY-FOUR
LONDON, 1992
LUCIA IS NINETEEN YEARS OLD

The waiting room is shabby. Plastic chairs are lined up against a peeling wall, and a stack of comics balances on a table in the corner. A plastic toy box sits next to them, with a naked Barbie doll sticking out and an Incredible Hulk with no head on. A rocking horse with a grey mane stands in the middle of the room.

Lucia waits.

Wearing her ripped 501s and her brother's 'King Kong Lives' bomber jacket, she wipes away the sweat above her top lip and then sips her Vimto.

A steady clunk echoes down the stairs. Lucia glances up and watches a chunky pair of legs in heels descend. She rubs her trouser leg back and forth, and looks up.

'Are you Lucia Goldman?'

'Yes, that's me.'

She stands.

'I'm Maggie. Please follow me.'

Lucia follows Maggie down the stairs to the basement. She doesn't understand why Maggie looks so emotionless: psychotherapists are supposed to be feeling people. Maggie is funny looking – with a chubby face, geeky specs, and dressed in a conservative blouse and skirt.

The hallway smells like a school, with that hint of disinfectant. Maggie leads Lucia into a bare room. Two orange-plastic chairs sit at a diagonal to one another and a wall clock ticks, with every second seeming hours later than the last.

Lucia sits.

She tucks her legs under the chair seat and looks down at the floor.

The bars outside the window are prison like.

Fuck, these seconds are long.

No one speaks.

At 4.07pm…

Lucia grips the metal chair legs and clenches them tight.

4.08pm…

She's got swollen ankles.

4.12pm…

Maggie coughs.

Lucia kicks the chair leg.

4.14pm…

She looks like a primary school teacher.

4.16pm…

I bet she's frigid.

4.20pm…

'Why are you staring at me like that?' Lucia asks.

'How am I staring at you, Lucia?'

'You look all stern. It's creeping me out.'

'I am holding the space for you, Lucia. This time is about you, not me,' Maggie says with a smirk that pisses Lucia off. It is as if she knows Lucia better than she knows herself.

'Is it?' Lucia replies.

4.25pm…

Maggie sits back and folds her arms.

Silly cow.

4.27pm…

What does she care about me anyway?

4.30pm…

Lucia looks out of the window and watches people's legs march past.

4.33pm…

It smells of mothballs in here.

4.35pm…

The street lights come on. An amber glow shines down on the pavement outside.

4.36pm…

'Are you angry with me?' Lucia asks.

'No, I'm not angry with you, Lucia.'

4.40pm…

Lucia winds her foot around the chair leg and slides her hands under her bum. What would happen if she told her the truth?

4.42pm…

'I am picking up a lot of hostility from you, Lucia,' Maggie says, pouting.

Lucia winds her jean thread around her finger. 'I don't know if I trust you.'

'Why is that, Lucia?'

Lucia looks down at the floor. 'I don't know. You're kind of unfriendly.'

4.44pm…

The radiator hisses. Lucia feels heat shoot to her shoulders.

4.45pm…

'Sorry,' Lucia says, 'I don't mean to be rude, but it's kind of weird sitting here in silence with you. What do you know about me anyway?'

'I know very little, but I am wondering how much you know about *yourself*, Lucia?'

'What do you mean?'

'Do you like yourself, Lucia?'

'What kind of question is that? No, not really, but who fucking does?'

'I ask because you come across as very hostile. I wonder if this anger is perhaps misplaced and you turn it in on yourself unnecessarily?'

'I dunno, maybe,' Lucia shrugs. 'How would I know? Everyone around me is so fucking angry. I don't know the difference. It's all anger.'

Maggie sighs and shows that wry grin of hers. 'That's very insightful of you, Lucia. Often when there is little separation or poor boundaries in relationships, it can be confusing to know what is our own emotion and what is not.'

4.48pm…

It grows dark outside.

Lucia brushes her boot across the floor and takes her hands away from under her bum. 'I blame myself for everyone's misery,' she says.

'Why?' Maggie asks.

'I just feel like everything is my fault.'

'But it isn't,' Maggie consoles, 'Adults are responsible for their own destinies.' Nothing moves when Maggie speaks, except her lips.

'Yeah, but I feel my Mum's unhappiness is my problem. I feel as if I am not allowed to be happy if she is not.'

'That's not very fair,' says Maggie.

'Well, life isn't fair is it?' Lucia replies.

There is a long silence. The second hand on the clock sounds even louder.

'You don't have to walk around with all of this anger, Lucia, not if it is not yours.'

Lucia presses her tongue against the inside of her cheek. 'Where do you suggest I deposit it? Any skips around?'

'Perhaps you can start by being kinder to yourself, by not being so very hard. You don't deserve punishing. You have done nothing wrong.'

'I have actually.'

Lucia looks up at Maggie for the first time.

4.50pm…

'That's our time, Lucia.'

'That went quickly,' Lucia says, 'I thought our session was one hour.'

'No,' Maggie says, standing. 'It's Freud's fifty minutes. Well done, though; you did very well today.'

'Shall I come back next week?'

'Yes,' Maggie says, straightening her skirt, 'same time each week.'

Lucia follows Maggie back up the windy stairway to the reception desk, where a pimply lady slides the glass window to the left.

'Same time, please,' Lucia says, watching the lady pencil her name into the diary. Lucia opens the front door and is hit by a blast of cold evening air.

Lucia nestles her chin into her scarf and strides down Lancaster Road. She passes the fruit and veg man, who winks at her and throws her a satsuma. She catches it and smiles, thinking how pretty the fairy lights look around his stall.

Ladbroke Grove is hectic as rush hour begins. Lucia does not feel ready to head back home yet. The circle line is shit at this time.

She walks into Mark's Joint, a greasy spoon next to the Tube station, where she orders a fried-egg butty and milky coffee. The cafe is busy. Lucia sits next to two middle-aged men, who are talking about their betting habits. Lucia laughs at their conversation, whilst watching people pass by. Her guard is down and that familiar knot in her stomach has gone away for now.

Sipping her coffee, Lucia feels more relaxed after her session with Maggie. She feels for a moment, for *just* one moment, that she has permission to be part of this world without apology.

*

Lucia has been out shopping in Camden Lock with Tiffany. Walking down King Henry's Road, she sees her mother pacing up and down in her slippers. She immediately thinks someone has died.

'Mum what are you doing?' she calls from several metres away.

'I've b-b-been wa-wa-wa-waiting for you. I have something to tell you; most bizarre, it is.'

'What?'

'I've had a very strange phone call from Colin.'

'Dad?'

'Yes, I think they're back from Spain, but he s-s-s-sounded most st-st-strange.'

'What do you mean?' Lucia asks, following her mother up the stairs. She closes the flat door and walks into the sitting room. 'What did he say, Mum?'

'He sounded deranged,' her mother replies. 'I think he was in a phone box and he kept asking for you. He was repeating over and over that he was in London, and that it was all to do with his wife.'

'What was to do with his wife?'

'I have no idea! He was very concerned about me, asking if I was keeping well, which was completely bizarre, and he gave me an address and phone number for you. He seemed to be reading it from a piece of paper. The whole thing was rather pathetic. I felt very so-so-sorry for hi-hi-him.'

Lucia snatches the piece of scrap paper from her mother's hand.

79 Markham Street, Chelsea, SW3 6PU
071 352 4445

'Is this where he is?' Lucia asks.

'Well, yes, as far as I can te-te-tell, bu-bu-but it was very hard to make sense of h-h-him. He doesn't sound well.'

Lucia takes the phone in to her room. She picks up the receiver. Her finger quivers as she dials.

It has been years since she has been allowed to phone her father, so why now?

*

Lucia can hear her heartbeat pounding in her ears as she turns off The King's Road and goes up Jubilee Place. A woman walks past, reeking of Chanel No. 5, and in a long black shawl and Hobbs boots. She asks the woman if she is going the right way. The lady tells Lucia to take a right after the church.

It feels as if someone is wringing a wet towel in Lucia's abdomen.

Markham Street is narrow, with Georgian terraced houses that are all kept spotless. Most have brightly coloured doors, but she cannot see number seventy-nine. Pacing up and down for the fifth time, she sees it. There it is, with a red door. The ground-floor windows are guarded by a thick net curtain, and there is no light on.

Lucia rings the lower bell with *'Goldman'* written on it, and steps back onto the pavement. She straightens her skirt. She has made an effort today, by wearing her Whistles blouse and skirt. She knows her father likes her to look ladylike.

The door brushes across the mat as it opens.

Yvonne holds the door open. She is in navy, pleated trousers; a polo neck; and slippers. Lucia's eye is immediately drawn to Yvonne's thighs, which are bulging in her trousers. Though she is immaculately coiffed as always, the streaks of grey are a new addition.

Yvonne's eyes narrow. 'Hi Lucia,' she says, with a warm glint that Lucia did not expect, 'come in.'

Lucia follows Yvonne through a narrow hallway into a small flat with plush carpet. They walk into a sitting room devoid of any character, with only a Heels sofa, an armchair, a dining table and chairs. There are no books, plants or pictures, and it is a definite drop from what Lucia imagined his poolside pad in Alicante had been like.

Her father is slouched in the armchair.

'Colin, it's Lucia here to see you,' Yvonne says.

He bounces out of his chair. He is unshaven. His shirt hangs out from his trousers. Smiling from ear to ear, he grabs Lucia by the neck. 'Hello, my darling one,' he says, kissing her forehead over and over.

Lucia withdraws from his clutch. 'How are you, Dad?'

His lips tremble, but no words come out.

'He's doing OK; aren't you, Colin?' Yvonne says.

Her father snarls and looks away.

'May I get you a tea or coffee, Lucia?' Yvonne asks.

'Yeah, a tea please, with milk and sugar,' Lucia replies, not quite sure what to do with herself. She walks over to her father, whilst Yvonne is in the kitchen. He is sitting with his head in his hands.

'It's nice to see you again, Dad,' she says.

Licking his lips, her father looks away with vacuous eyes. He then walks over to the patio door and guffaws. 'Look, they've come!' he says, pointing outside.

Lucia stands behind him and looks out at the two magpies sitting on the garden bench. She is sure that is the same bench they had at Lord North Street.

'They keep coming!' he laughs.

Lucia senses his volatility, so she goes along with his vibe. 'Yes,' she replies, 'the magpies are here.'

Unable to be present with her father's inner jitters, Lucia joins Yvonne in the kitchen. It is a blue-and-white galley kitchen, with everything in its place, but with no trace of any cooking smells. The kettle switch clicks, and steam rises. Yvonne stands at the sink, rinsing a mug.

'So, when did this all begin?' Lucia asks.

'It began shortly after we got to Spain,' Yvonne says quietly. 'He started to lose his memory rapidly and then became very volatile. I knew something was wrong when I came home one day to find him burning his robes.'

'The robes he wore as a judge?'

Yvonne puts the teabags in the mugs and makes eye contact with Lucia. 'Yes, he built a bonfire in the garden and threw them all in to it.'

'How bad is he?' Lucia asks.

'He's got no short-term memory now at all. He calls me Shirley most of the time.'

Lucia stares at the hob. 'So what are you going to do?' she asks.

'I don't know,' Yvonne replies, snivelling into the back of hand. 'I know I can't look after him full time because of work.

He needs twenty-four-hour care.' She wipes her mascara and pours the water into the mugs. 'I've had to go out after him in the early hours of the morning four times now.'

'What do you mean?' Lucia asks.

'He just goes out in his slippers, and starts banging on doors, shouting at the neighbours. I'm going to have to put him into a nursing home, but it will only be the best for him.'

This intimacy feels odd to Lucia. 'Shall I take the biscuits?' she asks.

They walk into the sitting room. Her father is knocking on the patio doors. Lucia walks over to him. There is only one magpie now.

'He's alone,' her father says, peering into Lucia's eyes.

She is unsettled, but takes in his gaunt, drawn face. 'Yeah, his friend abandoned him,' she replies. 'Shall we have our tea, Dad?'

Lucia leads her father over to the sofa. Yvonne is in the armchair.

Lucia sits down and picks up a biscuit. She bites into her fig roll. 'So how do you like Chelsea?' Lucia asks.

'We haven't seen much of it, to be honest,' Yvonne replies with that characteristic sarcasm, 'have we, Colin?'

Her father makes a deep low grumbling sound, and looks at the floor.

It goes quiet. There is an awkward silence. Yvonne brushes down her trousers.

Lucia screws up a ball of Blu Tack in her pocket, as she thinks of what to say next.

'And you?' Yvonne asks.

'I'm retaking my A levels at the minute.'

'Are you going to university?'

'I'm hoping to read history,' Lucia replies.

'Did you hear that, Colin? Lucia's off to university soon.'

Her father frowns; his eyes dart from side to side. He stands and bounces up and down in front of her. 'Who are you?' he snarls. 'Who are you?'

Lucia swallows and looks down.

'You know who it is, Colin; it's Lucia,' Yvonne says.

Her father stares at her and pokes his mouth, as if he has bad toothache.

Lucia's eyes sting. 'I better get going,' she says, picking up her bag.

'No, don't go; he'll settle in a bit,' Yvonne replies.

'I actually only popped in to say hi. I have somewhere I need to be.'

'Thanks for coming,' Yvonne replies, misty-eyed.

Lucia walks over to her father and puts her hand on his shoulder. She notices his arm shaking. 'Take care, Dad; nice to see you.' As she says those words her throat constricts. She realises that the dream she had of having an adult relationship with her father when he came back from Spain is now dead. He will just decline now. She saw it with Grandma Daphna.

'I'll see you out,' Yvonne says.

Lucia looks back at her father and blows him a kiss. He waves and nods as if she were a passer-by.

'Please let me know the details of the nursing home you choose,' Lucia says, opening the front door.

'I'll phone you,' Yvonne replies.

The air is crisp; the sky sapphire blue. Lucia's hands are trembling. She sits on the wall and lights a fag. It's a brief relapse. She'll quit when she's finished therapy. The smoke scratches her throat. Thoughts race in her mind. She wonders why Yvonne was so nice to her.

She takes a long drag and watches a bird peck an acorn. Lucia thinks about her father burning his robes, and she realises that, whilst she was living the life of a teenage poltergeist, her father was in Spain losing his mind. She thinks about the symmetry in their stories, yet there are so many questions that she will never get answered.

Why no phone number for so many years? And why did he stop loving her after he married Yvonne? Why did she used to kick him in bed and have the bruises the day after?

She cannot ask him now.

He has lost his mind. She'll have to fill in the gaps herself.

She stubs out her fag and walks off.

AND THEN...

CHAPTER THIRTY-FIVE

LONDON, 1992

LUCIA IS NINETEEN YEARS OLD

I've got a new boyfriend. He's called CJ.

We met at a seventies nightclub on Wardour Street. It was Tilda's eighteenth birthday. A big crowd of us went down there. I was looking hot in my gold lamé outfit; my ringlets were in fine form. I caught him out of the corner of my eye, grooving on the dance floor in his psychedelic shirt and cord flares.

He beckoned. I shook my head and beckoned him to come to me.

He walked over coyly. We danced, grinding our hips to Gloria Gaynor, and then gate crashed an all-night party in Baker Street, where we sat in the empty bath, drinking Heineken and laughing.

All I remembered about him was that he was a landscape gardener, and he had cold hands; a long, thin nose; and a sexy smile.

I bumped into him outside Camden Tube station a week or so later. He looked rough and ready in his Gore-Tex boots, after a long day at work. He invited me to the Dub Club the following night. The air was thick with pure weed. Those baseline beats were so loud that it felt like they lifted me off the floor.

We kissed on the dance floor. Out of all the boys I have snogged, that kiss with CJ felt different. It was softer and made me feel immediately wet between my legs.

He invited me back to his pad.

I went. He lived in a flat above a leather clothes shop on Camden High Street. We kissed some more. He pulled down my tracksuit bottoms, and went down on me.

His tongue was so soft, I came straight away.

Then we made love on his floor.

He told me nothing had ever felt so good. We lay awake all night on his futon listening to Van Morrison, and fondling.

We fell in love. The rest is history.

He doesn't know about my poltergeist. I still haven't told anybody. He just knows that I see a psychotherapist. I still see Maggie. I am convinced it is thanks to her that I have been able to recognise a loving man, instead of an abusive arsehole. She has taught me that I deserve to experience good things, and that abuse is not the norm.

I have moved in with him now. Mum didn't want me to go, but it was an escape from her clutches. I packed a few things and just turned up. It is pretty filthy (and mouse ridden), but I feel happier than I have ever felt before. I look forward to CJ coming home, us cooking together and making love throughout the night to the background noise of drunken people on Camden High Street.

We are saving up to go to India after my A-level resits in January. I am working shifts at a bakery, selling doughnuts and pasties between sessions of revision. CJ is doing extra time at work. He has always wanted to visit the Hindu temples in India and, most of all, to sit under the Bodhi tree in Bodh Gaya. We hope to fly out in March on a cheap Aeroflot flight and return in time for my start at Bristol University in September (if I make the grades).

CHAPTER THIRTY-SIX

GLASTONBURY, 1994

LUCIA IS TWENTY-ONE YEARS OLD

We wake to the sound of hippies doing a sun dance around last night's bonfire. Some of them chant, while the others play the djembe drum We slept under the stars up here in the Green Field. The feel of the morning breeze on my face is wonderful. I love feeling organically dirty with dried mud splashed across my legs. CJ has gone to get us breakfast. I watch the hippies doing somersaults over their van, and listen to the wind chimes ring in the tepee opposite.

We wander down to the main festival where we are drawn to an animated crowd. It is not just any crowd. They are singing and cheering in sync with one another. There is a feeling of unity amongst them. They look more alive than anything I have seen before. In the middle is a grey-haired man leading them. He is dressed in a multi-coloured jumpsuit and wearing a fool's hat.

We join in.

We are crawling on our hands and knees with hundreds of others, pretending to be fish, as the morning sun beats down on us. 'Niminee, nominee, nooooo,' we all babble.

'Come on!' the fool beckons. 'Let's go down there!'

We follow him. We sprint like kids to the bottom of the field, where the fool divides us into two sections and conducts us to sing 'The Birdie Song' in rounds. We sing and shake our bums. Ah! It feels great belting out this tune. More people join in as they pass by.

'I need two volunteers!' the fool calls. A man and a woman come forwards, and climb onto the top of the portable loo with the fool. I don't know if he has permission to be up there, but no one stops them.

He directs the musical *Grease* up there. We gather around and watch the play from down on the grass. Danny and Sandi, once strangers, are now lovers, snogging under the sun's rays. We sing 'Summer Loving', in unison. It's crazy! The crowd is so now huge.

This man is a genius. We have been running around in a field with a group of strangers for one hour, who all now feel like best friends.

He is called Cameron Cleeve – 'The Fool'. He is performing again tomorrow in the theatre tent at 3.00pm. We must come.

I need to do this again. Something inside me feels different.

*

It is a scorching June afternoon. The theatre tent is packed. We await the fool's arrival.

'You can't see me, but I can see you,' a voice says from above. The voice is gentle, like water flowing along a pebbly brook.

Everyone looks around.

'See I told you,' the omnipotent voice says. 'You can't see me.'

The tent goes suspiciously quiet.

'Hmm,' he says again. He's got a lovely voice – it's kind. Hearing it makes you want to meet him. 'So where do you think I am?' he asks.

The tent breaks out into a unified cackle.

I look up. The fool is swinging from the scaffolding across the dome above. 'Hello,' he chirps 'Aren't you going to say hello?' He is lowered down to the stairs by invisible strings. He walks towards the stage in the same outfit he wore yesterday: the jumpsuit and hat with a spike on top, and tassels flopping over his face. He is barefooted.

The crowd clap and whistle.

He stands in the middle of the stage. There are no props or set, just him. He opens his arms. 'Nice to see so many of you,' he says. 'You all look very nice. Are you?'

'Yes!' the crowd shout.

'Sorry, didn't hear you,' he replies, pushing his ear forwards with his hand.

'Yeeees!' the crowd roar.

He walks around the stage, talking to us. There is something raw and vulnerable about him that I connect with. 'I'm a fool,' he says. His voice turns deep and big. He stands still. 'I'm not very clever. I'm foolish. I don't know many things. I like it that way, to not know,' he says. 'When you know too much, you stop enjoying yourself.' He screws up his face, wiggles his tongue and twitches.

His eyes catch me through the audience. It is only for a second, but it is as if he can see right into me. 'You don't enjoy yourself enough, do you?' he says. I am sure he is addressing me. Blood rushes to my cheeks. I look behind. A Korean lady laughs uncomfortably. His eyes dart to the broad-chested man in the front row. Phew!

'Do you enjoy yourself?' the fool asks.

The man looks from side to side. 'Me?' he asks.

'Yes. What do you do for a job?'

'I'm a builder,' the man replies.

'Is that fun?' the fool asks.

'It's OK,' the man shrugs.

'Come up here,' the fool says and moves his arm as if hurrying water along.

The man walks onto the stage. The fool hugs him. They embrace for ages, really embrace, like old friends who are reunited after years. It is moving to watch.

'What you all staring at?' the fool asks. 'Why are you watching? Why don't you join in?'

A few people in the front row stand and walk onto the stage. Those behind them follow suit. CJ and I tag along, and follow the crowd. We hug person after person in a raucous love mash-up. The stage is rammed. People are tumbling onto one another, falling off the stage, laughing.

'It's better up here, than down there; I mean, just watching, isn't it?' the fool says, proving his point. 'It's boring just to watch. Shall we go outside and play?'

His gaze catches mine, again.

'Yeaaaah!' we cheer.

We shuffle out into the sweltering heat. Acrobats whizz past on unicycles, whilst clowns on stilts juggle with fire sticks. Young children are having their faces painted by colourful artists, whilst a dance troupe in catsuits perform to moody music.

The fool is not distracted by the activity round us. He gathers us around him in a circle. 'Come on,' he jeers. We all hold hands. 'What shall we do? You decide.'

CJ and I are dragged by the sudden force of the group, running in towards the middle and out again, belting out the 'Hokey Cokey'.

People stop and goggle at us with a look of awe. They would prefer to be part of our gang than be eating an ice cream, just watching. Some of them amble over, just like we did yesterday, and join in. We bounce through the field, all pretending to be chirpy bunny rabbits.

At the bottom of the field, the fool conducts us to sing the Pink Panther theme tune, and then gets us to applaud ourselves. The sound of us all cheering makes the blood race around my body fast. I don't want to leave this crowd.

CJ links arms with me. I focus on his Gore-Tex boot as we amble up the hill.

'Prrrhhh,' CJ sighs, blowing air up to cool his brow. 'That was incredible, Luce. I'm buzzing, are you?'

I am sweating. I sit down by a family's tent and listen to the echoing sound coming from the music stage. It is a male whining sound that travels up the hill. 'Yeah, I am,' I reply, running my fingers through my hair. 'I feel lighter, as if I have been on a crazy journey.'

CJ sits next down to me, and takes out his Golden Virginia to roll a ciggie. 'He was a find, wasn't he?' CJ says. 'A special human being.'

'Yeah,' I reply and lie on the grass. I keep thinking about the way the fool looked into my eyes as if he had known me for years. There is something special about that fool. He definitely made a connection with me. He looked at me twice.

There is something about him that I want to know more about.

On our return from Glastonbury, I write to Michael Eavis, and ask for the contact details for Cameron Cleeve. I don't expect a reply, but three days later an information pack arrives about Cameron Cleeve's theatre company. It's called Arcadia. The pack includes details of fooling workshops, and performances that he does nationally in schools and colleges. There is a picture of him on the front pulling his legs over his head and sticking out his tongue.

I write a heartfelt letter to Cameron, explaining how his performances at Glastonbury affected me, and how he opened something up inside me that I had never felt before.

I invite him to come to Bristol University to run a workshop with its drama students.

One week later, his administrator phones me to say that Cameron would be happy to run a full day workshop for £300.00. I have a meeting with Achir, the head of our student union, who approves a grant to fund the day workshop with Cameron Cleeve.

It's booked! It's official. Cameron Cleeve 'The Fool' is coming to Bristol University next term to run riot.

CHAPTER THIRTY-SEVEN

BRISTOL, 1994: 'HOMECOMING'

LUCIA IS TWENTY-ONE YEARS OLD

CJ is travelling in Latin America. He's gone trekking along the Inca Trail, planning to end up in Machu Picchu to watch the solar eclipse in November.

Tomorrow is the workshop I have organised with Cameron Cleeve.

The phone rings.

A light voice speaks. It's upper class sounding. 'Hello, it's Cameron, Cameron Cleeve. I'm… I'm… supposed to be doing a workshop with you tomorrow.'

What the fuck? It's him! 'Yes, that's right,' I reply politely. 'Do you know Bristol University?'

'Well, actually,' he sounds lost. 'I've just arrived and I

don't have anywhere to stay. I was wondering if you had a spare bed.'

The area around my rib cage turns to steel. I suddenly get really bad heartburn, like the worst indigestion. 'Yeah, course,' I reply. 'Come over. I'll sort you out a bed.'

'What's your address?'

'It's 31 Chantry Road, just up from Clifton Down station.'

'OK, I'll… I'll make my up way then,' he bumbles.

'See you soon,' I reply.

Shit! I run upstairs to check Tess' sheets are clean. She's at Mike's tonight. There's a blood stain on them, so I change her bedding to one of my flowery sheets.

I rush downstairs and straighten up the living room. There's barely anything in the fridge to offer him: half a packet of tofu, some eggs and two slices of stale Sunblest bread.

There is a knock on the door sooner than I expected.

I dash upstairs, spray on some CK One and throw on my handmade waistcoat over my purple shirt.

He's standing on the pavement in a dishevelled coat and with wild, grey hair. His sapphire eyes gleam at me.

'Come in,' I say, taking his coat.

I lead him downstairs to the living room. 'Sorry, it's a shabby student dive,' I say. 'I hope you weren't expecting four-star accommodation.'

He throws back his head and laughs. 'I was actually.'

'Well, sorry to disappoint you.'

He lights up this grim space with his magical presence. He is in green-velvet trousers and a white shirt, with a multicoloured fool's waistcoat over the top. He makes himself at home and slouches on my sofa. 'Put the kettle on, then,' he says, like he has known me for years.

That stabbing heartburn won't settle. I can't believe he's actually in my house. I wash up a mug and take the milk out of the fridge.

'So,' he says, slapping his hands together, 'this is you.'

'Yep,' I say turning to him. 'I guess it is.'

'Your name is Lucia, is it?'

'Yes. Yes, it is.'

'Pretty name,' he says smiling, showing me his yellowed teeth. 'Do you mind if I smoke?' He takes out his rolling tobacco.

'No, go for it.' I notice his delicate hands as I hand him an ashtray.

He takes a drag of his cig. 'That was a nice letter you wrote to me. You opened your heart.' He looks right at me.

'You touched me deeply at Glastonbury.' I say, sitting down and throwing off my Kickers. 'Something in me changed that day, and I can't stop thinking about it.'

'I'm glad you wrote to me,' Cameron replies. 'It was courageous of you.'

We talk about his theatre work until past midnight. I look at my watch. 'We should get some sleep,' I say. 'I'll show you to your room.'

He taps his fingers on the banister, as we walk up the stairs.

I lead him into Tess' bedroom. 'Is this all right?'

'Yeah, great thanks,' he replies, and stares at me with his sparkling eyes.

I look down at Tess' bed. 'Well, sleep well then,' I say, and walk out.

I walk into my room. As I pull back my sheets, I hear him walking about next door, restless. He sounds like a caged animal. There is no way I am going to get any sleep tonight with all of this excitement churning around in my stomach – no way.

*

It's a bare room on the second floor of the student-union building. It overlooks the university entrance and front lawns. The windows are large. The floor is wooden, and there is a smell of stale beer in here. Chairs are scattered around from yesterday's socialist-worker meeting. Cameron gathers them and lines them up in a row.

There are seven of us. Abigail, who I know from drama society. She is large, and has curly hair and a raucous laugh. The others are strange faces, who I have never seen before.

We sit in a line. Cameron stands in front in the same clothes he showed up in last night. We introduce ourselves. It's Rose, Kendrick, Sam, Adam, Abigail, Layla and me.

'So,' Cameron says, rolling up his sleeve. 'Here we are. I'm a fool. I appear just like that,' he clicks his fingers, 'and then I'm gone. I don't live by rules or expectations. I respond to things in the moment.' He looks up as if a shower of rain was coming. 'Think what we can do with all this space.' His eyes open wide.

We all stare at him like he is an alien.

'What can we create? You see, creativity is about being here now and stepping into the unknown.' He runs his hands over his mouth and swallows. 'The next moment is a beginning, an opportunity to discover something new. It's not something to be frightened of. Up here, you can allow yourself to say things you wouldn't be seen dead saying.' He points to his navel. 'Our inner world lies dormant most of the time. Here, we can give it free rein, but it's hard when we have the censoring voice in our heads.'

He walks around the room, talking to himself. He opens and closes his hands up by his ears, like they are the mouths of two Pacmen. 'Oh, I really feel like having a good boogie and kissing that fella.' His nostrils flare and he points his finger. 'No! You can't do that! What will people think of you, you stupid arse? They'll laugh, and say "Who the fuck does she think she is?"'

We giggle.

The room goes still.

'See that's what we are like with ourselves all of the time, censoring, censoring. You include that in your performance, all of it, and you must see the audience as your friend. They are part of your world. They want to get to know you, so interact with them.' He claps his hands. 'Right then, who wants to come up and have a go?'

No one answers.

'Don't be afraid. It's just a space and you. Come up and see what happens.'

Adam stands. He looks like a train spotter in his brown trousers and specs. He flaps his arms and runs around the room. He turns into Big Bird from Sesame Street, directing traffic in a squeaky voice. Abigail bursts out into a boisterous laugh.

We clap.

Adam sits.

I stand. 'I'll have a go,' I say as I pull my Aaron jumper down over my leggings.

I look at them one by one. Abigail is smiling at me with an empathetic 'brave you' kind of smile. Cameron's eyes are twinkling at me, so I focus in on him.

'It's rare I look into people's eyes,' I say, strolling around the room. I have command of the space. 'You see so much when you do, don't you?' I look into Cameron's eyes. 'I really fancy you,' I say.

He grins and rubs his lips together as if tasting something salty.

The group burst out laughing in unison.

'Shit! I shouldn't have said that should I?' I say. 'That's from the forbidden world isn't it?' I am enjoying this. 'But I do. I think you are beautiful.' I shudder a bit.

I look into their eyes and feel a deep connection with them all. You could hear a pin drop in here.

'It's nice telling someone when you fancy them, isn't it? It's freeing. Imagine how much sex you would have if you said it all the time?' I say.

Sam giggles into his hand.

The minutes pass. 'I've had my go,' I say, and sit down.

One by one, we open up part of ourselves that we normally hide. Layla has an imaginary conversation with her dead mother, verbalising the things she wished she'd said.

'Well done,' Cameron says. He stands and rubs his hands together. 'What shall we do now?'

'Sing a song,' Adam shouts.

'What shall we sing?' Cameron asks.

'Let's sing a song by Queen,' Layla says. "Bohemian Rhapsody."

'Come on then, let's stand.'

Is this the real life? Is this just fantasy? Sam bellows.

Cameron plays the conductor. He picks up a felt tip pen for his baton.

We join in.

Caught in a landslide,
No escape from reality
Open your eyes,
Look up to the skies and see.

Abigail gets down on her knees and crawls around the room. We crawl behind.

Any way the wind blows,
doesn't really matter to me, to me

Adam jumps up, opens out his arms out and spins around looking at the ceiling. We run over to the window, knocking on it at passers-by, and waving. They look down and shuffle along in their own world.

'Let's share this lovely singing with the world.' Cameron beckons us over to the door.

We go out of the door and walk down the stairs in a line. At the bottom, Abigail opens the door to the student-union bar. It is full of greasy-haired undergrads playing pool and drinking beer. We walk in. Sam leads. He spontaneously runs around the room with his arms outstretched, leaning from one side to the other. We all fly around the bar as Concorde planes, and sing.

I see a little silhouetto of a man
Scaramouche, Scaramouche, will you do the Fandango?

We crouch down, and walk like pixies, each with one finger over our lips.

The bar goes silent.

Thunderbolt and lightening,
Very, very frightening me.

Adam jumps up onto a table. *'Galileo!'* he shouts, flailing his arms in the air.

'Galileo,' we, the chorus, echo back.

'Galileo,' he belts out.

This feels so good. It's just like a play.

Cameron beckons us outside onto the lawn.

We skip out behind him. A long line of students from the bar follow us outside and join us for a singsong led by our new front man, Adam.

I'm just a poor boy, nobody loves me
He's just a poor boy from a poor family,
Spare him his life from this monstrosity.

A group of drunk blokes watch from the side. 'Who's that prick?' one of them asks Abigail.

'He's a fool.'

They laugh.

At the end of the song, we bow and curtsy. Everyone cheers. People peer out from classroom windows. It's crazy out here. No one wants to leave.

Cameron leads us back up to our room. As I walk up the stairs, it feels like there is a stone at the meeting of my thighs, with sparks of electricity flying from it into my abdomen. This attraction is insane.

We sit in a circle and hold hands. 'Have you enjoyed yourselves?' he asks.

I look at the clock. I can't believe it is lunchtime already.

'It's been the best morning ever,' Abigail says, beaming from ear to ear.

'We'll take an hour break,' Cameron says.

I walk through the fields behind the university, and go up the hill. There's no way I can eat anything; I've got adrenalin racing through me. I sit on the bench under the willow tree, and watch a sparrow nibble on some crumbs. A helicopter circles above, making me think danger is near, and I hear the distant rush of traffic from the motorway down there.

I have the worst cramp ever. I don't know how I can contain this energy or get through this afternoon with these feelings. The way Cameron looks at me with that glint in his eye – I feel it with a thump, right in my pelvis.

I've still got half an hour to calm myself down.

*

In the afternoon, we each perform a solo play about some part of our life. My play is called *Where Is My Devil in the Light?* I enact my mum and dad first meeting, and going out on dates. Then I play them making love. It's strange to act them together in that way. I never saw them happy. I certainly never imagined them having sex, although I know that's how they made me. I just recall the hatred between them. I feel settled after my performance.

Abigail re-enacts the death of her baby brother. He was a stillborn baby. It's moving to see how brave she is. At 4.00pm, we have a closing circle.

'Have you got a lot out of today?' Cameron asks.

'It's been amazing; thanks, Cameron,' Sam says. He doesn't look so pale.

'I'm glad you've enjoyed yourselves,' Cameron says. 'You can have a lot of fun when you let yourselves go, can't you?'

'I feel different inside,' Adam says.

'It's important to play and interact authentically. Remember others know your love, love knows you and see the shining world turn. Twisting stars are still,' Cameron concludes.

We leave.

*

Cameron and I walk out of the university campus. I begin my usual walk home up Woodland Road.

'Let's go a different way,' he says pulling me down University Road, towards the art gallery. 'You don't always have to do the same thing, you know.'

We link arms. My tummy is in knots. I haven't eaten since breakfast.

At the top of Park Row, he leads me along a footpath that runs along the A4018. Heavy trucks race by. It feels dangerous, but I kind of like it. 'Are you sure we should walk along here?' I ask.

He sucks air in through his teeth. 'Oh, I don't know. We may get into trouble.' Cameron pulls me close as we saunter along the dual carriageway. He smells of burnt chestnuts, like he's been around a bonfire all night.

'It was nice to see you open up today,' he says.

I kick a stone and nestle into him. 'It felt good.'

'It's good when your inner and outer worlds meet. You feel more integrated,' he says.

'I felt intuitive. I liked it.'

'Have you ever looked at the word "intuition" before?' he asks. 'It comes from *in-tuit*. It means your inner tutor. Inside you, you have a world. And in that world is tuition and in that intuition is a sense of self beginning to awaken. You need to follow that, because it leads to love and life.'

We walk through College Green and slow down at the cathedral.

It looks so beautiful here, in this early evening light. There is a nippy breeze. Bells are ringing. We walk behind the cathedral to a chapel, and sit on a bench under some trees. Cameron puts his arm around me and points to a flagstone on the ground. 'Look.' Engraved in that stone are the words '*Be still and know I am God*' (Psalm 46:10).

'Who do you think wrote that?' he asks, 'A stone mason? A carver?'

I twiddle the button on his coat and say nothing.

'What if God wrote that?' he asks. 'Can you make that leap of faith to think that God wrote that?'

The clock strikes and a flag dances in the breeze at the side of the chapel.

'You see, if we could just focus and feel the presence of stillness, so that your inner world is calmed by silence, peace is always here. "Know that I am God." What does that mean to you?'

I shrug.

'I'm just a person like you or the stonemason, but imagine if we were all still everywhere, we would all feel part of a universal stillness, and we would have a knowing quality. We would know that we are God.'

The air smells like cardamom. This feels like the safest place in the world. As I listen to Cameron's words, my emotional pain dissipates. It just fades, and I see the possibility of something pure, where I am someone who is happier. I feel full of hope that I can walk into a brighter world than the one I have known.

'You see, we have to break free of the idea that God is in a church or a mosque. It is nothing to do with church. God is within. If I got to know you, I would get to know myself, and if you get to know me, you would get to know yourself. That is the relationship. "Be still and know that you are God." Isn't that beautiful?'

I watch his thin lips move and look into his eyes. There are laughter lines ingrained around them. He has a piglet nose and a brown blotch on his cheek, like a faded mole.

I kiss him. I can't help myself; I just kiss him. 'Sorry,' I say pulling back. 'I didn't know what I was doing.'

'You don't need to apologise.' He kisses me on the lips.

We are still, our mouths moulded together. It is hard to be present. My lips are touching his, but my body has frozen. I can't believe I'm kissing this man. I have lost track of time. I am beyond starving hungry, but I have never felt so alive. We stay there for a while.

We head along Anchor Road, down to the river, and sit on a wall, looking across at the marina. There is a clinking sound coming from the boats.

'Are you married?' I ask.

'Separated,' he replies, 'but I still live with my wife.'

It sounds complicated. I ask no more. 'Do you have to get back tonight?'

'Nope,' he replies, 'I'm free as a bird.'

'I'm cold,' I say.

He takes off his coat and puts it around my shoulders. 'Let's go back to yours,' he says and takes my hand.

We walk up Church Lane to the top of town and get a chicken chow mein and some spring rolls from a takeaway.

'Aren't you going to eat?' he asks, holding a spring roll to my mouth.

'I'm too excited to eat, but I'll sip some cola.'

We wander back home. No one is in. I lead him up the stairs into my room and close my door.

He undresses me and kisses my neck. 'Enjoy yourself,' he whispers. 'Let yourself sink to the bottom of the pond.'

I think of CJ in the Peruvian mountains.

Cameron pulls me into bed.
I will tell CJ.
He kisses my breasts. I turn off the light.
I will.

CHAPTER THIRTY-EIGHT

LONDON, 1995

LUCIA IS TWENTY-TWO YEARS OLD

Camden High Street greets me with its usual bustle. Our meeting is at 2.00pm.

I enjoy the whiff of the pecan-chocolate mix as I walk past the creperie and the different shades of coloured denim hanging outside Rokit.

The fruit and vegetable stallholders yell out the best deal on two packs of strawberries, as I turn into Inverness Street, and I notice an avocado lying bashed under one of the wagons. I love that smell of earthy produce, and can't resist a bargain bunch of beetroot for only 40p.

Giovanni's Cafe is empty except for a business man devouring a sausage sandwich. I watch him gulp down his coffee and skim the headlines as I order a hot chocolate.

'With sprinkles, darling?'

'What?' I am lost in the stall holders heckling outside.

'Chocolate sprinkles on your drink?' he asks.

'Oh, yes, please.'

The waiter is beautiful. He is Mediterranean looking, with sturdy arms and bushy eyebrows. He has a cocky smile, and his white t-shirt is pristine under his chequered apron. He laughs at me as he catches me daydreaming and puts my mug of hot chocolate on the counter.

'That'll be 50p, darling,' he says cupping his palm.

I hand him the change and walk over to the table nearest the window. It's 2.00pm exactly.

Ben walks past the window and waves at me. He opens the door.

'Hiya,' he says, forcing a smile. I know something is up.

He never asks to meet me unless he wants something. He looks smart in a suede jacket and green loafers, and I smell his potent aftershave as he leans down to give me a peck on the cheek.

He orders a cappuccino and sits opposite me.

'You look smart,' I comment.

'Yeah, I've got a meeting after,' he says. His cheeks are rosy; his stubble is overgrown.

I want to ask what on earth this is about, but I wait for him to initiate it. He asked to meet me, so I sit back in my chair and tap my fingers on the table. The sexy waiter brings over Ben's coffee, and puts it on the table with two swirly biscuits.

Ben lurches forwards, pushing aside his coffee. 'So how's things, Luce?' he asks with an uncharacteristic warmth.

'All right, I'm just getting geared up to go back to Bristol for next term.'

'How's CJ?'

'OK,' I shrug. 'He's moving down to live with me in Bristol.'

He flicks his teeth with his finger. 'You don't sound thrilled. Is that what you want?' he asks, knowing it isn't.

'Dunno,' I reply. My chest stiffens so I change the subject. 'What about you?'

'Busy in rehearsals with *Top Girls*,' he sniffs. 'We open next week at The Gate Theatre.'

'You must be pleased that things are picking up,' I say.

He makes spiral shapes with his finger in the spilt sugar. 'They're not really going well, Luce. We are in financial shit. I may have to close the theatre company down. I'm going for an interview next week with The Royal Shakespeare Company up in Stratford.'

'Will that mean you'll have to move up there?'

'For a year, yes,' he replies. 'It'll be worth it for the financial security.'

Two ladies in their fifties walk in, cajoling one another. They order lasagne and chips. It makes me feel hungry, but I only have £3 on me.

'Listen, Luce...' Ben looks up, and establishes eye contact with me. 'There's something I need to tell you.'

A storm races across my lungs. 'All right, what is it?'

He scoops the froth off the top of his cappuccino and sucks it off his spoon. 'I've wanted to tell you for a while, but just haven't got round to it.'

'Well, what is it?'

'I'm gay.'

I'm not surprised. My cheeks blush as he waits for a response. 'Cool,' I reply. 'I'm glad you told me.'

He sips his coffee. A relief sets in across his face. 'Yeah, me too,' he says. 'You don't seem surprised.'

'I kind of knew.'

'How so?'

'I don't know. You always seem a bit cagey. I've never seen you with a girl, plus your Bowie collection kind of gave it away.'

He titters to himself and looks out of the window. 'I had a tough night with Mum last week when I told her,' he says.

The ice has broken between us. I want to know more.

'What do you mean?'

'Well, she was fine with me being gay, but I asked her why she had never told me she loved me. She couldn't tell me.' He pauses. 'We were both crying.'

I can just see the scene in my mind. I feel jumpy inside as I imagine how difficult it must have been for Mum. Then I start to wonder what makes a person gay. Does a man want to be with a man because they hate their dad or their mum? I can't remember which one it is.

'I don't get her, Luce. Why is she so incapable of loving us?'

I shrug and finger out the creased layer of skin on my hot chocolate. 'She's damaged, Ben. You know that. But just because she doesn't tell us she cares, it doesn't mean she doesn't.'

'I know,' he says. 'Her way of loving us has been through making sure we have wholesome food and giving us whatever pennies she has.'

'Exactly,' I agree, sticking up for her. 'It's not her fault, Ben. She's sad.'

'No excuse,' he replies. 'Lots of people are sad, but they can still express how they feel.'

The coffee machine churns in the background. A Soul II Soul song is playing on the radio.

'Have you told your dad?'

'No. I'm going round to see him and Angie next week.'

'Well, good luck with that.'

We sit in silence. Ben stares at the chequered table cloth. I brush the sugar off the table and listen to the ladies behind nattering about their niece's first day at school.

'So, have you got a boyfriend?' I ask.

'Yeah, I have actually. He's a lovely bloke called Jackson.'

'Oh, right. Where did you meet?'

'He was in my production of *Kiss of the Spiderwoman* at the Donmar Warehouse. He's a great person, Luce, with a lovely family from Trinidad.'

I'm happy for him and I'm pleased he's been open with me. An unusual feeling of intimacy dances between us that makes me want to confide in him.

'It's hard though,' he says.

'What is?'

'You know,' he ducks his head, 'being in a relationship with the madness we grew up with.'

'What do you mean?'

He runs his hand across his scalp and picks at his psoriasis scab. 'Well, I get angry sometimes, like Mum, and I find it hard to express myself and communicate with him.'

'Have you told him?'

'Told him what, Luce?'

'You know, about how mad Mum is.'

'Not yet. Anyway, there's mad and there's *mad*, Luce.'

It goes quiet between us.

'Listen, Luce, I need to shoot soon,' he says, glancing at his watch. 'I'll try to make it down to see you next term.'

He won't. He just says it. The short-lived connection between us quickly tears.

'What're you up to tomorrow?' I ask.

'I'm going to a party with Twiggy and Etta.'

My chair scrapes across the floor as I stand. 'Cool, I'll see you soon then,' I say.

Ben leans forwards and kisses my cheek. 'See ya, Luce,' he says and dashes out.

I feel lighter inside now that Ben has at least been honest. The bloke behind the counter is busy slicing cheese. I sling my bag across my shoulder and walk towards the door.

'Are you leaving, darling?'

'Yeah, I am. Where are you from?' I ask.

'Malta.'

'You're gorgeous,' I say with a swagger that surprises me.

'Thank you, darling,' he winks. 'Take care.'

He says 'take care' in a way that suggests I am not taking care. 'You too,' I reply and walk back out into the stir of Camden.

As I stroll towards the Tube to meet Nancy, I buy a slice of pepperoni pizza and crouch down by the railings to eat it. I feel different inside: lighter. I can see Nancy getting off the number twenty-four bus in her ethnic gear. We are off to Turnmills tonight for Tiffany's birthday, and are going shopping to buy Nancy a leather skirt. I can't afford anything. I've only enough for my Tube fare home.

'Luce,' she calls, running across the road.

'Hiya,' I say, standing.

'You all right?' she asks.

'Kind of.'

'What's up?'

'My brother just told me he's gay.'

I feel liberated as I say those words. If he can tell me that, maybe one day I can confide in him about things that I need to.

'Really?' she laughs. 'Did you already know?'

We walk towards the Electric Ballroom linking arms.

'Kind of, yeah, I did.'

*

The smell of mashed potatoes and urine hits me as we walk in. A dishevelled lady wearing a red skirt and slippers stands mumbling at the fish tank. I watch the zebra fish, with its bulky body and long tail, swish about as I listen to her monotone babble.

'Vera said she was marrying him you know, she did.' She pokes the fish tank and turns to me with sincere eyes. I don't know what to do.

'She did, she walked down the aisle with them.'

I nod.

'Yes, it was on Wednesday.'

This place reminds me of Grandma Daphna's nursing home; it's the smell, and the lost souls wandering about not knowing what day it is or who they are. This home is more up market, though, than the dingy Golders Green home Daphna was in.

The smell of urine is not as strong here.

CJ holds my hand as we wait for the nurse. More residents shuffle out of the day room mumbling and looking sad. This is the first time I have brought CJ to see my dad.

'Hi Lucia, I'm Debbie Sanderson,' says the nurse. She is dressed in white. Her hand shake is strong. 'I'll take you down to see Colin.'

CJ waits up here as I follow Debbie down a narrow stairway to the TV room. My heart hammers. I do not know what to expect. It has been a year since I last visited him.

Twenty or so residents sit in high-seated chairs in a square. Some rant and some whine. None of them pay attention to the mute cartoon on TV. I can't see Dad at first glance, but, in the corner, there he is, with his head down and scratching his knee.

'Colin, it's your daughter,' Debbie says in a shrill voice.

He looks up, his eyes flit from side to side and then he looks out of the window at the dustbins.

'Your daughter, Colin, has come to see you,' she says.

'Yeeees,' he says. A hysterical laugh issues from his gut.

He knows it's me.

'Do you know her name, Colin?' Debbie asks.

He laughs and jabs the air with his finger. 'They're coming today,' he growls. 'They're coming!' He pokes his armrest. 'They're coming,' he repeats, but now he strokes the armrest, as if it were his beloved cat.

Debbie helps him out of his chair. He is a child in a frail body. I am the adult. A ball of goo is trapped in my throat as I look at him – still dressed in his smart trousers, shirt and tie – but that gaping hole between his top button and his throat shows how thin he is. Time stills as Dad shuffles along in his slippers; Debbie chirps on about today's news. I follow behind.

'There you go, Colin,' Debbie says as she sits him down. 'Cup of tea, Lucia? Milk and sugar?'

'Yes, please,' I say, and sit next to Dad.

His bedroom is basic, with beige walls and a single bed tucked away in the corner. There are no pictures on the walls, just four framed photos of him and Yvonne on his table.

The photo of me isn't there anymore. The bitch got rid of it.

What's he doing?

Dad punches his knee with his fist. 'Bam! Bam! Bam!' he rumbles and looks into my eyes. He guffaws loudly.

I join him and cackle.

'Bam! Bam!' he laughs, pointing at the lampshade.

'Yes, bam, bam,' I say.

'Ra, rasa, rams bam.' His shoulders are joggling up and down.

He is laughing at himself, I think.

Debbie brings in a trolley of biscuits and tea. 'Are you OK in here on your own?'

'Yes,' I reply, not quite sure.

'He's all right,' she whispers, 'He's having an all right day, aren't you, Colin?' Her tone is patronising.

Dad points at Debbie, cackling like a hyena, saying 'Don't you find out!'

'You'll be fine. Call me if you need me,' she whispers and creeps out.

Dad breaks out into a tuneful hum, orchestrating with his fingers. His cheeks redden as they puff full of air. His foot taps up and down. *'Let's all go down the strand...'*

I recognise this song.

'Have a banana...' He grabs my hand and swings it as he bellows.

I join in. I quite enjoy singing with him for a minute or so.

His hum turns into a mumble as he simmers down.

We sit in silence, holding hands. His hand is warm and familiar, but the absence of his aftershave scent is odd. Navratilova makes a loud heaving sound as she serves on TV. I look at the bars outside the window. The courtyard wall shields any sunlight. I think how long these days must be with nothing to break them up, being trapped like a goldfish in the chaos of your mind.

His fingers begin scratching at my thigh. I don't know what he's doing. I gently lift his hand away.

He growls and shakes his head.

Oh no what have I done?

I clutch his hand forcefully, looking him in the eye. 'You do know who I am, don't you, Dad?' I say, 'I'm Lucia, your daughter.' I just want to connect with him, get him to say something truthful.

He is looking away out of the window.

Beads of sweat gather under my nose. Why the central heating in summer?

'Dad,' I say again, trying to bring him back, 'It's me, Lucia.'

He turns to me, and his face is so emaciated that it makes his nose look long. 'Ra! Raaah!' he roars and sticks his tongue out at me.

His teeth grate. They are chipped.

I stand and hold his grab rail. I know what's coming...

Dad stands. He punches the table. The photos fall off.

I back-step towards the door. 'It's been nice to see you, Dad.'

He turns to me, sniffling, and wails quietly as if he is trying to cry. I walk back towards him and touch his shoulder.

'Dad?' I say. I have never seen him cry before.

He punches his head. 'My mind... my mind doesn't make sense anymore,' he squeals.

I am confused by the sense he just made.

'You're ill, Dad,' I say.

His face convulses. He paces back and forth grimacing. 'Evil!' he spits. 'She made me evil.'

I am frightened. He has never hit me before, but I think he is going to.

'You don't understand.' His whisper is hoarse. 'You're not...' He bends down, shaking.

I grab the door handle and run up the stairs, two at a time.

'Lucia!' Debbie calls.

'Dad has lost it!' I call as I open the hall door.

CJ is reading the paper on the sofa. I grab his hand.

'Quick, let's go,' I say.

CJ opens the front door and we step out into the misty air. It's a relief to feel CJ's arms around me. His cagoule reeks of burnt marijuana.

'It's OK,' he soothes, running his fingers across my face. 'You're safe now.'

I stand in CJ's arms sobbing, and watch a young boy learning to ride his bike in the gardens over the road.

'Lucia!' Her voice is soft as she calls my name. I look up. Debbie is standing at the top of the stairs, holding Dad's hand. 'Your dad has come up to see you. He keeps asking for you.'

He is bouncing up and down like a child needing the loo. His eyes have settled.

'Hi Dad,' I say.

He nods as he wrestles to find words. He starts pointing at me, 'You must enjoy your life,' he says. 'Forget about me. My mind... my mind has gone.' His voice is guttural and throaty; his eyes are watery. 'I want you to be happy. Please, enjoy your life, for me; enjoy yourself.'

He walks back inside with his head bowed.

Debbie follows him.

The need to cry blocks my throat. I am in shock at the sense that Dad just made. Is he pretending to be senile? CJ holds me close as I sob into his chest, again. This is it. This was Dad's way of saying goodbye.

CJ lifts my head back. 'That was positive,' he says.

'Positive?' A salty tear rolls over my lip.

'Yes, he gave you his blessing to be happy.'

'How can I be happy when he is trapped in here?'

'Because that is what he wants for you, and the best way you can give it to him is to have a great life.'

I can't speak or even think. My hands are shaking.

'Please,' I say. 'Just walk with me; just walk.'

We hold hands as we stroll towards Battersea Power Station. It is the wrong way, but I don't care.

I need to walk.

I just need to walk.

CHAPTER THIRTY-NINE

HAVANT, 1995

LUCIA IS TWENTY-TWO YEARS OLD

CJ and I have split up. Things were never right after he returned from Peru.

I have been to three more of Cameron's workshops around the UK, and I am learning to open up more. My relationship with Cameron is developing into somewhere between lovers and friends. I call him every week, and we talk for hours. I felt I really needed to see him this week. I didn't know why, I just did. He told me to meet him at Havant, near his home. I packed a rucksack and booked an open-return train ticket.

I walk out of Havant station. It's like a ghost town. It reminds me of St Anne's by Sea when the amusement arcades are shut. It is cloudy. There is a light shower of rain spitting on me, and opposite is an ice-cream van with no customers.

Cameron pulls up in a huge, blue van. I don't recognise him at first because he is tanned and wearing shades. He winds down his window. 'Jump in then,' he says, and opens the door.

It's a high seat. The windows are huge, giving me a panoramic view. He is dressed in an old pair of jeans and a chequered shirt that is open, showing his chest hair. He doesn't say much. We drive along the coastal road towards Portsmouth. The sea is fossil grey and covered in a shroud of mist. He hums as he drives, and has one hand on the wheel and the other leaning out of the window – sexy!

I haven't got a clue where we are, but he parks up behind a wall by a pebbly beach. We are somewhere between Chichester and Portsmouth, but it's nice not knowing where.

'Out you get then,' he says, and turns off the ignition.

We walk along the beach in silence, throwing stones in the sea. The sound of my shoes crunching on the pebbles is both gritty and tinny. I have the taste of mint in my mouth from the Aero I ate earlier. I kneel down and watch the waves ripple to the edge of the shore; their whooshing sound calms my jitters. White froth gathers at my feet and wets my socks a little.

We sit on the shingly beach and listen to the wailing cry of the seagulls. Cameron picks up a pink shell with a green, glittery shine on its underside.

'Isn't that pretty?' he says.

It's so peaceful here on this beach, in this misty fog. I run my hands through the stones, and enjoy the grainy feel of the sandstone and shale beneath. I throw a black pebble into the sea and delight in its sploshing sound.

Cameron chucks a rock up in the air and catches it. 'So, why did you want to see me so urgently?'

I freeze inside. I don't know what to say, so I just enjoy the sensation of rain spitting on my neck and play with a slimy piece of seaweed.

'Are you feeling OK? You sounded like you were going round in circles when we last spoke.'

I burst out into a crackle of laughter to cover up the pain I feel. 'I still feel stuck,' I reply. 'It feels like I am chained to my mum's pain. I can't get away from it.' I sieve a handful of gloopy sediment through my fingers. 'I just don't know how to change. I keep trying, but then I fall back into old ways.'

'Just relax,' he says. 'Stop putting so much pressure on yourself. You can't make a flower grow any faster than it does.'

I huddle in close to him and lean my head on his shoulder. His scent is the same –yesterday's bonfire.

'People always talk about needing to change,' Cameron says, 'but we need to see how we are here, and notice how we think and feel. That way, we see how frozen we are in our perceptions and attitudes.' He lies back and digs his elbows into the shingle. 'Notice is a good word. It says, "*not ice*". It shows our thinking is frozen, and that we must warm up our feelings and thoughts. "*Notice*" is a signal that, if I notice how I feel, I melt a bit and then I feel love.'

A role of thunder echoes in the distance.

'How are you feeling?' he asks.

'I feel frustrated, like I have to say sorry all the time. I'm pissed off.'

'Why don't you let it out and have a good shout at the sea?' he suggests. 'The sea won't judge you.'

I look around. There is no one in sight. I stand.

'Go for it!' he encourages.

I open my mouth. No sound comes out.

I try again. I push for some noise, but I sound like a quietened foghorn.

'Go on, have a good scream.'

I dig for more force. An angry roar comes right from my gut. It feels good. My roar is bass sounding, with no rattle in it. I grit my teeth and throw a stone into the water. 'Fuck off!' I shout at the sea. My sound echoes into the mass of space before me. I bawl loudly, letting the sea catch my sound.

'It feels good, doesn't it?' he says, standing. 'You've got nothing to be sorry for.'

I look up at the mackerel sky. The horizon is covered in a fog of haze. Something inside me has softened. I don't feel so tense. My face muscles have relaxed. My mouth doesn't jar when I open it, nor does my jaw crack like it usually does.

'Fancy getting something to eat?' he asks.

'Yeah, OK.'

We walk, holding hands, to the cafe set back from the beach. It's the only building in sight for miles. The stench of chip fat hits me when we walk in. We sit at an orange-plastic table in red-plastic chairs, and order from the hamburger menu. There's only one bloke in here. He's reading the *Daily Mail*, and eating a full English breakfast.

'Everything OK in Bristol?' Cameron asks.

'Kind of,' I reply. 'My course is boring. I'm not sure I know what I am going to be when I grow up. History isn't what I want to do.'

'Hmm.' He sits back in his seat and taps his fingers on the table. 'What do you want to be… *to be… to be?*'

Our hamburgers arrive. His has extra cheese.

Cameron's nostrils flare. His stare is poised on me. 'Don't you think it is strange that "*je suis*" looks like "Jesus"?' he asks, sprinkling salt on his chips. "*Je suis*" means "I am" in French. It is not who you are, it is the fact that you have an "I am" that's important. I am.' He licks his lips. 'Do you ever say that? *I am* weary. *I am* lonely. *I am* in love. Love is blind, that's why it touches you. It calls to you when you are not judging, you find yourself in a state of not caring what people think about you and it clicks. It clicks that you are more an "I am" than anything else.' He takes a bite of his burger and sips his tea.

A space opens up inside me. My perspective on the way I have been living shifts. I see that I can be something different. Cameron's words make me feel I can walk freely; get away from my mum and my past. I can be my own person.

'Everybody is an "I am", you see,' he says. 'The deception is that "I am" is camouflaged by being a priest, a monk or a murderer. You think "I am a singer", "I am a house wife" or "I am an artist" are important, but they are not.' He wipes his mouth with a napkin. 'Next time you talk with someone, hear yourself say "I am". Allow it to just be like that. Then you're in time, in a space, and you are not looking for anything to happen; it's a beginning. The artist, the monk or the banker obscures who you really are. It is a signature, not the writing.'

I nod.

'So don't get tangled in knots about *what* to be – just be,' he says.

I look into his glistening eyes. He is present – here with me, right now. It's as if this shitty cafe is the centre of the world. He has no agenda and nowhere else to be. The moments pass with ease; each one is so lively. There is no need to run off to somewhere better. It is better here, eating this plastic-tasting cheeseburger with Cameron. It's the best place in the world.

I look at the clock. Three hours have passed since we walked in here. See what I mean? Time passes without you noticing when you are with Cameron. Doing something as mundane as sitting in this dead cafe is a beautiful experience.

Cameron walks over to the counter to pay, whilst I sing along to 'Common People', which is playing on the radio.

'Right, shall we go then?' Cameron asks, putting on his jacket.

We walk along the beach, back to his van. The air is dewy, and the light dim. It looks like a storm could be coming. 'Can we stay here for the night?' I ask.

'Yeah, we can do whatever you want,' he replies.

We remain parked here for the night.

*

It's cosy here, in his van. The side curtains are shut. We're in his double bed, tucked away at the back. The van rocks as the wind slaps against the bumper.

I peek out of the window. The tide is high. It's right up to the wall behind where we are parked. It's heaven. I could stay here forever. Who needs anything else? It's just enough to be lying on this foam mattress, looking at the full moon with Cameron.

I pull him towards me and run my fingers through his hair. That scent of his, of burnt kindling, is sour up close. I kiss his neck and then his ear. His taste is acrid too.

'You look beautiful in the moonlight,' I say.

'So do you. You glow with a silver shimmer,' he whispers, and kisses me from my breasts down to my tummy.

I flinch.

'Why did you do that?' he asks.

'I don't know.'

'You were all relaxed and then you jumped. Just enjoy yourself.' He grabs my sides, and circles my tummy button with the tip of his tongue.

I splay my arms out wide and moan, as he kisses me up and down the inside of my thigh.

I feel his stubble tickle my pubic bone. I tense.

'What's wrong?' he asks.

'What do you mean? Nothing's wrong.'

He gets off me and lies by my side. 'Didn't you like the way I was kissing you?'

'I did,' I reply, because I did.

'Why did you tense up like that then?'

I turn and look at the ray of midnight light streaking

through the back window. 'I don't know,' I reply. I'm frustrated because I don't know the answers to his questions. I know he is right. I am here with this wonderful man, yet I cannot be with him.

'You pull me towards you, ravage me, and then, when I touch and kiss you, you turn away and become vacant. Just relax,' he says.

I run my finger across his lips. He's correct, but I don't know why I do it. I want him more than anyone, but I don't know how to stop myself from blanking out. I was never like this with CJ. I kiss him. 'Touch me again,' I say. 'I won't jump. I do want you.'

He turns off the lamp and leans over me. 'Where do you go in your mind when I kiss you?' he whispers.

'I don't know, but something happens to me.'

'It's like you won't allow yourself to let go,' he says, stroking my breasts. 'You are so beautiful. Why can't you let yourself be happy?'

'Stop lecturing me,' I say.

He tucks my hair behind my ear. 'Part of you seems locked away. Have you been close to anybody before?'

'Only CJ, really,' I reply. 'But he never said this before about me.'

'Are you still together?'

'No, we split up a few months ago.'

He straddles me and looks into my eyes. I notice the moles on his chest. 'Have you ever looked at the word "intimacy" closely before?' he asks.

'No,' I reply. I know something wise is coming.

'It means "in-to-me-see",' he says.

'That's clever.'

'It's OK to let me see you, you know. I won't hurt you.' He puts his ear close up to my chest. 'I can hear your heart beating. It's beating fast.'

I think about how I could really let this man in.

'Are you getting used to me?' he asks.

'Yes,' I reply. 'Make love to me. I want to show you how I feel.'

'You don't have to, you know,' he says.

'I know I don't have to, but I want to. I love you.'

He picks his wallet up from the floor, and pulls out an old Mates condom.

'That looks like it's been there a while,' I joke.

He rips the packet and squeezes the condom out. I take it and roll it over his penis. He is already hard.

I lie on my back. *I won't freeze*, I tell myself. *I won't.*

'Just relax,' he says.

He penetrates me.

I squeal.

CHAPTER FORTY
DISS, 1996
LUCIA IS TWENTY-THREE YEARS OLD

It is mid-autumn. Lucia is house-sitting for a friend in Diss. It is a five-bedroom, stone-built house opposite a common, where red and brown leaves are scattered across the ground. The sitting room has an open fire, which Lucia is keeping alive with daily doses of kindling and wood. Her on–off lover, Cameron, has come to stay for the weekend to keep her company. After a lamb casserole and a bottle of Merlot enjoyed by the fire, Cameron and Lucia have come to bed.

It is a king size bed with Egyptian cotton sheets and a goose-down duvet. There is little furniture, only a lightly coloured pine wardrobe and a sturdy chest of drawers with African ornaments displayed on it. Cameron's jeans and sweater are strewn across the chair. Lucia's knickers and skirt are tangled on the floor.

The light is out.

The rain outside is heavy. The wind howls. The light on the landing shines through the crack in the door.

Lucia lies on her back as Cameron caresses her forearm with his fingers.

'That's nice,' she slurs. The hairs on her arm stand.

He pecks her neck with his lips and strokes her stomach. 'You've got lovely skin,' he whispers, circling her belly button with his finger.

'Stop teasing me,' she moans.

He kisses her ear.

His hot breath and dirty whispers tickle her eardrum. She stretches her arms back and spreads out her legs wide. 'Ah, that feels so good, Cameron. You're making me wet.'

He runs his fingertip up and down the inside of her thigh. 'How wet?'

'Touch me!' she groans and grips the brass headboard with her hands.

'In a bit,' he replies, sucking her nipples. 'I like teasing you.'

'Feel me!'

Cameron touches her clitoris without warning. She gasps. It swells and tightens.

He rubs it up and down, and licks her ear. 'Is that nice?'

She thrusts her hips in the air. 'Ah… yes… more!'

He penetrates her with his finger, sliding it in and out of her wetness. She groans. He goes faster.

Her body shudders. She follows the sound of squelching at the meeting of her thighs. 'Ah… yes, Cameron… faster!'

'Are you enjoying yourself?' he whispers, biting her earlobe.

The feel of his slender finger circling the opening to her vagina makes her body jolt. Close to orgasm, she moistens and throbs.

Suddenly, as if under a spell, her thigh muscles tighten. Lucia's legs drop down. She releases her grip of the headboard. Her mind goes blank. Lucia's body turns to stone.

Cameron slips his finger out of her and wipes it on the sheet. 'Are you OK?'

Rain whips the window in waves. The window pane rattles. Lucia flips over onto her side and pulls the duvet over her. It rustles in her ear. Practical lists race through her mind of things she must do on Monday. She must go to the job centre and phone the Citizens Advice Bureau about training programmes. It is like nothing has happened.

Cameron brushes his hand across her back and kisses her spine. 'Where've you gone?' he asks. 'You were in ecstasy a second ago and then you froze. He snuggles up to her, resting his hands on her tummy. 'Where are you?'

'Sorry' she murmurs into the pillow. 'I don't know what happened.' A tear drops from her eye onto her arm. She is miles away and has lost her connection with him.

'Talk to me,' he says.

She clutches Cameron's hand. 'I don't understand either,' she replies playing with his fingers. 'One minute I felt so free with you and the next I felt cold. I couldn't feel my body.'

'Did I hurt you?'

Lucia turns to face him. She leans on her elbow and tugs his grey hair. 'Jesus, no, you were lovely with me,' she replies. 'No one has ever been that tender with me before.'

'Come here.' Cameron grabs her. He holds her tight and tucks his face into the side of her neck. 'It's OK,' he says.

'I'm sorry,' she blubbers. 'It wasn't you.'

'You don't need to apologise. It's not your fault. I understand.'

'Understand what?'

'Well, something may have happened to you.'

She draws back suddenly from his embrace. 'What do you mean?'

'Don't get defensive. Something must have happened to you to make you react like that,' he says. 'I've noticed it with you before, when we were together in Havant.'

'What?'

'I've been aware you have tensed up before. It's like you can't let go.'

'When did you turn into Sigmund Freud?' Lucia replies.

He runs his fingers through her hair. 'Come here; let me hold you.'

She can still feel the moisture at the sides of her thighs. She nestles up to him, feeling more like an infant than a twenty-four-year-old.

'For someone to freeze that seriously must be connected to a trauma,' he says.

'Not necessarily.' Her voice is small.

'Has someone hurt you?' he asks.

She prods his belly button. 'Not that I know of, no.'

'Did anyone interfere with you when you were younger?'

'Not that I remember.' Lucia rolls over and takes a sip of water. 'I used to sleep in the same bed as my dad when I was younger. I used to kick his shins a lot.'

'And?' Cameron sits up and leans against the headboard.

She looks at him. The light from the hallway illuminates his squidgy body. 'I can't remember anything else, just the mornings after. I had bruises all over my legs.'

He scratches his chest. 'That's very common.'

'What is?' Lucia asks.

'It's common for people not to be able to remember childhood trauma. My ex-wife was sexually abused. Her memories didn't return until she was forty-one.'

'Great. So, I'm going to be flooded with memories at forty of shagging my dad?'

Cameron swings his legs out of the bed and scratches his back. 'Not necessarily, but maybe something happened with your father that you can't remember. He loved you too much, and in the wrong way.' He stands and puts on his boxers.

'Where are you going?' she asks.

'I'm going downstairs to make a cuppa.'

'You're wrong,' she shouts. 'High court judges don't fuck their daughters!'

'Don't they?' Cameron replies, raising one eyebrow.

He walks down the stairs.

Lucia punches the pillow. *For fuck's sake!* She picks up the duvet and walks over to the armchair. Lucia throws Cameron's jeans onto the floor. A pound coin rolls out of his pocket. She huddles in the chair and wraps the duvet around her. It stinks of duck feathers. Her mouth feels like cotton wool. Lucia retraces those nights in her father's bed.

I would go to bed early.

He would come to bed. His pyjamas felt furry.

441

I could hear him saying something.
Stop.
I was hot. His tummy was warm.
Stop.
I was kicking. I was kicking his bony shin.
She pushes for more memory, but, like with the worst constipation, as hard as you push, nothing moves.
Then it was morning. Daddy would say 'You kick a lot, darling.'
I had bruises on my legs.
It was scrambled eggs on toast for breakfast. I was frightened.

*

Downstairs in the kitchen, Lucia runs her hand across the smooth surface of the pine table. The grandfather clock ticks. The night is still black. Out of the window, she sees the outline of the branches waiting for spring to bring them into new leaf.

This house makes her think of *The Waltons*, with old-fashioned radios in every room.

Lucia feels unsettled by their failed attempt to make love. She feels it is her fault.

She sits, naked, in the carver chair, whilst Cameron spreads another piece of toast with strawberry jam. Her head rests in the palm of her hand, whilst he hums a happy tune from *Snow White* to distract her from brooding about herself.

He can read her and knows something is up.

Cameron sits on the chair at the head of the table. He chews on his granary crust and watches her tortured repose. He smells of burnt kindling and old coats.

She moans quietly.

'What's up?' he asks.

Lucia shrugs.

'You don't need to beat yourself up for everything, you know.'

'I'm not,' she replies.

'Aren't you?'

'Maybe, a bit.' Her arms fall flat on the table and her head drops. 'It's just that I really like you. I don't know what just happened upstairs. I checked out.'

'It will take time to understand,' he replies.

'What will take time?'

'If something happened with your father, recovering your memory will take time. Be gentle with yourself.'

Gentle is not a word Lucia readily understands. When Cameron says it, an image of a silk scarf blowing ever so slightly in the breeze comes to mind. 'Gentle?' she asks.

'Yes, gentle.' His eyes enlarge. 'You punish yourself for everything all the time. You don't need to worry about retribution. Your father can't hurt you. He's in a home, lost in his madness. Relax.'

Relax?

Lucia flicks her eyes up at him. Cameron has a way of looking at her that penetrates her. It is healing but uncomfortable. Her feet feel cold on the marble floor. She rubs the sole of her right foot up her left calf, and stares at the red spots on Cameron's shoulder.

'I still think there is a secret inside you,' he says.

She turns her head away from him.

'There is, isn't there?'

'No.'

'What is it? Go on, tell me,' he goads playfully.

'I can't!' she cries, and pulls at her hair.

'What's the worst thing that could happen? Hmmm?'

'I could go to prison.'

'Prison?'

'Yes, it's bad, Cameron.'

'Have you hurt someone?'

'Don't be daft; of course I haven't,' Lucia replies.

'Come on, it can't be that bad!'

'It is.'

'Look, whatever it is, telling the truth brings relief. I've known you for a while now, and something inside is keeping you trapped. Telling the truth about whatever it is will set you free,' he says.

Lucia looks into his searing, blue eyes. A whole world lives behind them.

He slams his hand on the table.

She jumps.

His face moves closer to hers. 'Come on, what is it? There is something you need to say, and, until you say it, you will never be at peace.'

Her gaze drops down to his beautiful, manicured hands; just looking at his hands makes her feel wet.

'Come on!' he shouts.

'No!' She tilts her head back like an angry stallion and lets out a forced laugh. 'I can't!'

His eyes scan her face for answers. 'Have you committed a crime?'

'No.' Lucia grips her neck with her hand. 'Well, kind of, yes. I faked something once. I told a bad lie.'

'Ah, this is more like it. What did you fake? Go on. I'm all ears.' Cameron asks like he is speaking to a young child.

Lucia bites her wrist, and bounces up and down on her chair.

'Go on, tell me.'

'I can't!' she squirms, twisting her body into knots.

'Yeah, you can; after three, ready? One… two… three.' He waits.

'I faked a poltergeist when I was sixteen. Everyone believed it. It ended up on TV.'

He breaks out into a wild burst of laughter and claps his hands. 'Ah, that's excellent!' he chuckles. 'What did you do?'

'Everything. I threw furniture around, moved things, poured water on carpets…'

Daylight breaks through. The birds tweet. Drops of condensation roll down the window, and the radiator lets out a hissing sound as it releases the first shot of morning heat.

Lucia looks at Cameron's rugged face. She is now able to fully take him in. She savours this moment of being loved for who she really is. 'Why do you love me like this, Cameron?'

'You are a very creative person,' he replies. 'I want you to know that and stop hiding.'

'Hiding?'

'Yes, you need to be who you really are. Your poltergeist was creative not bad. It was part of you.'

'Was it?'

'Yes. It was a creative outlet. Well done!'

Being congratulated after what had felt like a prison sentence for eight years is hard to take in. Cameron's words lift those years of burden. The weight of her guilt lightens.

A ladybird lands on Lucia's arm and crawls down to her hand. It tickles her skin.

'Now you must set yourself free.'

Lucia sits up straight. 'How do I do that?'

'You need to go to London and tell your family the truth.'

Telling them the truth is inconceivable. 'But they'll hate me,' she insists.

He licks his lips. They are already wet, but he moves them like a fish, making a popping sound.

'No, they won't. The truth heals,' he replies.

The way he taps his nails on the table ignites her sexual fire, but she knows that sex won't happen between them again. It is now 6.00am. Her head is tight from being awake all night, but she is running on adrenalin.

'And then you must write a play or a book about it,' Cameron continues.

'A book?'

'Yes, because it is about your creativity. What you did was creative, so you must create. Your story is a universal one. It feels personal to you, but it is about everyone.' He folds his arms. 'We feel alone with our stories, but they are interpersonal. If you have the courage to tell your story, you will help others.'

'How do I do that?'

He scratches his head and contorts his mouth to demonstrate that she knows full well how to do it. 'Just write it as *you* want to write it, but, before you do that, you need to go and speak to your family. You must tell them the truth.'

CHAPTER FORTY-ONE

LONDON, 1997

LUCIA IS TWENTY-FOUR YEARS OLD

It is a mild Saturday afternoon. Lucia has arranged to meet her brothers and mum at the flat at 3.00pm. She has come across especially from Bristol, where she now works for Oxfam. Lucia has not told her family what this meeting is about, but has stated that she has a *need* to meet.

She shuffles up the front steps. She can see Tim's bashed up Fiesta and Ben's Golf GTI parked opposite. Her hand trembles, which makes it hard to insert the key in the lock.

Lucia steps into the hallway and listens for voices upstairs.

That evening last year in Diss, talking with Cameron, floats in her head. Lucia grips onto the strength of Cameron's conviction as his words echo in her mind. *You must tell your family the truth.* She knows she is doing the right thing. With blood thudding in her ears, she marches up the stairs in spite of her fear. She stops just before the top step, and hears laughing. Lucia feels left out before she has even entered.

She opens the flat door.

'Hi!' they shout simultaneously.

Their cocktail of tones is upbeat on the surface, but laced with undertones of dread. They do not like her.

She turns the doorknob and tucks her hair behind her ears. 'Hiya,' she says.

'Hi Lucia,' Tim mumbles.

'Hi,' Ben says and smiles artificially.

Her mum says nothing and greets Lucia with a stare brewing anger.

Her mother is slumped in her armchair, Ben is sprawled out on the sofa and Tim sits cross-legged in the bespoke chair. Lucia walks over to the divan, sits down and stretches out her legs. She slaps her thighs and takes a deep breath.

'How are you?' Ben asks.

'All right,' Lucia replies, avoiding eye contact.

'So, what's this all about?'

Lucia wrinkles her face. 'I need to talk to you all.' She keeps her gaze fixed on the blue triangles on the Persian rug. 'It's important.'

'Yes,' Tim says. 'Go on.'

'It's about what happened here in 1989,' Lucia says, stealing a glance at Tim. His face is the most forgiving. She focuses on the mole above his lip.

'What about what happened in 1989?' Ben asks.

Ben's tone is tense and sets up a nervous reaction right under her heart. Lucia grabs onto the picture of Cameron's milky-blue eyes that moment she told him about her poltergeist story. The afternoon in Camden Town when Ben admitted he was gay flashes back to her as well. Ben needed her understanding then, so will he extend that warmth back to Lucia today?

'It was me. The poltergeist was me,' she says, meeting all of their eyes. 'I did it all,' she declares, as if under arrest.

The droning hum of the air purifier cuts the silence in the room.

'Poltergeists always focus around the teenager. We know you were at the epicentre of it. We always knew that. That's not news,' Ben replies.

'No, it didn't focus around me, *it was me*. I did all off those things. There was no poltergeist. It was me.'

Tim presses his knuckles against his lips and looks out of the window.

'You did every single thing?' her mum asks, purse-lipped.

'Yes. I have wanted to tell you all these years, but I just couldn't. Tears surge to Lucia's eyes, but she chokes them back.

'No, it's impossible,' Ben says, shaking his head. 'There is no way you could have done all of those things without us seeing.' He sits forwards. 'We saw things moving on their own accord. *I* saw your textbook fly across the room and the vase of dried flowers float.'

'I did do it all, but not consciously.'

'What do you mean "not consciously"?' Ben snarls. 'You were either conscious or not.'

Lucia counts the triangles on the rug to stop herself crying, and spreads her fingers like palm leaves across her lap. 'I couldn't control a lot of it,' she says. 'It just happened. I didn't plan any of it; something happened to me.'

Tim cocks his head and jerks out a smile that quickly turns stern. 'Well, come to think of it, that does answer a lot of the mystery.'

'No. I re-re-re-refuse to accept it was you. I *saw* things flying around with my very own eyes, day in, day out!' her mum bellows.

'Well, we all thought we did.' Tim replies. 'We were obviously wrong.'

Ben punches the coffee table. A marble egg jumps and crashes back down on the brass tray. He leans forwards and shows his teeth like a dog on the prowl. 'I want you to go over every *single* incident and say how you did each one, before you leave today.' He sits back. 'Well, go on; I'm all ears.'

Lucia presses the heel of her hand between her eyes. 'I can't! I can't go over every single one!' she shouts. 'It's impossible.'

'We've got all afternoon,' Ben replies.

Lucia's words escape downwards in slow bursts. 'Look, it-it-it was out of my control. I just found myself doing the things without thinking about them.' She lifts her head and kneads her eyebrows. 'But some of them, I really didn't do.'

'Like what?' Ben asks.

'That helicopter noise from your stomach! I didn't do that,' she pleads, as if on trial. 'And the messages, they just came through me. I couldn't control it. It was like another person was doing it.'

Tim folds his arms and lets out an affirming hum. 'What about the fire?' he asks.

'I did that.'

'You set fire to this room?' Ben asks.

'Yes. Look, I'm sorry; I'm sorry for it all!' Lucia replies, cupping her hand over her forehead.

Ben grabs a cushion and throws it on the floor. 'Have you any idea the shame you have brought on this family?' His face reddens. 'What are people going to think of us when we tell them?'

Lucia looks at him. Her face burns. She tries to swallow but can't.

'What about the trances?' Ben asks.

Lucia shrugs.

'"What about the trances?" I asked.'

'It was real and it wasn't. I didn't know what was going on.'

'I-I-I-I still cannot accept that y-y-y-you did it all, Lucia; I'm sorry,' her mother stammers. 'It's just not possible... not possible.'

'I agree,' Tim says.

Lucia feels the blood drain out of her face.

'I guess some of it makes sense,' Ben mutters under his breath.

'Wh-wh-wh-what do y-o-o-ou mean?' her mother asks. 'How can any of this *make sense*?'

'Well, we hardly wanted Lucia around, did we?'

Lucia feels relief at Ben's admittance.

'Wh-wh-wh-wh-hat o-o-on earth d-d-d-o you mean?' Her mother stammers, poking her chest with her finger. 'I-I-I wanted her. She's my d-d-d-daughter.'

'You've a funny way of showing it,' Ben replies.

Her mother looks at Lucia and swallows. 'Of course I wanted her!'

Ben raises an eyebrow. 'Strange, then, that she had to shit everywhere to get your attention.'

Lucia massages the skin under her jaw. She is relieved that the conflict has moved away from her, but feels that age-old protectiveness towards her mother, whose vulnerability Lucia understands better than anyone.

'It wa-wa-wasn't her!' her mother screeches. 'It *was* a poltergeist!'

'Fine, keep turning a blind eye,' Ben replies.

Lucia realises she is not going to get anywhere. They do not accept that the poltergeist was her. In not accepting her pain, they don't accept her. The stark realisation that it will never be any different hits her like a metal object falling and hitting her from above.

Lucia stands.

She slings her rucksack on her back.

'Wh-wh-where are you go-go-going Lucia?' her mum asks with bulging eyes.

Lucia looks through her mother's steamy glasses. The lines in her mum's face are deeper than ever before, and the rolls of tummy flab hanging over the elastic of her trousers show how much weight she has gained.

'I'm sorry, Mum,' Lucia says, 'for everything.'

Her mother shakes her head and wipes her nose with a tissue. 'No... no... no, its fine, Lucia,' she snivels.

'No, Mum, it's not. We need some time and space apart.'

'What do you mean, Lucia?'

'I'm going to go to Tiffany's for the night and then head back to Bristol, to give you time to think it all over.' Lucia walks towards the sitting-room door. 'It's for the best.'

Lucia sprints down the stairs and opens the front door. The clouds race high up in the warm spring wind. She opens her arms and allows that sweet-smelling breeze to blow over her skin. The irises look beautiful on the lawn across the road. A black taxi chugs over the speed bumps and Lucia watches its indicator flicker until it becomes more distant.

Lucia walks to the end of the road and stops at the house that looks like a chapel. She sits on the wall, watching the sway of a pussy willow. She takes a cheese sandwich out from her bag and bites into it.

She chuckles to herself as she looks across at the white houses she once coveted. She imagined, once, that perfect lives were lived in those. Now they are Noddy houses with no character, and, who knows, divorce and abuse could happen behind those doors too?

This place is dire. Even with the spring trees in bloom, her hopes and dreams don't live here. As long as she is linked to these family relationships, she can never be happy. She chucks her crusts into the litter bin and watches a plane cruise through the scatter of fluffy clouds. She is the only person who can turn her life around.

Lucia thinks about her psychotherapy with Maggie and now Francis in Bristol, and the encouragement it has given her to reach her potential. But she doesn't know how. Francis, her transpersonal therapist, has taught her that happiness is not about grabbing onto fleeting moments of joy, but about finding something meaningful to sustain you.

She swings her leg and feels the breeze creep up her skirt. How can she find something meaningful? Francis says that people from broken families can use their devastation to create something beautiful if they treat their pain as compost, and not as shit. She ponders that for several minutes and recalls the inspiring day Francis told her that.

Maybe it is possible for her! A rush of energy shoots up her spine. Yes, she *can* reach her potential, but she must set sail for new lands and make a fresh start, away from here.

Lucia heads towards the over-ground station. There is a nip in the air. As she strolls, she allows herself to dream of the roaring Pacific along Route One from Los Angeles (LA) to San Francisco. She's only seen it in films. She'd love to go there. She knows there are seals on the beaches not far from Santa Barbara, and don't Californians eat loads of sushi?

Now en route to Hackney, Lucia studies her reflection in the train window and recalls the look of desperation in her mother's eyes as she walked out. Nothing pulls at her more than her mother's need. She rubs her fingers across her eyebrows to dull the tension there.

As Lucia steps onto the platform at Dalston Kingsland, her red-haired heroine Annie springs to mind. She dribbles a Coke can along the platform with the side of her foot, thinking about the gusto with which Annie raises her fists to the boys who steal her dog, Sandy. She got away from the baddies and found her Daddy Warbucks, so, maybe, Lucia can too.

*

Back at her flat in Bristol, Lucia sits on the sofa, gazing out at the black night, whilst listening to Anand wash up in the kitchen. Rose-scented incense wafts in from the hall, whilst a Bhagwan Osho meditation plays in Anand's study. He does his kundalini meditation every Sunday night. Lucia hasn't got a clue what it's about, but this is the best a home can be.

Anand pokes his head through the hanging beads, 'You look shattered, Lucia; would you like a peppermint tea?'

'Yes, please,' she replies, misty eyed.

'Was it a long journey or just a difficult trip?'

Lucia holds up her hand and flops back onto the cushions behind her. 'Difficult trip,' she sighs. 'I saw my family.'

'Why don't you go and have a hot bath. I'll bring this to you when it's brewed. I'll make it from fresh leaves. Don't worry, I'll knock first,' he mocks.

'Thanks.' She appreciates her friendship with flatmate Anand. There is no sexual chemistry; he's just a decent bloke who rents her a room in his safe hippy haven.

The phone rings.

'I'll go,' Anand says and marches out to the hall.

She listens.

'Yep, hold on a minute.'

She knows it is for her. Lucia walks down the dusty stairway. Anand hands her the receiver. 'It's for you, Lucia. It's Ben. He wants a word.'

Lucia sits on the creaky chair and takes a deep breath. 'Hi Ben, I was going to call you,' she says.

'Well, I beat you to it.' Ben replies.

'I'm sorry, Ben,' Lucia says, rubbing her eyes.

'You don't need to be sorry Luce. I'm sorry that you were

in so much pain that you had to go to such extremes to get our attention. It's sad.'

The line crackles.

'Luce, are you still there?'

'Yeah, I'm just knackered; it wasn't a run of the mill weekend really.'

'Well, you know where I am if you need anything. Just call me.'

Lucia feels touched at her brother's gesture, but she is unable to take in his invitation for support. The hostility is still too close. 'Thanks, Ben. I appreciate it.'

'I love you,' Ben says.

She swallows. Her sticky breath coats the mouthpiece with mist. 'Love you too. And I'm sorry.'

'Listen, we do what we have to do to survive. None of us will go to our graves fully understanding what happened back then,' he replies. 'It was a mystery.'

She winds the phone wire around her hand and watches her fingers swell. 'You can say that again! Look, I can't really chat now, Ben. I'm knackered. I'll see you soon.'

'See ya, Luce. Take care.'

'You too.' She hangs up.

A glaze of peace settles within her. Lucia walks to the bathroom and turns on the hot water. She sits on the rim of the bath and watches the steam settle on the mirror.

She did it. She told her family the truth.

'Lucia, is everything OK?' Anand calls.

'Fine, thanks,' she replies, undressing.

Whatever happens from here on, Lucia has nothing to hide.

CHAPTER
FORTY-TWO

LONDON – HAIGHT ASHBURY, 1998

LUCIA IS TWENTY-FOUR YEARS OLD

I've spent the last year applying for post-graduate training programmes in California, and fundraising for my studies there. I chose the west coast because of the open space and wild coastline.

'Ha-ha-ha-have you got everything?' Mum asks. She is hunched over in her anorak with a drop of snot on the end of her nose.

I can't swallow. I feel torn inside as I look at her sagging face and lonely eyes. I don't want to leave her alone, but I know this is the only thing I can do. I watch a line of people wheeling their cases through to the departure lounge as I pick my nail.

'Ha-ha-have you got enough money, Lucia?'

'I'm fine, Mum, honest.'

'Ar-ar-ar-are you sure?'

Tears are brimming in my eyes. It feels like there is a block of cement in my throat. 'Yeah, I have my dollars. Please don't worry about me, Mum.'

'Shall we speak first thing tomorrow?' she asks with a dry mouth.

'I'll call you 6.00pm tomorrow evening, my time.'

She scrambles in her bag, pulls out her diary and writes, 'Lucia calling, 10.00am,' on 20th April. 'Ha-ha-ha-have we got time for one last coffee, Lucia?'

I have a prickling sensation in my throat. I can't prolong the agony. 'I'd better go through, Mum,' I reply, and heave my rucksack onto my back. I lean over and kiss her on the cheek. Her skin is soft and smells of D'Issey Miyake.

'Are you going to be all right, Mum?'

She gives me a hearty kiss back on the cheek. 'Of course I'm going to be OK,' she replies with watery eyes.

It feels as if I won't be seeing her again. I can't bring myself to walk away. I swallow down my tears and kiss her again. 'We'll speak tomorrow,' I reassure her and take a few steps forwards.

She blows me another kiss with her hand. 'Have a good flight,' she croaks and waits for me to walk through the doors.

I look back and wave. She turns away and waddles off through the crowds. Tears gush from my eyes. I hold onto a luggage trolley and bawl, oblivious to all of the flight announcements being made.

I look up. Mum has gone. There is no sight of her green-and-blue anorak or her duck like waddle. I start to imagine her alone on the Tube facing the lonely night ahead with me not there. I can just see her, with her dinner on her lap, watching *Coronation Street* with no sound on. I block out the thought and walk through security. I put my rucksack onto the conveyer belt, and hold my arms up as the uniformed guard runs her hands up and down my body. Tears stream down my face.

'Are you all right, petal?' the security lady asks.

I wipe my nose with my sleeve 'No, but I will be,' I reply and walk through to the departure lounge.

San Francisco flight VA4510 is on time. It's boarding at 3.20pm from Gate Forty-Two.

*

The plane drops into pockets of wind as we fly over the San Andreas Fault, which is a deep line surrounded by cracked earth. It looks like skin gone mouldy around a scab. The rusty-red, rolling terrain beneath is majestic. There are no boundaries; it extends for hundreds of miles.

My cheeks are soggy and my lungs are compressed from sobbing so much on this flight, but I feel my body expand and my tears settle as I look down at this vast land below. Looking down at this beautiful land, I feel I may have a chance of happiness now.

The plane takes a sharp turn left. I see the skyline and water beneath. It's wonderful.

This land invites me towards a better life.

*

I've found a room in Upper Haight. It's in a four-storey Victorian row house, with a blue-and-yellow exterior. Anna, the owner, is a seventy-four-year-old lesbian, who swims daily, has crystal clear skin and cooks the best crispy bacon for brekkie ever. The other flatmate, Caroline, is an oversized banker, who works in Sacramento and spends most of her time on her phone talking to her daughter in South Carolina.

There's a musty smell throughout the house. Each room has coloured wood panelling. There are comfy chairs in the hallway with rows of bookcases lining the walls. My room is tiny with only a desk, a bed and a wardrobe, but out of my window I can see the Berkeley hills across the bay. Their salmon-pink twinkle first thing in the morning, as the sun rises behind them, is a glorious sight.

It's the fresh smell of eucalyptus on the streets that I love here. It hits me every day as I walk through Golden Gate Park. I stroll through the arboretum in the early morning and sit under the oak trees listening to the birds. The minty smell is wonderful, especially in a gust of breeze. It has an unusual hint of citrus to its fragrance.

I've found a cafe down on leafy Cole Street, where I enjoy a peanut-butter bagel and a cup of Earl Grey on a bench outside. It's a meeting ground for political utopians and artists, who gather for lunchtime chats. Upper Haight is full of great thrift shops and funky bars.

I've started my training in arts consulting and education. My college is down in the Mission District, close to all the Mexican restaurants and small theatres. I've never seen so many homeless people before though; they wander through the streets with shopping trolleys full of black bags. It's so sad to see. We don't know how good we have it back in England.

I have met some cool folks on the programme. Kaitlyn and Alyssa are both great. Kaitlyn has high cheek bones and a cool dress sense. She's from LA originally, and lives in a quirky top-floor flat off Van Ness, with a roof terrace that looks out over the Golden Gate Bridge. It's heaven out there at sunset, with a glass of wine and one of her home-cooked chickens. Alyssa lives in a tree house outside Mill Valley. You have to climb a rope to get up there, and, once inside, you look out onto groves of lush redwood trees. Both women are training as therapists.

I can't get used to the way they do relationships here though. Everyone seems so boundary conscious. I don't like the 'we must do coffee' culture. I prefer just popping round for a cuppa. Nor do I like being called 'ma'am' by stern Muni drivers.

I've set up an agreement with Mum that we speak once a week, at a set time. That way, I don't feel like I am abandoning her *and* I don't feel as strangled by the relationship. It's a good balance, and it allows me to live with less guilt about her loneliness, though I still feel the wrench from her. I worry about her on her own, that she might do something silly. Yet, I am so relieved to be away from her pain, and that I have space to breathe. The conflict tears me apart, but the smell of lemon from the trees brings me solace as I walk along these colourful streets.

CHAPTER FORTY-THREE

SAN FRANCISCO, 1999

LUCIA IS TWENTY FIVE YEARS OLD

I've found a more permanent room to rent on Craig's List. I'm living with two women in a flat share in The Castro. It's a joy to walk these hilly streets, with the rainbow flags hanging from every lamppost. It's a testosterone overdose some days, with men with bulging biceps walking arm in arm, but it's never short of a bar playing cheesy house music.

I have finished my training, and I have got a job working for an arts organisation, teaching kids dance and theatre in elementary schools. I go to fifteen schools a week and deliver twelve-week arts residencies to children from the first grade through to the fifth.

I take the tram from Market Street up to China Town. I love the steep ascent up Powell and Mason Street, and the sight of the sparkling bay as we chug past Pacific Avenue. I stand, holding the pole, feeling that crisp air on my skin, and watch the grip man drop the rope at California Street as we crest the hill. It's always a spectacle.

I walk the rest of the way to North Beach, where I am teaching a first-grade class. I stop for a cheeky fig-and-rhubarb sorbet at Gelateria Del Gallo, which sells the best ice cream in town. I sit outside and listen to the bells ring from St Peter's Church, and watch the world go by.

As I climb up Filbert Street, a crowd of kids run to the fence of the school playground, shouting 'Miss Lucy, Miss Lucy!' and wave at me. I am dressed in more conservative clothes than usual because the principal is very strict. It's a Chinese school, though the children all speak English.

In the assembly hall, I prepare my CDs, and arrange my scarves and props, whilst enjoying the sweeping views of Coit Tower. A line of children walk in, led by their classroom teacher, Miss Mei. Their eyes light up when they see me.

'Good morning, children! Let's make a circle,' I say, beckoning to them.

We hold hands and sit down.

'Do you remember what we learnt last week?' I ask.

'Levels! High, medium and low, and shapes,' Huan shouts out, making his arms into the shape of a teapot spout.

'Well done!' I say. 'Today we are going to learn about locomotive movements.'

'What's that?' Xiang asks, with his finger in his mouth.

'Do you remember we learnt about stationary movements?'

'Yes,' they nod in unison.

'Well, locomotion is the opposite of stationary. Jiang, can you crawl across the floor for me?'

He crawls from the stage to the door. Everybody laughs.

'That is locomotion,' I say, pointing to Jiang. 'Please give him a clap for an excellent demonstration.' They all clap. 'Now, let's stand and move.'

The class walk around the hall. I bang the drum and shout, 'Freeze!'

They stop, and keep as still as they can. This helps them to learn about focus.

'This time, when I say "freeze", I want you to make a twisty shape,' I instruct.

They run and twirl around the room to the drumbeat.

'Freeze!' I shout.

Liling looks beautiful, standing tall, with her arms matted together like rope and her head tilted sideways. Godfrey crouches on his side, with his arms interwoven.

'Now I want you to line up in two rows. When the music starts, Cheng and Liling, you are going to skip across the floor.'

Lauren Hill's 'Doo Wop' starts with the harmonies and vocals. The drum beat kicks in. 'Off you go, bringing your knees up as high as you can!' I say over the music.

They hold hands and skip across the floor in twos, giggling. We repeat the exercise with hopping, jumping, rolling, leaping and spinning. Their cheeks are flushed.

'Now, kids,' I say, clapping my hands together. 'I want you to get into groups of four and choose three locomotive movements, two levels and three shapes, and put them together in a sequence. Do you understand?'

They nod.

I demonstrate skipping on a low level, jumping on a high level and then freezing in a spiral shape with my elbow on the floor.

I leave them to work together for eight minutes, whilst I prepare the music for their performance. When they have finished rehearsing, I gather them together in a line, to form the audience.

'Do you remember what you have to do in the audience?' I ask.

'You have to watch and be respectful,' Wei calls out.

'Well done, Wei. Who wants to come up and show their composition?'

Peng puts up his hand. 'We do,' he says. Peng has come on a long way. The school label him as a 'problem kid' with an attention deficit disorder, but in these movement sessions he comes to life.

I hand Peng's group a coloured scarf each. They stand in the performance space. Chopin's 'Nocturne Opus 9 Number 1' plays. They spin to the melodic music, changing levels and making imaginative shapes with their scarves. Wang lies on the floor and brings his knees into the air. The others gallop around him and freeze with their ears touching the floor and one leg raised in the air.

It's incredible. They are simple elements, but, put together, it is beautiful to watch.

They bow. The audience clap.

'Can you tell me what you saw in their performance?' I ask the class.

'Medium level!'

'Shape like a deer!'

'Spinning! Rolling!'

'Did you see any stationary movements?'

Daquan raises his hand and says in a quiet voice, 'when Wang was on the floor.'

'Well done, Daquan!'

The groups come up, one by one and perform their pieces. We end in a circle, catching a star and making a wish.

The bell rings. They leave as quietly as they came in, but smiling. It's wonderful seeing the kids thrive from these sessions. This is such a fulfilling job.

After work, I head down to Fisherman's Wharf for some seafood and watch a theatre troupe miming on the waterfront. I then wander down to the marina to look for a new skirt for tomorrow night. Kaitlyn and I are going down to the Mission District to see a Cuban band.

*

The Fillmore is heaving. Toots and the Maytals are on stage, singing their greatest hit, 'Take Me Home, Country Roads'. I'm swaying to the ska beat, smiling.

I move like I'm rowing a boat standing up, letting the waves carry my weight.

I feel a large man's hips grinding behind me. His groin is in contact with my butt. I move in sync with him, clapping to the beat. I feel his hot breath on my neck, as I wipe away the sweat from my face.

He hands me a fat joint. I take a drag and get an immediate rush.

I turn around, and notice his strong features and unusual style. He puts his arms around my waist. We dance to the reggae song, as if no one were watching. Beer spills on my shoulder from a couple grooving in front of us. I don't care. He holds my hips as they gyrate.

'What's your name?' I ask.

'Lennie,' he whispers in my ear. 'Do you want a drink?'

'Go on then, half a pint of lager.'

We walk to the bar. Lennie wipes his forehead with a beer mat and hands the bartender a $10 bill. *'Get your hands in the air, sir!'* Toots start to sing '54–46', another one of my faves. *'And you will get no hurt, mister, no no no.'*

Lennie puts a glass of Heineken in front of me and asks me my name.

'Lucia,' I reply.

'Loo what?' he laughs.

'Lu-ci-a,' I say with deliberate lip movements.

'That's a mouthful. Can I call you Lu?'

'If you must,' I reply, sipping my beer.

You give it to me one time (huh)
You give it me to two times (huh-huh)

I love this track.

54–46 was my number, yeah,

467

Right now, someone else has that number

Just in front of the bar, we jive around my handbag, with our hips linked.

And I said yeah! (I said yeah)
Listen to what I say…

This man has rhythm. Every one of his moves is in sync with the beat.

Lennie is black. He has a deep southern accent. He's wearing leather trousers, purple cowboy boots and a red waistcoat with a purple t-shirt underneath – all coordinated. He has a gold chain around his neck and a sovereign ring on his middle finger.

His hands are firm, and his build broad.

'Where are you from?' I shout.

'Alabama.' He talks right into my eardrum, 'the deep, dark south, baby.'

His accent turns me on, and so does his deep voice. I smell aftershave on him, under the heavy wave of body odour around us. We finish our drinks and go back to the dance floor. He holds me around my belly and kisses my neck. I lean back into him and let his sturdy body take my weight. His thick lips feel soft against my burning hot skin. We dance together until the end of the concert, past midnight.

'I'll take you home,' he says.

God! It's already 1.00 am. 'OK, thanks.'

We get our coats from the cloakroom and leave the club. The street lights make me blink fast for a few minutes as I get used to being outside. That message from primary school jumps to mind, the warning they gave us to never go anywhere with strangers. I don't know Lennie, but he feels like a safe soul.

We jump on a number twenty-two Fillmore bus. Lennie puts his arm around me as we ride the hilly journey home.

'What do you do?' I ask.

'I'm a drug and alcohol counsellor.'

'What does that involve?'

'It's helping young people with heavy addictions. I mean *heavy*.'

I knew he was good. We get off the bus at Market and Castro, just in front of The Castro Theatre, which is lit up in pink and blue neon lights.

'I'll walk the rest of the way,' I say. I don't want him to know where I live just yet.

'You sure?' he asks, flicking my hair away from my face. 'Boy, your eyes are beautiful, Lu-Lu.'

'Thank you.'

His eyes settle on my collarbone. Lennie leans towards me and kisses me on the lips. It's a long, wet, teasing kiss, and I enjoy the feel of his lips petting mine.

I pull away. 'Can I have your number?'

He writes it on the back of a Rizla packet. 'Don't be a stranger, Lu-Lu,' he says, and hands me his number.

We hug. His back feels like iron.

'I won't,' I reply, starting to walk away. 'Thanks for a great night, Lennie.'

'Hey, sister,' he winks. 'More will be revealed.'

*

We've been out on a date. We approach a run-down tenement block on Eddy Street, in the heart of the Tenderloin. A man with an eye patch staggers out of the liquor store. He kicks a whisky bottle up the street, swearing. Lennie puts his arm around me and opens the front door. The walls and floor are concrete, and need a new coat of paint. A woman in fishnet tights leans over some metal seats, whilst a man, with a scar across his cheek and wearing combat trousers, drinks a bottle of Strongbow and looks at her.

This is how I imagine a brothel in the Bronx to be.

We get in the elevator. The smell of stagnant piss hits me. It says *'Maximum load, two people'*. It jolts before it ascends. I worry we will get stuck because Lennie is so big.

The third floor is a long corridor. Hip-hop blares out from the room at the end. Lennie's bedsit is number 310.

'Make yourself at home, Lu-Lu,' he says and turns on the light.

It smells of old socks and paraffin. It's about four foot by three in here. There is a single bed in the corner, with an old blanket over it; an armchair in another corner; and a small kitchenette with a cooker ring, a fridge and a sink.

I sit on his bed. In front of me are colour-coordinated shirts and trousers hanging from a long rail. The purples are all together and merge into lilacs, then come reds, pinks and yellows, all in beautiful silk. Underneath must be fifty pairs of cowboy boots, in different colours of leather, even fricking green!

'Why do you have so many pairs of cowboy boots, Lennie?'

'Cos, I'm a cowboy,' he replies, swigging a can of cold lager.

Gold chains and scarves hang from hooks on the wall. I love his attention to detail. He takes pride in his appearance, but not with his home. I notice a painting on the wall of a black Jesus on the cross. 'Did you do that?' I ask.

'No, one of the kids I helped at work painted it for me. He said I saved his life.'

I hear men arguing out in the corridor. It sounds like one of them is being pushed up against a wall.

'Ignore them,' Lennie says, sitting next to me. 'You get used them.'

This place puts me on edge, but I trust Lennie. I see the man, not the surroundings.

He takes off his top. His black rippling chest is like a still-life painting. I run my fingers along the contour lines under his muscles and kiss his nipple. 'Do you work out?'

He unbuttons my blouse and bites the lace rim of my bra. 'Everyday,' he replies. 'Do you?'

'I'm not that committed, but I dance everyday with the kids.'

'Lie back, baby,' he orders, undoing my trousers with his teeth.

His spongy lips glide up and down my stomach. He grabs hold of my knickers and pulls them slowly down my legs. He eases my legs apart and nibbles my toes.

'I like you wet, baby,' he hisses, and places my feet on his shoulders.

I groan as I feel his warm breath blow against my vulva. I spread my legs out wider, so they can't open anymore. He wiggles the tip of his tongue around the hood of my clitoris. I heave. He licks me slowly from the opening of my vagina up to my clitoris, and then laps the area fast with his entire tongue.

'Lennie, that feels so good,' I pant and stretch my arms out in a star shape, so my hands are touching the walls. 'I'm coming!' I scream.

Lennie places his velvety lips over my labia as I throb in his mouth.

He tickles my inner thighs with his fingers, making me pulsate deeper. He stays down there for ages, nursing my orgasm.

'Someone enjoyed that,' he says, coming up.

He lies beside me with my juices smeared around his mouth and guides my hand down to his trousers. I feel warmth and hardness. I want to fuck him so badly. My past fears have gone. I climb on top of him, and yank down his boxer shorts.

His penis pops up. I kiss his foreskin and slide my lips downwards.

'Ah… yes; Lu-Lu, I wanna be inside you.'

I rip off his jeans and roll on a condom. He holds up his erect penis, as I slip down onto him. I grip his chest, and bounce up and down, burning and squelching inside.

'Roll over, baby,' he says. 'I wanna give it to you on top.'

I bang my head on the wall as we turn over.

His stomach muscles press into my ribs as he thrusts into me hard. I wrap my legs around his wide back. His breath quickens as he penetrates me deeper. The bed thrashes against the wall, but I don't care if anyone hears us.

'Yes, Lu-Lu; yes, baby!' he shouts, pulling my hair. His breath is rasping.

I feel the end of the condom go limp. He slows down, and collapses onto my chest. Wetness drizzles down my thigh as he pulls out of me. I am scorching hot.

Lennie lies on me for ages and then rubs his nose against mine. 'You're my Lu-Lu,' he says. He tears off the condom, throws it in the bin and walks over to the kitchenette.

I think to myself how I didn't flinch or jump once. I got lost in the sex. I must be healing.

'What you thinking about, Lu-Lu?' he asks, pissing in an empty milk bottle.

'I'm thinking, "Why don't you go to the restroom for a leak?"'

'Those jerks you heard earlier are probably in there, plus it's full of cockroaches,' he replies, putting the milk bottle under the chair.

I gag. 'Why don't you get somewhere to live with a toilet?' I ask. I don't understand why, with a good salary, he lives in this shit hole.

'Cos, we're not all from the land of milk and honey like you, sugar plum,' he says, flopping into the armchair and putting on his cowboy hat.

'Just cos my name is posh, I'm not rich, you know,' I pull the blanket over me. It stinks of mothballs. 'I had to walk to school cos my mum couldn't afford the bus fare.'

He lights a cigar. 'This place suits me just fine, Lu-Lu,' he says.

I burst into laughter.

'What you laughing at, Lu?'

'I'm laughing at you, sitting naked, with a cowboy hat on, puffing on an old man's cigar. You're a character.' I hear the sound of gunshots on the street. 'Is that what I think it is?' I ask, pulling my knees up to my chest.

'You get used to it in the ghetto, relax,' he replies.

'I don't understand how you could feel safe living around these streets.'

I hear more shooting outside.

'This is my 'hood. No one touches Lennie,' he replies, blowing smoke rings into the air.

I wish I had a paintbrush. He would make such a perfect still life, and this bedsit and the gunfire outside make it all the more perfect.

This is Lennie.

I turn onto my side and look at the painting of Jesus, whilst Lennie puffs on his cigar. I prefer the cedar scent of his cigar to the stale smell in here, any day.

CHAPTER
FORTY-FOUR

SAN FRANCISCO, SEPTEMBER 2001

LUCIA IS TWENTY-EIGHT YEARS OLD

I'm dating Lennie, but he doesn't want to live together. He likes his space because his 'crazy bitch' of an ex-wife messed with his head. That suits me fine. I've joined a women's theatre company down on Valencia. We're rehearsing a production of *The Skriker*, which we are touring around San Francisco and Berkeley this summer. I'm playing Josie.

I see Kaitlyn and Alyssa loads. Brooke and Aubrey are great women, too. We camped under the stars at Yosemite for Brooke's birthday last week. We sang around the fire, and lived off tinned tuna and burnt marshmallows. They take me hiking at weekends, all over Sonoma and Marin County. Mendocino is my favourite spot, because of that wild coastline.

It didn't work out with the two stern lesbians in the Castro – there was a solemn atmosphere there and a nasty dog. I've now moved into a former sex commune in Lower Haight. It's a sixteen-bedroom Victorian house, painted lilac on the outside with a fairly tired interior.

Eighteen of us live here. Gail is the youngest resident, an eighteen-year-old politics student at San Francisco State University. Joyce, our most senior housemate is an eighty-year-old writer, who has lived in a nudist colony, and is proud to have had a three-hour-long orgasm. She shares a room with her partner Walter (who is twenty years her junior) and comes down to dinner in her silk pyjamas with her glass of red wine.

The commune was set up in the sixties by a group of hippies from Berkeley, when the residents were all shagging as much as possible. No one seems to get any now, apart from Joyce and Wanda, who enjoys 'being done' by Bruce, a fifty-year-old banker from upstairs. She says his finger 'feels just as good as a cock'.

We have a resident chef, Rodney. We eat communal meals and take it in turns to help. Weekly meetings are held to clear the air, and the hallways are decorated with fresh flowers, picked and arranged by Giresha, our resident Taekwando lover. There is a hot tub in the garden and a dashing bougainvillea bush out there too.

I love Lower Haight. It's edgy. It feels unsafe, with drug dealing on the streets, but there is a buzz about it; there are late-night spoken-word gigs, a delicious Ethiopian restaurant and pub quizzes at the Mad Dog in the Fog.

Grayson's TV is on in the room next door. CNN are

still replaying the same shots of the twin towers falling and people jumping out of windows. I can't watch it anymore. Every shop door you walk by here has a Stars and Stripes flag in it, and the atmosphere on the streets is hostile.

Rodney is downstairs, chopping vegetables with Judith. His moods haven't been too bad of late. He is fairly volatile (which is down to his HIV meds), but we've been getting on well recently. He's bought me tickets to see Bob Dylan in Berkeley for my birthday.

The sun is streaming in through my window. I daydream on my bed in the warm pocket of the sun. Norah Jones' sultry tones block out the traffic noise from Oak Street.

My phone rings.

'Hello.'

'It's me,' Mum replies. Her tone is hushed and unusually kind.

I am shocked to hear her voice. It is 4.00pm, which means it's only 8.00am in England. We haven't arranged to speak. 'Is something wrong?' I ask.

'I-I-I'm so so-so-sorry to have to tell you this. It's Colin. He died in the night.'

I stand still and listen to a siren wailing past outside. My Buddha sits in the corner. That last shot of Dad on the steps of his nursing home, trapped by the chaos of his mind, flashes before me. He can't be dead.

'What do you mean, Mum?'

'He died of pneumonia. Yvonne said he wasn't in any pain. I'm so sorry, Lucia.'

Blood knocks in my ears. I don't know what to do with myself. 'Can I call you back, Mum?'

'Yes. Sh-Sh-Shall we speak later?'

'I don't know. I'll call you when I can, Mum.'

'Th-Th-The funeral is going to be sometime next week. Will you come?'

'Well, I don't know if I can get out. There are still no planes leaving America. Look, I'll call you.' I hang up, and run my fingers through my hair.

I feel winded. My mind has no thoughts, only that lasting image of Dad telling me to 'enjoy my life'. His tie was chequered, and his bony face was so gaunt. I didn't tell him I loved him. I just walked away. He can't be dead.

I have to move. I gather my belongings into my rucksack and run down the stairs. I mount my new racing bike, and head across Divisadero to Golden Gate Park. The force I use to peddle up Haight Street works up a sweat and pushes through the block of confusion I feel. I zoom past the homeless tribe, smoking skunk on the Panhandle. I don't care about them today.

The minty air soothes me as I enter the park. There is a bunch of people roller boogieing to Missy Elliott on Hippie Hill. I change gears and gather my speed, passing the cypress trees and taking in the scent of California lilac.

As I approach the Japanese tea garden, a wild peafowl walks out in its admiral glory. I brake suddenly, get off my bike and sit on a bench. I wipe the sweat from my forehead, and take in his lapis-feathered surround and majestic eyes. I watch him drift past me, with his long train of feathers shimmering behind. My legs are stiff. I forgot about Dad's death for a second. The redwood grove opposite is verdant. I am tempted to wander through there, but I mount my bike and head down Park Presidio Drive to the beach.

The ocean is calm. The waves have a grey shine, like a seal's fur. There is no one around, except for a couple walking their dog, and a bloke skateboarding.

I sit, shielded from the wind, in the middle of a sand dune, and rest my head on my knees. It just doesn't make sense. Dad has been trapped in his Alzheimer's for so long. It had become the status quo. I knew where he was. I knew I could see him if I wanted to. I knew the chair he sat in, and I knew that, even though he didn't know who I was, he was still there. He was still my dad.

He cannot be dead.

I feel the wind brush against my face. My stomach wrenches with cramps. I hold my tummy with my hands and lean over to subdue the pain. There has been no proper ending and no goodbye. He has just fucked off for good. I didn't think he would ever do that. I thought there would be some smooth ending to this story.

I can't bridge the gap myself; I just can't...

I run down to the water and remember that day in Havant when I shouted at the sea. This ocean is more heroic than the North Sea. I scream at the top of my lungs. Two surfers emerge from under a wave in the distance, but I don't care; I scream again. It's a hoarse sound that comes from me; one scream rolls into another until my sound becomes gravelly.

'Why did you fucking die?' I shout. 'No fucking answers, you bastard! What about those happy days you promised?'

I feel so small, my voice so insignificant as the Pacific breeze carries it away, but I keep shouting, with my desperation bursting out as I wait for some calm to arrive.

I look out at the vast space before me. The Golden Gate Bridge over there stands strong, linking us to Sausalito. I am alone now. There is no one there for me. It may have been an illusion that Dad was there when he was alive, but I prefer the illusion to the stark reality of aloneness.

I realise that I'd been thinking all along that he would recover from senility and become a loving Daddy again, but it's been one series of rejections after another. First, he married Yvonne, then he left for Spain and then he went mad.

Now he's dead; yes, dead.

I stand here for a while, trailing through my last memories of Dad, and I wonder how I could have done things differently, but each time I try to see an alternative I reach a dead end. I roll up my jeans and wheel my bike along the beach towards the Clubhouse. They do a nice Americano, and have a real fire on windy days like today.

My feet slush in the wet sand. I look up at the trees as I walk, and I can just about see a blue heron in his nest. Two boys are flying a kite in front of the windmill down there. They're a long way away, but I can hear the sound of their laughter being carried by the wind. I think of all my friends back home with their perfect mums and dads, and me out here alone, today, when my dad died. They are all so lucky to still have healthy, supportive parents.

I'll call Kaitlyn when I get back. She's such a great support. She has just started her placement in a high-dependency unit for boys, in Oakland. She's made of strong stuff. Kaitlyn is always telling me about the Saturn return, which happens now, at twenty-eight years old. She says it's a time of significant change and is supposed to set you off in a better direction.

I still can't believe my father is dead. He never kept any of his promises.

CHAPTER FORTY-FIVE

SAN FRANCISCO – LONDON, SEPTEMBER 2001

LUCIA IS TWENTY-EIGHT YEARS OLD

The funeral directors in Chelsea have told me that I can visit Dad in their chapel of rest. His coffin will remain open until the day before his funeral. I am welcome any time from 9.00am – 5.00pm.

I flew out from San Francisco on the first plane that took off from US soil after the bombing of the World Trade Centre. As jet-lagged as I am, I want to write a letter to put in Dad's coffin. I have come to our old haunt, the rhododendron bed at St James' Park. It is nippy for September. The crispy leaves skip across the ground in the breeze. I am on the bench where we used to sit and feed the ducks. It still stinks of sour pigeon pooh, and the green water in the duck pond is still full of slimy algae.

I take out my paper and pen from my bag, and I write this:

Dear Dad,

I always wondered how this day would feel. I could never have imagined this strange combination of betrayal and shock.

It's the gaps that you've left that hurt the most, Dad. The gaps I am left to fill in alone. You've left me with questions that I will never get answered. I hate you for that. There are so many things you said you would do, but never did; so many unfulfilled promises; and so much unexplained behaviour. Now, all I have is this silence with no apology or explanation.

I crunch a passing leaf with my foot. It's a satisfying sound. A harried businessman walks past, lost in thought. I can't believe the bandstand is still there after all these years. That lawn used to be full of deckchairs on those summer days when the band would play. I can remember the feel of Dad's happiness as he would tap his foot to the hooting trumpets.

I don't understand. You said that crazy night in Hunstanton, that we would one day have an adult relationship, when I was independent of my mum. I held onto that promise through many lonely years. I believed you. You said I could come and visit you in Spain. I never did. Why? And why on earth no phone number for all those years? How could you deny your own daughter the right to speak her father? It was cruel. Have you any idea how many days I came home from school hoping to find a letter from you? It was torture.

Why, Dad? If you really did love me, then why couldn't I contact you? Those years of enforced silence have seriously damaged me. I can't trust anyone now. So how do I walk on? What comfort can I find in any of this? Tell me, Dad, because I am confused. You abandoned me and left me wanting.

It was the biggest betrayal I will ever know.

It's so desolate here, the branches are becoming nude before winter arrives. That bitter smell of the water is exactly the same as it was. It is like no time has passed. I keep seeing Dad's smile as he watched me devour my strawberry ice and the vigour in his eyes the day he taught me how to spell rhododendron.

So, you've taken the easy route - you've just died and left it all incomplete.
At least this time it's final.

I loved you so much. I looked up to you.
Those holidays, running along the golden
sands in St Brelade's Bay, were the happiest
days of my life. They still make me feel warm
inside when I think of them now. I've got
to walk on now, Dad, and find something
true to hold onto. I don't know what that is.
   It's true that I loved you.
   I wanted you.
   I missed you.

My mouth tastes like when I had flu.

   I love you.
     I miss you.
     I wish it had all been different.
     Go well.
     Lucia x

My only memory of seeing a dead body was one I saw by accident, which I wish I had never seen. Mum's former cleaning lady, Trisha, lived in a flat on top of a funeral directors', which her brother Michael ran. We were there for tea one day, when Michael's son, Ross asked me if I wanted to see one of the embalmed bodies downstairs. I didn't really, but I was kind of fascinated. Mum warned me not to go, but when someone warns you not to do something, you normally do.

I did go. He was a well-built man, comfortably fitted into a shiny, wooden coffin, and dressed in a pinstripe suit, tie and pristine brogues. His face was all glossy looking. It was his eyes that haunted me. They were wide open and staring at me.

Ross gave his leg a hearty slap and said with bravado, 'Good old chap.'

I felt sick and ran out as fast as I could. To this day, Mum says she wishes I had never gone. I do too, actually, as his image has stayed with me – in a bad way – ever since. Bruno, I think he was called. He looked like he had been a banker or something financial in the City of London.

When I walk into the funeral directors on the Fulham Road, I am struck how welcoming it is. It is a quaint, white building with low ceilings. A bell chimes when you open the door. A well-groomed, lanky man walks out of a side room to greet me. He is so tall that he stoops, so as to not bash his head on the ceiling. He shakes my hand. 'You must be Lucia Goldman,' he says.

'Yes, that's me,' I reply.

He introduces himself as Mark Wilson.

His handshake is ever so soft, and behind him is a desk with stacks of papers on, with a spotlight shining brightly over them. He lowers his spectacles and nibbles their left arm. 'You have come to visit your father,' he says softly, 'in our chapel of rest.'

I swallow several times. 'Yes,' I reply, 'if that is OK?'

'Yes, I was expecting you,' he says, and guides me to the door. He turns the handle. 'If you walk through here, there is a small room just to the left. That is where your father is.' He pulls me back as I step through. 'I must just mention that your father is not embalmed. We have covered his face with a cloth as his face will not be as you remembered. We recommend relatives keep the memory of who their loved one was before they died. It is therefore advisable that you not remove the sheet from his face.'

'That's fine,' I say.

As I walk through the door, I get all kinds of horrible images in my mind of Dad's cheeks blackened and his face emaciated, like the images you see on the news when bodies are pulled out of the rubble days after an earthquake.

I look for Dad, but I can't see or hear him. I still expect to hear him ranting.

It is so quiet in here. The walls and floor are stone. There is no furniture, save for a stand with Dad's coffin resting on it. I see it now. I stand in the middle of the room and take in the silence.

I can't face looking at him, so I sit on the stone floor and fold my arms over my knees. The floor stings my buttocks as it is so cold, but this silence is so comforting that I don't care. I have never sat with my father in silence before. There has always been a chaotic hum coming from within him. I have always been clenched tight in his presence.

I look behind me at the arch-shaped window. Not much light comes through it, and on the windowsill is a vase of wilting flowers. I look up at the bare walls and feel the simplicity of my breathing: in, out, in, out. There is something both imprisoning and immensely freeing about this room.

My heart pounds as I stand up.

It is like there is no one here. It's hard to remember that he is lying right there.

I take two steps towards his coffin and look inside. The blood is pounding in my ears, and my breath gets out of step with itself.

I hold the sides of his mahogany coffin and stare at him, lying still. His face is covered with a large, white handkerchief. I can only see the point of his nose. There is no breath. His body is dressed in a cream-satin robe, and his mildly flecked hands are thinner than before and lie across his stomach. His fingers are clasped in a posture of peace.

As much as I hate Yvonne, she has made sure he is leaving this world with dignity.

I touch his stomach. It is sturdy and does not move. I keep my hand there; the fabric of his gown is so thick it is like a curtain. A salty tear falls from my eye onto his hand. I leave it there to soak into his dead pores. I feel the urge to peek at his face, but I refrain and put my hand in my pocket. I remember the last time I saw him, crazed, on the steps of his nursing home. 'Enjoy your life,' he said.

I can't get used to this stillness. I want him to sit up, breathe and say something, anything. My eyes sting as I struggle to grapple with this finality. Death is too long. The 'ever' of forever feels impossible to take in. Snippets of our history race through my mind, like that night in 1979, when he came to collect me after the flood.

He bought me two Yorkie bars on the way home.

Yet, I remember how he could turn: his loving glare juxtaposed with his menacing grumble.

Like a dam that bursts from the pressure of water, tears cascade down my face. I don't worry about the noise I make; I sob right from my gut and begin to grieve for all the lost years. It is a relief to really weep, not just half-cry to protect his feelings.

I reach into my back pocket, my body is jolting with sobs, and I pull out my letter. I steady myself, come back to the sound of silence and look for a place where I can put it.

There, around the inside of his coffin, I see a satin pocket. I could tuck it into there.

I lift my arm over his body and slip my letter into the stretch of pocket just behind his ear, where it will be safe. As I bring my hand away, so as not to touch the cloth over his face, I think of the game Operation, where if you touch the metal edges as you remove the patient's organ, his body buzzes and you get that awful electric shock! It's strange, the thoughts that come to us uninvited.

My letter is buried safely within the satin pocket, and I feel relief knowing that a part of my heart will go with him tomorrow. It feels like a step towards a resolution.

I look around. I don't want to go. I like it here.

As I turn away, I pause. I remember Dad's last words to me on the steps of the nursing home; how, in a brief moment of coherence, he urged me to enjoy my life. I can still taste the horrid, plasticky cheese lingering in my mouth from the McDonald's I had earlier. Chills wash over my body.

I walk back to his coffin. 'I will, Dad,' I mutter. 'I will enjoy my life.' I kiss the palm of my hand and hold it over his knuckles. They feel strangely warm. I pull myself away and walk out of the door, but trip on the step up as I come out of the chapel.

Mark Wilson scuttles towards me, rubbing his hands together as if he is cold. 'Everything OK?' he asks, with a forlorn look.

His sympathetic tone makes me crack. I bite my lip to stop the torrent of tears coming, but my floodgates burst. I grab his offer of a hand and weep with my head on his shoulder. 'No, I'm not,' I blubber.

He rubs my back. 'It's OK, Miss Goldman. The death of a loved one can be most distressing.' He guides me to a chair in the waiting room and pulls up a chair for himself. 'May I help with anything?' he asks.

I squeeze his hand so tight it goes pink. 'Yes, yes,' I wipe my nose with the side of my hand.

He hands me a Kleenex. 'Here,' he says. 'This will do the job better.'

I look into his eyes and see the genuine kindness there. I am reminded of the compassion of a stranger, and how much easier it is to show your wounds to someone you have never met. I try to compose myself, but I am finding it hard to catch my breath. I concentrate on slowing the rhythm of my breathing, opening my mouth like a goldfish to take in slow gulps of air.

'That's it,' he says. 'Breathe nice and slowly.'

I straighten my feet and let go of his hand. 'There is something you can do for me,' I splutter. 'I apologise, in advance, if it sounds stupid.'

'Fire away,' Mark says.

'I've put a note in my father's coffin, and I really need to know it will go with him tomorrow.'

'Of course it will,' he replies, 'without a doubt.'

'No, you don't understand,' I say. 'My stepmother, Yvonne, could remove it.'

'Remove it?'

'I'm sorry, I know it's hard to comprehend,' I say, snivelling, 'but the woman is a real bitch. She has stopped me seeing my dad for years. I know she would stop me from having my letter in his coffin if she could.'

Mark Wilson leans forwards and pats my hand. 'Lucia, I do understand how complex family relationships can be, especially in the aftermath of a death, but it would be very unlikely for anyone to do such a thing.'

'Seriously!' I exclaim. 'She would. She's a bitch!'

The front door opens. Two suited men walk in.

'Lucia, if it would put your mind at ease, I will check your father's coffin before I close it to make sure your note is there.'

My breathing steadies. 'I'd appreciate that.'

'Where did you put it?' he asks.

'In the side pocket, to the left of his face.'

'Very well,' he says, and stands to go and greet the new clients. 'Would you like to give me your mobile number? If there are any problems, I will phone you.'

I write my number on a sheet from my diary and hand it to him. 'Thank you,' I say.

'You're welcome,' he replies. 'If you don't hear from me, please rest assured that your letter will go with your father.'

'Thanks Mark,' I say, and open the door.

I walk out onto Fulham Road. A lorry drives past, blowing grit into my eyes. I wander towards the bus stop, but feel too vulnerable to go back to Tiffs. I think I'll go back to the rhododendron bed and spend some time there before dark.

CHAPTER FORTY-SIX

LONDON – SAN FRANCISCO, 2001

LUCIA IS TWENTY-EIGHT YEARS OLD

After Dad's funeral two days ago, Yvonne asked to meet me. She said she had some belongings that my father wanted me to have. We've arranged to meet at Dad's favourite place, the coffee shop at The Army and Navy on Victoria Street.

These South West London streets bring me great comfort. You could trace my father's and my footsteps all around here, to and from the Tate Gallery, and along the bank of the Thames.

The espresso maker steams and that pungent smell of coffee beans makes me gag. It's still got that old-fashioned feel up here; it's a proper coffee shop with triangular sandwiches and apple turnovers on plates with doilies.

I order an Earl Grey tea and find a table in the corner. I feel that familiar dryness of mouth and racing heart that

I can't control, so I try to make myself look busy by sorting through my bag.

I hear the heavy clunk of heels and smell the strong whiff of Yves St Laurent behind me.

My stomach lurches. I turn my head.

Yvonne is carrying a Jaeger bag, and is smartly dressed in a tweed suit and heels. In her other arm, she holds a box close to her chest. She greets me with a warm kiss. 'Hi Lucia,' she says in a buoyant tone, and puts down her things. She undoes her blazer and hangs it around the back of her chair. 'I'm just going to grab a coffee; do you want anything?'

'I'm OK, thanks.' I am relieved by her warmth.

I guess now Dad is dead, there is no one to fight over anymore.

She returns with a black coffee and an oily flapjack. 'Here, help me eat this,' she says and breaks it in two.

I take half and bite into it. 'It was a nice service on Tuesday,' I say.

'It was what your father wanted,' Yvonne replies. 'He made it clear in his will that he wanted a humanitarian service. I knew Christopher would do a good job. He did a service for one of Colin's colleagues.'

It goes quiet.

Yvonne taps her red nails on the table. She is still wearing her wedding ring.

'So how are you?' I ask.

She flicks her eye up at me. Her mascara moistens 'It's hard,' she shrugs. 'So much of my life has been centred on looking after Colin; I feel lost.'

'It must be difficult,' I say. 'You did well. He looked beautiful in his coffin.'

'Thank you,' she replies. 'I wouldn't have had it any other way.'

'Did he suffer?'

'What?'

'At the end, I mean. Was he in any pain?'

She adjusts her neck scarf. 'He struggled to breathe right at the end, but that was only for a short while. Other than that, he was comfortable. They looked after him well.'

This flapjack tastes of honey and flax seed. I chew my way through another long minute of silence. I haven't really come here for small talk. I've come to find answers. I ask myself what is the worst thing that could happen if I ask her for truth?

I take a deep breath.

'Yvonne, there are some things I need to ask you now Dad's gone.'

She presses her lips together. 'Like what?'

I run my fingertip around the rim of my cup. 'There are just things… things that…' My heartbeat quickens. I stumble on my words, hesitate and fall silent.

'What things?'

I look at her. 'I never understood why Dad cut off from me when you moved to Reigate; why I was not allowed your phone number or your address in Spain. Was it because of you?'

'Because of me?'

'Well, you were hardly my number-one fan were you?'

'God, you were a little swine,' she sniggers. She hesitates as she catches herself and tries to patch over what she has said. 'At times… at times you could be…'

'So is that why, Yvonne? Did you stop him from seeing me?'

'No, I didn't.'

'So what was the reason then?'

'Perhaps you should try asking that question closer to home,' she replies.

'What?' I feel a jab in my chest. I know she is referring to Mum, whom I instantly feel protective of. She may be an ogre at times, but she is my ogre. 'Do you mean my mother?'

'Yes, she'll tell you.'

I gaze over at the ladies behind the counter. They look so content talking to one another and pouring coffee.

'So, it was all to do with my mother?'

She scratches her arm. 'Look, it is not my place to say, but your mum wouldn't give us any peace; she phoned all the time. It drove him mad.' She leans forwards. 'It wasn't that he didn't want *you*, Lucia,' she nods. 'I promise you, he did.'

I look into her watery eyes and see the sincerity there. I believe those words, but I don't believe the full story. I still think she played a key role in the drama. 'He loved me then?'

'He loved you, Lucia, most certainly. He thought the world of you.'

My head suddenly feels hazy and my energy drops. I won't get any further with her and I know Mum won't tell me anything, so I draw my own conclusion that I was caught between the daggers behind the scenes.

I gaze down at the box on the table. 'Is this box for me?'

'Yes, it's his poetry books, which he wanted you to have, and his framed photo of Marti's horse, *Silver Beauty*.'

I can see his Phillip Larkin collection amongst others, all underneath a square frame covered in bubble wrap. 'Is this the photo?' I ask.

'Yes. I know how you loved *Silver Beauty*.'

'I did.' I am back there now with Granddad Marti at Southport, looking at *Silver Beauty*'s gleaming coat and wild mane.

'Thanks,' I say sliding the box towards me. I inhale a slow breath. 'Is there any money, Yvonne?'

'No,' she replies, with absolutely no hesitation.

I don't believe her. There must have been. 'How come?' I ask.

'It all went on his nursing home fees.'

I know she is lying. She probably rewrote his will when he went senile. There is no way I would not have been mentioned in his will. I look at her poised face, now turned stern, and realise that there are some battles not worth fighting. 'Ah, right,' I reply.

Thank God for the chit chat around us.

'It's been nice seeing you again,' she says and smiles. It's not a genuine smile. It's a frosty smile: a front to hide the cracks.

'Yeah, it's been good to meet,' I say, because it has.

'When do you go back to San Francisco?'

'I fly back on Friday. I only get one week's compassionate leave.'

'Are you happy, Lucia?'

'Happy?' That question is a hard one to answer, because I'm not skipping around blowing bubbles, but I am kind of content. 'Yeah, I guess I am.' I reply. 'I love the fresh air and blue skies, and I enjoy my job.'

'You dad would be pleased.'

'I guess so,' I say, and flick a crumb off the table.

She writes on a notelet and hands it to me. 'Keep in touch,' she says.

I look at it. It is a Greenwich address. 'You're leaving Chelsea?'

'Yeah, I'm moving to a flat in Greenwich. I don't want to stay where I nursed your father or I will never be able to move on.'

I understand.

'Are you still a shorthand typist for the courts?' I ask.

'Yep, my work is still the same.'

She'll probably bed another judge and wreak havoc on his poor daughter's life. I slip her notelet into my bag and stand.

'Do keep in touch,' she repeats.

I know I won't. I don't want to lie. 'All the best, Yvonne,' I say, picking up the box.

She kisses me on the cheek.

'Bye,' I say and walk out of the cafe, through the lingerie section, towards the lift.

The lift doors open. Two old ladies exit as I walk in. I am surrounded by mirrors. I look at myself. *It wasn't that he didn't want you.* At least I got another piece of the jigsaw.

Maybe I should have fought harder for the money. I should have at least asked to see his will, but karma will come round and bite her on the bum for that one. All in good time…

*

Back home now in San Francisco, I've come down to Ocean Beach with two of the poetry books Yvonne gave me: a Faber collection of English love poems and Joseph Brodsky.

I am sitting in the sand dune shielded from the wind. The ocean is grey and choppy, but awesome in its infinite mass. Two surfers are braving the waves. A putrid smell of fish wafts around me. Flies hover over a bonfire that must have died days ago, and cans and a pair of tennis shoes lie desolate. I can hear the pneumatic hiss of the F Muni behind, as its door closes.

I open the old edition of love poems. Dad has written in capitals on the inside cover:

163 — JULIET
174 — TWO POEMS
180 — IN A BATH TEASHOP
For Lucia
Dad

I turn to page 163 as a gust of sand flies into the fold of the book. I brush it away.

H. BELLOC
1870—1953
JULIET

How did the party go in Portman Square?
I cannot tell you; Juliet was not there.
And how did Lady Gaster's party go?
Juliet was next to me and I do not know.

These are the words of someone so blinded by love they cannot see anything else.

Is he referring to me? Am I Juliet? No, he can't mean me. He can't…

As I read the 'Two poems' on page 174, I battle with myself, trying to figure out what my father is trying to say to me through these poems. I am still decoding his messages, even when he is dead.

FRANCES CORNFORD.
1886-
TWO POEMS

She Warns Him
I am a lamp, a lamp that is out;
I am a shallow stream;
In it are neither pearls or trout,
Nor one of the things that you dream.

Why do you smile and deny, my lover?
I will not be denied.

I am a book, a book with a cover,
And nothing at all inside.

Here is the truth, and you must grapple,
Grapple with what I have said.
I am a dumpling without any apple,
I am a star that is dead.

I read the last verse again. *'A star that is dead'*? I imagine
Dad's face lit up in the black, starry sky. What is *'a dumpling*
without any apple? I try again to understand these covert
messages and fathom what on earth he is trying to tell me,
but I can't quite succeed. Nothing is ever straightforward
with him.

> All Souls' Night
> *My love came back to me*
> *Under the November tree*
> *Shelterless and dim.*
> *He put his hand upon my shoulder,*
> *He did not think me strange or older,*
> *Nor I, him.*

This one is definitely about illicit love. The creepy image of
an older man seducing me storms through my mind. Perv!
That forbidden kiss outside the cash machine near Overton's
creeps back to me.
Was it really like that?
No, no. His tongue wiggled…
No!

The brakes of another F Muni screech as it rattles back along the line into town. It's turning chilly now. The cloud is covering the sun. The surfers emerge from the water, holding their boards. I bet they're on their way to the Java Cafe, where it always stinks of wet dog.

I turn to page 180:

JOHN BETJEMAN
1906–
IN A BATH TEASHOP

Let us not speak, for the love we bear one another—
Let us hold hands and look.
She, such a very ordinary little woman;
He, such a thumping crook:
But both, for the moment, little lower than the angels
In the teashop inglenook.

I imagine being in that cosy inglenook with Dad, both of us huddled away from the world, with no bitch of a wife. We had lots of moments together, just the two of us, before she arrived.

I run my fingers through the sand and lick my salty lips before opening Joseph Brodsky's *Selected Poems*. Dad has left me another message on the back page:

This is a wonderful book, but, at this moment in time, I think you could best concentrate on 'A

Slice of Honeymoon' on page 53. In the future,
do take in page 168.

  Dad

This one pulls me in straight away. There is no mystery to
page 53.

A Slice of Honeymoon
To M.B.

Never, never forget:
How the waves lashed up the docks,
And the wind pressed upward
like submerged life-buoys.

– How the seagulls chattered,
Sailboats stared at the sky.
– How the clouds swooped upwards
like wild ducks flying.

May this tiny fragment
Of the life we then shared
Beat in your heart wildly
like a fish not yet dead.

May the bushes bristle.
May the oysters snap.
May the passion cresting
at your lips make you grasp

— without words — how the surf
of these breaking waves
brings crests to birth
in the open sea.

Oh my God! Fuck!

'May the passion cresting at your lips make you grasp.' Jesus. That kiss at Victoria comes back to me again, with his steak smelling breath. I watch the long grass sway. *'Never, never forget.'* Is that what he is referring to? Did he love me in that way?

I howl at the sea. Why was I so stupid? Did he? *'May this tiny fragment of the life we then shared.'* I punch my knee. I can never get that time back now. It's gone. I bawl with no inhibition. The frothing waves carry my sound. *'May the passion cresting at your lips make you grasp.'* Maybe Cameron was right when he said, 'He loved you in the wrong way.'

But why did I never realise?

Photos of me at seven years old drop out of the book. I am posing naked in the bath, pouting at the lens. I can remember that day. Something went on. I'll never understand what.

Were all those weird, silent moments with him about his 'passion cresting'?

I listen to the long drift of the waves brushing against the shoreline. This is my ocean, where I come for refuge. That bracing breeze runs over my naked scalp. I shaved my hair off yesterday to mark Dad's death, and donated my locks to a leukaemia charity that makes wigs for children. My new friend Lacy says I look like Antigone.

I flick to page 168, and close it again. I saw the last two lines:

'Away from me, you are safe from my oedipal passions.'

Odysseus to Telemachus

My dear Telemachus,
The Trojan War
is over now; I don't recall who won it. [Does that refer
    to Mum, Yvonne and him?]
The Greeks, no doubt, for only they would leave
so many dead so far away from their own homeland.
But still, my homeward way has proven too long.
While we were killing time there, old Poseidon,
it almost seems, stretched and extended space.

I don't know where I am or what this place
can be. It would appear some filthy island, [His mental
    state?]
with bushes, buildings, and great grunting pigs.
A garden choked with weeds; some queen or other.
Grass and huge stones… Telemachus, dear boy!
To a wanderer the faces of all islands
resemble one another. The mind trips
when it counts waves; eyes, stung by sea horizons,
must weep; and flesh of water stuffs one's ears.
I can't remember how the war came about [This line
    makes me sad.]
even how old you are – I can't remember. [I was four,
    Dad.]

Grow up, then, my Telemachus, grow strong. [I have a
    lump in my throat.]
*Only the gods know if we'll see each other
again. You've long ceased to be that babe
before whom I reined in the pawing bullocks.* [What
    an image.]
*Had it not been for Palamedes' trick
we two would still be living in one household.* [Who
    is Palmedes?]
*But maybe he was right; away from me
you are quite safe from all oedipal passions,
and your dreams, my Telemachus, are blameless.*

Was I right about what used to happen in his bed when I
was four?

I push for more memory. All I can remember is kicking
in my sleep. My memory jumps to the bruises the next day
and those uncomfortable breakfasts. I force the boundaries
of my mind and concentrate hard:

1. His stripy pyjamas.
2. The smell of an unmade bed on his skin.
3. His tummy.

Then my mind goes blank.

Love is love though. *He thought the world of you.* That is
enough for me. I'll never get further than that, nor reach
any better resolution than this. I have to look forward
now.

It's my turn to cook tonight with Rodney. I'm on chard-chopping duty. I stand, wipe down my damp skirt and walk over the dune to the main strip, where the surfers gather.

I walk into Java Cafe, and order a bagel and chai latte. The smell of wet fur is gross.

Chard chopping can wait.

I sit on the leather sofa by the window and watch the world go by.

CHAPTER
FORTY-SEVEN

MARIN COUNTY, JUNE 2002

LUCIA IS TWENTY-NINE YEARS OLD

Lucia has finished a seven-day retreat at Green Gulch Farm, a Zen monastery in Marin. Waking to the sound of the deep gong at 7.00am each morning, she sat zazen in the morning and evening, and helped with weeding in the gardens during the afternoon.

Her skin glows from the days spent out in this glorious sunshine. Her body feels supple and alive from all the work she has done on the land. Leaving Green Gulch Farm, she ambles along the winding track, which runs alongside the organic farms, and feels the hot sun shining on her skin. She is headed for her favourite spot – Muir Beach.

She hears the buzzing of a bumblebee as she stops to

look at the wild horses grazing in the distance. Crinkly heat lines cruise vertically in front of everything she sees. She sits on a boulder and watches a red-tailed hawk soar overhead.

It's a beach in a quiet cove, and a place she often comes to for reflection and peace. As Lucia gets through the rushes, she kicks off her flip-flops and runs over the dunes. She strolls barefoot along the beach, enjoying the feel of the warm sand under her feet. It's crowded here today, with families picnicking and several boats out sailing.

A light breeze blows, wafting that medicinal scent of eucalyptus over her. Lucia throws off her rucksack, and sits on her sleeping mat, which she'd been using all week to soften the hard mattress. She digs her hand into the sand, whilst looking out to sea. Stars of sunlight hop on the waves as a falcon does a kamikaze dive from above. She loves it here.

London feels far away. Her mum's pain lives in an entirely different land. They still speak at set times. Lucia still gets that funny feeling between her legs when her mum is aggressive, but she just hangs up now and walks forwards into this beautiful scenery.

The more accustomed Lucia gets to living her own life, the more she feels part of the world and less trapped in *her own* world.

Lucia leans back and watches a couple paddle and splash in the water. She listens to the squawking of the California gulls circling her and eats the hummus baguette she couldn't manage at breakfast.

The tremor from her father's death has settled now. That lasting image of him at peace in his coffin has helped her to let go. She has grieved for the lost years of her adolescence and is getting used to a new emotional landscape. It is easier to live now he has gone, instead of having his tormented shadow existing in the background. There was a guilt pulling at her whilst he lived, telling her that she should visit him more or make amends. That pressure has gone. She can be who she likes now, even a complete failure if she wants.

Lucia gets up and brushes the sand off her shorts. She walks along, dipping her feet in the cold water as she goes. She takes in the wonderful coastal cliffs with their rugged ridges. Clusters of redwood trees stand along the cliff edge, with wooden chalets dotted in between.

A young boy in shorts and a baseball cap runs up to her, and throws a colourful beach ball. She catches it and throws it back to him. They play catch for a while. The child bursts out into laughter and points at an aeroplane cruising above.

'Yes,' Lucia says. 'That's an aeroplane.'

'Airplane,' he replies, watching it's contrail in the sky.

She looks at his innocent face. Sun-kissed all over, he has snot dripping from his nose and not a care in the world.

'Ball,' he says, handing it to her.

'Toby!' his mother calls from a few metres away. 'Come and finish your sandwich.'

'Off you go, Toby,' Lucia says, leaning down and giving him back his ball. 'It's been lovely to meet you.' She starts to walk away.

He runs after her, jumping in the wet sand. 'Ball!' he shouts.

She keeps walking, listening to the sweet sound of him cheeping away to himself. She looks back. Toby waves at her and throws the ball into the sea. His mother runs and fetches it, and carries Toby back to their picnic table.

She smiles.

Lucia wipes her feet and puts on her flip-flops. She walks across the pedestrian bridge and along a shady grove lined with lush Monterey pine trees. She is enamoured by the orange-and-black butterflies fluttering around the shiny, green leaves, as she breathes in that rich pine aroma.

Lucia hikes up the ridge trail towards the coastal path. She may be able to see some whales from up there today. The sun beats down on her as she looks up at the mighty oak trees. They must be at least 100 feet tall. She picks off a piece of chequered bark and slides it into her pocket. Lucia puts on her headphones and sings along to Dido.

I know I'm not perfect, but I can smile
And I hope that you can see this heart behind these
tired eyes.

She takes a sip from her water bottle and ploughs on uphill.

Cause I'm no angel, but please don't think that I won't try
I'm no angel, but does that mean that I can't live my life?

Up on Coyote Ridge, she enjoys the flat walk along the coastal path. The ocean is sparkling. The sky is Persian blue, with not a cloud in sight. Lucia stops to look for whales, but she can't see any today. She saunters along into the open land, wondering how Lennie got on with his interview for the new job. She'll call him when she gets home.

She is now only a dot in the distance, but you can still hear her belting out Dido.

I'm no angel, but does that mean that I won't fly?

She walks.

LITERARY ACKNOWLEDGEMENTS

1. Two poems 'She Warns Him' and 'All Souls' Night' by **Frances Cornford** are reproduced with the permission of the trustees of the Frances Crofts Cornford Will Trust.

2. 'Juliet' by **Hilaire Belloc** is reprinted with the permission of Peters Fraser & Dunlop (www.petersfraserdunlop. com) on behalf of the Estate of Hilaire Belloc.

3. 'In A Bath Teashop' by **John Betjeman** –© copyright 1957 The Betjeman Literary Estate – is reproduced with the permission of Aitken Alexander Associates.

4. 'A Slice of Honeymoon' by **Joseph Brodsky** – © copyright Joseph Brodsky Article Fourth Trust, 1964–

is reproduced with the permission of The Wylie Agency (UK) Limited.

5. 'Odysseus to Telemachus', *Collected Poems* by **Joseph Brodsky** – © copyright, 2001 The Estate of Joseph Brodsky – is reproduced with permission from Carcanet Press Limited, Manchester, UK.

6. 'Happiness' from *When We Were Very Young* by **A A Milne** – Text © copyright The Trustees of the Pooh Properties, 1924. – Published by Egmont UK and used with permission.

7. 'Happiness' from *When We Were Very Young* by **A A Milne** – © copyright 1924, Trustees of the Pooh Properties – reproduced with permission from Curtis Brown Group Ltd, London, on behalf of the Trustees of the Pooh Properties.

8. 'The Left Hand and Hiroshima', *Breakfast for Barbarians*, 1966 by **Gwendolyn MacEwen** is reproduced with the permission of Mosaic Press, Ontario, Canada.

9. 'The Doppelganger' by **Daryl Hine** – © copyright The Estate of Daryl Hine – reproduced with the permission of the Estate.

10. The three speeches spoken by the character of Cameron Cleeve that appear in chapters thirty-seven and thirty-nine are taken from 'Will I am' and 'I am God; A Series

of Conversations with you, the observer' (YouTube videos) – © copyright 2010 **Jonathan Kay**. These lines are reproduced with the permission of Jonathan Kay.

11. The line on page 189, in chapter eighteen is from Playboy Magazine, 1976; an interview with David Bowie#2.

MUSICAL ACKNOWLEDGEMENTS

PERSONAL ACKNOWLEDGEMENTS

Thank you to Jonathan Kay for inspiring me to write this book.

Thanks to David Ford at The Marsh, San Francisco, California, US, for your brilliance, and for turning on the creative 'light' inside me.

Thanks to The Mary Anderson Centre, Southern Indiana, for giving me such a beautiful space to write, and to The Rotary Club for the bursary award, which allowed me to reside there for two months.

Thanks to Cynthia Fuller at the University of Newcastle for helping me to find both my voice and the narrative perspective for this novel. Thanks to my Master of Arts (MA) supervisors, Jane Rogers and Linda Lee Welch, for the care with which you always read my work, and for pushing me to be the best I can be. Thanks, also, to the writing team at Sheffield Hallam University for your sharp eyes.

Thanks to Drew Johnson, Gill Marshall and Penny Heald for your typing support when illness struck. This book would never have been finished without you.

Thanks to Christine Williams, Tracey Holland and Howard Earl for your encouragement, and to my scribing buddy, JM, for the laughter along the way.

Thanks to Student Finance England for the financial assistance you gave me during my post-graduate studies, particularly mid-way when I fell ill.

To The Snowdon Award Scheme, The Professional Classes Aid Council and The Bradford Jewish Benevolent Society for your generosity in helping fund the tuition fees for my writing MA. Thanks also to The League of The Helping Hand and Elizabeth Finn Care for your kindness and assistance, whilst I wrote this novel.

Thank you to Troubador Publishing for being so fabulous to deal with, and to Hannah Dakin, for simply being a ray of sunshine.

Thanks to Helen Macfarlane, at Music Sales, for all of your help with the copyright leads, and to Luca Balbo for being so helpful, too. Thanks to Leah Mack at Sony ATV and Tim Hayes at Warner Chappell for being so great to deal with. Thanks, also, to Elke Inkster at Porcupine Quills for guiding me to that last but vital permission lead I just could not find. Whhhooooooaaaaaaaaaaaaaaaa!

Thank you to Evan Jones for your generosity.

I, lastly wish to acknowledge and thank, The South West Yorkshire Partnership NHS Foundation Trust for your support over the years. Thank you to Doreen Farooq, Toklis Tombros and Kelly Savery for your care.